Return to

Willow Tree Cottage

Also by Elise Darcy

The Living Apart Together series

Living Apart Together

It Takes 2 to Tango

Dear John

Love on the Rooftop

Standalone books

Lola & The Man

A Mallorcan Affair

The Villa in Sicily

We'll Meet Again

The Sunrise Coast Series

New Beginnings at the Harbour Inn

The Secret of the Summerhouse

The Cottage by the Sea

The Guest House at Shingle Cove

The Houseboat by the Quay

Return to Willow Tree Cottage

A Novel

ELISE DARCY

ISBN 978-1-913147-17-4

Life takes you unexpected places, love brings you home.

1

Margot picked up one of the library books that Meredith had delivered the previous afternoon. She knew Meredith hadn't wanted to collect them for her. She imagined what Meredith had been thinking: *you should be spending your time writing your own books, not reading other people's.*

Margot sighed. It was Monday morning, a work day. She sat at her desk, looked at the typewriter, and picked up the novel instead. *Perhaps reading one will give me some inspiration,* she thought, realising even as she was thinking this that it was a load of old claptrap. She was just avoiding what she knew she had returned there to do.

She sighed heavily and cast the book to one side. Her mind kept wandering back to the same time the previous week, when she'd returned to Willow Tree Cottage, and to her conversation with Meredith.

'Why are you so late?' Meredith had said.

Margot recalled frowning at her housekeeper. She hadn't felt inclined to give an explanation.

'I cooked dinner. When you didn't arrive, I thought you'd changed your mind.'

'When have I ever?'

'Well, there's a first time for everything,' Meredith had said.

There had followed a heavy silence. Margot had still felt annoyed by the question. 'I always return to Willow Tree Cottage for the summer – you know that. Why should this summer be any different?'

Meredith had shrugged. 'I think the dinner is spoiled. I was expecting you hours ago.'

Margot recalled that Meredith had waited for an explanation. Margot had sighed, and given her one. 'I stopped in Southwold on the way here.'

'Why?'

'To get some paper.'

'Why?'

Margot remembered frowning at her. She also recalled getting tired of the game of twenty questions. 'How long have we known each other?'

'That's a silly question, Margot. All our lives.'

Margot had smiled affectionately at her best friend. They'd grown up together in this cottage. She'd sighed. 'Sometimes I can't believe how quickly the time has flown, and we're now in our mid-seventies.'

Meredith had frowned at that thought. She'd asked, 'What is your point, Margot?'

'Well, what's with all the questions? You know why I bought paper for the typewriter.'

'It took you all that time to shop for stationery?' Margot had asked.

'I fancied seeing a film, so I popped into the cinema in Southwold on the spur of the moment and saw a morning matinee.'

'You did *what*?'

Margot had shrugged at that point.

'Did you walk into Southwold with your suitcase?'

'Of course not. Why would I do that? I left it in the porch.' Margot had stood in the hall and indicated the porch, from where she'd picked up her suitcase on her way in.

'Why didn't you call in and let me know you'd arrived?'

Margot recalled looking at her sheepishly when she'd asked that. 'I was only intending to be quick.'

'Your neighbours in the houseboats on the quay think you spend your summers in London.'

'I know that,' Margot had snapped. She didn't need to be reminded of the ruse she'd concocted. It was a stupid little lie she'd told them years ago, that she spent her summers with family in London. Now, of course, that was where they assumed she'd be when she went away each summer.

Why hadn't she told them the truth from the off, that she wasn't in London but returned to the home she grew up in, Willow Tree Cottage, just a few hundred yards up the street in Walberswick? It had been easier to spin a lie because she hadn't wanted to get into the reasons why she couldn't bear to spend the summer on the houseboat.

'What if someone had seen you?' Meredith had asked.

'Ah, I'd already thought of an excuse. I would have said that I'd had the taxi stop on the way to the train station because I needed something in the shop.'

'And the cinema?'

'That would have been a bit more tricky.'

'I bet.' Meredith had added, 'It's not as though you need a taxi. You just have to walk from your houseboat into Walberswick.'

'Yes, I know that,' Margot had snapped again. 'I've done it enough times over the years.'

'Yes, every summer. Don't remind me.'

'What's that supposed to mean?'

Meredith had frowned at that point. 'Do you know how long it takes to uncover all the furniture from the dust sheets, and get this big old house liveable again?'

'Yes, but do I need to remind *you* that I pay you all year round to look after the place, and wait on me hand and foot for one summer every year. I don't think that's a bad deal – do you?'

Margot had caught her best friend smiling at her. Meredith said, 'I suppose not.' They could never remain cross with one another for long.

'If you're going to keep up this summer charade – which, quite frankly, is ridiculous – you know that you can't go into Southwold. It's just across the footbridge from Walberswick. If someone spots you ...' she'd trailed off.

'Yes, I know, I know.' Margot had kicked off her shoes and walked through the hallway, past the stairs with old stair treads and past the kitchen, which she had recently updated.

Margot was a writer. She'd been a struggling writer for years, until her mid-fifties, when she'd turned her hand to writing children's books. She'd published three, and as a consequence of the success of her trilogy, and the large advance following the runaway success of the first book – not to mention the royalties which, even now, twenty years after she'd stopped writing, were still coming in – Margot had brought Willow Tree Cottage into the twenty-first century.

Little had changed on the exterior of the property since it was built in 1905, but inside, the five-bedroomed property had been renovated and updated. It had a large modern kitchen with an extension on the back, overlooking the gardens. The bathroom had been modernised, and an ensuite had been added to the master bedroom, along with complete rewiring, gas central heating, and underfloor heating in the kitchen and bathrooms. In all, it was a rather modern property on the inside, but was still masquerading as a period property on the outside.

Margot was sitting in her study at the back of the house and trying not to think about that conversation with Meredith on her arrival a week earlier. She glanced through the French doors into the back garden with the weeping willow tree as she set the stack of blank white paper down beside the typewriter. Just then, she heard Meredith's footsteps, and her study door opened.

'What is that for?'

Margot turned in her seat to find Meredith standing in the doorway. 'I told you that I bought some paper. Don't you remember the conversation this time last week when I arrived at the cottage?'

Meredith looked at her blankly.

Margot sighed. 'What do you think it's for?'

Meredith rolled her eyes. 'Every summer you come back and say you are going to write another book. And you know what happens?'

Margot averted her eyes, embarrassed.

'Nothing.'

Margot rolled up the sleeves of her jumper. 'Well, this time is going to be different.'

Meredith folded her arms. 'How so?'

Margot shrugged. 'I don't know yet.' She fell silent, her eyes roving to the inbuilt bookshelves lining one complete wall. The study had been her grandfather's, back when the cottage was used as the family's holiday home. The bookshelves were still full of his books, and in the recent past her own trilogy had been there too. It was the one room in the house that Margot had hardly touched when renovating, apart from the necessary work like rewiring. The room remained very much as it had always been.

Margot swivelled her chair back to the desk and stared at the selection of small, framed photos in front of her, some dating back many years. Hers had been an unconventional upbringing for the times. She reached for an old photo of two children. The same age, they could have been sisters – twins, even – but they weren't. Margot looked at the image of her ten-year-old self, at the casual arm she'd had draped around Meredith's shoulders. Both were wearing pinafores, little jackets, boots with laces, and berets. They wore thick mitten gloves and long hand-knitted scarves. The photo had been taken in the garden of Willow Tree Cottage in the mid-fifties.

They had known each other all their lives, knew one another's secrets. Meredith's mother had been the housekeeper. She lived in, which meant Margot and Meredith had grown up together in the old cottage given to Margot's mother, Esme, by her late father.

Built in the style of the Arts and Crafts houses popular at the time among the wealthy, the house was rendered and painted yellow, with leaded windows, turrets and dormer windows in the sloping tiled roof. It formed an L-shape, with a little one-storey double-fronted entrance porch. Surrounded by walled gardens, the secluded property sat in its own grounds of half an acre, and the upper storey had uninterrupted views of the sea.

When she was older than in the photograph, Margot had found out the truth as to why she had been brought up in Willow

Tree Cottage by her mother, rarely seeing her maternal grandparents, who lived in London. The house wasn't a gift that her grandfather had bestowed on her mother, his only child, as some may have supposed. It was a solution to a problem that had needed to be swept under the carpet.

Margot's mother had been whisked away from London's civilised society, where girls her age, in their late teens, were coming out; it was the first season after the Second World War. In effect, she'd been banished there, to live a life under the radar with her illegitimate child. It hadn't really been a home, but a prison.

Her mother had been given no choice but to move out of London to Suffolk. She'd been provided with staff; her family hadn't expected an eighteen-year-old to live on her own. She wouldn't have known where to begin. A local gardener was employed to take care of the grounds. The only live-in staff member, though, was a housekeeper. And it had needed to be somebody who could keep a secret.

One of the maids from her grandfather's household had volunteered, practically begged to be given the position – so the story went. But little did anybody know that she had found herself in the same predicament as her wealthy counterpart, but with nothing and nobody to fall back on.

And so two women and two children had lived in Willow Tree Cottage. The issue of where the fathers were was never discussed. Margot stared at the photo of Meredith and herself when they were ten. It was around that time that Meredith's mother had met a local man and they had married. Meredith's mother couldn't abandon Esme and Margot by leaving her position as housekeeper, so she moved into a house in the village when she married and continued to work for Margot's mother until she retired, and

Meredith took over the position. Still employed by Margot on a part-time basis, now Meredith only worked at the house each summer when Margot returned.

'You know they were calling you the next C.S. Lewis.'

Margot turned around to find Meredith staring at the bookshelves.

'Perhaps you need a change of scenery to write, Margot.'

'Are you suggesting I take a holiday?'

'No, I'm suggesting perhaps you should return to the houseboat with your typewriter, and have a go at writing there.'

Margot's eyes went wide. 'Are you out of your mind, after what happened there that summer?'

'That was years ago, Margot.' She sighed and turned around to face her. 'It was just a thought.'

Margot frowned at her. 'Perhaps you should keep your thoughts to yourself.'

Margot's words went unheeded. Meredith continued, 'The royalties are going to run out one of these days.'

Margot didn't need to be reminded.

'What are you going to live on then?'

Margot didn't want to think about that. Meredith hadn't seen her bank statements. The large advance for the second two books in the trilogy had gone years ago. And she was right: the royalties were dwindling. The books were in libraries, and still stocked in bookshops, although if it wasn't for the merchandise that was an offshoot of the books, which her publisher at the time had cleverly persuaded her to agree to, she'd have no income. But the income she did receive barely covered her food and electric bill and the mooring fees for her houseboat. She was aware that if it wasn't for paying Meredith to work part-time for her, things wouldn't be so ridiculously tight. But Margot couldn't let her go, even though she knew she didn't need to pay her all year round when Margot was only living in this house each summer.

Meredith had no idea that Margot was living on her savings, and had been for years, and that now her not-insubstantial inheritance from her late grandfather was dwindling fast too.

Every summer, she returned to attempt to write a novel, but nothing happened. This summer, she was determined she would make a start. She had to. That was why she'd walked into Southwold and bought the paper – and lots of it.

Meredith walked over to the desk and looked at the old typewriter. 'Don't you think you should buy a computer or a laptop?'

'Why would I do that?' *More to the point, where would the money come from?*

'Because it's what people use now, to write, I imagine. No one uses an old-fashioned typewriter, Margot.'

'Well, I do!' Margot pursed her lips, aware that in actual fact she didn't use the typewriter, because she hadn't written a damn word in twenty years. If she hadn't stopped writing, perhaps she could retire now, like people her age or younger did, and be enjoying her life rather than worrying about money. She looked at Meredith, and realised that she wouldn't be surprised if her friend could retire now, if she chose to.

Meredith rolled her eyes. 'Fair enough. Do you want dinner, Margot?'

'No, I'm not hungry. I ate a tub of popcorn in the cinema.'

'Suit yourself.' Meredith walked over to the door. She turned around. 'You know, sitting here all summer won't bring them back.'

Margot turned in her swivel chair to face the garden. She could sense Meredith still standing in the doorway.

'I'll be off then.'

Margot didn't answer.

'I think you should return to the houseboat this summer, Margot. Just tell your neighbours the truth.'

The truth? How could she tell them that she'd lied for years? Margot thought back to that morning just over a week ago when she'd packed her suitcase to leave. Her closest neighbour and good friend, Ray, a couple of houseboats down, had spotted her leaving. 'Say hello to your grandchildren from us,' he'd said. He'd even asked her if she needed a lift to the train station.

It had taken her a bit by surprise when he'd said that. He hadn't lived on his houseboat for as long as some of her other neighbours. A retired police officer from London, he'd followed his soon-to-be ex-wife, Sarah, down here from London. He'd mentioned that she lived in her own flat along the coast in Aldeburgh. They still hadn't divorced, as far as she was aware. In fact, from what she'd seen – intimate romantic candle-lit dinners with his wife – she guessed the divorce was on hold for now.

Her thoughts turned to his comment. Margot hadn't told him where she supposedly spent the summer. She'd guessed that one of her other neighbours had mentioned it.

Margot cringed. It had started years ago, the little white lie she'd told that she returned to London every summer to spend the long school holidays with her grandchildren. She wished she'd never said that. She couldn't even remember why she'd blurted that out when one of her neighbours asked her where it was she went each summer.

In hindsight it was a stupid, stupid thing to say, especially under the circumstances. She'd mentioned London, the first place that popped into her head when they'd asked where they lived. It did make her wonder about the reason they'd never asked why her family didn't visit her on the houseboat. She raised an eyebrow. Perhaps they were too polite to ask.

'You have to let people in, Margot.'

'I do. I live on a houseboat, surrounded by lovely neighbours.'

'Oh, yes. The houseboat people who have no clue who you are. Why don't you tell them the truth?'

'What? That every summer I pack a suitcase full of clothes and retreat to a house nearby that no one knows I own, and live like a recluse away from the hordes of children who descend on the Suffolk Coast in the school summer holiday, just reminding me of what I lost—'

The words caught in her throat. She changed tack. 'I have to lie to my friends and houseboat neighbours so they think I'm one of them, that my houseboat is my permanent home.'

She turned around and caught Meredith's expression. The look on her face said she was not sympathetic to Margot's plight. After all, it was of her own making, and it was she who had perpetuated her own lie.

2

Meredith walked into Margot's study and caught her sitting at her desk, staring out at the garden, the library book she'd brought over yesterday afternoon cast aside on her desk. Even though she was sceptical that Margot would start writing again, Meredith still hoped she might get over her writer's block and make a start.

Margot had been back an entire week, and from what Meredith had seen, she hadn't used a single sheet of typewriting paper she'd bought in Southwold the previous Monday, save for the sheet she'd threaded through the typewriter. That sheet was still blank; not a single word had been typed. Meredith had spotted that earlier in the morning when she was dusting the desk.

Meredith shook her head. 'You still blame yourself, don't you, over what happened on the houseboat that summer?' she said softly.

'You can go now.'

Meredith wasn't offended by Meredith's dismissive remark. She'd done her work there for the day, cleaning the cottage and preparing Margot's lunch; she'd made a stew and left it cooking in the slow cooker for Margot's dinner that evening. She also knew why her friend wanted her to go. She didn't want to have a conversation about that summer – not now, not ever.

Meredith didn't budge from the doorway. 'I don't know why you keep that blasted houseboat.'

Margot swivelled around in her chair to face Meredith. 'You know why. My mother would wonder what had happened to it. Besides, you know I can't sell it. It belongs to her.'

Meredith sighed. She knew that wasn't the issue. Margot loved the houseboat, even though she couldn't bring herself to remain there each summer. Thinking of Esme, Meredith asked, 'How is your mother?'

Margot groaned.

Meredith could tell by the look on her face that she didn't want to get into that either.

'Oh, Margot. Esme is not getting any younger. When are you two going to patch up your differences?'

'Differences?' Margot scoffed at that word. 'It's a feud, more like. I know that she doesn't want to see me. I put her in that home. She wants to go back to her houseboat. After all these years, she still won't accept that she's too old and frail to live there anymore.'

'I know,' said Meredith. 'I could help look after her if she lived here, though. I would have the time in between the bit of cooking, cleaning and shopping.' Meredith thought back to years ago when they had both been young mothers and she'd helped Margot out. She had remained living in the village once she'd married, and had only lived a few doors down from Willow Tree Cottage, on the opposite side of the street. It meant that she had not only helped out with cooking and cleaning as the housekeeper, but also child-care when Margot's husband had died unexpectedly of a heart condition and Margot had been left a single parent. She had needed all the help she could get. Meredith also remembered that unfortunately, Esme hadn't gone out of her way to lend a hand. In some respects, she was surprised that Margot wanted her mother back. Even so, Meredith said, 'Why don't you ask her again if she will come and live here?'

'She might have no choice,' blurted Margot.

Meredith pursed her lips. She knew what that meant. She imagined that Margot didn't want to talk about money, but with her dwindling savings, Meredith imagined she didn't know how much longer she could fund her mother in that care home.

It wasn't just about money. She knew that Margot didn't like seeing her mother in a care home; it was one of the reasons the visits were so difficult for her. But Esme refused her offers to return to live in Willow Tree Cottage. That came as no surprise. Meredith understood why Esme didn't want to return to the house her father had banished her to. It would just dredge up memories of the past.

She stared at her best friend, feeling sad when she thought about her childhood there. Although Margot had had a happy childhood at Willow Tree Cottage, one summer her mother had bought an old houseboat and had started renovating it. She'd spent weeks on the houseboat, often sleeping there. Esme had spent less and less time at Willow Tree Cottage, practically leaving her daughter to be raised by the governess and Meredith's mother.

'You visit my mother more than you do your own.'

'Yes, Meredith, and you know why that is. She was more like a mother to me than my mother ever was.'

Meredith remained silent, although she nodded in silent understanding. She asked, 'Did your mother ever answer your question?'

Margot shook her head.

'Is that why you won't visit her, because she still won't tell you who your father is?'

'I don't know anything about him. How they met. Who he was. Where he came from. Absolutely nothing. She won't speak of him.'

'Why do you think that is?'

'Honestly, I don't know.' Margot frowned. 'Like you said, she's not getting any younger. I might never know if she—'

Meredith nodded. 'Look, have you thought of joining one of those DNA sites? There may be a way of finding him without relying on her to tell you. What if it was a one-night stand and she never knew his name, but is too embarrassed to tell you? It was the end of the Second World War. It could have been, you know, a one-night stand on VE day, during the VE day celebrations.'

Margot had thought of that.

'Joining one of those sites might be your only way.'

'I know. I thought of asking Ray, my neighbour. It's what he does now, he runs a little business tracing long-lost relatives of people who have died intestate.'

Meredith looked at her blankly.

'Without a will.'

'Ah. I see. Well, that won't happen to me.'

'Or me. I've left you everything.'

'What?' Meredith looked at her taken aback. 'You can't. What about—?'

Margot held up her hand. 'I've left you the cottage. You've always been like a sister to me, Meredith. You're the only family I've got now.'

Meredith said, 'Sorry to ask a really dumb question, but has your mother left you this house in her will?'

'Yes, she has. I have left you my entire estate, which should include the cottage if my mother dies before me.'

'Don't get me wrong, I'm not suddenly interested because you've just told me about *your* will, and god knows I'd much rather I go first – I can't imagine life without you, Margot. It just made me wonder if she has spoken to you about her wishes? Perhaps she mightn't want you to leave me her house. Have you thought of that?'

'Well, no, but—'

'I think you should go and see her, Margot. And if I were you, I'd ask Ray if he could help you with joining one of those DNA websites.' She paused. 'What's stopping you?' She had intended it to be a rhetorical question, but Margot answered.

'What if I find out who he was, and he's ...'

'He's *what*?'

'Dead.'

'Oh, Margot. If that's what you're worried about, the longer you delay ...'

Margot could see her point. 'I'll have to wait to see Ray until after the summer holidays when I go back to the houseboat.'

'You really need to end that charade.' Meredith shook her head. 'While we're on that subject, I've been meaning to ask – did you remember to pick up the spare key from under the flowerpot?'

Margot raised her eyes.

'Oh, Margot. You do this every time. It's all well and good leaving it there in case you get locked out, but now you've gone for the summer, don't you think it's risky leaving it there? You don't know who might happen along and find it.'

Margot sighed. 'No one is going to find that key. Besides, it's not as though there's anything much to steal apart from some old furniture and clothes in the bedroom cupboard. Oh, and I think I left a jar of pickles, a jar of coffee, some teabags, and a pint of milk in the fridge.'

'This is no joking matter, Margot. Times have changed. Someone might move in and refuse to leave.'

'A squatter?' Margot could see her point. 'The trouble is I can't go back now.'

'All right. When I've got a chance, I'll walk to the houseboat and pick up the key.'

'Thank you, Meredith. What would I do without you?'

❖

Margot swivelled in her chair and stared out of the window at the garden. It seemed like no time had passed at all since she'd sat in this study writing her last unfinished novel. She could almost hear the children's voices in the garden, playing around the weeping willow tree. Oh, how they loved the garden, just as she and Meredith had when they were children.

Margot listened to Meredith's footsteps heading away down the hall, and heard the front door click shut as her friend left. She turned to the typewriter and looked at the single A4 sheet of paper. Her fingers hovered over the keys as her eyes roved to an unfinished manuscript sitting on her desk. It was yellowed with age. Her eyes shifted to the newest photo on her desk, taken twenty years earlier, of two small children, the eldest with her arm around her little sister's shoulders. Their pose was much like that of herself and Meredith in the photo behind it, taken decades earlier. Margot wiped away a tear. When would she accept that they were gone? And, no matter what Meredith said, she would always blame herself – it was all her fault.

She looked at the typewriter, and removed her fingers from

the keys. When would she come to terms with their loss and write again? Margot got up from her chair, walked out of the study and shut the door. Perhaps Meredith was right: she should return to the houseboat, spend the summer there, deal with her grief, and put behind her what had taken place there one summer, all those years ago. Then, and only then, would she be able to write again.

3

Lexi carried her bag of shopping across the footbridge, called Bailey Bridge, from the Southwold side of the River Blyth into Walberswick. She couldn't stop smiling. She now had a job. It wasn't just a temporary summer job, which was what she'd expected to find if she was lucky. This librarian apprenticeship could be a new career, and the start of a new life here in England, if that was what she decided she wanted.

It would be a huge change from the long hours she'd worked in publishing, and the glitzy fast-paced life she had been leading in New York, but as she'd discovered, that life wasn't all it was cracked up to be. And neither was Brandon. Lexi dismissed him from her mind. She did not want the thought of her ex spoiling the moment and her happy, carefree mood.

As she turned onto the path along the quay where the houseboats were moored, Lexi thought of Hazel at her little publishing house in London. Lexi had flown over from America to hand-deliver a letter to a woman in order to fulfil her late mother's wishes. Her mother had left her some money for the trip. She'd had no idea who this woman was or where she lived – there was no address on the envelope apart from her name, Margot

Dorey, and the word *England.* However, the lawyer who'd handled her late mother's estate had discovered there was a reclusive English writer by that name. There was an address for the publisher in Bloomsbury, London who had published her books years earlier. Lexi had visited the little publishing house, which was owned by a lady called Hazel, and had discovered that Margot Dorey had been their star writer. She'd published a very successful children's trilogy, but had stopped writing twenty years earlier – due to a family tragedy, Hazel had surmised, although she didn't know any details.

Hazel had been able to supply her last known address; a houseboat on the quay in Walberswick.

Lexi still didn't want to think about what she had done next. She'd felt like a naïve American abroad when she'd realised that an innocent question from a passer-by on the street wasn't innocent at all; she'd been pickpocketed, and all her money and bank cards had gone.

Leaving her hotel in London without paying, Lexi had used her pre-paid train tickets and taken the train from Liverpool Street to the Suffolk Coast, where she'd found Margot Dorey's houseboat – unoccupied, with a key under the flowerpot. She hadn't intended to become a squatter, but when she'd spoken with the owner of a neighbouring houseboat, Ray, she'd discovered that Margot Dorey would not be back all summer – according to him, she spent her summers with family in London. Lexi had decided to stay on in the houseboat until she returned, telling Ray a fib that she was houseboat-sitting.

That had been the plan until she had discovered that Margot Dorey was not in London. It was just by chance that she'd been working at the library when a lady called Meredith had visited to collect some library books for her friend, Margot Dorey. Lexi had followed Meredith, and had discovered that Margot Dorey was not in London, but right there, a few hundred yards from the quay, just up the street in Walberswick.

Lexi's first instinct had been to run back to the houseboat, gather her things, and leave as quickly as she could before she was discovered. But then it dawned on her that Margot Dorey wouldn't be returning to her houseboat any time soon – she wouldn't dare to show her face until the end of the summer at the earliest.

Whatever Margot Dorey's reasons were, Lexi knew she'd lied to her houseboat neighbours, and had been doing so for years, by the sounds of it. For that reason, Lexi knew with certainty that Margot would not be back right away, so she had time to figure out what she would do about accommodation. And the discovery had worked in her favour in another way: now she didn't have to wait for Margot Dorey to return to the houseboat – she just had to walk up the road and deliver the letter.

Lexi's thoughts turned to Hazel at the publishing house in London. She wanted Margot Dorey back on her books, if she started writing again. *Can I persuade her to do that when I deliver her letter?* thought Lexi. Hazel had made no formal offer of a job; it had just been a throwaway remark regarding the need for more staff if Lexi were to find Margot Dorey and persuade her to write another book. Lexi got the impression that Hazel thought the scenario was highly unlikely. She recalled the conversation about the finder's fee, though. Wouldn't that be the icing on the cake if she met Margot Dorey, who agreed to write another book in her series and let Hazel publish it?

Lexi was already thinking ahead. That finder's fee might amount to a couple of thousand pounds, which would pay for a deposit on a rental and perhaps even a couple of months' rent. Lexi hadn't researched the local rental market, but she imagined that Jill, the librarian who had hired her at the local library in Southwold, was right: she couldn't live on the wages from the librarian apprenticeship – certainly not if she had to pay for accommodation and bills. Would Hazel offer her a job? Could she drop a few hours at the library and work for Hazel too, remotely?

Lexi's mind was racing. She really didn't want to spoil the moment by thinking what would happen at the end of the summer, when she imagined Margot planned to return. Lexi knew she would go and hand her the letter before that happened, but right now she was happy in the houseboat, and whatever was in that letter, she didn't want to risk precipitating Margot's return any earlier, before she figured out what she was going to do after she had vacated the houseboat. She had solved her immediate predicament; she had somewhere to live, and she'd just have to let the end of the summer look after itself. Things were looking good – perfect, even – at the moment, and that was all she wanted to focus on.

Lexi was almost skipping down the path. As she neared Margot's houseboat, she noted that nothing had changed – the curtains were open, and there was no sign of anybody inside. The gate to the boat's little gangplank was securely shut, just as she'd left it that morning.

She stole a furtive glance up and down the quay, checking for anybody walking along who might live in one of the neighbouring houseboats and might question why she was there. Lexi had told Ray she was houseboat-sitting. She imagined that word would soon spread within the little houseboat community, but for now there was nobody around, apart from a group of teenagers who had approached the bridge from Walberswick as she crossed from the other direction.

Lexi opened the gate, closed it behind her and walked down the gangplank to step on the boat. She put the bag of shopping she'd bought from the Co-op in Southwold on the little wooden garden table on the deck outside the cabin door. She bent over to tip the flowerpot, putting her hand underneath to retrieve the small plastic bag containing the key. It was where she had originally found it, and she left it there each time she went out. It made sense to do so; she was afraid she'd lose the key if she took it with her.

'That's odd.' She could not feel the bag. She lifted the flowerpot up. Nothing. She was sure it was the right flowerpot. She looked at the other one, sitting by the door on the other side. She lifted that one too. There was still no sign of the door key. She put the flowerpot down and thought back to that morning. 'Did I take the key after all?'

Lexi emptied her handbag on the table. No key. 'Damn! What could have happened to it?' She looked about the deck and under other pots, even though she knew where she had left it. She stood up and scratched her head.

'Oh, god,' she said under her breath. There was only one explanation – someone had been here and taken the key.

4

'Everything okay?'

Lexi turned around at the sound of a familiar voice. Ray had a newspaper tucked under his arm and a bag of shopping from the local Co-op, just like hers.

'I'm locked out,' Lexi called out. *If someone has been here,* she thought, *have they been inside and seen my suitcase?* She'd left her case by the stairs. Perhaps if they'd looked in at one of the windows, they wouldn't have spotted it, and nothing would have seemed amiss. She expected that if whoever had been there had discovered her belongings on the boat, they would have stayed and waited for her return. The fact that no one was there, waiting for her, said they hadn't been inside. They'd just been sent to collect the key.

Why Lexi hadn't thought of it before, she had no clue. It made sense. She expected that Margot left the spare key under the flowerpot in case she mislaid her keys and locked herself out. But she wouldn't leave it there over the summer when she wasn't around. There was only one explanation; she'd forgotten to take it with her.

It couldn't have been Ray who'd taken the key. The look on his face was just one of concern.

'I don't know what to do,' said Lexi. All her belongings were on the houseboat. But it wasn't just that fact that had spoiled Lexi's perfect morning – there was the issue of what she would do for accommodation if she had to leave.

'I'm just going to pop my newspaper and shopping home. I'll be right back,' said Ray. 'Just hold tight.'

Lexi watched him walk past the houseboat next door, which the little girl and her father were renting, and disappear inside his boat.

A moment later, he appeared at the gate. 'Permission to come aboard?'

Lexi stared at him. Was he having a joke at a time like this? Or was this some kind of English tradition among the boating community. 'Er, yeah – sure.'

Ray smiled as he opened the gate. He stepped aboard. He'd brought with him what appeared to be a black toiletry bag. Lexi frowned. 'What's that?'

He walked over to the table and unzipped the small cotton bag. Lexi watched in surprise as he placed it on the table and rolled it out, revealing little pockets with small stainless steel tools.

He picked one up that resembled a long pair of tweezers and turned around. He must have noticed Lexi's surprised expression.

'Are you going to pick the lock?'

'Now, I did tell you that I'm a retired police officer, didn't I?'

Lexi nodded.

'I don't know why I kept them when I retired. Well, actually, I do. For just this scenario. Not you, I hasten to add – it's me. I do tend to put things down and then I'll be darned if I know where they are – including my door keys. It's very expensive to call out a locksmith, so these have come in handy from time to time.'

He knelt down at the door, then glanced over his shoulder. 'Do you mind if I pick your lock?' He grinned. 'Sounds silly to ask, but the look on your face says to me you didn't quite expect this.'

I'll say, thought Lexi. She bit her lip. He only ought to know that it wasn't her lock he was picking. He was a retired police officer aiding and abetting breaking into someone else's property for a squatter.

He stopped. 'If you prefer to call a locksmith ...'

Lexi's expression had given her away, but not for the reasons she knew he would be imagining. 'Er, no – I'm quite happy *not* to call a blacksmith. Please go ahead.'

Lexi didn't have the money for a locksmith. She glanced at her plastic bag full of shopping. She barely had the money for grocery shopping. Pay day wasn't until the end of the week. It was only Monday. She was lucky that she still had five pounds left in her pocket and that it had bought some necessities from the local grocery store.

Lexi stepped back and looked about her, hoping no one, especially a nosy neighbour, happened to be passing and saw what was going on. She took a seat at the table and watched as Ray turned around several times to try different instruments.

'There, all done.' Ray pushed the door wide open. He turned around and handed Lexi the lock.

Lexi looked at him in surprise. 'Oh, I didn't realise you'd have to take it apart.'

He sighed. 'These things happen, I'm afraid. The lock is quite old. It kind of fell apart as I was, er, doing my thing. Sorry about that.'

Lexi looked at the broken lock in her hands. *Now what was she going to do?*

'I have a friend in the local hardware store. I could ask him to pop along and fit a new lock with a new set of keys?'

Lexi finally had to explain her financial predicament. She couldn't see any way out of it.

Ray noticed her hesitate. 'Ah, would you need to contact the agency?'

'Agency?'

'The agency for the houseboat-sitting?'

'Oh, yes – right.' Lexi had completely forgotten about that little white lie. 'Er, no … that won't be necessary.'

She caught his confused expression.

'Um, what I mean to say is that I can tell them about it when I leave.' Lexi wasn't exactly sure how she would go about telling Margot Dorey that she'd had her locks changed. She looked at Ray. Perhaps she could leave the keys with him, and then Margot would be none the wiser as to who had been living in her houseboat these past few weeks.

Lexi still had to explain why she couldn't afford to get the locks changed.

'Look, the problem is, I haven't got the money to have it done.'

'Yes, they are expensive. I imagine the agency could contact Margot and—'

Lexi quickly said, 'But I lost the keys, so it's kind of my responsibility, isn't it?' For once, Lexi told the truth.

'Ah, I see what you mean.'

'The thing is, when I arrived in London, I must have looked like a gullible tourist because I had my purse stolen and all my money.'

'You were pickpocketed?'

'Yes.'

'Did you report it to the police?'

Lexi could feel her face going bright red at the thought. Of course Ray would say that. She couldn't report it because she still hadn't paid for one of her nights at the hotel. She had received quite a few text messages and phone calls demanding that she get in contact to pay her bill, all of which she'd deleted. They had been rather nice to begin with, saying they imagined that it was most probably an oversight on her part, and would she be so kind as to get in touch. But they had become increasingly demanding until the last one said they were going to call the police. Lexi looked wide-eyed at Ray and lied. 'Yes.'

'There's not a lot they can do, I'm afraid. Hopefully your bank might be able to reimburse the money. Did you cancel your cards?'

'I did, yes. They will send out new ones in the post, but of course that will be to my address in the States. In the meantime, I thought I would open a bank account here.'

'That's a good idea – then the agency can pay your wages into that account.'

'Yes.' She avoided eye contact. Ray seemed like such a nice man, and she felt so guilty for telling all these bare-faced lies. Her stated intention to open a bank account wasn't a lie, but pretty much everything else was. Although she was being honest when she said, 'I can't possibly let your friend fix the locks and not pay him. But I've got no money to pay the locksmith until payday.' Lexi frowned when the word *payday* slipped out of her mouth. She hadn't intended to mention her new job in the library. But then she remembered that he thought she was houseboat-sitting.

'Look, I'd strongly advise you to get the lock fixed. I'm afraid you don't know who might happen along, see an opportunity, and take advantage of my very lovely neighbour, Margot.'

Lexi didn't know where to look. She wished the ground could swallow her up.

'So, I'll tell you what. Why don't I pay for it?'

Lexi shook her head.

'Hear me out. I'll lend you the money and you can pay me back. How about it?'

'Really?' Lexi didn't mind so much if it was a loan.

'What are neighbours for?'

'That is so kind of you.'

Ray grinned. 'And talking of neighbours, it really is quite handy that he lives on a houseboat just a few doors down.'

Lexi looked at Ray bemused. 'Who does?'

'My friend who works at the hardware store in town. The guy who will be coming to fix your lock. Between you and me, I think he's got a bit of a thing for Margot. He's going to be very pleased to hear that someone is looking after her home while she's away.'

Lexi swallowed. The last thing she needed was to get involved with any more neighbours – especially someone who had a 'thing' for Margot.

'Don't look so worried. He'll get that lock sorted in no time. Are you in this evening?'

Where else would I be? Lexi thought. She loved the houseboat, even though she really didn't like that it was on the water, but the thought of sitting in there all evening on her own wasn't exactly filling her with warmth – although she was rather enjoying catching up on some reading. In between her high-flying job and demanding boyfriend, Lexi had rarely had any time to herself in New York. Now she had a lot of time to sit and read. Hazel, Margot's publisher, had given her a copy of the first book in Margot's trilogy when she'd visited the small publishing house in

Bloomsbury. Lexi was rather enjoying it.

'I'll give him a ring and see if he can pop round after work.'

Lexi heaved a sigh. She couldn't very well say no. 'Sure – why not? Thank you.'

'He's a lovely guy – very chatty.'

Lexi said, 'Oh, great,' hoping Ray didn't catch the sarcasm in her voice. That was all she needed; a chatty neighbour. She imagined word was going to spread around the little houseboat community.

'His name is Alan.'

'Okay.'

Lexi watched Ray step off the boat as she picked up her bag of shopping.

'I forgot to ask, are you okay for an evening meal?'

Lexi turned back to find Ray standing at the gate. 'I'd invite you over, but Sarah is coming over this evening for a meal. I can pop you something round. We're having linguine with garlic butter prawns.'

Lexi's mouth watered. It sounded delicious. She shook her head, far too embarrassed to admit that she only really had the money to buy breakfast and lunch. She imagined her evening meal would consist of cheese on toast and a cup of coffee. 'No, I'm fine.' She held up the plastic carrier bag of shopping, thankful he couldn't see its contents. 'I've got plenty.'

'Okay. Well if you need anything, you know where I am.'

Lexi smiled. It was nice to know that he was there. Lexi frowned when she thought of her family and how unhelpful they were being. She'd told her sister, Andrea, to keep it a secret that she was going to England. It was all rather petty and childish, but for some reason her maternal grandparents, along with her stepdad, Mitch, frowned at any mention of her returning to England.

She had been born in England and had lived there until the age of six, when her English father had died. Lexi's American mother had taken her and her sister, Andrea, back to America to live in Connecticut with her wealthy maternal grandparents.

As soon as they'd found out she'd taken a trip to England – annoyingly, her sister just couldn't keep a secret – they'd booked her a one-way ticket, travelling first class, back to America. Lexi knew she shouldn't have told anyone. Her mother had told her in the note that came with Margot Dorey's letter and the money not to tell anyone about her trip. She'd stupidly told her sister.

Then she'd had to ask Andrea for help after her money had been stolen, but she'd refused. Worse still, when her grandpa had found out she was in England, he'd cut her off from the allowance that was normally deposited in her bank account every month. Andrea had checked her account in America; the allowance had been stopped. For the first time in her life, she really was on her own.

The only person who would help her out, bizarrely, was Brandon, even though they'd split up. He'd texted, called, and left voicemails, all of which Lexi had ignored and then deleted. The problem with Brandon was that he never had any money. She knew that for a fact because during all the years they'd been together – since high school – he had never once got a job. After college, when they'd moved into an apartment in New York, paid for by her grandfather, Lexi had ditched her part-time jobs after college and started working full time while Brandon continued to write music; he was convinced that one day he would be discovered by a record label and get a recording contract from one of his demos or the gigs he'd played in bars around New York. Ten years after forming a band at the age of sixteen, he was no closer to that elusive recording contract. Lexi thought it was probably time for him to get a proper job, echoing just what her family had been saying for years.

Lexi watched Ray walk down the path to his houseboat. She looked at the broken lock in her hand and put it on the table. There was no point taking it inside with her.

5

'What happened to your door?'

Lexi whirled around. 'Oh, Charlie! You gave me a start!' Lexi had had her back to the door, reaching for her shopping on the table, but had got side-tracked by her mobile phone. She'd received another text from Brandon. When would he get the message that she did not want to speak to him? She put her phone away and looked at Charlie, who had clearly slipped onto the houseboat when Lexi wasn't looking and had caught sight of the broken lock on the table. She picked it up.

Lexi's eyes drifted from the curious ten-year-old girl to the Airbnb houseboat next door, where Charlie was staying with her father. They'd arrived the same day as Lexi, the previous Thursday. She had seen the two of them arriving late that night.

Lexi had invited Charlie over on Friday because she had felt sorry for her. She'd heard the row next door and had seen Charlie storm out and sit alone on the deck, crying. So, Lexi had introduced herself and asked her over for some lunch, unbeknown to her father. In hindsight, it had been a stupid thing to do, not telling her father where she was, but Lexi's actions hadn't been completely selfless. She was lonely, and it had been lovely to have some company. Charlie had enjoyed herself, nosing around someone else's boat, preferring the cosy, homely feel of Margot's little place to their big, bland houseboat with the very boring beige interior.

Charlie said, 'Aren't you going to tell me what happened?'

Lexi looked at Charlie, who was holding up the broken lock.

'Oh, yes.' Lexi had been lost in thought. She hadn't told Charlie her secret – that she was squatting – so she couldn't tell her that someone had come by and taken the key. She looked at the lock. 'I lost my key, so Ray, who lives next door to you guys, picked the lock. But as you can see, that didn't go so well.'

She expected Charlie to look a bit surprised that someone had picked the lock. Instead, she said, 'You could have asked my dad. Daddy can open anything. He has the tools.'

'Tools? Were they like in a little bag that unrolls with lots of different implements?'

'Yes.'

'Is your dad a police officer?'

'No.'

Lexi stared at her. 'What does your dad do?'

Charlie put the lock down and ran over to the cabin door. Was she avoiding the question? Lexi remembered when she had visited before and had shared a secret that Lexi had to promise not to tell; Charlie had confided in her that they moved around a lot and that she thought her dad was on the run. Lexi had smiled at Charlie, the little girl with the overactive imagination. That was the trouble with spending far too much time on your own, she had thought; you could start to imagine all sorts of crazy things.

Lexi had found her own imagination running wild when she thought of the letter that she needed to deliver to Margot Dorey to fulfil her late mother's wishes. She still didn't know what was so important about it that she'd had to travel to England herself and give it to the lady in person. She had often felt like unsealing it and reading the letter to find out; at least that would stop her imagination working overtime. But she wouldn't open someone else's letter and read it.

Perhaps Andrea was right; perhaps there was a simple explanation, and it was written in her own letter. Lexi and Andrea had each been left a personal letter from their mother. Andrea had opened hers months earlier, but Lexi had not. *Maybe I should open it and find out,* Lexi mused.

'I'll do it later,' Lexi said under her breath, knowing that one day soon she really would have to confront the final letter her mother had written to her. Perhaps if she did read it, it would shed some light on who Margot Dorey was.

Lexi remembered the call from the lawyers who'd handled her mother's will. It had been six months since she'd passed away, and the letter had only just come to light. She'd met the grandson who had taken over running the law firm in Connecticut. His grandfather had recently retired. The young lawyer had told Lexi that he'd been doing an audit and had discovered an irregularity – at least, that's what he'd called it. There was a suggestion that the letter for Margot Dorey had been misfiled on purpose. Lexi's grandparents were wealthy, and were the oldest clients of the family firm of lawyers in Connecticut. They were also good friends of the old man who'd founded the law firm.

The young lawyer had immediately contacted Lexi when the letter, along with the money and her mother's wishes, had come to light. Lexi didn't want to think that there had been a conspiracy between her grandparents and Mitch, who had warned her off returning to England. She hoped it had been the case that it had just been accidentally misfiled, and that it was simply her imagination that had her thinking all sorts of crazy things – just like the little girl on the houseboat next door. Although there was no getting away from the fact that her family did not want her to return to England, that didn't mean it had anything to do with the woman she was there to find.

What if Margot was just an old friend that her mother had not kept in touch with over the years, and to make amends she'd sent her eldest daughter to hand-deliver an apology? Lexi knew that her mum had been aware of her desire to return to England on vacation, but that she had just never seemed to find the right moment. Perhaps this was her way of just forcing the issue; getting her to drop everything and just go.

Of course, it hadn't quite worked out that way. But she was there, wasn't she? Perhaps her own personal letter from her mum explained all this, and who Margot was. *So, why not read it?* She had brought it with her. But why did she have this sinking feeling every time she thought of opening it?

Her sister's letter had been no big deal. It had been exactly what she'd expected, all about her impending wedding and her mum's sorrow at not being there for her. Lexi knew that when she opened her own letter, she would open up her heart to grief again and an awful wave of loss at her mother's passing. She was afraid of that. But she was more afraid of her mother's last words to her. Would they be kind, or would they berate her for the things she had or had not done? Would she ask of her something that she could not or would not be able to fulfil? *Perhaps,* thought Lexi, *I should read my letter, just to put all these wild imaginings of what it might contain to rest.*

Lexi followed Charlie down the wooden steps into the houseboat. Although she was more than happy for her to visit again – Lexi wasn't really looking forward to another evening all on her own – she did wonder what Charlie was doing there. She wondered if Charlie was just as bored and lonely as she was.

Lexi had found out during Charlie's last visit that she was home-schooled, but not through choice. She really wanted to go to school. Lexi had suggested she speak to her father, and tell him how she felt, but she'd said she'd already tried that; he wouldn't listen. Although they weren't there on holiday as Lexi had first thought – Charlie had said this was their home now – Lexi got the impression that Charlie's father was not putting down roots.

Lexi walked through the small lounge across the wooden flooring, taking off her shoes before she stepped onto the brown woven rug. She passed the beige sofa and its white throw, which had a yellow daisy pattern that matched the curtains, recalling when she'd first stepped into the houseboat. She hadn't been surprised it was so small inside, but she had loved the cosy feel. She enjoyed sitting on the sofa, facing the two cabin windows that looked out over the River Blythe. She had a perfect view of the bank on the Southwold side and the fishing huts where they sold fresh fish, caught that day. She also loved The Harbour Inn, which was right on the quay.

Late in the evening, as dusk approached, she loved sitting there looking at The Harbour Inn lit up in the dark, and watching the cars arriving outside on the quay as people arrived for evening meals or just a drink with friends.

Lexi walked around the trunk that sat in front of the sofa. It felt a bit chilly, so she stopped in front of the small wood burner in the corner of the room, but changed her mind about lighting it.

She did that every evening. Lexi knew why she refrained from lighting it; she was afraid something would happen. What if a spark from the fire damaged the wooden flooring or the lovely rug?

She didn't see how that would happen, as the little log burner wasn't an open fire, but she didn't want to risk it; the last thing she wanted to do was cause any damage on the houseboat. She was being really careful.

She walked behind the sofa to the small kitchenette on the other side of the room, where there was a window overlooking the riverbank path. The door at the end of the narrow cabin led to a tiny toilet and shower room, and one double bedroom that just fitted a double bed and an inbuilt wardrobe that she had to crawl over the bed to get to.

Lexi put her handbag and the shopping bag on the kitchen counter. She glanced at Charlie, who had kicked off her trainers and had sat down on the sofa, making herself at home.

'Have you told your dad that you were coming over?' Lexi asked.

Charlie turned around, resting her chin on the back of the sofa, bright blue eyes staring at Lexi. 'Yes.'

'Good, because you know what happened last time.'

Charlie rolled her eyes. 'He gets cross about the least little thing.'

'I don't think he was cross really. I think you scared him, disappearing like that. He didn't know where you were.'

Lexi recalled what else had happened – she'd felt a little embarrassed and tongue-tied under the good-looking young man's gaze.

Lexi had been surprised; she'd just split up with Brandon, whom she'd known since school and whom she'd thought was the love of her life, and there she was finding herself attracted to a man she'd just met.

'I wish we didn't have to move around all the time. I like it here.'

Lexi liked it there too. She glanced at Charlie as she unpacked the shopping. A small, skinny slip of a girl with blonde pigtails, she was still wearing the oversized jean dungarees and t-shirt that Lexi had seen her in the first time they'd met. It had been hard to gauge her age; she looked younger than ten.

Lexi smiled at her, thinking back to the secret that Charlie had told her about her dad being on the run, and believing he was in some sort of trouble. 'I imagine there's lots of reasons why you and your dad have to move around. Your daddy's work, for one.'

'But he works from home. It's not like we have to move around the country for that.'

'Well, finding a rental these days isn't always easy. Sometimes landlords want people to leave, and then you have to find somewhere else. As I said, there are all sorts of reasons.'

'Why can't he just *buy* a house?'

'Well, um, that's a good question.' Lexi was fast coming to the realisation that Charlie was very smart, and that she was not easily fobbed off with lame excuses. 'Maybe your father is looking for the perfect little home for you both in the right area. That could take a while.' Lexi caught the sceptical look on Charlie's face.

'How long does *that* take?'

'I don't know, Charlie. I guess it depends on where he is looking. Why don't you ask him? And while you're at it, you could remind him that you'd like to go to school.'

Charlie pulled a face. 'I have! He never listens.' Charlie changed the subject. 'Do you like it here?'

Lexi looked around the houseboat. It was growing on her, that was for sure. But the problem was that every time she walked down that gangplank, she was scared of falling into the water. Petrified, actually. She knew she had a phobia of water.

'Do you wish you didn't have to move again?' asked Charlie.

She looked at Charlie. Lexi reckoned that most school-aged children had been taught to swim. But Charlie didn't go to school, so she might not have had lessons. Lexi wondered if Charlie's father ever took her swimming. She imagined that if he did, Charlie didn't throw a huge strop and refuse to get in. Lexi had been doing that ever since she could remember.

'Yes, I do like it here,' said Lexi, in response to her question. 'But unfortunately I will have to leave soon too.'

'When?'

'When Margot returns.'

'Who's Margot?'

Lexi grimaced. She hadn't meant to say that. It just slipped out. 'She's the lady who owns the houseboat.'

'So, you're renting too?'

Lexi bit her lower lip. She hated spinning so many lies. She looked at Charlie's innocent expression, and thought *I can't do this – lie to her anymore.* Lexi put the last of her shopping away, closed the kitchen cupboard door and turned to Charlie. 'Can you keep a secret?'

6

Lexi sat down on the sofa next to Charlie. She took a deep breath, gearing up to telling her the truth. She just hoped Charlie could keep a secret. 'Do you know what squatting means?'

Charlie thought about it for a moment. She suddenly scrambled off the sofa and stood in front of Lexi. 'Like this?'

Lexi watched her start to do squats.

Charlie stopped. 'What's so funny?'

'That's not the sort of squatting I meant.'

'Oh.' Charlie sat back down on the sofa next to her.

'I'm squatting on the houseboat. That means I ...' Lexi frowned. There was no way of sugar-coating what she was doing. It was wrong, and that was that. 'I'm not meant to be here. I found the key and let myself in. Doing that is ... against the law.'

Charlie's big blue eyes stared at her.

Lexi continued, 'I'm not excusing what I did, it's just that I came all the way from America to see the lady who lives here in order to deliver a letter. Then I found out she's away for the summer, so I'm staying here until she returns. She just doesn't know that.' Lexi added, 'And neither do the neighbours, like Ray. I lied and told him that I'm looking after her boat until she comes back.'

Charlie was uncharacteristically quiet. Lexi wasn't surprised, after what she'd said.

Charlie said, 'I don't see why that's against the law if you're looking after her houseboat. You're a nice person. What if a horrible person came along and found the key? They might not look after Margot's houseboat like you.'

'That's true, but it's still wrong. I haven't got her permission to be here.'

Charlie brow furrowed. 'Why can't you get her permission then? Oh, wait. She's in London. Well, it's not your fault, then, is it?'

Actually, it is, thought Lexi. She knew exactly where Margot was. All she had to do was walk up the road and ask her if she could stay on her houseboat, but unfortunately things were never that simple. Margot wouldn't let her stay there for free, and Lexi didn't have much money. But that wouldn't be the main issue if she did deliver the letter and ask Margot if she could stay on her houseboat for the summer; the problem was that she was already there. Lexi knew that if she was in Margot's shoes, she wouldn't take too kindly to a stranger squatting in her home.

Charlie asked, 'When did you say that Margot comes back?'

'At the end of the school summer holidays.' Lexi hoped that Ray had got that right. She added, 'In a few weeks.'

'Good, because I don't want you to leave. I like you.'

Lexi smiled. 'I like you too. Charlie reminded her of someone. Lexi frowned. She couldn't think who.

'What's the matter, Lexi?'

'Oh, it's nothing.' *But it was something.* Lexi smiled at her. 'So, shall I make a drink? Would you like a cup of tea?' Lexi remembered her last visit. She hadn't had any squash to offer her, but

Charlie didn't mind; she liked a nice brew, as she'd called it. Charlie had said. *For an American, you make rather a good brew.*

'Yes, please,' said Charlie.

Lexi smiled. 'One brew coming right up,' she said. She returned to the kitchenette, flicked on the kettle, and made them both a drink. She returned to the sofa carrying a tea-tray with two mugs and a plate of biscuits. Lexi set the tray down on the old trunk in front of the sofa and handed Charlie a cup of milky, sweet tea. Lexi picked up her tea.

'Do you have a boyfriend?'

Lexi kept a smile on her face. She turned to Charlie. 'No.'

'Don't you want one?'

What Lexi wanted was to change the subject. She reached for the plate of biscuits. 'How about a custard cream?'

'May I have two?'

'Of course you can.'

Charlie took the biscuits. She sat munching on one, eyeing Lexi.

Lexi avoided her gaze. She sat and finished her tea hoping that her little friend didn't bring up the boyfriend thing again.

'Do you have to go back to America? Can't you stay here?'

'I *can* stay here in fact. Well, not here on the houseboat, but in England. You know, I was born in England. I have a British passport. I lived here until I was six.'

'Why did you leave and move to America?' Charlie rolled your eyes. 'It was your dad, wasn't it?'

Lexi looked at her.. 'How did you know?'

'Well, my daddy makes us move around all the time.'

'Ah, I see.' Although Lexi had already told Charlie that her father had died, she looked at her and decided not to tell her when it had happened. It seemed that she had enough on her plate without putting it in her head that a healthy man who wasn't even middle-aged had died suddenly of a heart attack. If Charlie thought her life was pretty crap just then, Lexi did not want to send her home with the thought in her head that it could possibly happen to her father. Charlie already had an overactive imagination.

'I guess I don't sound very English to you.' When Lexi had first moved to America and started school, she'd been teased about her English accent. But rather than imitate her classmates to try and fit in, Lexi had made a point of trying her hardest to keep her cute English accent, as Brandon had called it. He was the only one who hadn't teased her. It was little wonder he'd become her best friend. They'd been inseparable since they were six.

Lexi rolled her eyes, wishing her thoughts didn't keep going back to Brandon. But it was little wonder. Every memory of her time since moving to America involved her best friend, one way or another.

'You sound like people on TV.'

Lexi smiled. She guessed Charlie was referring to American TV programmes and movies.

Charlie finished both her biscuits and looked at the plate.

Lexi followed her gaze. 'One left each.'

Charlie didn't need to be asked twice. She grabbed another biscuit.

'Eww! Why did you dip your biscuit in your tea?' asked Lexi.

'I didn't dip it.'

'But I just saw—'

'It's called *dunking*. You dunk your biscuit in your tea. Give it a try.'

Lexi looked at her tea. Charlie put her mug down on the trunk and sat watching Lexi tentatively dunked her biscuit. When she took it out, half was missing.

When Charlie saw half of Lexi's biscuit missing she fell about laughing.

'What did I do wrong?'

Charlie shook her head. 'Here, let me show you.' She looked at the empty plate.

'Shall I get some more biscuits?'

Charlie nodded enthusiastically.

Lexi returned to the sofa with the packet of biscuits. She'd just put them on the table, when Charlie reached for the packet and knocked over her mug of tea. It was still half full.

'Oh, no!' Charlie stared at the tea pouring over the side of the coffee table.

Lexi ran over to the kitchen to grab some paper towels from a roll on the kitchen worktop.

'Sorry!' said Charlie, backing away from the table. 'I'd better go.'

'It's okay, honestly. It's just a little bit of tea. There's no harm done. Here, why don't you wipe some of that up from the table while I sort out the floor – huh?' Lexi didn't want her to think she was in trouble just because of some spilled tea. They were having such a good time, and she didn't want a little accident to spoil the day.

Charlie took some kitchen paper off the roll and started to mop up the tea.

Lexi did her best to keep her expression neutral when she saw the tea-stained rug. *God, now what am I going to do?* The paper towels were useless.

Lexi returned to the kitchen and ran some water into a bowl.

She squirted some washing-up liquid in the water and brought over the bowl. She had an idea. If she mopped up the tea on the rug with a wet cloth, perhaps she could take the rug upstairs to dry out on the deck?

'Where's the bin?' asked Charlie. She had a handful of wet kitchen paper.

Lexi pointed at the cupboard under the sink unit. 'It's over there under the sink.'

Charlie came back a moment later. Lexi was on her knees scrubbing the rug. She looked up at her. 'Thank you, Charlie. I've got an idea. Let's move the coffee table off the rug, then I can take the rug out on deck to dry.'

Charlie stood there staring at the tea stain on the rug. 'Sorry.'

Lexi shook her head. 'Don't be silly. You don't have to apologise. Accidents happen. It will be as good as new when it's dry, just you see.'

'I hope so.'

So did Lexi. She got off her knees and carried the bowl over to the sink. 'Right, nearly done.' She sounded a lot more cheerful than she was feeling. Lexi didn't want to take the rug outside. What if someone spotted it who knew Margot was away? But there was a nice breeze outside and Lexi knew the rug would dry much quicker in the fresh air.

Together they lifted the trunk off the rug and placed it under a window. 'Right, I think we should roll up the rug, then we can spread it out on the deck,' Lexi said. They pushed the sofa back to release the rug from under the feet. It was awkward trying to keep hold of the rug so it wasn't dragged along with the sofa, but they managed it.

Lexi stepped back on the corner of the rug that had been

under the sofa. She felt something give way beneath her foot.

'What was that?' asked Charlie.

'Oh, no!' Lexi lurched awkwardly to the side, catching herself on the sofa arm so she didn't fall. She removed her foot from the area where the rug had sunk a couple of inches and knelt down. She gingerly lifted the rug back. 'Oh, dear.' Lexi realised her day was going from bad to worse.

Charlie walked over to take a look.

Lexi held out her hand for her to stop. 'Let's not have any more accidents.'

Charlie stayed where she was but peered over Lexi's shoulder. 'What is that?'

Beneath the wooden flooring they could see the hull of the boat. But it wasn't the hull that had immediately grabbed their attention.

Lexi discovered she had stepped on a loose floorboard, but it didn't look as though it was loose by accident. On closer inspection, she realised that one of the floorboards had been sawn through and fitted back in place.

'It looks like a secret compartment.'

Lexi glanced over her shoulder at Charlie. 'So it does.'

7

'Is there something inside the secret compartment?' Charlie looked in her shoulder bag and found her phone. She switched the light on and shone it into the gap. 'It looks like a box.'

'A tin?' suggested Lexi. She didn't really want to reach inside in case there were spiders.

Charlie noticed her hesitation. She said, 'I've got small hands. I can reach inside and get it out.'

Lexi stood up and let Charlie kneel down in front of her. 'Be careful. Watch your hands. You don't want to get a splinter.'

'Okay.'

Lexi knelt down beside Charlie and took her phone. She held it up, shining the light so they could both see.

'You're right, Lexi – it's a tin.'

Lexi watched her reach inside. The tin seemed wedged. Charlie groaned. 'It's stuck.' She ran her little fingers around the edge.

'There might be something in one of the kitchen drawers that we could—'

Charlie suddenly shot backwards. Lexi caught her.

'I got it!' Charlie held up the tin. There was a thick layer of dust on the top. They both coughed.

'Let me get a cloth and wipe that,' said Lexi. She stood up and walked over to the kitchen area, reaching for the kitchen roll again. They both retreated to the coffee table, the rug forgotten.

Sitting cross-legged on the floor in front of the coffee table, Lexi wiped away the dust, which looked like it had built up over decades. 'You know, I don't think this box has been touched in years,' she said.

Charlie's eyes went wide. 'Do you think it's like a time capsule? Where I used to go to school we did a time capsule and put important things in like photos and the newspaper and other stuff, and we buried it in the playground under a tree.'

Lexi looked at the tin. It did look *very* old. It appeared to be a vintage tin, the scratches and worn appearance showing its age.

Charlie grabbed the tin and tried to open it. 'There's definitely stuff inside.' She shook it.

'Charlie, I wouldn't do that.'

'Why?'

'I think we should treat the tin gently. If the age of this is anything to go by, the contents inside could be quite fragile.' *Or could have disintegrated by now*, she thought. 'Here, let me see if I can open it.'

Charlie reluctantly handed it over.

The first thing Lexi did was to examine the tin. Although it was scratched and worn, and even a little rusty in places, the gold flower and leaf pattern was still visible. 'Oh, my goodness.'

'What is it?'

'This is actually a biscuit tin.'

Charlie's gaze shifted to the packet of custard creams on the table. She looked at Lexi and grinned.

Lexi grinned too, silently sharing the joke. All this – spilling the tea all over the coffee table and on the rug, and then finding the tin hidden under a floorboard – had started with a custard cream.

'How do you know it's a biscuit tin?' asked Charlie.

'Here, on the back – you can just read the gold lettering.' They both looked at the writing. *MacFarlane Lang & Co Ltd, Biscuit Manufacturers, Glasgow & London.*

'Who are those people on the front?'

Lexi turned over the tin and took a closer look at the picture. It was inset, as if in a small photo frame. 'Well, I do believe that's a picture of King George VI and his family. That was the late Queen Elizabeth when she was young.'

'So King George was her dad?'

Lexi looked at Charlie and guessed that history was not on her home-schooling curriculum. It made her wonder what was.

'Do you think this belonged to the king?'

Lexi smiled and shook her head. 'No. These were probably sold in shops up and down the country, just like our biscuit tins now.'

'It's quite big.'

'Yes, it is.' Lexi guessed it was a family-sized biscuit tin. She guessed something else too. Going by the ages of Princess Elizabeth and her sister, this tin was old – *very* old. From the 1940s.

'I want to open it.'

Lexi grinned. 'Me too.'

'Do you think there're still biscuits inside?'

Judging by the weight of the tin, Lexi guessed not. Besides, why would someone go to the trouble of hiding a tin under a floorboard if it just contained biscuits? Lexi had a go at prising off the lid, but it was stuck fast. Unless she wanted to break a fingernail, she'd have to find some other way.

'What about a knife?'

Lexi looked at Charlie. 'Good idea.' She went to fetch a knife from the kitchen drawer. Carefully holding it under the lip of the lid, Lexi started to prise it off. 'It's working!' She put the knife down and pulled off the lid. They both stared at the contents.

There was something wrapped in a muslin cloth. Lexi got it out. 'I think it's a book.' She carefully unwrapped the cloth to reveal what at first glance was a notebook.

In the bottom of the tin, under the notebook, Charlie found a small envelope, yellowed with age. She put it on the table. 'Can we open it?'

Lexi looked at the envelope. It appeared to be a letter. Although the writing was barely legible, it had faded with time, she could make out the name – *Esme*. Lexi thought of the letter she was supposed to deliver to Margot. Ordinarily, she would not open someone else's mail, but this had lain here undiscovered for years. What was the harm in opening it now?

Lexi looked at the notebook. Was this Esme's too? Her attention shifted to the envelope. It was still sealed, suggesting that Esme had never opened the letter. Had she been given the letter and never bothered to read it? Or had someone found the hiding place of her secret diary – stored in a biscuit tin – and placed the letter under her notebook for her to find? The fact that it hadn't been opened suggested that Esme may never have known it was there, hiding under her notebook.

Lexi examined the tin and then cast her gaze around the houseboat. She doubted this houseboat dated from the 1940s. She reckoned Esme, whoever she was, had either owned or lived on this houseboat quite some time after the war, and had stored the tin in a secret place. Why she'd done that was anyone's guess.

'Here, let me open it.' Charlie was getting impatient.

'No, it's okay. I'll do it.' Lexi did not want over-enthusiastic little fingers tearing the paper. She kept it out of her reach as she opened the flap and peered inside.

Charlie leaned forward. 'What's that bulge in the envelope?'

Lexi wondered the same thing. She put her hand inside. 'Ah.'

'What is it?'

Lexi withdraw her hand. Between her fingers was a small white metal band inset with colourful stones that looked like gemstones – sapphires and rubies. 'It's a ring.' Lexi held it up to scrutinise it. The ring was quite ornate, with a hand-carved design on the band which looked like a daisy chain, or maybe ribbons. Lexi couldn't tell. What she did discern, though, was that the design – in fact, the whole ring – seemed very feminine.

'It's not very pretty.'

Lexi looked at Charlie. The ring was quite heavy and bulky, but she imagined that was the popular style back in the day.

'I prefer gold rings.'

Lexi smiled. 'So, do I. But I think this *is* gold.'

'Huh? It doesn't look like gold. There's some gold, but it's also ...'

Lexi smiled wondering when she was going to say the word.

'... white.'

'Bingo!' said Lexi. 'It's white gold.'

'White gold?' Charlie looked at her sceptically. 'There's no such thing.'

'Oh, but there is.' Lexi remembered her history lessons at school. If this was from the period around the time when the biscuit tin was made, the 1940s, then a couple getting engaged or married might exchange rings of white gold, instead of gold. 'It is gold, but with a coating to make it look silvery.'

'Why not just use silver?' Charlie asked, taking the ring from Lexi's fingers.

Lexi smiled at her very bright young friend. She did have a point. However Lexi had an idea what was so special about white gold. It was very pretty, and did resemble silver and platinum, but it was cheaper.

She had some white gold jewellery herself that she'd bought with her wages when she'd first started work. She had been so proud of herself, earning her own money from a part-time job as a student, that she'd splashed out on a treat from her first wage packet and bought a pretty necklace.

Lexi stared at the ring. 'It's very old – that's why it's changed colour over time.' As Charlie turned the ring over in her hand, Lexi caught the golden hue in the light. 'I think it might be an engagement ring or a wedding ring from the 1940s.'

Charlie looked at her. 'Was that when there was a war?'

'Yes, the Second World War.' Lexi picked up the envelope and carefully took out the single sheet of yellowed, lined paper. She held her breath, hoping it didn't disintegrate when she unfolded it.

Charlie scooted closer to Lexi's side and leaned over her arm to inspect it. 'What does it say?'

The writing was faint, but just legible. Lexi read it aloud.

'To my darling Esme. I found your hiding place, in a biscuit tin! You do make me laugh, my dearest. I didn't read your notebook, I promise you, but I have left you something. They're coming for me, so this letter has to be short. I love you, Esme. I want to marry you, and live with you for the rest of my God-given days. This ring is my promise to you that I will return. It was my

mother's ring. It was my most precious possession, and now I entrust it to you. If I am not here when you get back, I will find you. We will be together again. I will put this ring on your finger when we marry.' Lexi took a breath. *'Yours, Kit.'*

'Is that it?'

Lexi thought it was the most beautiful thing she'd ever read. It was the sincerest of love letters. 'It's a love letter, Charlie.'

'Yes, I get that, but—'

'But – what?'

'What happened to Kit and Esme?'

Lexi shook her head. 'I don't know.' Lexi re-read a line in the letter – *They're coming for me.* The young man who had written this letter, Kit, had obviously been in some kind of trouble.

Charlie looked crestfallen for a moment. She shifted her attention back to the letter. 'Oh, look – there's a date.'

'Where?'

Charlie pointed at the top left-hand corner of the letter.

The writing was so faint that Lexi had missed it. 'Oh, yes. You're right.'

'It says *April 8th 1945.*'

'One month before the end of the Second World War,' said Lexi. 'If I remember my history lessons correctly.' She looked at the old notebook. 'Perhaps we can find out more about Kit and Esme in here.' Lexi opened the notebook. It looked like an old school exercise book. The cover was green, and the notebook was lined. She'd expected to open it and find lines and lines of writing.

'Hey, there're drawings,' remarked Charlie.

There was writing on one page, but there were also pencil drawings. She had a quick flick through. Although faded, the pages were still legible.

Charlie said, 'Let's read it!'

Lexi began on the first page. There was a pencil sketch of a barge with three young women sitting on the roof. They were dressed in what appeared to be overalls and heavy boots, their short hair covered in handkerchiefs, like the sort of clothing the Land Army girls wore. The sketches were very good. Below each girl, their names were written – Esme, Joan, and Margaret.

Lexi read from the notebook. *'This is us. We are the new IWs. I must confess that I am a bit apprehensive. My older sisters think I'm mad to become an IW. They said why couldn't I join the Land Army or something? But then they know me – I always have to be a bit different. They're wondering why I'm volunteering at all. But I want to do my bit for the war effort.*

'I know that while they are going to parties I will be working long hours on the barge, transporting coal and steel up and down the country. It's going to be hard work. But I don't care. I hate parties anyway. That's what I said to Mama and Papa when I told them I'd signed up. They were so cross. They said I was too young.

'I don't know why they were making such a fuss. It's not like I was going to war. I wasn't joining up. I was volunteering. I didn't tell Mama and Papa that you had to be seventeen and a half. I couldn't wait six months. By then, the war might be over. I didn't think I'd get away with lying about my age, but I did, and here I am.

'I like my new friends. We only met today. I am the youngest of our crew. I think I am the youngest of all the IWs although I don't think there are that many of us – not as many as the land girls. Joan is funny. She is the oldest of the three of us. Her husband went to war. She hasn't got any children yet, so they let her volunteer. Margaret is twenty. She's like the captain. She isn't married yet, although she does have a fiancé. He went to war. She has a little photo of him. She keeps it in the top breast pocket of her overalls, close to her heart. He is very handsome.

'Oh, I nearly forgot to add that today we start our training. It's only for a few hours. I hope I make a good IW.'

'What are IWs?' asked Charlie.

'I honestly don't know.' She'd heard of land girls, everyone had, but she'd never heard of young women volunteering on canal barges during the Second World War.

Charlie looked closely at the drawings in the notebook. 'There are badges on their jackets that say *IW*.'

Lexi looked closer at the talented young woman's drawings. 'You're right. Perhaps when we read on, we'll find out. But we know one thing for sure. This is Esme's diary.'

'Do you think we will find out who Kit is?'

'I hope so.'

Lexi was about to turn the page when she heard someone shout out, 'Charlie!'

Charlie rolled her eyes. 'That's my dad. I don't want to go. I want to read the notebook. Can I take it with me?'

Lexi shook her head, no. 'It doesn't belong to me, I'm afraid.' Despite confiding in Charlie her secret – that she was squatting on Margot's houseboat – Lexi refrained from telling her that the lady who did own this houseboat was living just up the road in Walberswick. Lexi didn't know how long Margot had owned the houseboat, but she imagined she had no idea what the previous owner had left behind. It made her wonder what had happened to Esme.

8

'Daddy, please can I stay a bit longer? We found this amazing diary under the floorboards all about an IW called Esme and a man called Kit. There was an old ring and a love letter.'

He frowned. 'What's an IW?'

Lexi said, 'We haven't found out yet. We were about to when you—' Lexi had been going to say, *when we heard you shouting*. She said, 'When you called.'

'Oh, Daddy, please let me stay! Lexi doesn't mind. You're busy, and there's nothing for me to do on that houseboat. It's boring. I promise I'll be back for teatime.'

'Teatime? I'm sure Lexi has things to do this afternoon. Besides, I think you've taken up enough of her time already.'

Lexi shook her head. 'No, it's fine, really. I have a completely free afternoon.' Lexi was just as keen as Charlie to find out about Esme and Kit. Of course she could have sat and read it on her own, but it wouldn't be the same. It would be much more fun reading it with Charlie.

Charlie's father looked at his watch. 'All right. But I want you back here by five-thirty exactly – do you understand?'

Lexi found herself nodding vigorously along with Charlie. She said, 'I'll send her over on the dot.'

He eyed Lexi, giving her a wisp of a smile. 'Good.' His gaze shifted to Charlie. 'When you get back, you can tell me what an IW is.'

Charlie grinned. 'I will, Daddy.'

He lingered a moment, staring at Lexi.

She felt uncomfortable under his gaze, wondering what he was thinking. Was he thinking about the first time they'd met, as she was? He'd been very abrupt when he'd discovered she'd invited Charlie over. She didn't blame him; Charlie had given him quite a scare by disappearing. Lexi knew she should have gone next door and introduced herself before inviting his daughter over. It was little wonder he hadn't been happy.

Charlie's father's name was Scott, and Lexi still had that funny tingly sensation she'd had when she'd first set eyes on him.

He was still eyeing her suspiciously, just like in that first meeting. Lexi still wished he wasn't so good-looking. She tried not to stare. In his early thirties, he was a tall man, his blonde hair quite short, close-cut. He had an angular nose and high cheekbones, and Lexi could see that Charlie took after her father, especially with the piercing blue eyes.

She saw his gaze shift to Charlie. 'Five-thirty, remember!' And with that he turned on his heel and walked back into the houseboat next door.

Lexi stared after him. She had been hoping for an invite to dinner again. The first time around, she'd been out at work, so Charlie had left a message with Ray to pass on to her, inviting her to dinner with them. It had turned out that it wasn't Charlie's father who had invited Lexi to dinner. Unbeknown to Lexi at the time, it had been Charlie's idea. She'd been mortified when she'd found out it hadn't been Scott's idea, although he had seemed to enjoy their evening together as much as she had. He had certainly seemed to be having a good time.

The fact that the invitation had come from Charlie hadn't been the only reason for her acute embarrassment. There was also what had happened on the way over. Charlie had slipped and fallen in the water. Lexi had frozen with fear, unable to move. She had shouted for help, and Scott had come running. She hadn't been able to explain why she was paralysed with fear, although she had always been frightened of the water.

She still felt terribly embarrassed about it now, but what had started out as a disaster had turned into the best evening she'd had in a long time.

He'd cooked an amazing curry, and although the frightening incident had ruined her appetite, one taste of Scott's delicious homemade curry, which they'd persuaded her just to try, had sealed the deal.

'Lexi, let's go!'

She turned around to find that Charlie had disappeared down the stairs. Lexi followed. Charlie picked up the notebook.

'Let's put the sofa back first,' suggested Lexi. 'It's way more comfortable than sitting on the floor.'

Lexi put the floorboard back in place, and together they dragged the sofa back to its original position. Lexi didn't bother rolling up the rug and taking it outside. Instead, they just avoided walking on the wet patch. They shifted the coffee table back in front of the sofa. 'There, that's better,' said Lexi. 'Now, what shall I make for lunch?' She remembered that Charlie liked cheese sandwiches. That was what they'd had the first time Charlie had come over and they'd had lunch together.

Charlie wiggled her nose. 'Can we have lunch later? I can't wait to read the notebook.'

Lexi smiled. 'I suppose lunch can wait.'

'Would you like to share the rest of my crisps?' Charlie got out a large, crumpled packet of crisps from her bag.

Lexi smiled. 'That's very kind of you.' She fetched a bowl from the kitchen and watched Charlie empty the large bag into the bowl. She shook the crisp packet over the bowl. The remnants at the bottom of the packet spilled out over the trunk, and on to the floor. Charlie's eyes went wide. 'Oh.'

'Never mind. I'll clear it up later.' Lexi leaned forward and took a crisp while Charlie opened the notebook on her lap. She turned to the next page.

❖

'Charlie!'

Lexi quickly got to her feet, with a feeling of déjà vu.

'Charlie!'

Lexi looked at the time. 'Oh, no. Have you seen the time?' She couldn't believe they'd been sitting there on the sofa that long; apart from toilet breaks and a pause for Lexi to make them drinks and cheese sandwiches, they hadn't shifted from their spot on the sofa. The large bowl of crisps was empty.

They'd read the notebook and enjoyed the story of Esme and her pals Joan and Margaret. The IW on their badges stood for Inland Waterways. They were the Inland Waterways Women, but there was a nickname that the new recruits taken on by The Ministry of War Transport were known by – the Idle Women.

According to Esme's account, the nickname came from the boat people living and working on the canal system at the time.

Perhaps they were not that keen on the new recruits, Lexi had thought as they'd read the account of Esme's time as a 'boater' – but they needed these so-called Idle Women to work on the canals when the men went to war.

Lexi thought that they were anything but idle after reading Esme's account of their life onboard a canal boat. It had been tough. They had worked up to fourteen hours a day, taking two or three weeks to travel the Grand Union Canal between London and Birmingham or Coventry.

It didn't seem possible that these women had once been housewives, nurses, teachers and factory workers, with no experience of working on boats. They had travelled over one hundred and thirty miles of waterways, operating one hundred and sixty-six locks, according to Esme's account. After what sounded like a short training scheme, they had been let loose on the waterways, and had been in charge of delivering food, coal, flour and all sorts of other supplies that were vital during the war. It seemed quite a responsibility for young women. *Some were younger than me*, thought Lexi.

Their living conditions were equally tough. Joan and Margaret had shared the extremely cramped living quarters on the main boat. It was only the fact that Esme had sketched pictures in the notebook that made it clear what she was talking about. There were two boats, both carrying cargo. The one in front, called *The Motor*, had the diesel engine, and it towed the barge behind, called *The Butty*. They were both full of supplies. They were joined together by a seventy-foot rope.

Charlie had laughed when she heard the name *The Butty*. She'd said, 'Not a chip butty then.'

Lexi had laughed too, and had made Charlie roll about

laughing when she'd said, 'They might have been carrying potatoes on *The Butty*, so I suppose you *could* call it a chip butty.'

It was that part of Esme's story that had started to get really interesting. While Joan and Margaret shared the cabin in *The Motor*, Esme had the tiny cabin in *The Butty* to herself. And that was how she had met Kit. Christopher was his real name, and he was a stowaway.

One night, after a long day off-loading their cargo in Birmingham, before they set off for Coventry to collect coal and then to make the journey along the same route back to London, Esme had returned to *The Butty* for a nap, leaving Joan and Margaret in their cabin on the boat in front. That was when Esme had discovered an intruder hiding in her cabin.

'Charlie!'

Lexi sighed. She heard Scott shouting for his daughter again, his voice sounding cross and impatient. She wasn't surprised they'd lost track of time. Esme had described in her notebook having a hand clamped around her mouth and feeling a hot breath on her neck as a young man said, *Please don't scream.* Lexi honestly didn't know how Esme had kept quiet when he released her.

Kit was seventeen, the same age as Esme. Like her, he'd wanted an adventure, so he'd enlisted in the US army at sixteen. You had to be eighteen to enlist. Kit knew other boys who were younger, fourteen or fifteen, who had enlisted. So he too had lied about his age and not long afterwards had found himself on a boat bound for France.

He'd confided in Esme that it was the worst decision of his life – that and deserting in France. He'd fallen in with a group of other American deserters hiding out in Paris. They were older than him. He'd told her they were a bad bunch. Esme had drawn sketches of a bombed-out Paris with American servicemen hiding in the shadows, reaching out to pick people's pockets. But she'd also written in her notebook that she wasn't sure exactly what Kit meant when he said they were a 'bad bunch'. He wouldn't go into detail.

Lexi had smiled when she'd seen heart-shaped drawings further on in the notebook. It was obvious that Esme had been falling in love. Some of the entries talked of their clandestine trips outside, late at night when Joan and Margaret were asleep in their cabin. Sometimes, they'd lain on top of the barge's roof and stared up at the stars, imagining they were on a beautiful hillside and planning what they would do after the war was over. But as Lexi read on, she'd discovered how Kit had come to be in England and the darker story that would unfold on the Grand Union Canal.

Lexi looked at the open envelope and the letter lying on the coffee table. They'd discovered that Kit had written on the back of the letter too. It was Charlie who had picked up the letter and discovered they'd missed something. Lexi stared at the second page. Esme hadn't read the letter. Lexi had suspected she might not have even been aware that he'd found her tin and placed the letter with the ring under her notebook. Because Kit's letter was dated, Lexi knew that the very last entry in the notebook was the day before Kit had written his letter. It meant that Esme would have gone through the rest of her life believing Kit had betrayed her, and she would never have known what had really happened one terrible night on *The Butty*.

Charlie ran up the stairs and opened the door, shouting out, 'Daddy, I'm coming!' She backed down the stairs and glanced over her shoulder at Lexi. 'We *have* to find Esme and give her the letter, and tell her what really happened to Kit.'

Lexi smiled affectionately at Charlie. Lexi didn't know how to tell her that Esme was probably long gone. She did a quick mental calculation. If she had just turned seventeen when she volunteered towards the end of WW2, then that meant she was born around 1927, and would now be ninety-six. She could still be alive, but Lexi thought it was more likely, sadly, that she was not.

9

'Esme, stop being a nuisance this morning. You need to get dressed. Your daughter is coming to visit you.'

'Oh, la de da. Just because she decides to grace me with her presence once in a while, I've got to dress up as though the Queen is coming to tea.'

'Now, Esme, that is not the right attitude, is it. I'm sure your daughter is busy.'

'Busy doing what?'

'Well … I don't know.'

Esme threw her blouse on the floor. It wasn't a particularly good throw. She knew that. It just dropped to the floor. She didn't have strength in her arms like she used to. 'I wish she wouldn't come.'

'Now, Esme that's not the …'

'Right attitude,' said Esme, mimicking the care home manager. She knew why it was the manager herself who came to help her dress, rather than the younger staff members in the care home. Esme was aware that she had a reputation for being difficult.

'I think you should count yourself lucky you have a visitor. Some of our residents don't, you know.'

'I don't care.'

'I'm sure you would if you were all alone at your age.'

Esme watched her pick up the blouse from the floor. She sighed and held out hand. 'Give it here, then.' She knew she couldn't sit in just a bra all day. That wouldn't do. Besides, she was feeling decidedly chilly. And she'd had her spell of rebelliousness for one morning. Now she wanted to hurry up and get dressed, otherwise she'd miss breakfast.

'There, now. Isn't that better?'

'Don't patronise me, Nicki.'

'I wouldn't dream of it. Now, do you want to sit in the chair, or are you walking to breakfast this morning?'

Esme looked at the walking sticks. She was in good health for a ninety-six-year-old. Surprisingly, she didn't have any particular ailments, bar one very big unsurmountable one – old age.

Esme slipped her legs out of bed and reached for her skirt, slapping away Nicki's hand. 'I can do this myself.' Esme awkwardly pulled on her skirt as she sat on the bed. She looked at the wheelchair. There were two things that made her feel her age; one was the mirror, and the second was that blasted chair. 'Hand me my sticks.'

'Of course.'

Esme frowned. 'What are you hanging about for? I can make my own way to breakfast.'

Nicki hovered by the door.

Esme walked towards her and stopped. 'What is it?'

'I know it's none of my business, Esme, but why do you never want to see your daughter?'

Esme tapped her on the leg with one of the sticks. 'Out of my way.'

Nicki sidestepped and opened the door for her.

Esme said over her shoulder as she walked out of the room. 'You're right: it's none of your business.'

❖

'So, you're off then?'

Margot frowned. 'I don't want to go.'

'I know. You say that every time.'

Margot was stalling – and she knew it. She stood by the front door and looked at Meredith. 'I feel like giving it a miss this week.'

'I know.' Meredith didn't have to ask why, but Margot said it anyway. 'Every time I ask her the same question, I get nowhere.'

'Maybe this time will be different.'

Margot threw her hands up in frustration. 'How can you say that? She's not going to change – ever.'

'Stranger things have happened.'

'Really? Like what?' Margot wasn't surprised when Meredith didn't answer. She watched her friend take the raincoat down from the row of coat pegs by the door. 'Here. You'll regret it if you don't go.'

'I'll regret it if I do.'

Meredith smiled. 'Look, just tell her how you feel.'

'Like that is going to make a difference. You remember when we were children. She spent most of her time on the houseboat. I swear she didn't want to be around me, and didn't even like the sight of me. Your mum was more of a mother to me than she ever was.'

Meredith sighed. 'I know. But put yourself in her shoes. Her family basically banished her to this big old house, so far from London. She must have felt very alone, unwanted, unloved.'

'She had your mum and the staff, and she had those two women, her friends, who used to visit her on the houseboat. What were their names?'

'I can't remember.'

'Jane or Joan, was it? And Margery. Or was it Margaret?'

Margot had always wondered just what her mother's fascination was with the boat and why she had spent so much time there when Margot was growing up. To Margot's utter disappointment, her mother had hardly ever taken her along to the boat when she was a child. She seemed to spend a lot of time there with her two friends. Rather than staying in the big house, as Margot had once called her childhood home, the three of them would stay in the cramped houseboat.

She knew they were Mama's friends who went way back to the war. She remembered Mama saying that she wanted to spend time with her friends without children under her feet. They rarely ventured up to the house when they visited, so she never got to know her friends, or how they'd all met, and what exactly bound them all together in such a tight-knit friendship.

In hindsight, Margot wished she'd had the opportunity to get to know them better. Perhaps they knew who her father was.
Meredith said, 'Look, did it ever cross your mind that your mother was nursing a broken heart? And you—' Meredith stopped short.

Margot eyed her. 'Go on. What were you going to say?'

Meredith sighed heavily. She said in a small voice, 'You just reminded her of her lost love.'

'You mean I looked like my father.'

Meredith nodded. 'You don't take after Esme. You know that.' Meredith held up her raincoat. 'You'll miss visiting hours if you don't get a move on.'

Margot rolled her eyes. 'Give it here, then.' She slipped on the coat and opened the front door. It was drizzling with rain. The weather reflected Margot's foul mood. She always felt like this on a Tuesday.

'Why don't I drive you? I'm heading there to do some shopping.'

'Don't be silly – it's only a light drizzle.'

'But if it really starts coming down, you'll get soaked walking into Southwold.'

'I'll be fine.'

Meredith looked at her in surprise. 'Have you forgotten something? What if you're seen?'

'Well, that's the beauty of the weather. With my large hood up, and my umbrella, no one is going to realise it's me. Besides, it's not as though my mother is living in the heart of the town where the shops are, is it?'

'All right. Well, I'm off then.' Meredith stepped out with Margot. 'You know, it's really not necessary for me to come every day and clean. You are wasting money. I think I spend more time making tea and chatting.'

Margot smiled.

Meredith looked up at the cloudy sky. 'You know, it isn't really that bad, is it? I was going to drive into Southwold and do some shopping, but I think I'll walk. Can I join you?'

'Of course. Would you mind picking up a couple more library books that I ordered online while you're there?'

Meredith nodded. 'Yes, of course.'

'Are you sure you can manage them if you're walking into town?'

'Yes. I've got a couple of books to return, so I was intending to pop into the library anyway. Are they paperbacks?'

'Yes.'

'Then I'll be fine carrying them back.'

Margot caught Meredith frowning. 'What's the matter?'

'I take it if you're not writing, then?'

Margot swiftly changed the subject. 'Shall we meet back here?'

'All right. I'll make some lunch. You can tell me about your visit to your mother.'

'I'd like that, Meredith – not that there will be much to tell.'

'But you do like to have a good moan afterwards.'

'Yes, I do, don't I?'

They exchanged a knowing smile as they set off.

10

'Tell me about my father.'

Esme sighed. *Not again.* Every time Margot visited, she knew the question would come up. This was the reason she always had mixed feelings about seeing her daughter. Of course, the care home manager, Nicki, wouldn't have understand how she felt if she had responded to her nosy question, but as Esme had quite rightly told her, it was none of her business.

'I don't want to talk about it.'

'But you're not getting any younger, Mama. Please, I want to know.'

'No.' Esme gave her daughter a sideways glance. It was the same conversation every time, and her daughter was getting more persistent with the passage of time. She understood – of course she did. But what was there to tell? Esme changed the subject. 'I want to go back to my boat.'

'Mama, you know you're too old to live on a houseboat now.'

'You sold it, didn't you?'

'Of course I didn't.'

'That's only because I own it, and you can't do that until I die.'

'You know that's not true.' I live on the houseboat most of the time. I wouldn't sell it. It's my home now.'

'Why?'

Margot stared at her mother. 'Why – *what*?'

'Why do you keep coming if you are going to ask the same question?'

'You know why.'

'I'll have you know that I don't plan on kicking the bucket any time soon. Perhaps I'll outlive you.'

'That's not a very nice thing to say.'

'Why?'

'Because as a mother, you shouldn't be thinking about outliving your child. You shouldn't be able to bear even thinking about it.' Margot knew what it was like to lose a child. It didn't matter how old they were; you should not outlive your children.

'I'm sorry. You're right, Margot – that wasn't a nice thing to say.' She caught a look on Margot's face. Her daughter was surprised that she'd elicited an apology.

There followed the usual uncomfortable silence when they ran out of things to say to each other. Esme knew why that was; it was because she refused to tell Margot who her father was. She'd told her, in the past, that she'd had a one-night stand and had never known his name. It was an outright lie, but she'd hoped that it would stop all the questions about him. It hadn't. Perhaps it was the way she'd said it; she had not sounded as convincing as she should have. No matter how many times she'd repeated the story over the years, her daughter didn't believe her. Margot had always sensed that she was lying.

Esme stared at Margot, who was looking out of the window. It was a nice view from one of the cosy lounges in the large Edwardian house; it was situated in one of the poshest streets in

Southwold. The detached property sat in a commanding position overlooking the sea.

At first glance, no one would think it was a care home. The property was set in lovely lawned gardens. There was no tell-tale sign outside to suggest it was anything other than someone's private, albeit large, residence. She knew it must have cost Margot a fortune to get her a place there. A sizeable chunk of her daughter's royalties must have been swallowed up in the cost of her living there for the past fifteen years.

Esme had refused to live with her daughter, despite Margot's wish for her to return to Willow Tree Cottage. She'd told her it had nothing to do with the cost. Her daughter simply did not want to see her living in a nursing home. Esme would much rather be in the home, though, than move back into that house – that prison where she'd been forced to live years earlier.

She knew some people would think it wasn't bad for a prison; in fact, they'd swap their house for that prison any day. *Well, go have it!* Esme thought, echoing the words that Kit used when he talked about the chance that he would be discovered and dragged back to the army. He said he'd refuse to fight and become a conscientious objector. *If they want to fight their stupid war, then go have it.*

Esme's father had left her a small inheritance. It was more than she'd expected, given that he'd appeared to virtually disown her. Other than Willow Tree Cottage, and the staff he'd paid for, she hadn't expected anything more, so she was surprised she'd been named as a beneficiary in his will. With that money, she'd bought the rundown houseboat that had set her free.

She hadn't been able to go anywhere in it; the houseboat was permanently moored to the quay. But that wasn't the point. It had set her free from that house. She'd had somewhere to go, to be herself, and to spend time away from the biggest mistake of her life.

Esme gave that mistake a sideways glance. *What a terrible mother am I to still think of her as that, all these decades later.* But she couldn't help it. Whenever she saw Margot, who looked so much like her father, all she saw was Kit and his betrayal.

But that wasn't Margot's fault – was it? She didn't choose to be born. She didn't choose to have a bad mother and an absent father.

Esme followed Margot's gaze out of the window. If it wasn't for Margot, she'd be completely alone. Meredith wouldn't visit. She had her own family. And even if she didn't, she wouldn't come and see her. Years ago Meredith had told her to her face, what a terrible mother she'd been to Margot; so different to Meredith's own mother. Esme knew Meredith wouldn't come to visit if her life depended on it.

Esme's two best friends, Joan and Margaret, who knew what had happened on *The Butty* when they'd worked together as IWs all those years ago, were long gone.

She looked at her daughter and thought, *I can't lose you too.* What if she walked out of there one day and decided not to come back? Every Tuesday, Esme put on a show for the care manager, pretending she didn't want to see her daughter, acting like she didn't care. It was true that she didn't want the question of Margot's father to come up when Margot visited, as it always did, but she still secretly hoped she came. She expected her to come. But what if one day she simply didn't? What if one day, like Margot's child, her own grandchild, Margot was suddenly gone?

Margot got out of her chair. 'I'm going.'

Esme looked up. 'No – wait!' She grasped her hand.

Margot's face was a picture of surprise when she saw her

mother holding her hand. Esme was never the demonstrative type. She knew that.

'Please, don't go.' She watched as Margot took her seat, a bemused expression on her face. 'I want you to fetch something for me.'

'Can't one of the care assistants fetch it from your room? Do you need your cardigan? It is a bit chilly in here.'

'No, I don't need a cardigan. When you get old, why does everyone fuss so, like you're a small child?'

'Sorry.'

Esme shook her head. 'It's not in my room.'

'Then, where—?'

'I need you to fetch something from the houseboat.'

'From the houseboat?' Margot looked at her as though she had a screw loose. 'Pardon me, but you've been living here for *fifteen* years – what is it that you could possibly need from there after all this time?'

'It's not for me.'

'But you just said—'

'Just go and fetch my notebook from the houseboat.'

'Your notebook? I'm sorry, but I don't know what you're talking about. After all these years, I've never come across—'

'You wouldn't. I hid it years ago.'

'You hid it? Where?'

'Under a floorboard in the lounge. It's in a biscuit tin.'

Margot stared at her.

'I'm not going senile, Margot, if that's what you're thinking. It's there. Move the rug and look for the floorboard with two seams where a bit of the board has been cut out and replaced. You can't miss it.'

'But I've never come across it before, and I've moved the rug from time to time to hoover the floor.'

'Have you ever got down on your hands and knees and closely examined the floor?'

Margot frowned. 'Of course not.'

'Well, there you go.'

'Look, I won't be returning to the houseboat just yet. You know I live in the house for the summer, so it will have to wait until—'

'All right then.' She watched Margot rise from her chair. 'It's a shame, though ...'

Margot looked at her mother. 'What's a shame?'

'I wanted you to bring me the notebook to tell you about your father. But as you said, it can wait.' Esme watched Margot's reaction. She immediately took her seat again. 'You're going to tell me about him?'

'Margot, I must warn you that our story does not have a happy ending and it's not all roses around the door. You won't like what I tell you about him.'

'I don't care. I just want to know.'

Esme said, 'Fetch my notebook first.'

'Of course. Oh, god … I can't believe it.'

Esme was taken by complete surprise when Margot got up from her seat and threw her arms around her mother. 'Thank you. You don't know how much this means to me.'

Tell me that when you find out what a liar and a scoundrel he was, and how he betrayed me. Esme kept her mouth shut. She knew Margot would want to know everything. She also knew that if she didn't tell her about the notebook, one day she'd be gone, and it would be lost forever. As Margot said, she'd never have found it.

Margot sat back in her seat and got out her phone.

Esme looked at her. 'What are you doing?'

'Meredith is in town as we speak doing some shopping and collecting some library books for me. I'm just going to phone her and ask her to pop into the houseboat.' Margot scrolled through her phone to find Meredith's number. 'I'll explain to her where it is.'

'No!'

Margot looked up. 'I'm sorry, what did you say?'

'I don't want Meredith to find it.'

'But that's stupid. She's in the town. She can walk across the bridge and fetch it. She wouldn't be long, and I can wait here with you until she—'

'I said no!'

'Why ever not? She wouldn't read it, I promise.'

'I want *you* to go and get it, and that's final.'

Margot lowered her phone. She breathed a heavy sigh. 'All right.'

'Promise me that you won't send Meredith, because if I find out—'

'If it means that much to you, of course I'll go and get it myself.'

Esme stared at her a long moment. 'Do your neighbours know why you won't spend the summer on the houseboat?' Esme studied her daughter when she got no response. 'You still blame yourself, don't you?'

'I don't want to talk about that.'

'You can't keep blaming yourself.'

Margot stood up. 'I'm going to find your notebook.'

Esme pursed her lips. It was the first time she'd brought that subject up with Margot. She remembered that summer twenty years earlier when she'd gone away on holiday to Italy, and Margot had decided to spend the summer on the houseboat by herself. Esme knew it had been a revelation. Margot had loved it. That was why, when Esme had moved out of it five years later, when she turned eighty – she'd been forced to move out because she could no longer manage the gangplank or the awkward stairs down to the cabin – Margot had moved in.

Esme had been surprised by that, considering what had happened there. But she knew Margot had never spent another summer there. She'd always wondered what she told her houseboat neighbours. Were they aware of the tragedy that had unfolded there all those summers ago? It had always been a close-knit community. Did they know about the house in Walberswick?

'When will you be back with the notebook?' Esme asked as Margot walked to the door.

'As soon as I can.'

Esme nodded. As she turned to look out of the window, she sensed that Margot hadn't left. Esme turned in her seat to find Margot standing by the door, staring at her.

'Well, what are you waiting for?'

'Will you tell me my father's name?'

Esme stared at her daughter. She had his eyes. Esme took a deep breath. 'His name was Christopher, but he preferred his childhood nickname, Kit.'

11

'Meredith, you'll never guess what! She told me his name.'

'Slow down. Take a breath.'

Margot took a breath as she shut the front door behind Meredith. 'I still can't believe it.'

'Well, there you go. I told you things can change. A leopard can change its spots.' Meredith handed her the library books.

'Oh, thanks for collecting these.' Margot cast them onto the sideboard in the hall and took off her coat.

'I bet you're pleased that you decided to visit this morning. I knew you were indecisive. Nothing new there,' Meredith joked as she walked into the kitchen. She popped the kettle on and got out two teacups and a teapot. 'Let's celebrate with a nice cup of tea.' Meredith glanced at her and noticed a frown. 'So, what else did she tell you?'

Margot took a seat at the kitchen table. 'I never knew this, but apparently my mother kept a notebook. I think probably her memory isn't what it once was, and she wants to read her notebook before she tells me all about him.'

Meredith took two teabags out of a ceramic jar on the work-top and placed them in the teapot. She glanced at her best friend.

'So, when is she going to do that? When you next visit?'

'Well, that's the thing. It's not that straightforward.'

Meredith sighed as she opened another kitchen cupboard and took out a loaf of bread. 'Why am I not surprised? When it comes to Esme, nothing is ever straightforward. Would you like me to make you a sandwich?'

'I thought you were staying for lunch too?'

'Okay, I'll make two.'

Margot stood up and walked over to Meredith. She took the loaf of bread out of her hand. 'How about you sit down and I make the lunch?'

'But—'

'No buts. Now, what would you like?'

'What have you got?' Meredith asked with a straight face.

'Well, er ...' Margot looked at her friend. 'What have I got?'

Meredith laughed. 'I bought you some corned beef the other day. There's cheese, tuna or salmon. I know you're rather fond of salmon and cucumber sandwiches.'

'Ah, salmon and cucumber is just the ticket. Now, where would I find the tin of salmon?' She raised her eyebrows at Meredith.

Meredith pointed at the cupboard behind her.

'Great.' Margot turned around and opened the cupboard. She got out the tin. In the fridge she found the cucumber and margarine. 'Right, I'm all set.'

Meredith took off her coat and draped it over the back of the chair. 'So, you were saying something about a notebook?'

'Oh, yes.' Margot took a knife out of the kitchen drawer, stood at the kitchen island in the centre of the room, facing Meredith, and started buttering slices of bread. 'Apparently, her notebook is on the houseboat.'

'What's it doing there?'

'Good question. I didn't even know it was there. I thought she took all her personal belongings with her when she moved to the care home.'

Meredith glanced out of the window. It had started to rain. She stood up.

Margot started opening the can of salmon. She glanced at Meredith. 'What are you doing?'

'I'll fetch it while you make the sandwiches. I've still got the key in my bag from when I collected it the other day.'

'Oh, I didn't realise you'd done that already.'

Meredith got the key out and held it up.

'Oh, good. That's a relief.' Margot nodded as she drained the can of salmon in the sink. 'She wants me to find the notebook. It's hidden, you see, and she's told me where it is.' She returned to the centre island and emptied the can of salmon into a bowl. She started chopping up some cucumber. 'I knew you'd offer to go, Meredith, but what if something were to happen to the notebook?'

'Like what? Are you saying that you don't trust me?'

'Of course I do, Meredith. It's not you. Mama said that if she found out it wasn't me that went to collect it, then ...'

'Then what?'

'I don't know what she'd do. Perhaps she'd throw it away and there goes my only chance to find out about my father?'

'Surely not?'

'I don't want to take the risk, Meredith.'

'Okay. Right, here are the keys.'

Margot shook her head. 'I don't need it. Why don't you keep hold of that key for safekeeping? I've got one somewhere in the house.'

'I know, but rather than you having to go and find it, you can just take this one. I'll finish making lunch, and we can have it together when you get back.'

'Oh, that's very thoughtful of you, Meredith, but I'm not going right now.'

'Why not? You'd be back to see Esme straight after lunch.'

Margot pursed her lips.

'Really, Margot? At a time like this, when you've waited years for your mother to open up about your father, you're thinking about your neighbours and what they will say when they see you returning to the houseboat?'

Margot bit her lip and looked at Meredith sheepishly.

'Margot, you really are making a mountain out of a molehill. You don't need to explain yourself. If someone does say something, you can just tell them you cut short your holiday in London to return home. Simple as that.'

Margot frowned. 'It's not as simple as that.'

'Why ever not?' Meredith stared at her. 'Oh, Margot, it's about that summer, isn't it? How many times do I have to tell you that you can't blame yourself? It wasn't your fault that—'

'But I do blame myself, Meredith. I'm the one that gave them the key to the houseboat and let them go ahead. It was so stupid of me. And look at the price I paid.'

'We both lost a grandchild that day. I've come to terms with it, Margot. Why can't you?'

12

'Oh, before I forget, Alan is going to nip round and fix your lock.'

Lexi rolled her eyes when Ray wasn't looking. That was all she needed. They had been having a pleasant conversation about The Sunrise Coast until Ray brought up the broken lock.

Lexi and Ray had bumped into each other on the footbridge across the river to Walberswick, both returning from a morning in Southwold, and had fallen in step, walking together back along the quay to the houseboats.

The Sunrise Coast was what Ray called this part of the world. Apparently, this stretch of coastline on the Suffolk Coast had a reputation for its beautiful sunrises. Lexi could vouch for that. Waking up in the early hours, her heart beating rapidly at the thought that she really was a squatter, and recalling a bad dream about someone trying to break in, Lexi had sat up into the early hours on the sofa, legs curled under her, staring out of the window towards The Harbour Inn. She had been rewarded by the most beautiful sunrise. One of these evenings, she intended to venture out and see the sunrise from the beach in Walberswick.

But with the mention of Alan coming to fix the lock, Lexi wished she hadn't had a free afternoon. If she'd known when he was coming, she would have asked if she could do some overtime at the library after her shift ended at midday. Or perhaps if she'd just dawdled in the town, looking in Southwold's interesting shop windows rather than heading straight back to the houseboat, then she would have been out when Alan called round.

She wanted to avoid any awkward conversations about Margot and living on her houseboat. Browsing the little boutique shops in the town would have been much easier. Besides, she wasn't sure what she was going to do with herself anyway, hanging around the houseboat all Tuesday afternoon.

'Is that okay?' Ray peered at her.

'Oh, yes.' Lexi looked at him sheepishly. While she really wanted to avoid getting into a conversation with Alan – especially as he had a thing for Margot, according to Ray – she was relieved that he was coming to sort the locks. She hadn't liked leaving the houseboat unlocked overnight or when she'd gone to work that morning. What if someone came along and stole her suitcase, with all her belongings? She was also worried about a stranger walking in and causing any damage to the lovely little place.

Lexi sighed, thinking about the tea she'd spilled on the rug and the loose floorboard she'd put her foot through. Thankfully, she hadn't damaged the floorboards; she'd managed to put the loose board back just as she'd found it under the rug. Nobody would be any the wiser that it had been disturbed and she'd discovered what was in that secret hiding place.

Thinking of hiding places, Lexi reckoned she'd solved the mystery of what had happened to the key under the flowerpot. She bet Margot had sent her friend, Meredith, to collect it. Margot wouldn't come herself. Lexi imagined she wouldn't risk being seen.

'You don't have to worry about paying for it now. I've sorted that out with Alan. He's doing it privately, not through the shop, so that will save you a fair bit of money, and you can just give him the cash when you next see him.'

Lexi smiled at Ray. 'Thank you so much.' He was such a nice neighbour, and she felt constantly guilty about the lies she'd told him.

'Well, this is me,' said Ray, stopping on the path opposite his houseboat. It looked quite different from the other boats moored on the quay which were narrow boats of varying sizes. Ray's home looked like a clapboard floating house. Lexi remembered thinking when she first saw it that it wouldn't have looked out of place in somewhere like Florida.

She looked past Ray's home to the Airbnb houseboat next door, where Scott and Charlie were living. The next boat along was Margot's. Lexi was about to say goodbye when Ray suddenly waved, and shouted out, 'Oh, hello!'

Lexi turned around to see an older man walking towards them. He was around Ray's age, but shorter and with a heavier build.

'It's Alan!'

'Oh, right,' Lexi said.

'He's come to fix the lock, by the looks of it,' commented Ray.

Lexi saw Alan heading towards them carrying a toolbox.

Ray chuckled. 'What a stroke of good luck that he's turned up just when you arrived home.'

'Yes, isn't it?' Lexi sighed. She slapped a smile on her face as Alan approached.

The first words out of his mouth were, 'Margot would never let out her houseboat.' He eyed her suspiciously.

Lexi forced a grin. 'There's a first time for everything.' *Like, for instance, having a squatter*, she thought.

'That's just what I said when I found out,' Ray intervened, 'I think it's good to have someone looking after her houseboat. She's away for a number of weeks, so it does make sense to have a houseboat-sitter.'

'A what?'

Ray replied, 'You know, like a house-sitter – same principle.'

Lexi avoided eye contact with Alan. What if Alan had Margot's mobile number – assuming she had a mobile phone – and called her to check this out? Lexi could feel her heart pounding in her chest and her cheeks flushing bright red as Alan got out his mobile phone. Lexi stared at him. *Here we go, I'm in trouble now.*

'I'm switching this damn thing off now,' said Alan. 'I only have it for work. Don't see the point in 'em.'

'Oh, thank god!'

'Everything all right, Lexi?' asked Ray, turning to look at her.

'Oh, yes, sure.' She pretended to swat something in the air. 'I thought there was a wasp, but there wasn't – thank god.' She eyed Alan and quickly thought up an excuse not to hang around while he fixed the lock. 'You know what? I'm going to Aldeburgh this afternoon. In fact, I'm going right now, so I'll leave you to it. If that's all right?'

Alan slowly nodded his head, still eyeing her suspiciously.

Ray said, 'I fancy a trip to Aldeburgh too.' He turned to Lexi. 'Shall we go together?'

Lexi nodded enthusiastically. She didn't know why Aldeburgh had popped into her head. Chatting to Ray had brought to mind her late father. She hadn't been back to the graveyard since her first visit, and she did want to take some fresh flowers.

'Visiting your ex?' Alan asked Ray.

'Yes, actually, that's not a bad idea. I think I'll surprise her while

Lexi does some shopping.' Ray did an about-turn to walk back along the riverbank towards the bridge. Lexi quickly followed. As they fell in step, he whispered, 'I hope you don't mind that I didn't mention the reason you're probably going to Aldeburgh.'

'Oh, not at all.' Lexi smiled at Ray. 'Thank you so much for taking me in your car, Ray.' It had just occurred to her that the journey time on the bus to Aldeburgh meant she really wouldn't have been able to go by public transport that afternoon. It was a three-hour journey by bus through all the little villages, but took just thirty minutes by car.

'Don't thank me. I wanted an excuse to get out of here. I mean, I love the guy, I do, but Alan can talk for England, and he'd be here all night, and you still wouldn't have your lock fixed.'

'Sounds like I've had a lucky escape.' Lexi meant that in more ways than one. She cast a glance over her shoulder. She could see Alan making his way towards Margot's houseboat.

'He'll be finished when we get back.'

Ray paused to look at Lexi. 'Sorry, that was a bit forward of me. I am assuming you don't mind my accompanying you to Aldeburgh again?'

'Oh, not at all.' Lexi offered him a smile. It was so sweet of Ray. He made it sound as though he wasn't making a special trip just for her – which she knew he was.

13

Lexi followed Ray to his Volkswagen, which was parked on the quay. They both got in, and as he manoeuvred the car out of its space, Lexi recalled their first trip to Aldeburgh together. She'd bumped into him on the way back from her first morning working in the library after being offered an apprenticeship to become a librarian. She had a good reference from her previous position in marketing at a large publishing house in New York, where she'd been living with her boyfriend, Brandon, who had been her best friend since childhood.

Lexi would rather not think about Brandon and that horrible Monday morning just over week ago when she'd been fired from her job through no fault of her own – the company was going through restructuring. It didn't help, though, that her manager told her she'd been chosen for redundancy because, as part of a very wealthy family, she could afford to lose her job – unlike others who depended on their wage. Which reminded Lexi that she was still waiting on the two months' severance pay and the small redundancy payment she was due. At least in England no one knew the surname Harrington and the massive real estate business her maternal grandfather had built from the ground up.

That Monday, she'd arrived home mid-morning to surprise Brandon with a coffee and a bagel – and the news that she'd lost her job. She'd still had her monthly allowance from her grandparents, not to mention the apartment in New York they'd let her use, though. It was the only way she could afford to live in Manhattan on her salary and support Brandon.

She didn't want to think about that either – what her family had said about him; that he had been using her. It was true that she'd supported him – or rather her allowance had – so that he could spend all day writing songs and looking for that elusive recording contract.

Now she realised that what her family thought of him was true. She had believed they were best friends, that they were in love, until her unexpected arrival home that morning. She'd found a young woman in their apartment, in their bed, and had discovered she wasn't the first. He'd been going to gigs and hooking up with women; she'd had no clue that he'd been sleeping around while she'd been hard at work in her nine-to-five job.

And now that job, the life she had with Brandon, and her allowance were all gone. She'd told Brandon to stay in the apartment in New York for as long as he needed. Andrea, her younger sister, had said she was a soft touch.

Lexi hadn't told her grandparents she'd let Brandon stay on. She hoped they wouldn't find out. They lived in Connecticut, which was where she would be right now, living a comfortable life in the cottage in the grounds of their property, if she hadn't decided to jet off to England.

She was intending to return to New York after her trip to England, and to tell Brandon he had to leave the apartment, but she was rather enjoying her new job in the local library and the lovely people she had met, not to mention the beautiful Sunrise Coast. There was just one problem – if it wasn't for living rent-free on the houseboat, she couldn't support herself on the apprenticeship wage.

'Penny for your thoughts.'

Lexi just smiled at Ray. She was thinking about Margot, a few hundred yards away, up the street in Walberswick, living in a grand old ivy-clad cottage behind a wrought iron gate. Lexi even knew the name of the cottage. She'd seen the name engraved on a slate sign attached to a pillar by the entrance gate – *Willow Tree Cottage*.

Lexi had discovered that finding a place to live in the area wasn't easy. She'd looked in some estate agent windows and had been surprised by how expensive the properties were.

She thought of Margot in Willow Tree Cottage, and Charlie and Scott in their Airbnb, and imagined that the other houseboat owners were in for a rude awakening when they discovered that not all the houseboats were people's main residences.

Ray had spoken of how the little houseboat community frowned on second-homers or holiday lets. Not that he had a problem with people holidaying in the area or even on one of the houseboats. Lexi was thinking of Ray's new next-door neighbours, Scott and Charlie. But Lexi imagined it was more the case that there were so many second homes and holiday lets in the area, that there was good reason the people who lived on the houseboats preferred permanent residents; she imagined there was more of a sense of community.

Lexi still couldn't believe Margot was right there in the little Georgian seaside resort of Walberswick. Now, all she had to do was decide when she would return to Willow Tree Cottage and hand her the letter. Margot need never know that it was she who had been on the houseboat. Lexi glanced at Ray, who raised his eyebrows at her. She still hadn't answered his question. He was obviously wondering why she was so deep in thought. 'I'd like to visit my father's graveside again.'

'I assumed that would be the case. Would you like to visit The Potting Shed too?'

Lexi caught him grinning. She joined in. She recalled what he'd said about bombarding his soon-to-be ex-wife with flowers in the hope that he would win her back. That had been a big fail. Sarah had just got annoyed. However, since he'd backed off, it sounded as though their relationship had gone from strength to strength. Although they were still living apart – he lived on his houseboat and she lived in a flat in Aldeburgh, on the promenade, overlooking the sea – he said they'd never been happier.

She gave him a sideways glance. He certainly liked to have any excuse to visit Sarah, and she also came over to his on occasion for romantic dinners on the deck of his houseboat.

'Are you going to buy Sarah some more flowers?'

'Ah, silly question,' said Ray.

Lexi smiled. She'd bought a bouquet the last time she'd visited the town, and had laid it on her father's grave. It was the first time she'd been back since his funeral when she was six. She had assumed he was buried in a cemetery in London where they'd lived, so it was a surprise to discover through her research at the library that his grave was so close by.

She recalled the visit to The Potting Shed in Cobblers Yard. She'd suggested Ray buy flowers for Sarah, which he'd done – and they'd gone down a treat. She could tell he was looking forward to surprising Sarah again with an amazing bouquet.

It was only the previous Saturday that Lexi had visited the

churchyard with flowers for her father's grave and had discovered that there were already fresh flowers on his grave. She hadn't expected to discover that someone else was still visiting her father after all these years. She was keen to return, and very interested to find the person who had left the flowers. Ray had suggested it was either a close friend or, more likely, a relative.

As far as Lexi and Andrea were concerned, they didn't have any living relatives in England; at least, their mother had never mentioned anybody. Lexi recalled phoning Andrea on the way back from Aldeburgh the previous Saturday to tell her all about it. She was hoping to find the person who had left the flowers.

That was when Andrea had said something that hadn't occurred to Lexi. *Do you think that whoever laid the flowers, assuming it's a relative, is the reason our grandparents have always been so against us returning to England?* Lexi hadn't wanted to admit it, but she had wondered that too. But it had just made Lexi even more determined to find them.

'So, how's it going with AncestryDNA?' asked Ray, as if reading her mind.

'I haven't joined yet.' Lexi had been so busy with work that she hadn't got around to it, although it was at the top of her to-do list. She was still thinking about those flowers left by a stranger. They had been so fresh that Lexi had wondered if she'd passed the person on the street on the way to the graveyard.

She'd told Ray that she wanted to see if she could find some English relatives. Ray ran a small business as an heir-hunter, searching for the lost relatives of those who had died without leaving a will. Ray suggested that she should join a site like AncestryDNA. She'd told him that her sister in America had done just that a few years back when she'd got one of the DNA kits as a present from her fiancé, Chad. Nothing had come of it. Even so, Ray had pointed out that things could change, and more people could join, so it was possible that she still might find some relation, or even her paternal grandparents.

'I will take your advice and join.'

'That's wonderful, although ...' He trailed off.

Lexi noticed his ready smile falter. 'Although – what?'

'May I add a caveat?'

'What does that mean?'

'You will notice that the site has a disclaimer. While for many the search for long-lost relatives has a happy ending, I'm afraid for some ... well, the disclaimer applies.'

Lexi quickly grasped what he was trying to say. 'I might not like what I find?'

'That's the risk everyone takes when they start a search for the truth. No one knows what they will discover – good or bad. We have to be prepared for that.'

'You mean *I* have to be prepared for that.'

'Yes, hence the disclaimer. Once you've found what you're looking for, there's no going back.'

Lexi stared at Ray. Although it was he who had suggested joining, perhaps, from what she'd said, he'd got the impression that there were secrets in her family's past. Lexi pursed her lips. She was still set on finding out. 'I'd rather know the truth – whatever that is.'

'You might not find anyone through those sites, I'm afraid, but—'

'If I do, I'll be prepared,' said Lexi. She caught Ray's expression. 'What?'

Ray pulled the car to a stop at the end of the country road.

They were at the junction with the main road to Aldeburgh. He looked at her. 'Do you know how many people have said that to me in the course of running my little business?'

Lexi pursed her lips. 'So, I guess you're saying they weren't prepared?'

'No. They never are.'

14

Lexi glanced out of the car window at the familiar rolling countryside, the green fields interspersed with fields full of yellow rapeseed. She could see a church spire in the distance, in a small village nestled in the countryside. She loved the Suffolk scenery, all soft rolling fields and gently undulating countryside.

It wasn't long before they arrived in Aldeburgh, the pretty seaside town where Sarah lived. The first time Lexi had visited, she'd commented on how lovely the properties were that fronted the small promenade overlooking the pebbly beach. She hadn't expected to see a little street on the promenade comprising of two-storey terraced cottages along with three and four-storey Victorian townhouses painted in pastel shades of blue, pink and yellow. Sarah's place was one of them.

'So, if we go and get some flowers first, how about we meet back at Sarah's after you've visited your dad?'

Lexi smiled. 'Sounds like a plan.'

Ray brought the car to a stop in a parking space overlooking Aldeburgh's pebbly beach. Lexi could see that people were queuing to buy some fresh fish from one of the huts on the beach.

'I don't want Sarah to go to too much trouble,' said Lexi.

He switched off the car engine and turned to Lexi, smiling.

Lexi couldn't help but smile too. He knew what she was getting at. The previous Saturday, when she'd met Ray at Sarah's flat, she had thought she was just meeting him there and that they would set off straight away to Walberswick. But they'd stayed for lunch. Sarah had served homemade scones with jam and cream, and she'd also made finger sandwiches.

Ray said, 'You're talking about the cream tea.'

Lexi nodded.

'Don't worry, I'll be sure to tell Sarah that it wasn't to your liking, and you'd much prefer not to have—'

'No, don't do that!'

Ray's lips curled into a naughty grin.

Lexi didn't want to offend Sarah, but it wasn't just that. Her scones and finger sandwiches were delicious. She imagined they'd stop for lunch again. 'Well, as long as she doesn't mind ...'

'I'll let Sarah know that there will be two for lunch.'

The last time Lexi had visited Aldeburgh, she had rather fancied having lunch at a little café she'd spotted as she walked along the street – The Two Magpies. She'd have to save that for another time.

'So, did you go for dinner with your next-door neighbour?' Ray said conversationally as they headed towards the high street just behind the promenade.

Lexi loved all the little boutique shops. She couldn't afford to shop in them on her library apprenticeship salary, but she enjoyed passing them by and seeing the lovely window displays.

She looked at Ray and raised an eyebrow at his question, but she knew he wasn't talking about the previous evening. When she had seen Charlie the previous day, and they'd spent the afternoon reading the diary they'd inadvertently stumbled across on Margot's houseboat, Lexi had hoped she would be invited to dinner again. Being on her own was not something Lexi was used to after being in a long-term relationship, so she wasn't about to turn down another dinner invitation from her good-looking neighbour next door. But it wasn't to be. Perhaps she wasn't surprised.

'Lexi?'

'Oh, yes – right. What were you saying?'

'Your dinner date with your next-door neighbour.'

Lexi frowned. 'It wasn't a dinner date.' Although, saying that, Lexi thought back to that evening, when Charlie had taken herself off to bed, and she and Scott had talked into the early hours.

She still didn't know what Scott did for a living, or why they moved around a lot, or how come Charlie was home-schooled. Lexi felt like she had done most of the talking. That evening, she'd ended up apologising for telling Scott almost her entire life story. She'd jokingly told him that it was his fault for being such a good listener, but he'd said he was genuinely interested in her life in America. He'd never met anyone before who was an heiress to a fortune. At first, Lexi wished she hadn't told him that, but Scott hadn't seemed to look at her any differently when he'd found out. On the contrary, he'd said, *with great wealth comes great responsibility*. He'd said he had read that somewhere. He hadn't seemed fazed by it, although she had also mentioned that her allowance had been stopped. She still didn't know why her grandparents were so against her returning to England. She'd told him that too.

So ask them, Scott had said.

Lexi didn't want to phone them and ask. She knew what grandpa would do – persuade her to return to Connecticut. He could be very persuasive. Besides Lexi knew where she hoped she'd find answers – in the letter her mother had left her before she died six months earlier. Lexi hadn't yet had the courage to read her mother's final words, and with them truly accept that she was gone.

Since that evening with Scott, Lexi had been hoping for another curry night; Scott cooked a homemade curry from scratch every Friday evening. Lexi imagined it could fast turn into the highlight of her week. Although it wouldn't just be the delicious curry that appealed, but spending time with Scott and Charlie.

Lexi walked with Ray along the high street. She didn't lose sight of Ray like she had last time – one minute he'd been right beside her, the next, he'd gone. Lexi hadn't realised there was a secret alleyway. That's what she called it. The sign for Cobblers Yard was almost invisible. She imagined most people blinked and missed it, which she thought was a shame. This time she knew where it was, and turned into the narrow lane between two shops in the high street that led to the cobbled yard.

In the yard were old shop fronts with bowed, leaded windows that surrounded the cobbled square. It wasn't very large. She glanced in the window of the charity shop and passed the shop selling musical instruments on her way to The Potting Shed.

Across the square was the old antique store. There was also the old arts and crafts shop that was now a solicitor's office, and there was a bookshop that Lexi remembered from her last visit. It was still closed. She came to a halt in the middle of the yard and stared at it.

'That's The Bookshop of Memories.'

'The what?'

'It's the name of the bookshop. You can just make it out on the sign above the door.'

Lexi looked at the old-fashioned sign as it creaked in the breeze. The place made Lexi shiver. She wandered over to look in the window. It wasn't completely empty. She could just see through the dirty window. 'Hey, these are really old books,' she said.

'One day someone will turn up, I'm sure. I can speak for all the shop owners, myself included, when I say I'd be very interested to know who owns that place. I'm not sure what to think, though.'

Lexi looked at him curiously. 'What do you mean?'

'I run a business where I find people who are beneficiaries of wills, but just don't know it yet.'

Lexi nodded. Ray had mentioned his business.

'Like this, for instance. I might see an obituary in the local paper for someone who has died intestate – without a will – and without any close relatives, so I trace them.'

Lexi looked at The Bookshop of Memories. 'You've tried to find who owns this place, haven't you?'

'Oh, yes. I have made inquiries, but it's very odd. I can normally turn up something. But it's as though the person who owned it has disappeared into thin air.'

'So, what will happen to it, do you suppose?'

'I guess it will just sit there deteriorating until by some miracle someone turns up.'

'How long has it been?'

Ray walked over to the shop window. Lexi followed. She remarked, 'Those books displayed in the window – I guess they were the bestselling books from ... well, quite some years ago, judging by the yellowed pages.' Some of the hardbacks in the window display had been left open, presumably for passers-by to stop and read a taster.

'Twenty-five years that display has been sitting there.'

'Wow – that long?'

Ray nodded. 'I'll tell you what's really odd, though. Lili, who runs The Potting Shed – her best friend had a wedding not too long ago, and she posted wedding invitations in all the doors of the shops here.'

'Yes?'

'She received a reply, with no name or return address, to say they would not be able to attend.'

'No way!'

'Yep. As I said, it's all rather strange.' They both stood outside The Bookshop of Memories for a few moments, staring at the window display and its covering of dust and cobwebs. Lexi thought it looked like something out of a Hallowe'en display.

'Right, well, I've got a bouquet to collect,' said Ray, beaming.

Lexi turned to Ray, saw his expression, and smiled. She could tell he was looking forward to visiting Sarah and giving her flowers. 'Are you collecting one too?' he asked.

Lili shook her head.

'Well, hopefully Lili can make you one up,' Ray said as they walked across the yard. Lexi smiled. She hoped so too.

15

They both stepped inside the small flower shop, and Ray walked up to the counter at the back of the shop. 'Hello, Amy. I've ordered some flowers.'

'Hi, Ray.'

'Look, I'm, er, a bit early. I wasn't due in until tomorrow.' He glanced at Lexi. 'It's a bit of an impromptu trip, so if they're not ready to collect, I quite understand.'

'Lili made it up already, so they are ready to collect.'

'Wonderful!' Ray got out his wallet and paid for the bouquet. He turned around to Lexi. 'This is Lexi. She's come for a bouquet too.'

Amy turned to the order book in front of her and frowned. 'What was your last name?'

Lexi glanced at the beautiful bouquet Ray had pre-ordered. 'Ah, I haven't ordered one to be made up. Last time, Lili made me one when I came into the shop.'

Amy closed the order book and looked up. 'I'm afraid that Lili isn't here today – she's out working on a landscaping job.'

Ray turned to Lexi. 'She runs a landscaping business too.'

Lexi did recall that Ray said she also worked on people's

gardens in the local area. She'd forgotten about that. It hadn't crossed her mind that she wouldn't be there today.

'Would you like to order one now?'

Lexi looked at the order book. The trouble was that although it was very kind of Ray to give her a lift into Aldeburgh, she didn't know when exactly she'd be back to collect a bouquet.

The young assistant saw her hesitate. She reached below the counter and brought out a small booklet. 'Here – these are the types we do. You can have a look through and just phone us to order one when you're ready. Our number is on the back.'

Lexi smiled. 'Thank you.'

'You're welcome.' She turned to Ray. 'Would you like a message with your bouquet?'

'Yes, I would.'

Lexi said, 'I'll wait outside.'

Ray nodded. 'I won't be a moment.'

Lexi walked out of the shop and had another wander around the small, cobbled yard. She stopped outside the bookshop and stared at the cobwebs in the window and the old books covered in years' worth of dust and grime. She wondered who owned the place and why it had closed down. But most of all, she wondered how it had come by its name – The Bookshop of Memories.

'Lexi!'

She heard Ray calling her from across the yard. 'Coming!'

As she turned to go, she thought she saw the flicker of a light inside the bookshop, but when she turned back, all was quiet and dark in the window. She shrugged. *Just my imagination.*

She walked over to Ray. 'I'm going to visit my father.' She looked at Ray's beautiful bouquet and felt guilty she wasn't taking flowers. She glanced at The Potting Shed. Outside, there were hanging baskets and some potted plants on a small trestle table. There were also two buckets on the floor, full of small bunches of freshly cut flowers. She had an idea. 'Hold on a minute, would you?' she said to Ray. She walked back to the shop. She took two bunches of flowers, each made up of colourful freesias interspersed with roses. She turned to Ray. 'I'm going to buy these and then visit my dad.'

Ray smiled. 'Good idea. I'll head off to Sarah's, if that's okay.'

'Of course.'

'I'll meet you there in a while.'

Lexi smiled. 'Great.' She secretly hoped Sarah did provide lunch again.

After she had paid for the flowers and Amy had wrapped them in cellophane, Lexi left Cobblers Yard and walked along the high street towards the church. She passed a group of people waiting outside one of the fish and chip shops, their orderly queue snaking around the corner. Jill the librarian had highly recommended fish and chips in Aldeburgh when Lexi visited next. Lexi's mouth watered at the thought, but she knew it would have to wait for another time.

Eventually she reached the grounds of St. Peter and St. Paul's church. It was no less impressive on her second visit. She recalled the first time she had seen it; she had been surprised at the scale of the church and the churchyard in such a small seaside town. At least this time she didn't have to spend time locating her father's grave.

She walked past the church and the very old headstones, skirting the walled perimeter. Past the church, she could see the stone wall at the end of the graveyard and the fabulous views to the sea beyond. She'd been struck the first time around by how much the graveyard reminded her of a garden, with its different areas sectioned off by hedgerows. Her father's grave was located in the last garden, as she liked to think of it, right next to an old bench under a chestnut tree.

Lexi smiled as she approached, recalling how she'd sat down on the bench on her first visit. She'd been unable to find her father's headstone, but a conker had fallen from the tree, hitting her on the head. It wasn't officially conker season, but it wasn't unheard of to get conkers falling in August. Her first thought had been: *it's a sign.*

Although she didn't believe in that sort of thing, it did awaken a memory of standing at her father's grave after the church service and picking up conkers from the damp ground. She'd stood there running her fingers over their smooth surfaces while the vicar had read some words at the graveside before her father's coffin was lowered into the ground.

The memory had caused Lexi to discover his headstone, right there in front of her. Now, Lexi stepped in front of it once more. Although it wasn't even a week since she'd last visited – it was only Tuesday – she was still interested to see if there had been some more fresh flowers put there since her visit. At least this time it wouldn't be such a shock that someone else had been visiting.

The same bouquet of flowers that she'd discovered there the previous Saturday was still there. On her first visit, she hadn't had the heart to remove them, so she had placed her own bouquet on the grave next to her dad's; the resting place of a young woman called Billie who had been laid to rest with her parents.

Lexi's bouquet was still there too. She wasn't surprised. No one came to visit that grave. She didn't know who the woman was, but it was obvious that she received no visitors. Lexi had cleared away the overgrown grass and had cleaned down her grave – something she'd thought she'd be doing to her father's headstone before she had discovered that someone else was looking after it – and had proceeded to arrange her bouquet in the little empty grate on the headstone of her father's neighbour.

Neither her bouquet nor the mysterious one on her father's grave had yet wilted much. Lexi was intending to visit as often as she could in the hope that one day she might time it right and discover the person who'd visited her dad's grave – assuming they'd be back, of course.

Lexi frowned. She knew she'd be lucky to bump into them, no matter how many times she came. *If it's meant to be, it's meant to* be, she thought. She glanced up at the old chestnut tree, thinking of that conker and serendipity. She turned to her father's grave and looked at the bunches of flowers in her hand. She placed one at the base of the headstone. The other flowers she was going to take back with her to the houseboat, hoping she could find a vase.

Lexi stood back and stared at her father's headstone. She smiled when she discovered that her conker was still there, the one that had fallen on her head, along with the painted stone that she had decorated at a beach stall the last time she had visited.

Lexi picked up the conker which had rolled on to the grass and put it back on the base of the headstone beside her little bunch of flowers. She stood back and looked around her. There was no one about, so Lexi didn't feel self-conscious about having a word with her dad before she left. 'So, I'm back again.' She stared at the headstone. 'I have some news. That lady, Margot – she's not in London. She's right here. Well, not here in Aldeburgh, but in Walberswick, literally just up the street from the quay where her houseboat is moored. How crazy is that?'

Lexi glanced about her, checking she was still alone. 'I have no idea why Mum wanted me to hand-deliver a letter. I haven't visited England in twenty years, not once.' Lexi frowned at the thought. 'I should have come back earlier, but everyone discouraged me, so the last thing I expected was that mum would leave me this letter for that lady and some money for the trip.'

Lexi sighed. 'It's lucky I've got the job in the library. I've started an apprenticeship, but it can lead on to further qualifications, like a masters, to qualify as a librarian. I'd like to do that. Once I'm qualified, it pays a decent salary. Right now I'm only surviving on the low wage because I'm squatting on Margot's houseboat. Once she comes back at the end of the summer, I'm stuffed. I'll have to find somewhere else to live.'

Lexi paused. Not for the first time, she wondered why Margot would lie to her neighbours and tell them she spent the summers in London. It did occur to Lexi when she'd followed Meredith and discovered Margot in Walberswick that the sprawling, detached cottage in grounds might not be Margot's property at all. Maybe she was looking after it for the summer for a friend, or perhaps house-sitting. Maybe she was just too embarrassed to tell her neighbours that this year there had been a change of plan, and that she wasn't going to London after all, and that she'd be just up the road. Lexi frowned. These didn't seem like good enough reasons not to tell them. What was the big secret?

She stared at the grave. It was no good asking Dad. She sighed, wondering what he'd say, what his reaction might have been to the predicament she found herself in. She had no idea. She wished he hadn't died so young; that she could have got to know him better. Perhaps, if she managed to find the person who had left the flowers, they would be able to tell her all about him.

She stepped to her right and sat down on the bench under the chestnut tree, hoping that no more conkers landed on her head. She wanted to sit there for as long as possible and see if someone came. She glanced over at the stone wall that marked the boundary of the church grounds. She could see the rooftops of the cottages in the street below, and the sea beyond. She'd sit there all afternoon if she could, listening to distant cries of the seagulls and the occasional hum of a car going by on the nearby street, enjoying the peace and tranquillity.

Lexi got out her phone and looked at the time. There was only so long she could keep Ray waiting. She had his phone number. She could text him and let him know that she wanted to stay on there until it was time to return to Walberswick, but she knew he'd twist her arm to go to Sarah's and join them for lunch.

She took a last look at her father's gravestone. *Why are you laid to rest here?* she wondered, as she had done many times over the past few days. Her father had been an illustrator and had lived in London. It was where Lexi and her little sister had both been born and had lived with their parents.

It occurred to her that there must be some link to his past. 'Perhaps he grew up here in Suffolk,' she said out loud.

There was a sudden *thud* near her foot that made her jump. She looked at the grass by her foot and discovered another conker. 'Really?' Lexi tried to ignore the coincidence that a conker had fallen just as she had spoken. *What did it mean?*

Lexi shook her head. 'It meant nothing,' she convinced herself. 'It was just a coincidence.' Although something else did occur to her. She cast a glance around the graveyard. 'Perhaps my paternal grandparents are buried here.' Lexi knew she'd had a hard enough time locating her father's grave. How would she find theirs?

But I could find out about them, she thought. She did intend to join AncestryDNA. It wasn't just about trying to connect to relatives in the land of the living. She was looking forward to trying to build a family tree on her paternal side. It occurred to her that she had no idea who her paternal grandparents were. She didn't even know their names.

Not for the first time, Lexi had regrets over the fact that she'd left the important conversations with her mum until it was too late; all the things she wished she'd asked her, the conversations they could have had. But Lexi had been busy with her life in New York with Brandon. She had never thought about the past much, even once she knew her mum didn't have long, although there had always been the yearning to return to England.

Now she had all these questions, and there was no one to ask – well, no one who would tell her the answers. Neither her maternal grandparents nor her stepdad could be approached about it. Her thoughts returned yet again to the mystery person who had left the flowers. She had a sudden thought. Had they been purchased from The Potting Shed here in Aldeburgh? Lexi took a photo on her phone of the flowers. The assistant had said that Lili would be returning to the shop. Perhaps she'd be there now? Maybe she could tell her if the flowers had been purchased in her shop.

Lexi had another thought. She sat back down on the bench and opened her bag. She took out the little booklet the assistant had given her with the different types of bouquets they made up and flicked through the pages. Her breath caught in her throat. 'That's it! That's the one!'

Lexi checked the time on her mobile. She hadn't been too long, unlike her last visit when she'd popped in to see the church, and had then spent quite some time in the graveyard looking for the headstone. She'd have time to return to Cobblers Yard.

She stopped in front of her father's grave before heading off, and stared at the flowers, her eyes roving to the decorated stone and her conker. 'Well, I'm off now, Dad, but I will be back. I promise.'

She left the graveyard and hurried down the street towards Cobblers Yard. It occurred to her that most people who were new to the area, who were just visiting on holiday, would pass the entrance to Cobblers Yard and not notice. That meant it might well be someone who lived in the area. She quickened her pace.

16

Lexi stepped into The Potting Shed and was immediately greeted by Lili, who was standing at the counter. 'Oh, hi Lexi. Ray not with you today?'

Lexi smiled. She couldn't believe her luck. Lili was back. 'Yes, he is. We came in earlier and he collected a bouquet. I bought some lovely bunches of flowers.'

'Great. So, how's things?'

Lexi's smile faltered. Things were okay if she didn't think about the fact that without the allowance from her grandparents she couldn't afford to stay in her new life on the Suffolk Coast in England indefinitely. Soon the summer would end and so would her time squatting on the houseboat – that was if something didn't happen in the interim, like Margot returning to her boat early for some reason. Or one of the neighbours spotting her entering or leaving the houseboat, and didn't believe the story she'd spun about houseboat-sitting.

'Are you all right, Lexi?'

Lexi shoulders sagged. 'I'm a terrible person.'

'No, don't be silly. I'm sure that's not true.'

Lexi's frown darkened. 'You've all been so nice to me.

Everyone I've met since I came to Suffolk has been so friendly, and so willing to help me out. But you, Ray and Jill at the library don't really know me.'

Lili put the flowers down that she'd been arranging in a bouquet. 'I'll tell you what, I haven't had a break since I arrived back from my landscaping work this morning. How about a cup of tea?' She went to turn the sign around in the door to *Closed* and locked it.

'You don't have to close the shop on my account,' Lexi said.

'It would be nice to have a cuppa without being disturbed,' Lili replied. 'I haven't had any customers since I arrived back and Amy left. I know what will happen if I don't close the shop. We'll just have sat down with a cuppa and someone will come in.' She smiled. 'Come on.' Lili opened a door, behind which Lexi saw there was a narrow flight of stairs. 'My little office is up here, where my friend, Abigail, helps out with my accounts. You might meet her one day when she comes round to work on my computer.' They started up the stairs. 'Like me, she moved to Suffolk to live permanently too.'

'I didn't realise you weren't from around here,' Lexi said to her back.

'I used to live in London until my long-term partner and I split up.'

'Oh, I'm so sorry.'

'Yes, so was I, to begin with.'

They reached the top of the stairs. Lexi followed her into a cosy room in the eaves with a sofa and matching armchair, along with a desk under a small window that overlooked the yard. An old computer sat on the desk. Lili must have caught her staring. 'Abigail brings her laptop to do my accounts. She won't touch that thing. I'll probably chuck it out.'

'Does it still work?'

'Surprisingly, yes. You can get online and surf the internet, so it's good for something, although it is rather slow. Anyway, take a seat and I'll put the kettle on. We've got a little kitchenette through there,' Lexi pointed at a wooden, panelled door. 'And there's a little bathroom too.'

'It's like an apartment,' commented Lexi.

Lilli walked into the kitchen and put the kettle on. 'Milk and sugar?'

Lexi said, 'Yes, please,' as she took a seat on the sofa.

Lili chatted while she pottered about in the kitchen, putting the kettle on and spooning coffee and sugar into the mugs. She turned around, leaning against the kitchen counter and looking through the open door at Lexi. 'You know, when I first came here it was meant to be a holiday with my boyfriend at the time, Alex. He'd booked a hotel in Aldeburgh. It was a surprise – something he'd done on the spur of the moment, which was so unlike him because he was normally so up to his eyes in work that we hardly went away. I thought we were getting engaged, but he was celebrating his new job in Washington.'

'Washington!'

'Yes. I knew nothing about it. He just expected me to drop everything and go with him. I couldn't. So we ended up splitting up, and I came away on the holiday to Aldeburgh without him. The trouble was, I couldn't return to London. I had nowhere to live. It was the summer, and when I had to leave the hotel, I couldn't get a rental anywhere.'

Lexi stared at Lili. Her situation wasn't that desperate. All she had to do was use her flexi-return plane ticket and go back to Connecticut, to the cottage in the grounds of her wealthy maternal grandparents' home. There was a job waiting for her in the family business, although she didn't want that. She wanted to stay where she was. But the sort of situation Lili was talking about was exactly what Lexi was afraid of. Where did local people live, and how did they afford the rents or the cost of property in the area?

Lili walked out of the kitchen with two mugs of tea and set them down on the little wooden table in front of the old sofa. Lexi wasn't keen on the flowery chintzy cover on the sofa and matching chair, but it was comfy. Lili nipped back into the kitchen and returned with a plate of biscuits.

Lili picked up her tea and took a sip. 'I was lucky. An old gentleman who used to run the antique shop across the yard took me in to live in the flat above his shop. I don't know what I would have done otherwise.'

'And then you met Ray's son.'

Ray had told Lexi on their previous visit to Aldeburgh that his friend, Lili, now ran The Potting Shed in Cobblers Yard, and that she was engaged to be married to his son, Nate, who worked as a doctor at the local cottage hospital.

'Yes, and the rest is history.'

Lili showed Lexi her engagement ring.

'That's just great.' Lexi hoped she didn't sound bitter. She'd been with Brandon for years, but he'd never proposed; the idea of getting married just never seemed to come up. She hadn't been bothered, always believing that one day he would propose, and they would marry. She had thought he was just too busy with his music to propose and set a date. Looking back on it now, she knew why marriage never came up. He wasn't in love with her.

Her family had been right all along. Her mum, her grandparents, her sister, even Mitch all said Brandon had just been sponging off her for her money. She'd been such a fool for supporting him all those years.

'At least your boyfriend didn't cheat on you,' blurted Lexi. She immediately regretted saying that. 'Sorry.'

'Is that what happened to you?' Lili asked softly.

'Yes. I lost my job and discovered my boyfriend was cheating on me all in the space of one horrible day.'

'Oh, that's awful. So you came here to get away for a bit?'

Lexi nodded. Lili was aware that she'd returned to England from America for the first time since she was a child, and that she was born in England and had lived there until her father had passed away. Lili had said to her, 'Welcome home,' which Lexi had thought was quite lovely. She'd felt she was arriving home when the plane had touched down at Heathrow and she'd looked out of the rain-lashed cabin window as it taxied to a stop.

Lexi didn't mention the reason she was there – to deliver the letter. She didn't think Lili would be really interested in hearing all about that. Lexi was taken by surprise when Lili reached across the table and took her hand. 'We girls gotta stick together. Talking of which, you must come out with us one night.'

'Huh?'

'We make a point of having a girls night out – me, Abigail and Hannah. They're my two best friends. You must come with us next time. They'd love to meet my new friend – and Ray's.'

Lexi offered up a weak smile. She'd like nothing more. Apart from her sister, she'd never had any close girlfriends to go out with and confide in. She'd just had Brandon. He'd been her best friend, her everything. She'd like nothing more than to make new friends, especially if Lili's two best friends were anything like her – Lili was lovely, trusting, chatty, and obviously very caring.

Would Lili still call her a friend when she found out Lexi had lied to Ray about houseboat-sitting? Lexi heaved an enormous sigh and decided to tell Lili now, before she was introduced to her friends. She didn't want to find herself deceiving them too. She just couldn't do it.

She'd just opened her mouth, gearing up to tell the truth, when Lili said, 'Maisie mentioned that Ray said there's a girl around her own age living next door to you, and that she might like to meet her and have a playdate together on his boat. Maisie can't wait.'

'Oh, you're talking about Charlie. Yes, Ray talked of his grand-children, Maisie and William. I think Charlie would love to meet Maisie, and have some girls around her own age to make friends with.'

Lexi stared at Lili and thought *I could do with that too*. She wished she could stay longer, chat more, go on a girls' night out with Lili and her two best friends, but she knew she couldn't.

'So, Maisie and William's mum ...' Lexi knew that Lili and Nate were engaged to be married, and that Maisie and William must be Nate's children from a previous relationship.

'Ah, yes Maisie is my best friend's little girl. They moved down here too, and Hannah runs the old antique shop.'

Lexi touched the amber necklace that Lili was staring at.

'You've got an amber necklace. Did you buy it in the old antique shop across the yard?'

'Yes. Ray mentioned that his granddaughter makes them and sells them in the shop.'

Lili laughed. 'I remember. I think I chided him over it – because they are his granddaughter's he thinks they're amazing.'

'Oh, but they are,' said Lexi. 'I bought Charlie one too. She loves it.'

Lexi smiled. 'I'll let Maisie know. She might bring Charlie a matching bracelet to their playdate. She's just started making those too.'

'She's very talented,' commented Lexi.

Lili smiled to herself. 'Oh, you have no idea.'

'I didn't realise that was Maisie's mum.' Lexi thought she looked quite young, around her age, to have a ten-year-old.

As if Lili guessed what she was thinking, she said, 'Nate and Hannah met at high school, but it didn't work out. Maisie is his first child. My friend has done well turning the antique shop around. Once she's sold all the antique odds and ends, she's going to expand Maisie's range of jewellery and look at turning the shop into an arts and crafts store like Ray used to run next door.'

Lexi looked at her and nodded, realising she'd quickly changed the subject. Lexi understood. Nate and Hannah had been so young when they had a child. Just teenagers. Hannah had obviously become pregnant with Maisie at high school.

'Nate's first wife passed away. He was a widower with a child, William, when we met. Maisie lives with her mum part of the week, and then her half-brother, William, and her dad, Nate. And me of course, which is lovely. I have a close bond with Maisie. And William. I know it all sounds rather complicated, but sometimes that's just the way things work out. I'm hoping to adopt William when we marry.'

Lexi nodded. For some reason, Scott and Charlie came to mind. Their situation was complicated too.

'Hey, if you're meeting Ray at Sarah's for lunch again, you'll get to meet them.'

'I will?' Lexi said in surprise.

'Yes. Sarah is looking after the grandchildren this afternoon.

Nate is dropping them round to Sarah's before his shift at the hospital begins after lunch. He's on a late shift today. I think they've got something nice planned for lunch. Maisie texted me. She's been told they've got a special guest for lunch.

'Who – me?' Lexi stared at her. She could not believe she'd met such wonderful people. Lexi breathed a sigh, wishing that she hadn't lied to Ray. What would they think of her when they all found out she was abusing their kind, generous, giving natures?

'In case you returned to the shop for some reason, I'm sworn to secrecy and mustn't tell you because it's a surprise.'

'Oh, no.'

'What's wrong?' Lili asked, putting her tea down.

'I didn't want them to go to too much trouble on my account.'

'Oh, it won't be any trouble. Besides, it was the children's idea, something they love to do.'

'Okay.' That made her feel better if it was something they were going to do anyway.

17

Lexi finished her cup of tea and put it on the table.

'Would you like another cup of tea, Lexi?'

She shook her head. 'It's been lovely chatting, but I'd better get going soon.' She paused and looked at Lili. 'This is going to sound so silly, but I feel like Ray and Sarah are like substitute grandparents, taking me under their wing.'

Lili grinned. 'That's how I felt when I first met them. Aren't they the best?'

Lexi frowned, to the point of becoming a bit tearful.

Lili noticed. 'Oh, Lexi, what did I say?'

Lexi breathed a huge sigh. 'I'm a terrible person.'

'No, you're not.'

'But I am. You don't know the half of it.'

Lili smiled. 'You sounded very English there all of a sudden.'

Lexi's lip curled in a little smile. 'I did, didn't I?'

Lili stood up and walked round the coffee table to sit next to her on the sofa. 'What is it, Lexi, what's wrong? We can help you. Whatever it is, we can sort it out.'

Lexi furiously shook her head. 'You can't. You'll all hate me. You've been so nice and all along I've lied to Ray.'

Lili went quiet.

Lexi took a deep breath and spilled the beans. 'I'm not house-sitting. I'm squatting in the houseboat.' *There. I've said it*, she thought. She avoided eye contact. 'I'm putting money on one side to pay for anything I've used, and some rent money.' Lexi was aware that it didn't touch a market rent. She added, 'It's not much, but it's all I can afford. But that's beside the point. I'm there and I shouldn't be, and I've lied to Ray and Sarah who have been so lovely. I feel so bad.'

Lexi sighed heavily. 'The trouble is I don't want to leave the houseboat. I can't. I'd have nowhere to go. Then I'd have to return to Connecticut and lead a life I'd hate.' She stopped rambling and stared forlornly at the floor. 'I'd better go now.' She looked up at Lili, expecting to see a cross, angry expression on her face. Surprisingly, Lili was smiling. Was she finding this funny?

'I'm afraid this isn't news to me, Lexi.'

'Huh? You know?'

'I didn't know you were squatting, but I think Ray suspects there's something going on you aren't telling him.'

Lexi wasn't really surprised to hear that. He'd been a police officer. She expected he could tell just by her body language that something was amiss.

'He told me you'd been mugged in London. He saw you arrive in the rain, sitting out on the houseboat deck as though you were waiting for someone. I think I can guess what happened.'

'I didn't break in, I swear. There was a key under the flowerpot. I wasn't even looking. I just knocked the flowerpot over with my case by mistake, and there it was. Then I went into the houseboat and fell asleep. When the owner didn't turn up, I found out they were away for the summer.' Lexi realised she was rambling again.

'Sorry, that doesn't excuse what I've done. Am doing.'

Lili shook her head. 'No, it doesn't – on the one hand. But you know what? I've been in the same position, with nowhere to stay. I was lucky.'

Lexi said, 'The guy who used to run the antique shop took you in.' She remembered that Lili had mentioned that.

'It wasn't quite as straightforward as that, I'm afraid. Joseph had an accident and ended up in hospital, and I kind of used his flat, even though it wasn't official, and we hadn't drawn up a contract. He wasn't even there. I know the family were suspicious of me at first, but just like you, I intended to pay my own way.'

Lexi stared at her. 'I had no idea.'

'Well, needs must, you know.'

'I do,' said Lexi nodding her head vigorously. She sighed. 'You'd better tell Ray.'

'I'll leave that to you, when you're ready. Now, don't take this wrong, as I am in no way condoning squatting, but—'

'But—?'

'Well, if the person is away all summer, then you are doing them a favour.'

Lexi frowned. 'How so?'

'You're looking after the place.'

'So they don't end up with squatters?'

Lili burst out laughing.

Lexi smiled.

'Look, Lexi, I've got an idea. Sounds as though you've settled into the houseboat.'

'Yes, that's the unfortunate thing. I don't even like boats, never did like the water.' She shuddered at the thought of the dream, or more like a nightmare she kept having, since she'd returned to

England; a child was drowning, and she couldn't save them.

'One day soon, Lexi, the summer is going to come to an end, and you'll need to move out.'

Lexi breathed a heavy sigh at the thought. 'Yes, that's true.'

'I guess you've had a look in some estate agents' windows.'

'I honestly don't know how people afford to rent, let alone buy.'

'I know, it's crazy. It's little wonder there's a thriving houseboat community.'

Lexi thought of Margot spending her summer in a huge cottage in grounds up the road in Walberswick. She'd seen a small cottage for sale in the village, and it was over half a million pounds. It didn't seem right for Margot to own that cottage and the houseboat too. And it certainly didn't seem right that she'd strung along her neighbours who lived in their houseboats full time. Lexi hoped she was just jumping to conclusions.

'Lexi?'

'Oh, sorry, I was miles away.' She added, 'You were lucky, meeting Nate.'

'Sounds to me as though you're rather friendly with the single dad next door – what's his name?'

'Scott.' Lexi furrowed her brow. She reckoned Ray had mentioned the dinner date to Lili – which wasn't a date. 'It's nothing like that.'

Lili just nodded and smiled. 'If you say so.' She changed the subject. 'Look, Nate and I live in quite a big place, with plenty of spare bed—'

'Oh, no, no. I couldn't possibly impose.' Lexi wouldn't impose on her sister and her fiancé, so she wasn't about to accept an invitation to live with Lili and the fiancé she'd never met.

'I knew you'd say that. Look, it isn't much, but Abigail doesn't have to work here to do my accounts. She just nips round as an excuse for a natter. She lives in Southwold too, you know. I only come up here to make a cuppa when the shop is open.'

Lexi looked at her.

'I know this sofa is old, but it is a sofa-bed. There's a bathroom with a little compact shower, and a kitchen. Of course the views are not that great, I'm afraid, nothing like being on a houseboat on the river, overlooking the quay.'

'Oh, I love Cobblers Yard,' Lexi said.

Lili smiled. 'So do I. It's where my life changed for the better.'

Lexi smiled too. She thought about discovering her father's grave and its mystery visitor, and wondered whether her trip might well change her life too.

'I know it's a bit pokey, and the furnishings are old, but you can stay here as long as you need, while you get on your feet.'

Lexi felt tears in her eyes. 'That is so kind of you.'

'Not at all. What are friends for?'

Lili surprised her by leaning over and giving her a hug. 'I've been where you are now, and it's a scary place, finding yourself in a strange town, and going it alone. But know this. You're not alone. You have friends here.'

Lexi draw back and wiped a tear from her eye. 'I don't know what to say.'

'You don't have to say anything. You can just turn up with your bags whenever you like, and the flat will be waiting for you.'

Lexi looked about her.

'I get that you prefer the houseboat.'

Lexi looked at her sheepishly. 'Sorry.'

Lili laughed again. 'Don't apologise. I bet I would too.' Lili stood up and walked over to her bag on the kitchen counter. She came back with a set of keys, prising one off the key ring. 'Here.'

'What's this?'

'A spare key to the shop.'

'Oh, I couldn't possibly ...'

'Yes, you could.' Lili thrust it at her. 'I won't take no for an answer.'

Lexi took the key. Her eyes drifted to the old computer. 'I don't suppose I could pop in and use your old computer?' Lexi knew she could use the computer in the library to join AncestryDNA, but she didn't want to do it on work time. Besides, it was private here and she imagined she could spend as much time as she wanted researching her English family tree. 'I want to join AncestryDNA.'

'Of course you can. Come along any time.' Lili glanced at her watch. 'Right, well I've got to go back to work, and you've got a lunch date with Sarah and Ray. Oh, and Maisie and William.'

Lexi stood up. 'I hope Maisie and William don't mind me joining them.'

'Of course not, why would they? You're in for a treat, by the way.'

'I hope they haven't gone to too much trouble on my account,' Lexi said again.

'It's no trouble at all – you'll see.'

As Lexi followed Lili down the stairs into the shop, she caught sight of one of the booklets filled with photos of bouquets that they made up in the shop. 'Oh, I nearly forgot, there's something I wanted to ask you.'

Lexi got out her booklet. She'd turned down the corner of the page she wanted to show Lili. 'Someone laid some flowers on my dad's grave. I don't know who it is, but they must have bought the bouquet from here. It's the same as the one in your booklet. Look.' Lexi showed her a photo on her phone of the bouquet that had been left for her father. 'It was last Saturday. Can you tell me who bought these flowers?'

'Hold on. Let me look in the order book.' She reached for the order book on the counter. 'Last Saturday, you say?'

'Well, that's when I saw them, so whoever left them could have visited on that day, or perhaps a day or two before. I don't really know. But the flowers are still very fresh, so I imagine they hadn't been there long when I visited.'

Lexi watched her run her finger down a column. 'Ah, here we are.'

Lexi held her breath. She knew that she'd be asking a lot for their name and address. She imagined Lili wouldn't give out any personal information of her clients, although if she could at least tell her whether the person was a local, then she'd know they weren't just visiting the area and it was a one-off. In which case, she wouldn't be wasting her time waiting to see if they turned up again.

Lexi looked at the order book. Perhaps they had put in another order and Lili could tell her when the customer was due in next to collect their bouquet. She looked at Lili and caught her shaking her head.

'They paid in cash, I'm afraid. In those cases we just keep a record of the transaction.'

'But wouldn't you have the name of the person who'd ordered for when they came in to collect?'

'Yes, we would have, but when paid in cash we don't keep the customer's details once they've collected.'

'Oh, I see.' Lexi had a thought. 'Do you remember the person who bought that bouquet of flowers?'

'Amy was here. She took the order. She's gone for the day. She's a student, so she only works here part-time. I can tell you when she's next in.'

'Sure.' Lexi wanted to know today, now, but she supposed it would have to wait.

'Unless the person is a regular customer, I'm afraid she probably won't be able to shed any light either.'

'Thanks for looking anyway.' She watched Lili close the ledger. Lexi put her booklet back in her bag. When she knew what day she'd return to Aldeburgh, she intended to phone through an order to pick up. 'I'd better get going. Ray will wonder where I am. Oh, and thanks for the key!'

'Don't mention it. Although I do expect something in return.'

Lexi's smile faded. It suddenly brought to mind her grandparents. Her grandpa used to say, nothing in life is a free ride. Why did everything come with strings attached?

After she'd left Brandon, Lexi had returned to Connecticut to the cottage in the grounds of her grandparents' house where she'd grown up. She'd assumed that she could live there for a time while she sorted herself out and applied for other jobs, but that wasn't how things had worked out. Her grandpa made it clear that if she was back, she'd have to start work immediately in the family business. She could apply for other jobs in her spare time.

Lexi stared at Lili. She wondered what it was she wanted in return. Lexi didn't want to be rude or come across as ungrateful, but she felt inclined to hand the key back.

Lili said, 'You are coming on a girls' night out with me and my friends. Is it a deal?'

Lexi hadn't expected her to say that. She grinned. 'It's a deal.'

'Good, now let's swap mobile numbers.'

Lexi got out her phone and discovered a text from Ray asking if she was okay, and whether she was ready to pop round to Sarah's for lunch yet. Lexi quickly replied, and then swapped mobile phone numbers with Lili.

Lili looked at her phone. 'Good.'

Lexi said. 'I haven't got a car, but I can get a taxi when we go out.'

'Don't worry about that. Abigail always picks us all up. She loves any excuse to take out Penelope.'

'Penelope?'

'Oh, that's the name of Abigail's old Beetle.'

Lexi smiled. 'Okay.' Her phone buzzed with a text. 'That's Ray. I said I was on my way.'

Lili surprised her again by giving her a hug. 'Take care. If you need anything, or just want a chat, I'm always on the end of my phone, or here most days.'

'Thank you, Lili. That's so kind.'

'Now, go and have lunch – you'll enjoy it.' Lili grinned.

'You're still not going to tell me what they're doing for lunch, are you?'

Lili vigorously shook her head. 'Oh, but that would spoil the surprise!'

18

Lexi stood outside the Victorian townhouse on the promenade and rang Sarah's doorbell. The townhouse was divided into two apartments. Sarah lived on the top floor in the eaves.

Lexi remembered the bright white and airy space with wooden floors, colourful rugs and the most gorgeous view of the beach and the sea. She recalled thinking at the time that it was little wonder Sarah wouldn't move out and live with Ray on his houseboat if it meant she'd have to leave her lovely little apartment. Ray didn't seem unhappy about their living arrangements; he'd said it had strengthened their relationship. They were happier than ever.

Lexi waited outside the door. She could hear children's voices. Ray opened the door. 'Ah, hello Lexi.'

'Hello.' She looked at the two children standing beside Ray. 'Hi, I'm Lexi.'

'I'm Maisie.' She held out her hand. 'Pleased to meet you.'

Lexi smiled at her and shook her hand. 'I'm pleased to meet you too.' Lexi shifted her gaze to the little boy, William, who she guessed was around six or seven. Unlike his sister, he looked at her shyly. 'And you must be William.'

'Yes.'

Maisie surprised Lexi by grabbing her hand and pulling her inside. 'Come on. I want to show you Grandma's studio.'

'Oh, I'd have to ask Sarah, er, your grandma if she wouldn't mind me seeing—'

'No, it's fine. She's not running any classes today. Do you like art? I love art. I paint all the time. Do you paint?'

'Well, I'm not sure.' Lexi didn't like to say that it wasn't something that had been encouraged when she was a child.

Maisie ran ahead up the stairs.

Lexi paused at the bottom of the stairs and glanced behind her at Ray. 'Is it okay if I see Sarah's studio?'

'Of course.'

'Lexi – hurry up!'

Ray shifted his gaze to his granddaughter, who was standing halfway up the stairs. He whispered, 'You'll have to excuse my granddaughter – she can be quite exuberant.'

Lexi smiled. Maisie reminded her of Charlie. She hoped a play date could be organised for them because she imagined they'd have a great time together.

She was about to start up the stairs when she realised Ray wasn't closing the front door. 'Can we go now, Grandpa?' she heard William say as he stepped outside.

Lexi looked at Ray. 'Are you going out?'

'Yes, we won't be long. Maisie, tell your grandma that we'll be back soon.'

'Okay, I will. Lexi, come on.'

Lexi followed Maisie up the stairs to Sarah's apartment.

'Hello, Lexi. It's lovely to see you again.' Sarah stepped forward and gave her a hug.

'Nana, I want to show Lexi your studio.'

Lexi looked at Sarah. 'Is that okay?'

'Of course, go right ahead. Would you like a cup of tea, Lexi?'

'Oh, yes please.'

'Here, let me take your jacket.'

Lexi slipped off her jacket and handed it to Sarah. She followed Maisie through a door opposite the lounge into a similar room in the eaves with freshly painted white walls, oak flooring and the most marvellous views of the promenade and the beach from the picture window.

She glanced around the room. She counted six painting easels set up with canvases at various stages of completion.

Maisie sat down on a stool in front of a canvas and picked up a paintbrush.

Lexi rushed over. 'Oh, Maisie, I wouldn't do that if I were you!' Lexi's eyes went wide at the thought of her dabbing paint on someone's beautiful watercolour. She'd didn't want her to get into trouble.

'It's fine. I'm just putting some finishing touches on my painting. You can watch if you like.'

Lexi stared at her. '*Your* painting?'

'Yes. I know what you're thinking. It's not my best.'

Maisie had no idea what Lexi was thinking. When Lili had said Maisie had hidden talents, she hadn't been joking. Lexi was no art expert, far from it, but she knew a prodigy when she saw one – anyone would be amazed that a ten-year-old could paint something like this. 'Your painting is just amazing.'

'Oh, thanks. But I'm going to do it again.'

'Really? You're not happy with that?' Lexi said in astonishment.

Maisie huffed and turned her head this way and that, examining her painting. She tapped the end of her paintbrush against her cheek. 'Something isn't quite right.' She put the paintbrush down and picked up the canvas.

'What will you do with that canvas?'

'Oh, I don't know.' She turned around on her stool. 'You like it, don't you?'

'Oh, Maisie. I love it.'

'Would you like it?'

'Really?' Lexi reached inside her bag. 'I want to give you something for it.' Lexi knew she didn't have a lot of cash on her, and it would in no way be a reflection of what she thought the painting was worth, but she had to offer her something.

Maisie shook her head. 'It's a present for you.'

'Oh, Maisie, that is so sweet of you. Will you sign it for me?'

Maisie grinned. 'Yes.'

As Lexi watched her sign the painting, she got the impression that this wasn't the first time that Maisie had signed one of her paintings and given it to someone. The painting hanging in the little flat above Lili's shop came to mind.

Lexi had noticed the watercolour when she'd sat on the sofa and waited for Lili to make a cup of coffee. She'd admired the painting of a pebbly beach with beach huts and little fishing boats bobbing on the water. It also beautifully captured the amazing big sky that Lexi had discovered this part of the world was renowned for. The painting reminded her of Aldeburgh, and Lili confirmed that it was. Lexi recalled Lili's reply when she'd asked her who had painted it – Lili had said cryptically, *you wouldn't believe me if I told you.*

Maisie took the signed painting down from the easel and gave it to Lexi. 'Grandpa says my signed paintings will be worth a lot of money in the future.'

Lexi nodded. 'I get the feeling he's right.'

'Is it because I'm a child prodigy?' asked Maisie.

So, she does know, thought Lexi. 'Yes, I imagine so. But it isn't just that. I wouldn't be surprised if you could give Picasso or van Gogh a run for their money.'

Lexi saw Maisie frown. Ray's granddaughter didn't understand what she was going on about.

'Oh, you mean I'm, like, as good as them.'

Lexi looked at the small watercolour Maisie had given her. It really was breathtaking that anyone could paint like this, let alone a ten-year-old child.

'I prefer Constable,' commented Maisie. 'Do you know that East Anglia is called Constable Country because he painted some famous scenes here? He enjoyed painting the open spaces and our big Suffolk sky.'

Lexi had heard of Constable. She thought she might have even seen some of his work in a gallery in New York. She'd visited lots of galleries over the years, but unfortunately she couldn't remember the names of the artists.

'Do you know,' said Maisie, 'that he was a landscape painter in the romantic tradition? Like me, he was self-taught.'

Lexi didn't think anyone could teach that sort of talent.

Maisie picked up a new, blank white canvas and put it on the easel. She thrust a delicate brush at Lexi. 'Here – your turn.'

Lexi backed away. 'Oh, I couldn't possibly. I've never been to an art class in my life.'

'What's this about an art class?'

Lexi swivelled her head to find Sarah standing in the doorway.

William came running into the room, squeezing past his grandma.

'Maisie, Grandpa's on his way to find a table. We've got to go.'

Lexi looked at Maisie and was relieved to find her putting the paintbrush down. She'd had a lucky escape from completely embarrassing herself.

Maisie said, 'Come on, Lexi, it's time for lunch.'

'I'm hungry,' said William as they walked out of Sarah's studio.

'You're always hungry.'

'Am not!'

'Am too!'

Lexi smiled as she listened to the children arguing. Maisie and William ran ahead down the hall.

Sarah said, 'Sorry, but we haven't got time to stop for a cup of tea after all.'

Lexi turned to Sarah. 'I heard that Ray has booked a table. I really hope he – well, you both – haven't gone to too much trouble over lunch.' She imagined he'd booked a table at one of the restaurants, or perhaps The Two Magpies, a café she kept promising herself she'd stop at for lunch. Even so, she'd much prefer something low key. She would have settled for a sandwich at Sarah's.

'It's no trouble at all – you'll see.'

'Where are we going?'

'Fish and chips is my favourite!' William sang out in a sing-song voice.

'Mine too, especially when we eat it on the beach.'

'Hey, you two. This was meant to be a surprise for Lexi.'

'Sorry, Grandma!' Maisie and William said in unison.

'Fish and chips on the beach!' exclaimed Lexi, her mouth watering.

Sarah rolled her eyes. 'Sorry, Lexi, it was going to be a surprise. That's the thing with children. They can never keep a secret.'

Lexi laughed. 'Oh, don't worry. Although I am intrigued. If we're having fish and chips on the beach, why is Ray reserving a table?'

'Reserving a table?' Sarah smiled. 'Oh, I think you've got the wrong end of the stick. There are some wooden picnic benches on the beach. We're going to walk along the promenade to find him further along waiting with the fish and chips. Is that okay with you? I know you enjoyed my finger sandwiches and scones last time, but today we wanted to do something a little different.'

'Oh, it's just perfect. I'd like to bring Charlie – that's my neighbour's little girl – and show her Aldeburgh.'

'Perhaps she'd like fish and chips on the beach too.'

Lexi grinned. 'I'm sure she would.'

Lexi showed her the canvas as they walked down the hall. 'Maisie gave me this, but I really can't accept it.'

Sarah stopped in the hallway, surprised. 'Why not? She loves giving her art to friends. Don't you like it?'

'Oh, it's not that at all. I adore it. It's just she is so talented, and I imagine this is going to be worth a lot of money in the future,' said Lexi repeating what Maisie had, quite rightly, told her.

'Did she sign it?'

'Yes. I really want to pay for it.'

Sarah held up her hand, waving a stern finger in front of Lexi's face. 'Absolutely not. It's a gift.'

Lexi smiled. 'All right. I'll cherish it. When I get my own place, it will be the first thing I hang on the wall.' She looked at Sarah, taken aback at what she'd just said. She'd never had her own place, a home she'd chosen and worked for herself. She grinned, glancing around Sarah's little apartment before they followed the children out of the door. She wondered what her first home would be like.

19

'Oh, hello Alan.'

They'd arrived on the quay in Walberswick, and Lexi had her hand on the car door handle, ready to get out of the car, when Ray's phone rang.

'Yes, she's right here.'

Lexi rolled her eyes and turned to look at Ray. She really did not want to speak to Alan again.

'Okay, I'll give her the message.' Ray ended the call. 'That was Alan. He's fixed the lock.'

'Great.' It was very kind of Ray to offer to pay for the lock, but Lexi didn't like owing anybody. Her thoughts momentarily drifted to the hotel in London and the night's stay she still hadn't paid for. She wondered when that would eventually catch up with her. She could fix that if she had her allowance. Although she'd receive her pay at the end of the week from her job in the library, it wouldn't cover the cost of that night.

Lexi chose to ignore that issue for now. 'Did Alan mention how much it will cost for the job?'

'He did. He hasn't gone back on his word to do it privately, saving you some money compared to what the shop would charge.'

'Okay, that's good.' It was better than good when Ray told her how much Alan had charged for the job. Although it meant she wouldn't have much change from her pay that week, it did mean she wouldn't be in debt to Ray. Alan had said she could give him the cash.

Lexi did want Ray to do her a favour though. She wanted to hand over the payment to Ray to pass on to Alan when she got paid. She didn't want to get into another conversation with Alan; didn't want him eyeing her suspiciously again and asking for more details about how, exactly, she had come to be looking after Margot's houseboat.

Lexi hastily said, 'Can I give you the money to pass on to Alan when you see him, and say a big thank you from me?'

'You don't want to do it yourself? He's only a few doors down. I could point out his houseboat.'

Lexi shook her head. 'You know what? I'm out a lot of the time. I'll probably keep missing him.' She knew it was just excuses not to call on Alan. 'I'd much rather Alan gets paid as soon as possible, and it's just easier if I hand you the money as you're just next door.' She was relieved when Ray agreed.

Lexi had a thought. 'Where are the new keys? Can he pass them on to you and I'll call on you and collect them later?'

'That won't be necessary. I nearly forgot to tell you, didn't I? He said he'd left the new key under the flowerpot by the door.'

Lexi pursed her lips and frowned.

'Is that okay?'

Unfortunately, Lexi remembered what had happened last time she'd left the key under there. Someone had come along – she knew now that it must have been Meredith – and had taken it. But she didn't anticipate Meredith would show up again. 'Oh, er … yes, sure.' This time she wasn't going to make the mistake of leaving the key under the flowerpot.

'Did something happen to your lock, Lexi?'

Lexi glanced in the back at William and Maisie. It was Ray's turn to look after them in the afternoon while Sarah ran her art class.

'Yes – I, er, lost the key.' Lexi inwardly cringed at that outright lie.

Ray said, 'But Alan – you guys know Alan – has fixed the lock.'

Maisie said, 'Can we see your houseboat?'

'It's not *my* houseboat.'

'But you're living there, aren't you?'

Lexi nodded.

Ray got out of the car and opened the car door. 'I'll tell you what. How about I go and pay Alan for the lock while you fetch your key and show these two around? They'll be pestering me to let them come and visit you and see the houseboat anyway.'

Maisie and William scrambled out of the back seat.

Lexi breathed a heavy sigh and gave in when Maisie and William jumped up and down, shouting, 'Please say yes, Lexi!'

'Yes, all right.'

Ray looked at his grandchildren. 'You'll be as good as gold for Lexi, won't you?'

Lexi watched them both vigorously nodding their heads at their grandfather.

Ray led the way down the path towards the houseboat. 'Well, this is Alan's house,' he said, stopping in front of a large barge-like boat that was painted dark red and black. It was the first boat along the quay.

'Now, you two behave yourselves and do exactly as you're told while I pop in and see Alan. Remember, you are on a boat, so no larking around near the water.'

Lexi shuddered when that recurring dream suddenly came to mind. She couldn't get past the bit where she was reaching out, trying to save someone as they disappeared under the water.

'Are you okay, Lexi?' Ray asked, catching her expression. 'You know, you don't have to take them both. They can stay with me.'

'Oh, no – it's fine.' The children had given her an excuse to head off and not hang around to talk to Alan.

'Here's the key to my houseboat for when they've finished looking around. Would you mind putting my kettle on? I can't wait for a cup of tea. I'm parched.'

Lexi took the key and hurried down the path, putting some distance between her houseboat and Alan's. She heard Ray calling out to this friend and trying her best to catch up with William and Maisie.

'Is this the key?' asked William, pulling it from under the flowerpot. They'd both stopped and waited for her to catch up so they could all board the houseboat together.

'Yes, I believe so.'

'Can I try it in the lock?'

Lexi nodded. 'Go ahead. Let's see if it works.' *It better had*, she thought. The last thing she needed was to have to pay Alan a visit.

'It works!'

'Oh, thank goodness.' Lexi remembered to breathe. Maisie and William walked down the steps to the cabin below. Lexi heard the creak of the door to the inner hallway that led to the bedroom and shower room. She waited on deck for them.

'It's quite small,' said Maisie. Her head popped up at the top of the stairs.

William followed. 'It's cool. Bit small.'

Lexi smiled. 'It's a narrowboat.' It was nothing like their grandpa's boat, which was basically a floating, single-storey house.

'Can we go to Grandpa's now?' William asked.

'Of course. Let's go.'

'Who are they?'

Lexi recognised Charlie's voice. She turned around to find Charlie standing on the deck of the boat next door. 'Hey, Charlie. This is Maisie and William. They're Ray's grandchildren.'

'Okay.'

Maisie stepped forward. 'Do you want to come and play with us?'

Lexi remembered that Ray had said he'd arrange a playdate so Charlie could meet Maisie. She guessed it was as good a time as any, if Ray didn't mind three kids on his houseboat. 'Shouldn't we ask your Grandpa first?'

Maisie frowned at Lexi. 'Why?'

Lexi shrugged. 'I don't know.'

Maisie turned to Charlie. 'I'm ten. This is my brother. He's seven.'

'I'm nearly eight.'

Masie threw her little brother a look. 'Are you Charlie?'

'Yes, I'm ten too. How did you know my name?'

'Grandpa said he had new neighbours and I might like to invite you over next time I'm on the boat.'

Charlie grinned. 'I'm coming right over.'

Lexi said, 'Charlie, you have to ask your dad first.'

Charlie frowned at Lexi.

'Go on now, go and ask. You'll need to let him know where you are.'

Charlie's shoulders sagged. 'Oh, all right.'

Lexi watched Charlie go back inside the houseboat. She turned to Maisie and William. 'Come on, you two – let's head to Ray's. I mean your grandpa's.'

'But what about Charlie?' asked Maisie as they stepped off the houseboat.

'She's only next door. She can come and call on you if her dad says it's okay.'

They headed down the riverside path, past the houseboat that Charlie and her father were renting and towards Ray's place next door.

William said, 'Why has she got a boy's name?'

Lexi glanced at him. 'You mean Charlie?'

'Yes.'

'It's short for Charlotte, but she prefers Charlie.'

'But it's a boy's name.'

Maisie heaved a sigh and pulled a face. 'If she prefers her nickname Charlie, then that's what we'll call her, William.'

'Why haven't I got a nickname?'

Lexi found their sibling banter amusing. She remembered that she and her sister had often had these sorts of silly arguments and disagreements.

'I don't know.' Maisie's voice sounded a bit irritated. 'Would you like one?'

'Yes.'

Maisie grinned. 'I know. We could call you Willy.'

William, who was walking in front, turned around and gave his sister a cold stare. 'I don't want that nickname.'

Maisie rolled her eyes. 'I know. It was a joke.'

'That was a stupid joke.'

'How about Will?' suggested Lexi. 'It sounds quite grown up. You did say you were nearly eight.'

William puffed out his chest. 'Yes. I am nearly eight. I'm going to be called Will from now on.'

Lexi and Maisie exchanged a smile.

Up ahead, Lexi could see Ray coming down the path on his own. There was no sign of Alan. 'Was he home?' Lexi asked as Ray approached.

'Yes.' Ray handed her a slip of paper as they all stopped outside Ray's houseboat. 'Here's the receipt for the work. It's guaranteed for a year.'

'Okay.'

'Lexi! Dad says it's fine.'

They all looked over at Charlie racing along the path towards them. Lexi turned to Ray. 'Sorry – I hope it's okay for Charlie and come over and play with Maisie and William.'

'Of course, the more the merrier. I did say I was going to arrange a playdate.'

'Have you got a phone?' Charlie asked Maisie.

'Yes, this is mine.'

'Are you on Facebook or Twitter?' asked Charlie.

'I've got YouTube. I like some of the videos.'

Charlie said, 'Me too.'

Lexi watched Maisie and Charlie walk on to Ray's houseboat together.

'Do you like art, Charlie?'

'I like drawing.'

'Cool. We could do that too, if you like.'

'Cool,' said Charlie.

Lexi smiled.

As they all stepped on to the houseboat, Maisie said, 'Lexi, when we do some drawing, you can do some too.'

Lexi thought back to the offer for her to do some painting in Sarah's studio. Maisie obviously wasn't going to take no for an answer. 'Oh, please, Lexi.'

Charlie came over and took her hand. 'Come on, let's all do some drawing.'

Lexi stepped aboard Ray's boat. 'Are you sure you checked with your dad and that he knows where you are?'

'Yes, look.' She pointed. 'See.'

Scott came out on deck and looked at his watch. 'Just an hour.'

Ray waved. 'It's no trouble, Scott. She can stay as long as she likes.'

'Oh, please say yes,' Charlie called out.

Maisie joined in. 'Yes, please let Charlie stay all afternoon.'

Scott shifted his gaze to Ray. 'Are you sure?'

'It's no problem.'

'You be good, Charlie.'

'Yes, Daddy.'

Lexi stared at Scott. Then she lowered her eyes, becoming embarrassed the moment he shifted his gaze to her. She had a free afternoon and would have loved to spend it with Scott, just the two of them, although she guessed that whatever he did for a living, he probably wasn't free for the afternoon.

'Come on, Lexi.' Maisie grabbed her hand.

Ray said, 'Maisie, let her be. She can't play with you all afternoon. I expect she's got things to do.'

'We're not playing right now. We're drawing.'

'It's all right, Ray – I'll pop in for a bit and try my hand at some drawing, but I have to tell you now, Maisie, I think you're going to be disappointed with my efforts. I'm no artist.'

'How do you know? Have you tried?'

'No, actually.'

'Well, come on then.'

Lexi glanced over at Scott, who was standing on the deck, staring at her. She wondered what he was thinking. Was he thinking about the other night? She had loved his curry, but she had loved his company more. She knew the feeling was mutual.

She hoped she was going to get another invite to dinner.

20

'I had such a good time. Maisie is, like, my best friend now. She's the best,' said Charlie.

Lexi stared at Scott across the table. She still couldn't quite believe she was sitting there having dinner with them again. Charlie was still talking about her fantastic afternoon.

'Your drawings were so good, Lexi. You looked surprised. Maisie did too. She showed her grandpa. You're going to start classes with Maisie's grandma, aren't you? I heard Maisie tell her grandpa you'd enjoy it, and learn more about drawing and painting. Are you going to go, Lexi?'

'Huh?' Lexi tore her eyes away from Scott, just for a moment. 'Er, yes. I am.'

'Good because Maisie says you've got talent, and it should be nurtured. Maisie is going to show me how to—'

Charlie continued to talk about her exciting afternoon with her best friend ever, but Lexi was no longer listening. She'd had the best afternoon ever too.

She'd left Ray's after he'd phoned Sarah and arranged for Lexi to start attending her art classes on Thursday afternoons. Lexi expected that suited Ray perfectly – it was another excuse to call on

Sarah every week if he still had to give her a lift into Aldeburgh.

Although their relationship was going from strength to strength, Lexi could tell that Ray was still wary of things falling apart again. Apparently, he'd stuffed the divorce papers into a drawer. She guessed he wanted to rip them up or burn them, but didn't want to jinx what had turned out to be the start of a new chapter in his relationship with Sarah.

Charlie had stayed on for the rest of the afternoon, playing with her new friend while Lexi returned to the houseboat, walking on air at the discovery of her hidden talent.

She was so shocked to discover she could draw. She had a natural talent. That's what Maisie had said. And that was quite something, coming from Maisie. She was no prodigy like Maisie, but she had talent. What thrilled her most of all was that she must have inherited it from her dad. She'd told Maisie and Ray that her father had been an illustrator.

That's when Ray had asked her, 'What did he illustrate? Have you ever seen his drawings? Perhaps some are still in print?'

She knew he'd illustrated books. He'd worked for a publisher in London. It had never occurred to her to ask her mum where he'd worked and what he'd illustrated.

She'd told Ray her thoughts. He'd suggested doing a search online to see if her father's name came up and if the books he'd illustrated were still for sale. They both knew that books had the illustrator's name on the cover if the illustrations were central to the story, or on the back if they'd illustrated the cover, or inside the pages if there was a dedication to other collaborators on the book. They'd both thought it was worth a try.

Lexi hadn't got around to that yet. She'd returned to Margot's houseboat, and within a few moments, there had been a knock at the door. Her first thought had been that it was Alan, visiting to see how the lock was. She had been worried that he would use it as a ruse to question her further over what she was doing on Margot's houseboat. She'd recalled what he'd said: *Margot would never let out her houseboat.*

Now, though, she was sitting at the dinner table across from Scott, and they were staring adoringly into each other's eyes. It had been him knocking at the door, inviting her to join him on a walk.

'Aren't you working?' she'd blurted in surprise.

He'd said, 'I thought that as Charlie was busy next door, and you seem to have a free afternoon, you'd like to have lunch with me? I was going to eat it at my desk, but it seems a shame to eat alone.'

'Shall I come next door?' Lexi had asked eagerly. She'd just eaten fish and chips on the beach, but she wasn't about to tell him that. Besides, she'd find the room. If his amazing curries were anything to go by, she bet he made lovely lunches too.

From behind his back, he'd produced a picnic hamper. He'd opened it to show her the contents.

'You eat a lot for lunch,' she'd commented, seeing freshly made sandwiches in a lovely, seeded bread, homemade cakes, fresh strawberries and cream, and lots of other treats. That was when she'd realised it wasn't a lunch he'd been planning to eat at his desk. He'd made it up especially for her, and had assumed she'd say yes. Which she had, although she'd had no idea how she'd get through all that food. When Scott had called on Ray to check on Charlie, and to tell them that they were going for a picnic to the beach in Walberswick, and to give Ray his mobile number just in case, Lexi could tell that Charlie was torn. She'd wanted to go with them but also wanted to stay with Maisie.

Maisie had begged Charlie not to go.

Lexi had told Charlie that they would all go out on a day trip somewhere special, and have a picnic too, so that she didn't feel as though she was missing out. That had made up Charlie's mind.

Lexi was still smiling at Scott across the table. It had been such a lovely afternoon. They'd strolled along the path, past the other houseboats moored at the quay, into the small village of Walberswick. Lexi had picked up her pace as they'd walked past Willow Tree Cottage. She hadn't been able to help stealing a glance through the double gates as they'd walked by, her gaze settling on the branches of the willow tree in the garden as she strode past.

They'd continued past more cottages and the pub on the corner before turning down a wooden boardwalk between high reed beds. It took them to the beach with the sand dunes that Ray had mentioned when they'd driven through Walberswick in his car on their first trip to Aldeburgh.

They had chosen a nice picnic spot amongst the dunes with views of the sea, but sheltered from the wind and away from passers-by. Scott not only had the picnic basket, but a small backpack. Out came a soft picnic blanket to sit on, a bottle of wine, two glasses and a bottle opener.

Scott had thought of everything for a perfect picnic on the beach. There were plates for the sandwiches and even little cotton napkins.

She'd watched Scott pour the wine. He'd held up his glass. So had she, wondering what he was going to say.

Now, still smiling at him across the table, she gave Charlie a sideways glance. She was still talking about her afternoon next door with Maisie and William. And Lexi still wasn't listening. She was thinking about the afternoon on the beach, and the toast Scott had raised. 'To new friendships,' he'd said, 'And living in the moment – for who knows what is around the corner?'

'Living in the moment,' Lexi had said, smiling at him even though she was a little disconcerted by that comment – *who knows what is around the corner*?

Her smile faltered as she remembered what had happened next. She'd been carried away by a perfect day, the sun beating down on her shoulders as she'd sat in her bathing costume. When he'd suggested they have a picnic on the beach, she'd changed into a swimming costume, shorts, and a flowing white shirt over a camisole before they'd set off. They'd had lunch, chatted, laughed a lot, and then he'd suggested they go swimming in the sea.

Lexi never swam in the sea. She could swim. She'd learnt in school under duress, but that didn't mean she'd ever get over her fear of the water. It wasn't something she ever chose to do on holiday with her sister, mum, and stepdad Mitch, or with her grandparents on the occasions that her grandpa hired an expensive yacht and the crew moored it off the coast in beautiful inlets in Hawaii or the Bahamas.

She had wanted to join Scott for a swim in the sea and not put a dampener on the afternoon by raising her fear of the water, but she just hadn't been able to do it. She couldn't go in.

Instead, she'd sat at the water's edge, letting the gentle surf wash over her feet as she watched Scott swimming, waving, and at one point scaring the crap out of her when he'd dived over a wave and hadn't resurfaced for a moment or two.

When he'd finished swimming and had walked out of the water, smoothing his wet hair down with the palm of his hand, his tanned physique dripping with water and glistening in the sunlight, Lexi had burst out laughing.

Scott had run up to her and had lain down beside her in the sand. That had made her laugh even more.

He'd turned to her, and propped himself up on one elbow. 'Was it something I said?'

'I'm sorry,' Lexi had replied. She hadn't meant to laugh at him and make him feel self-conscious. 'You coming out of the water like that reminded me of a scene from an old Burt Lancaster movie. I used to sit and watch old movies when I was a young child. God knows who with, because my mum, stepdad and grand-parents were just too busy to sit around the TV. Anyway, there was this scene where he came out of the water and lay on the sand next to the young lady, and they kissed in the sand.'

'What – like this?' Scott had said, taking her in his arms and kissing her, dripping sea water all over her.

'Hey!' Lexi wasn't objecting to the sudden display of affection, although his wet skin on hers sent shivers down her spine. 'You've seen the movie!' she'd exclaimed when they'd managed to prise their hands off one another.

'Oh, yes – but the lady went for a swim too. Didn't they kiss in the surf first?'

'Yes, they did.' Lexi had frowned. 'I'm afraid you still can't tempt me into the water. Although, saying that, another kiss might be quite tempting.'

He'd kissed her again. When he drew back, he'd said, 'I can't remember the name of the movie either!'

'It's bugging me,' Lexi had said.

'Me too!' Scott had replied, his breath hot in her ear.

A child's voice had interrupted them, shouting out, 'What are they doing?'

They'd quickly parted, throwing apologetic looks at the

parents of the small child as they raced each other up the beach and fell in an excited heap on the rug behind the sand dunes where they'd left the picnic basket and backpack. There had been no chance of them carrying on being intimate among the dunes, with children running up and down them, playing hide and seek. One youngster had run around a sand dune to hide, not realising they were there. He'd stopped abruptly. 'Sorry.'

Lexi remembered thinking at the time that Charlie would love to go there and play among the dunes with Maisie and William. Perhaps it was something she could arrange with Ray when his grandchildren visited next.

She'd had such fun that afternoon – until Scott had brought up her fear of the water, and her extreme reaction when Charlie had fallen into the water on the way back to her own boat. She'd confided in Scott that since returning to England, she'd been having a dream about a drowning girl, but when Charlie had fallen in, she knew it wasn't a dream, but a memory. It was haunting her, not knowing who the girl was and what happened to her.

'From here to eternity.'

Lexi's thoughts were interrupted by Scott. 'I'm sorry – what did you say?'

He put his knife and fork down on his empty plate. 'The movie. It's called *From Here to Eternity*.'

Lexi thought, *I'd love to spend an eternity with you right here in this beautiful part of the world.* Her smile faded for the first time that evening. What had Scott said when they'd toasted each other on the beach? She remembered his words: *To new friendships*. He'd also said, *And living in the moment – for who knows what is around the corner?*

She watched him get up from the table and start to load the dirty plates into the slimline dishwasher in the galley kitchen.

What had he meant when he'd said, *who knows what is around the corner?* It reminded her that she still really knew nothing about him, whereas she'd practically told him her life story, glossing over what had gone on with Brandon. She did not want to talk about him. It wasn't just that he was an ex-boyfriend, and she was pretty sure Scott didn't want to talk about past relationships. It was what had happened – his betrayal. It was still very raw. But it was something more. She still missed him. She didn't want to admit that to herself, let alone Scott.

'What movie?' asked Charlie, looking from Lexi to her dad.

Scott laughed. 'Oh, it's just a private joke.'

Lexi exchanged a smile with Scott before glancing sheepishly at Charlie. She expected Scott's daughter to be quite cross that her dad had had a private joke with her. She imagined that Charlie might be feeling left out and even a little upset at their friendship. After all, Lexi got the impression that it had been just Charlie and her dad for a while. How would she feel about the possibility of her dad having a female friend, let alone starting a relationship?

Lexi raised her eyebrows when she saw Charlie grinning. Lexi narrowed her eyes. 'You look tired.'

Charlie yawned quite theatrically, Lexi thought. 'Early night?' Lexi asked innocently.

'Oh, yes. I think that would be a really good idea.'

Lexi caught Charlie grinning when she thought no one was looking.

Scott looked at his watch. 'Aren't you having pudding?'

'No, I'm bushed.'

'Bushed?' Lexi asked, wondering what she meant.

'Exhausted.' Charlie yawned again.

Scott nodded. 'I think Maisie's a bit of a livewire, and William too. I'm not surprised you're tired. You're not used to being around people your own age.'

Charlie said goodnight. They'd had dinner quite late. Charlie had stayed next door for hours. Eventually, Scott had gone to collect her.

'Goodnight, Lexi, Dad.'

Charlie hugged her dad, then came over and put her arms around Lexi, giving her hug too.

'Sleep tight,' said Lexi.

'Do you want me to read to you before lights out?'

Lexi smiled to herself. She got the impression that Scott asked her that question every night, and each time Charlie said, 'Dad – I'm ten. I can read a book myself.'

'I know, honey.'

Lexi caught the expression on Scott's face; his little girl was growing up, and there wasn't a thing he could do about it.

Lexi stared after Charlie, knowing what she was up to; she was getting an early night so Lexi and Scott could spend some quality time together. Although there was something else; that evening, Lexi had noticed her looking at her phone as she walked out of the room.

A mobile phone buzzed with a text. Lexi looked at her phone, wondering if it was her sister, texting her with a message that she'd got it wrong, and Grandpa hadn't stopped her allowance. *No such luck*, she thought.

There were no texts from Andrea, although she had got several texts from Brandon over the last few days, asking her to stop ignoring him and please get in touch. Lexi had deleted that text, and she hadn't bothered to read the others that had come through.

'It's not my phone,' said Scott. He glanced at the door.

'Charlie!'

Charlie appeared at the door. Lexi noticed she quickly hid her phone behind her back.

'Are you and Maisie texting?'

'No.'

'But I heard—'

'It's WhatsApp. Maisie made a private group just for me and her. William isn't very happy about it. He wanted to be part of our chat too, but it's girls only.'

'Oh, okay. Well, er … don't chat too late on WhatsApp, will you?'

'No, Dad.'

They heard another message ping on her phone as she walked out of the door. Lexi smiled. Charlie wanted friends. She needed friends her own age. And she needed to go to school.

Lexi eyed Scott. It wasn't her place to bring up what Charlie needed. But she was dying to ask him why they moved around a lot, and why he home-schooled her. She hadn't asked yet, afraid of what he might say – *who knows what is around the corner?*

Lexi was afraid that one day she'd return to the houseboat, and Scott and Charlie would be gone.

21

Meredith walked into Margot's study. 'So, where's Esme's notebook?'

Margot turned around in her chair. She'd been staring out at the garden, recalling happier times when she'd sat in this very chair writing, her work interrupted by the sound of children's laughter in the garden. All she saw now were dark clouds gathering.

'Did you find it?'

Margot looked sheepishly at Meredith. 'I haven't been to the houseboat yet.'

'Why ever not? Look, if it's about one of your neighbours spotting you – so what? It's your houseboat, you can come and go as you please. If you really feel you need to give an explanation then just say you forgot something and had to pop back and collect it.' Meredith smiled. 'You're not exactly telling a lie, are you? I mean you are going there to collect something.'

Margot remained quiet.

Meredith folded her arms. 'What is it? Come on, spill the beans.'

'It was something Esme said.'

'Oh, you know what your mother's like! Negative and

argumentative to the last.' Meredith shook her head. 'What did she say?'

'That I won't like it when she tells me about my father.'

Meredith sighed. She looked at her friend sympathetically. 'This picture you've built up over the years of who you imagine your father to be ...' She trailed off.

'What are you trying to say, Meredith?'

'Can I be blunt?'

Margot rolled her eyes at her friend. 'I wouldn't expect anything less.'

Meredith threw her a look before she continued. She didn't take it as an insult or a criticism. They'd known each other far too long for that. They'd been through the ups and downs of life, the good times, and the heartache and tragedy, but they'd always stood by one another – as best friends do. And Margot knew that Meredith was doing that right now, telling her something she needed to hear.

'And don't mince your words, Meredith.'

They exchanged a smile, both aware that she never did.

Meredith pulled up a chair at the desk and sat down opposite Margot. 'I think it's little wonder that over the years, because your mother has been distant and cold towards you, that you've built up this picture in your mind of your father as the hero, the good guy.'

Margot sat back in her chair, staring at her friend, wondering where this was leading.

'The question you have to ask yourself, Margot, is do you want to know the truth, or stick to the little fantasy of him you've built up in your mind? I wouldn't blame you if you decided to let sleeping dogs lie. The truth can hurt. I think that skeletons in closets are best left where they are, behind closed doors.'

Meredith had something else to add. 'Have you ever thought that perhaps Esme wasn't being difficult and mean all these years when she refused to tell you about your father, but rather that she was trying to protect you from the hurt of knowing the truth?'

Margot stared at her. It was something she'd never, ever considered. 'What do you think I should do?'

'I can't answer that, Margot. You know I can't. Only you can decide. But Esme isn't getting any younger, and each passing day brings the possibility that ...' Meredith trailed off. 'Well, you know what I'm saying. If you want to find out, then time is passing by. I suggest you make up your mind as soon as possible, today, and if you do want to avoid the neighbours, I would go after dark.' Meredith glanced out of the window. 'I think it's going to pour.' She turned back to Margot. 'If you're still concerned about being spotted, you can wear your big raincoat with the hood and take an umbrella.'

Margot stared at her good friend. She had a feeling there was something more she wanted to say. 'What is it?'

'I'm not trying to put you off, but what if he really wasn't a nice person? What if something happened between them to make your mum who she is today, who she's been for as long as we can remember – bitter and resentful. I know I'm pointing out the obvious, and you know this too, but I don't think it helped that every time she looked at you, she must have been reminded of him.'

Margot knew what she meant. They had no clue what her father looked like. There were no photos, and her mother would never speak of him, but the fact was that when Margot looked in the mirror it wasn't her mother eyes or high cheekbones or angular nose she saw. And she guessed that the resemblance became more striking as she grew older.

'What becomes of the broken-hearted,' commented Meredith. She sighed. 'If you want my two pennies' worth, I think she loved your father terribly, and he broke her heart. That's why she's always been so unhappy.'

'Apart from when she spent time on her houseboat,' Margot observed. 'I just wish she'd included me. She was like a different person whenever she packed her things and went to spend the summer there. I always felt like she did that to get away from me during the long school summer holidays.'

'It's one of the reasons you don't spend the summer there, isn't it, Margot?'

'One of the reasons ...'

They turned to look out at the garden. Margot knew they were both thinking of their terrible loss; of the summer when they were robbed of their grandchildren. It seemed like no time at all since the children had been running around in the garden, playing hide and seek around the old willow tree. Two decades had passed in a flash, and yet despite all those years, the pain of their loss had not diminished; it was still as raw as if it had only just happened.

'What's this?'

Margot turned in her chair as Meredith picked up the stone on her desk.

'I found it on his grave.'

Meredith said, 'When was this?'

'I got a taxi there yesterday afternoon.'

'You went to Aldeburgh on Friday? Don't you think someone might have seen you and thought it odd you were there when you're meant to be in London?'

'I just fancied paying him a visit.'

'But you went there just the other day to lay flowers.'

Margot shook her head. 'That was a week ago. Last Saturday, to be precise. I was surprised how long my flowers had lasted. A whole week is quite impressive. They do such lovely bouquets at The Potting Shed, don't you think?'

Meredith nodded. 'I guess so.' She raised a questioning eyebrow.

'I just … I wanted to lay some fresh flowers and have a chat.'

'You wanted to tell him about the notebook, didn't you?'

'Yes. Have you read what's been written on that stone?'

Meredith looked at the stone in her hand, and shrugged. 'No – should I?'

'Yes, I think so.'

Meredith put on her reading glasses that had been hanging by the cord around her neck, and read the inscription out loud. 'Always in my heart.' Meredith turned the stone over and read the simple message on the other side. 'Luv you, Dad. Miss you.'

Meredith slowly took off her glasses and looked at Margot. She shook her head. 'Margot, it's just kids, you know? They probably left it there for others to find. You do know about that don't you, about the decorated stones?'

'Of course I do,' Margot snapped. 'But why would they leave one in a graveyard?'

Meredith could see her point. 'Perhaps it was just kids larking around, or maybe a dog picked it up somewhere and dropped it there.'

'A dog?'

Meredith breathed a heavy sigh. 'Oh, Margot, you can't possibly think—'

'Why not?'

Meredith rubbed her temple. 'She's gone, Margot. You know

that. And she's never coming back.'

'But what if—?'

'What if – *what*?'

Margot leaned forward and opened her hand.

Meredith glanced at what was in her hand and looked at her best friend. She threw up her hands. 'Really, Margot. It's a conker.'

'Yes – don't you get it?'

The look on Meredith's face said she was losing patience fast. 'No, I don't get it, Margot. Why don't you enlighten me?'

'Remember my son's funeral?'

'Of course I do. I was there, wasn't I?'

'Remember Alexandra picked up a conker and wouldn't do as she was told and put it down?'

'Yeah, vaguely. I think I recall.'

Meredith held up the conker.

Margot frowned. 'That doesn't mean anything. The headstone is under a chestnut tree, for god's sake. Of course there's going to be conkers lying around.'

'But it wasn't just lying around, Meredith. I found it carefully placed on the base of the headstone next to the hand-decorated stone! God, just think, she must have decorated the stone on the beach. I could have passed her on the promenade and—'

'You can't be serious!' Meredith slowly rose out of her seat. 'Have you lost your marbles?' She stared at Margot. 'She's gone, Margot. It wasn't her – I'm telling you. *That*—' She pointed at the stone. 'And *that*—' She pointed at the conker. 'It's just a coincidence, one of those things you are reading way, *way* too much into, because you want it to be true.'

Her voice softened. 'I get it, Margot, I really do. But it isn't her. It can't be, Margot. You *know* that. You lost your grandchild the day of the accident, and she's *never* coming back.'

'But—'

Meredith slammed the stone down on the desk, making Margot jump. 'Just stop! I don't want to hear another word about it!' She stormed out of the room, slamming the door shut behind her.

Margot put the smooth conker carefully down beside the decorated stone and turned in her swivel chair to look at the garden once more. She stared at the willow tree that Alexandra had loved so much, playing hide and seek amongst its long branches. Someone had left that stone and conker on her son's gravestone, and she was determined to find out who that person was.

22

'Come on, Lexi!'

She was just locking the door when she heard Charlie. She looked up to see her with Scott, waiting on the path.

'I'm coming!'

Lexi couldn't believe how quickly the rest of the week had gone by since she'd had that lovely picnic with Scott on the sand dunes in Walberswick on Tuesday afternoon, while Charlie had played next door with Maisie and William. Lexi no longer had to worry about where her evening meals were coming from until pay-day. Scott had insisted, as had Charlie, that she went to dinner each evening.

Apart from curry nights every evening at Scott and Charlie's – although they still called them curry nights, he cooked a variety of delicious meals – she'd been so busy with work that they hadn't had another day out together since Tuesday.

It was now Saturday, and although she'd seen them each evening since, and it had only been three days, each day felt like an eternity before she saw Scott again.

Lexi was looking forward to the weekend. They'd planned to spend all weekend together, although she was feeling a little tired.

They'd stayed up late the previous night. After dinner, they'd walked into Walberswick to show Charlie the sand dunes. Scott had made hot chocolate in two flasks, and had brought along a packet of large marshmallows. Lexi had asked what the marshmallows were for. They were too big to pop on the top of a hot chocolate. She knew a handful of the mini marshmallows would be needed for that.

Charlie had said, 'You'll see,' smiling at her dad.

After they'd walked along the wide stretch of sandy beach, watching Charlie running up and down the sand dunes, they'd stopped in a sheltered spot amongst the sand dunes and reed beds. Scott had got out a little contraption from his backpack. It looked like a small barbecue. He also had a wind-up lamp.

'Where did you get those?' Lexi had asked. She remembered thinking that she'd never seen that sort of thing in a shop.

'Daddy got them from work when he used to be in the—'

Scott had immediately cut off his daughter, interrupting her.

As the sun went down, Scott had set up the little camping stove. They'd roasted marshmallows while they sat watching the sunset. Apart from a single solitary dog-walker, it had been just the three of them sitting in the dunes on Friday night, drinking hot chocolate as the wind picked up. Lexi had been surprised at how quickly the temperature had dropped at sunset.

She smiled when she recalled that Scott had thought of everything. He'd brought along a cosy blanket for them all to sit under. He'd put his arm around Lexi's shoulders and pulled her close.

Lexi was still thinking about the events of the previous night as she checked the door was locked before pocketing the key. Alan had done a good job, but she'd made sure for the rest of the week that she hadn't left the key under the flowerpot when she went to work. She didn't want a repeat performance of Alan having to come and change the locks, although she couldn't imagine Meredith would have a reason to return to Margot's houseboat for the rest of the summer. She'd already collected the spare key. There was no way of her knowing that the lock had been changed and there was a new key.

At the end of the summer – which Lexi didn't want to think about – she'd leave the keys in a plastic bag under the flowerpot where she'd found the original key, along with an apology for changing the locks. She didn't plan to sign the note, even though Ray knew her; that was why she was still doing her best to keep her work life in the library and her home life at the houseboat separate.

She was hoping Ray didn't visit the library any time soon. So far, she hadn't seen him, but she was keeping her eyes peeled in case he did. That would be her cue to disappear behind a bookshelf or nip for an extended loo break. As far as Ray was concerned, she was houseboat-sitting; that was her job. She wasn't quite sure how she'd explain away her job in the library, although she imagined that one day Charlie or Scott would mention it. So far, that hadn't happened. But she was aware, from what Lili had said, that Ray already suspected there was something she wasn't telling him.

As soon as Lexi stepped on to the path, Charlie threw her arms around Lexi's waist as though she hadn't seen her in an age.

Lexi was enjoying herself a little too much, and was pushing some things to the back of her mind – like the fact that her sister hadn't been in contact since she'd let her know that the allowance from her grandparents wasn't in her bank account.

She'd tried phoning Andrea to speak to her about it, but she wasn't answering her calls or texts. Lexi guessed it was because it was bad news about the allowance, and her sister didn't want to talk about it. She wasn't surprised. Perhaps Andrea was afraid that Lexi would ask her to try and persuade Grandpa to change his mind. Andrea had tried already, and it hadn't worked. The trouble was that they both knew when Grandpa made a promise – good or bad – he never went back on his word.

Even so, Lexi had hoped Andrea would get in touch, even if it was to say that there was no point asking her to speak to Grandpa again. But she had heard nothing.

She was okay for money now, though. Friday was payday. Jill had been an absolute angel and refused the fifty pounds back that she'd lent her to tide her over. Lexi still intended to pay her back, even if it took a bit of time on the low wages.

Lexi had given Jill her new bank account details for the account she'd opened in Southwold. Payroll had managed to get the money into her bank account. It meant she could now use her bank card. The bank had been so helpful in explaining how to download their app, which she'd done, so she could use their banking app to check her balance on her phone – when she had a signal, of course.

Lexi had yet to check her bank balance, but she wasn't worried. She knew what had been paid in from her job. But she could now use her brand-new UK bank card.

Apart from the fact that she knew she wasn't getting her allowance, her week had been really good. It hadn't been her intention to get involved with someone in England, but there was no denying the mutual attraction. She had only known Scott for a couple of weeks, but after Charlie had taken herself off to bed without being asked – Lexi was starting to suspect she was doing it on purpose – they'd sat on the sofa enjoying what was left of the evening after their hot chocolate under the stars on the beach in Walberswick last night. They had started watching a late-night movie, keeping the volume down so they wouldn't disturb Charlie, when Lexi had had the sudden urge to kiss Scott.

He'd been sitting with an arm draped along the sofa, as he had each evening, but yesterday evening she'd picked up his hand and moved his arm around her shoulder. He hadn't objected. She'd known he wouldn't. Then she'd asked him a question. 'Can I kiss you?' She'd just blurted what she'd been thinking, staring at his profile while he watched TV.

She'd been so embarrassed at her question. She didn't know why; they'd already kissed on the beach. But because Charlie was just in the next room, she'd held back. She had been shocked that she hadn't felt guilty over Brandon. But then, why should she? He'd cheated on her. They were no longer together. She didn't know why she'd even been thinking about him at that moment.

Scott had turned his head and looked at her a long moment before he said, 'I've been dying to ask you that question too.'

'Did you watch a movie last night?' Charlie asked as they walked along the path towards Scott's car parked on the quay.

Lexi exchanged a glance with Scott. After they had started kissing, they hadn't exactly been paying attention to the movie the previous night. They hadn't been able to keep their hands off one another. 'Er, yes – we did.'

'Great.' Charlie looked from Lexi to her dad and smiled a knowing smile. She recalled getting up early in the morning and creeping into the lounge for a glass of water, not wanting to wake her dad in the bedroom next door. It was the weekend, and she always went back to bed and watched YouTube or TikTok on her phone until around seven, when she normally heard her dad up and about making breakfast.

When she'd walked into the lounge, she'd found them. Her dad had been fast asleep on the sofa, lying on his back. Lexi had been on her side, wedged between the sofa back and Scott, an arm and a leg draped over him. They were both still fully clothed, just as she had left them the previous night, but their clothes looked ruffled; her dad's shirt was untucked, his buttons were done up the wrong way, and Lexi's hair was no longer tied up in a ponytail.

Charlie had quietly closed the door and crept back to her room. When her dad had called her for breakfast, she'd returned to the lounge, expecting Lexi to be there and had blurted, 'Where's Lexi?' Her dad had replied, 'She went home, like she normally does.'

Charlie had stared at her dad, who was busying himself making breakfast. He'd glanced at her sheepishly. She'd noticed he hadn't mentioned when, exactly, Lexi had gone home.

Charlie smiled at the thought that Lexi must have stayed the night the previous night. She skipped ahead and said, 'This is going to be the best day ever.' It was the weekend, and they were going for a day out in Aldeburgh in Daddy's car. Lexi had said she had something to show her; she'd called it *The House in the Clouds*, then they were going to have fish and chips on the beach, and watch a movie afterwards at the cinema.

'Oh, this is going to be the best day!' said Charlie again. But it wasn't just about all the things Lexi had planned for their day.

She glanced behind her and caught her dad and Lexi holding hands. She grinned. All those boring early nights had paid off. Leaving them alone in the lounge for some adult kissy kissy, smoochy smoochy had worked.

23

Lexi cast a glance at Ray's Volkswagen, which was parked on the quayside, as she walked towards Scott's car. She knew Ray had been disappointed when he'd discovered he didn't need to give her a lift to Aldeburgh anymore. She knew that she only had to ask Scott and he'd drop everything and drive her there.

Lexi had told Ray that he didn't need an excuse to visit Sarah anymore. It was obvious they were both still deeply in love with each other, and that was reason enough to visit her.

Lexi had decided not to ask Scott to take her to Aldeburgh when she wanted to go to Sarah's art class the previous afternoon, although he had offered. Charlie wanted to go too, although Sarah only ran adult classes. Charlie had said she'd just go along for the ride, but Lexi knew that if Scott took her to Aldeburgh with them, she wouldn't end up attending the art classes with Sarah – she'd want to spend the time with Scott and Charlie.

That was why she'd arranged to attend one of Sarah's classes on her own, straight after her morning shift at the library the previous day. She'd paid for a taxi to take her to Aldeburgh, tipping the taxi driver with a takeaway coffee and a large slice of cake from The Two Magpies Bakery. She hadn't forgotten his kindness when she'd first arrived in Southwold looking for a hotel, still hoping her sister could help her out with money after she'd been pickpocketed in London. She'd had all of five pounds left. Sensing she was in some kind of trouble, the taxi driver had taken pity on her and had refused payment for the journey. Since she had arrived on the Suffolk Coast Lexi had met so many generous, warm-hearted people. When she'd asked how she could repay him, he'd given her his card and said she could buy him a cup of coffee.

When she'd phoned the taxi company for her trip to Aldeburgh, she'd asked for him by name. When they'd arrived, she'd asked him to wait a moment while she went to the bakery. She'd not only paid for her fare this time but had bought him coffee and cake, and a freshly made baguette too. She'd also slipped twenty pounds she could ill-afford into the crease of the serviette she'd handed to him. She knew he wouldn't accept the generous tip otherwise. He'd remembered her, and the coffee she'd promised she'd buy him. 'I didn't ask for the cake and baguette,' he'd said. 'It's too much.'

Lexi had smiled. 'Nothing is too much for a good Samaritan. I really appreciate what you did for me. I wanted to repay you.' She'd then made her way to Sarah's. Lunch was provided, and it had been a chance to meet the other people in the art class.

She was absorbed in her thoughts about how the previous day's class had gone as she, Scott and Charlie settled into Scott's car for a trip to Aldeburgh.

'You're quiet,' observed Scott.

'I was thinking of my art class yesterday afternoon.' She'd been home the previous night in time for dinner with Scott followed by the walk to the beach with the flask of hot chocolate to watch the sun go down.

'Do you like your art class?' asked Charlie as she pulled the seat belt around her and clipped in.

Scott started the car.

'Oh yes. At first I was a bit worried about meeting the other people in the class.'

Charlie asked, 'How come?'

'I've never been to an art class before. I thought everyone would be better than me.'

'You've got to believe in yourself. Ain't that right, Dad?'

'Yep, that is very true, Charlie.'

Lexi exchanged a smile with Scott.

'So, did you do some drawing, like of the sea or something?'

She turned in her seat to look at Charlie. 'Yes, I did, but it wasn't in Aldeburgh.' They'd started off the afternoon in Sarah's studio with the amazing views through the picture window of the promenade, the shingle beach, and the sea. Lexi had enjoyed sketching the little brick-built hut, which was a little artists' hub where local artists displayed their work. Apparently, some of Sarah's former students had displayed their art there, and sold pieces too. It was the same hut that Lexi had stopped outside to decorate her stone to take to her father's grave on her first visit to Aldeburgh with Ray.

It had seemed quite peculiar to have Maisie pop in during the art class and walk around looking at their work, giving pointers and very helpful feedback. Lexi noticed that none of the members of the class batted an eyelid at the young artist. Sarah had commented to Lexi that her granddaughter could easily run the art class. Nobody took offence at any criticism – far from it. The students were mostly retired, although there were one or two international students. Lexi realised that different people attended all the time, so she imagined that no two days would be alike.

She had also discovered that Sarah often took her budding artists on the road to different locations in Suffolk, hiring a little minibus and driver from the local taxi company. That afternoon, she was open to suggestions about where they should go. Lexi had taken a book with her, the first of the children's book trilogy written by Margot Dorey. Set on the Suffolk Coast, Lexi rather fancied visiting some of the places in the book and seeing the locations for herself.

Sarah had thought that it was a marvellous idea, and so they'd set off for a place called Minsmere, a little further up the coast from Southwold. A nature reserve run by the Royal Society for the Protection of Birds, it wasn't just bird-spotting that had people flocking to one of the RSPB's most scenic and important nature reserves, but the beautiful and tranquil location. Lexi enjoyed the walk along the wooden boardwalks through the tall reed grasses to the viewing huts.

There was a windswept beach that could be reached from either the Minsmere bird sanctuary or Dunwich Heath, where they went afterwards for tea and scones in the Coastguard Cottages tearoom. Lexi had a peculiar feeling that both places were familiar, as though she'd been to both Minsmere and Dunwich Heath before.

She'd drawn some sketches while the others had set up easels and painted the landscape. Sarah had tried to entice her to paint, but Lexi was quite happy to sketch and then take herself off for a walk through the incredible scenery, along the well-defined paths through the heathland and down to the beach that seemed to stretch for miles; that part of the coast was quite a contrast to the cosy, quaint town of Aldeburgh, and the equally small and intimate Victorian seaside resorts of Southwold and Walberswick.

She'd ended her afternoon in the National Trust second-hand bookshop on Dunwich Heath, near the tea rooms, where she'd been surprised the find the second book in Margot Dorey's trilogy. She'd nearly read to the end of the first one. It was serendipity that she should come across the second one when she wasn't even looking.

She'd thanked Sarah for choosing to take them to Minsmere and Dunwich Heath. There were other locations in the book she wanted to visit, and she was now heading to one of them with Scott and Charlie. They were off to Thorpeness to see The House in the Clouds.

As they left Walberswick behind, taking the main road up the coast towards Aldeburgh, Lexi heard a ping on a mobile phone.

Scott sighed. 'Put the phone away, Charlie.'

Lexi looked at Scott. He glanced in his rearview mirror.

'But Maisie just texted me. I'm texting her back to tell her where we're going today.'

There was another ping. 'She says she's been there. There's a boating lake in Thorpeness.'

Lexi sighed too. She had wanted that to be a surprise.

'Can we take a boat out on the lake? Maisie says it's fun.'

Lexi caught Scott glancing her way before he replied, 'I don't think Lexi will fancy that.'

'Why not?'

'Because Lexi doesn't like the water.'

'Oh, yes. I forgot,' Charlie said in a small voice.

Lexi sat there, her face growing hot with embarrassment. They were both thinking of the episode when Charlie had fallen in the water.

'Me and you could go boating on the lake, Dad.'

Lexi said, 'It's fine. I don't mind coming too.'

Scott glanced her way. 'Are you sure?'

Lexi grinned mischievously. 'There's no fear of any of us drowning. The lake is only about three feet deep!'

She recalled what Ray had told her about the village of Thorpeness. As they made their way towards Aldeburgh, she told Scott they could drive to the beach in Aldeburgh and then take the lovely coast road hugging the shore that ran for a mile or so from Aldeburgh straight into the village of Thorpeness.

Ray had suggested doing the walk from Aldeburgh along the beach into Thorpeness, which Lexi thought sounded wonderful. He'd told her it was a very popular walk. The problem was that they were all a little tired after their late night – especially Charlie, who Lexi could hear yawning in the back of the car. She thought they could save that walk for another time.

Going by car instead meant they could spend time in Thorpeness and then drive back along the coast road into Aldeburgh, have fish and chips on the beach, and catch an afternoon movie in the old independent cinema in the town. That was the plan.

Lexi had something else planned for later in the afternoon, but she didn't want to broach that with either of them just yet.

As they drove into Aldeburgh, Lexi gave Scott directions. They passed the church on their way into town.

'Look, there's the cinema,' said Lexi, pointing as she directed Scott straight across the road and down a little side street with a pub on the corner.

'Where's the cinema?' asked Charlie, turning in her seat to look out the back window. 'I don't see it?'

Lexi grinned. Charlie wouldn't expect a cinema to be in such an old building. Her generation, just like Lexi's, were used to large modern multiplexes. The little independent cinema had a website. Lexi had looked up what films were showing on the cinema over the summer and discovered there were plenty of new releases, from summer blockbusters to family films suitable for all ages. There was a family movie showing that afternoon at two-thirty.

While she was on the website, Lexi had discovered that the independent cinema opened its doors in 1919, starting life showing silent black and white films. Now it not only showed movies, but also live performances on screen of opera and theatre, and hosted some special events with famous stars of stage and screen who visited for film premiers and Q&As.

She'd got the impression from what she'd read that the little independent cinema was an important part of the local community; there were over one thousand Friends of Aldeburgh Cinema who supported it.

Lexi didn't tell Charlie what she'd read about it. She imagined she'd hear her yawning with boredom if she told her all that. Instead, as they passed the magnificent Wentworth Hotel, Lexi recounted what Ray had told her about the holiday village, the boating lake and The House in the Clouds.

'Ray told me that Thorpeness was built in the nineteen twenties as a holiday village.'

'Is that The House in the Clouds!' exclaimed Charlie.

Lexi glanced at Charlie. She was looking out of the window, pointing. Lexi smiled. 'Yes, that's it.'

'It's so high up!'

Lexi remembered the first time she'd caught sight of it on her visit to Aldeburgh with Ray. She'd asked Ray if it had a boating lake. That was when she'd realised she must have been there before as a child. She thought again of the discovery that her dad was laid to rest right there in Aldeburgh. He'd had a connection there, perhaps had grown up in Aldeburgh. It would explain why someone was still visiting his grave, an old friend from years ago, or a relative perhaps.

'How come the house is so high, Lexi?'

Scott joined in. 'Wow, would you look at that? I'd like to know too, Lexi. Have you any idea?'

'Ray told me that it was a water tower, but they disguised it as a house by weatherboarding the building so that it's similar in appearance to the mock-Tudor and Jacobean style houses in Thorpeness.'

Lexi had read about it in a Suffolk guidebook she'd come across in the library when she had been returning books to the shelves. She'd checked the book out for herself and had read more about the famous water tower, built in 1923 for water pumped from Thorpeness Windmill – another landmark she was looking forward to seeing. It had been converted to a house in the late 1970s when the village got a mains water supply and the water tank was removed.

'How high do you think it is?'

Lexi turned to Scott. 'I believe it's seventy feet high.'

Scott shook his head. 'Amazing.'

'It's now a holiday let. You can stay there if you want.'

Charlie said, 'I don't like heights. I prefer the houseboat.'

'Me too,' agreed Lexi, even though she still had an aversion to the water.

Up ahead, the road veered away from the beach to pass detached houses, some weatherboarded, their exteriors painted white or shades of pastel blue. The style of the houses reminded her of New England, and the clapboard beach-fronted homes she'd seen when taking a road trip one year with Brandon. These properties sat well back from the road. She caught glimpses of gardens leading down to the beach.

They parked near a café that overlooked a green and the boating lake. The village was familiar to Lexi.

Scott turned in his seat and looked at Charlie. 'We're here.'

Charlie looked up from her phone. 'Oh, okay.'

He looked at her a long moment. 'Are you going to put that away now?'

Lexi glanced over her shoulder and saw Charlie frowning at her dad as she reluctantly put her phone away in the little handbag she'd brought with her.

As they got out of the car, Charlie said, 'Maisie is in her mum's shop making her amber jewellery. Can we go to Aldeburgh and see Maisie afterwards? I've brought my pocket money with me. I'd like to buy some more jewellery.' Charlie fingered the necklace that Lexi had bought her on her first visit to Cobblers Yard.

Although Lexi wasn't surprised that Charlie wanted some more of Maisie's exquisite amber jewellery, she imagined that what Charlie really wanted was an excuse to see her new friend.

'We'll see,' said Scott.

Lexi pursed her lips. 'Actually, I think that's a good idea. Aldeburgh was going to be our next stop for fish and chips for lunch, and I'd love to show you both Cobblers Yard. That's where Maisie's mum's shop is.' Like Charlie, she was also looking for an excuse to visit Cobblers Yard. She had something she had to collect from The Potting Shed today, and somewhere she wanted to go.

Charlie came bounding over and gave Lexi a hug. 'If Daddy

doesn't want to go then we can go on our own. He doesn't like shopping.'

Lexi looked at Scott.

'I think I've been outvoted,' he said light-heartedly. 'Charlie's right, though – I'm not a fan of shopping.'

'We won't be long – will we, Charlie?'

Charlie shook her head. She took Lexi's hand. 'Come on, I want to see the boating lake.'

24

'Oh god!' exclaimed Lexi.

'Come on, Lexi.' Scott held out his hand. 'You did say you were looking forward to it, didn't you?'

Lexi had been quite blasé about going with them in a boat on the lake until she saw the colourful little boats all lined up in a row along the shore. She imagined the setting might be quite tranquil out of season, but the little café and ice-cream parlour were heaving with long queues, and all the benches situated along the grassy bank were taken.

'There's nowhere for you to sit, so you might as well come with us,' said Charlie.

They'd stood in a queue for the boat, watching families with children and couples get into the little boats and head out. Up close, the lake was bigger. The large expanse of water was putting her off, along with the way she'd seen the little boats rocking quite precariously as people got settled in.

'You can't back out now,' said Scott, taking her hand.

You wanna bet, thought Lexi, dragging her feet as the orderly queue moved forward much quicker than she wanted.

She couldn't deny that the setting was gorgeous, and she

could see the little islands that the writer J.M. Barrie had named after places in his Peter Pan stories. Even so, she was still having second thoughts. She wished she'd never suggested taking a boat out on the lake.

Scott said, 'Didn't you mention the lake was only three feet deep?'

Lexi nodded. 'That's what Ray told me.' She recounted what Ray had said, the momentary distraction keeping her mind off that big lake and those little boats. 'The author of Peter Pan, J.M. Barrie was good friends with the wealthy Scottish barrister, Stuart Ogilvie, who wanted to create an olde-worlde village and playground for the well-to-do. The mere, or lake, with its creeks and islands was inspired by J.M. Barrie's Neverland. Apparently, the writer named the islands – Pirate's Lair, Wendy's Home, and Captain's House were some of the ones Ray could remember, although he thought there were others.'

'That's interesting – isn't it, Charlie?' Scott frowned when he saw Charlie with her phone.

She glared at her dad. 'I'm taking a photo.'

'Oh, all right.'

Lexi continued. 'Ray said that Ogilvie's original idea was that children could go out on the lake and safely learn to sail or row boats which was why the lake was designed to be so shallow.'

'Didn't you say that the lake was only three feet deep?'

'Yes, but you can drown in three feet of water,' she blurted.

Scott smiled. 'I think whoever said that, and I have heard that myself, was talking about children and toddlers. And I think it is three *inches* of water, or perhaps it's two?'

'Oh, god.'

'But neither of those scenarios apply to you. Nobody is going to fall in. And you know what will happen if one of us does?'

Lexi shook her head, staring wide-eyed at Scott, hoping the word *drown* didn't pass his lips.

'We will suffer from a severe case of wounded pride.' He grinned at Lexi.

Lexi managed a smile.

'What does that mean?' asked Charlie.

Lexi turned to her. 'It means you'd be very embarrassed.'

Charlie nodded. 'Oh, look – we're nearly at the front of the queue.'

Lexi sighed. 'Great.' She looked about her, hoping one of the benches near the lake was free. There wasn't one.

Scott climbed into the boat first and took up two oars. Charlie was next, sitting in the middle. The young man helped Lexi step aboard.

She hurriedly took her seat, the little rowing boat rocking back and forth. 'Make it stop!' exclaimed Lexi grabbing the side of the boat, her knuckles growing white.

'Everything is going to be fine,' said Scott as the boat stopped rocking.

As they set off down the middle of the lake, towards the little islands, Lexi reminded herself that nothing bad was going to happen if one of them fell overboard and the boat sank.

Neither of those things happened during their hour-long boat ride on the lake. They skirted the little islands and headed back to the shore, where others who'd been on the lake were disembarking.

Lexi couldn't have been more surprised. She'd had the most relaxing time; the best time she'd ever spent out on water. And she'd discovered she was rather good at rowing, unlike Scott, who – for someone who was quite outdoorsy and enjoyed sport – had discovered he was not. They'd done a swap around on the boat, Lexi and Scott carefully switching places so Lexi could row, after she'd got fed up with him steering the boat the wrong way. Once she had the oars, they made it to all the little islands. Even Charlie had a turn, and although she found the rowing hard work, she also piloted the boat far better than her dad.

'Daddy, you are rubbish at rowing!' Charlie had said, laughing. 'It's lucky Lexi came, otherwise we'd have been stuck out here on the lake, and I'm hungry.'

'Me too,' said Lexi.

'Can I have an ice-cream?'

'We're going to have fish and chips.'

'But, Dad, can't I have an ice-cream first?'

'Okay.'

Scott insisted they swap seats before they arrived back at the shore.

'Daddy – it's going to take a lot longer if you do it.'

'I insist.'

Lexi caught him looking around at the other boats heading back towards the shore. She noticed they were all being rowed back by the man of the boat. Lexi rolled her eyes when she realised why Scott was insisting. He didn't want to be seen having his girlfriend row him back.

Lexi smiled to herself when she remembered what he'd said about wounded pride. She realised that he didn't have to fall in the water for that.

Lexi stood up carefully to swap seats.

'Oh, Lexi, don't let Daddy row us back.'

She looked at Scott. 'I think we should let your dad have some practice. Obviously it comes naturally to you and me, so it's only fair to let Daddy have another turn and see if he can get the hang of it a bit more.' Lexi gave Scott a sideways glance as she sat down.

Charlie folded her arms in a huff. 'I don't think he will.'

Scott did seem to get on better on the way back, but he only had to row in a straight line. Lexi decided not to point that out. She didn't need to anyway because Charlie piped up, 'That's a lot better, Dad, but you're steering needs some work, obviously.' She'd said that as they'd arrived back to shore, Scott bumping into an empty boat.

Lexi had turned around, stifling a smile so Scott didn't see, but he'd been good-humoured about it, and had laughed when Lexi had said, 'I don't think it's the water I needed to be afraid of, but your rowing!'

Once on shore, they joined another queue for Charlie's ice-cream, and then headed back to the car. Lexi felt quite proud of herself for getting over her fears to get in that boat. It had been fun.

Their next stop was Aldeburgh. 'I want to do something with Charlie while you get the fish and chips – is that okay?'

'Of course.'

Lexi turned to Charlie. 'I've got an idea – something we can do while your dad walks into town to get the lunch.' They'd started walking along the promenade towards the flat where Sarah lived. She pointed down the side street. 'Scott, if you go down there, you'll come out in the town and see a fish and chip shop on the corner, and another one across the road.'

'Okay.'

'We'll be right here.' Lexi pointed at the trestle table on the beach with the stones and the paintbrushes and little paint pallets. 'Do you want to decorate a stone, Charlie?'

'Yes please.'

Lexi smiled.

Although Lexi had discovered that the summer weather in England was unpredictable, today there wasn't a raincloud to be seen. It was perfect weather for a day at the seaside – all blue skies and sunshine. It meant they could eat their takeaway fish and chips on the beach, before heading to the cinema for an afternoon movie. Lexi smiled as Charlie chose a stone. It was turning out to be a perfect day.

25

'Are you sure this is okay? I know it's not really the best way to round off a lovely day at the seaside, but as I'm here ...' she trailed off.

'Of course it's okay,' Scott replied.

They were in the old antique store in Cobblers Yard after a relaxing couple of hours seeing a family movie at the cinema in Aldeburgh. Maisie was spending some time showing Charlie how she made her amber necklaces while Lexi and Scott browsed around the shop. He was standing admiring an old wooden globe.

'Great. I won't be a minute. I've already ordered the flowers, I just need to collect them from The Potting Shed across the yard.' She paused. 'You don't have to come with me to the graveyard. I can go on my own. You could take Charlie back to the beach, and I'll meet you there.'

Scott shook his head, and took her hand in his, giving it an affectionate squeeze. 'I want to come with you.'

Lexi smiled at him. 'Okay.'

She left Scott and Charlie in the old antique store and headed over to The Potting Shed. Lili greeted her warmly at the counter. She'd ordered the flowers over the phone earlier in the week when she and Scott had made plans to spend Saturday in Thorpeness and Aldeburgh. As she waited for Lili to bring her bouquet from the back of the shop, she thought about the perfect day it had turned out to be. They had done all the things that Lexi had promised Charlie they would.

'Here we are, Lexi.'

'Oh, they are just lovely.' She'd chosen white flowers this time, thinking that Billie, the young woman buried in the plot next to her father, might have liked them.

Lili looked past her. Lexi knew she was looking for Ray. 'I didn't come with Ray today. I came with my—' Lexi was about to say her boyfriend. 'Friends, Scott and his daughter, Charlie.'

'Oh, yes – I've heard all about Charlie. Maisie never stops talking about her. She says she's her best friend ever.'

'Really? That's what Charlie says about Maisie.' Lexi didn't add that Maisie was Charlie's only friend.

'Maisie is going to invite Charlie to her birthday party.'

'Oh my goodness, really? Charlie is going to be so happy when she finds out!' Lexi glanced behind her. 'She's over there now in the antique store. Maisie is showing her how she makes her amber jewellery.'

Lili smiled. 'Maisie is getting a special something for her birthday this year.'

Lexi leaned forward. 'What is it?' she said in a hushed voice, although she had no idea why she was whispering.

'We lost our dog, Bella, whom she was very attached to. She was getting on in years and unfortunately, we knew her time would come sooner rather than later.'

Lexi frowned. 'I'm so sorry.'

'We had a plan for when that happened. The fact that it

happened near her birthday ...' Lili trailed off and grinned.

'Oh, my god, you're getting her a puppy!' Lexi clapped her hands. 'Charlie, she is going to be *so* envious.' She recalled mentioning that she'd asked her dad for a puppy, but he'd said no because they moved around a lot.

'She doesn't have to be,' said Lili.

Lexi said, 'Huh?'

My friend, Abigail – she's a vet, she runs a veterinary practice and a pet hotel in Southwold – you'll meet her when we go on our girls' night out.'

Lexi had forgotten all about the girls' night out Lili had invited her on with her two best friends. She didn't have a close circle of friends. Perhaps Lexi, Abigail and Maisie's mum, Hannah, would become hers.

'Well,' continued Lili, 'one of Abigail's pet hotel clients has a sweet Labrador who has just had a litter of puppies, and they said that Abigail could have the pick of the litter. She's chosen one for Maisie. I could always ask her if she could have two picks of the litter?' Lili grinned. 'I know for a fact there are puppies still available.'

'For Charlie?'

'Yes, for Charlie.'

Lexi frowned. 'I'd have to ask her dad.'

'I take it he might have an objection?'

Lili really didn't want to get into what Charlie had said about the reason she couldn't have one, or be reminded of just how much she still didn't know about Scott. She didn't even know what he did for a living, and why they moved around a lot. Was it just for his work, as Lexi presumed, or was there something more?

Suddenly, Charlie's words came to mind. When they'd first met,

Charlie had told her something that she made Lexi pinkie swear not to repeat. *My dad is in some kind of trouble, and we're on the run.*

'So, are you having a nice day in Aldeburgh?' Lili interrupted her thoughts.

'We spent the morning in Thorpeness and took a boat out on the boating lake.'

'You certainly chose the right day. The weather is beautiful.'

'Yes, it is,' agreed Lexi, managing a smile. She tried to push the thought of Scott, and all not being quite as it seemed, to the back of her mind. Lexi had convinced herself that what Charlie had said to her was just a child's overactive imagination. She did not want her uneasiness to resurface and ruin a beautiful day.

'Rain tomorrow and for the rest of next week, apparently.'

'That is a shame.' Lexi fancied doing the same trip again when she had an afternoon free the next week. Perhaps they could visit some other places along the coast, like the beautiful Minsmere and incredible landscape around Dunwich.

Lexi handed over her bank card.

'Ray said he has you to thank for suggesting that he buy Sarah flowers. I heard she loved them.'

'Has he been back?'

'Oh, yes.'

Lexi smiled. She had guessed as much. When they had been to decorate a stone on the beach, Lexi had noticed more flowers in Sarah's window.

'Those for your dad?'

'Um, sort of.'

Lili smiled.

Lexi guessed Ray might have told her about what she'd done with the last bouquet. She picked it up.

'See you again, Lexi.'

Lexi stopped at the door and turned around, throwing Lili a smile, thinking about how Lili had two new regular customers.

Charlie and Scott were waiting outside the flower shop. Charlie looked at her dad. Can we give it to her now? Please.'

Lexi looked from Scott to Charlie. 'Give me what?'

'Daddy and I bought you a present.'

'Really? You didn't have to.'

'But we wanted to – didn't we, Daddy?'

Scott smiled. 'Yes.' He glanced across the cobbled square. 'Cobblers Yard is quite a find, isn't it? It's got a lot of atmosphere with the old-fashioned store fronts.'

Lexi thought so too.

'How did you find this place? It would be so easy to miss if you didn't know it was here.'

'I know – right? I came here with Ray. He showed me where the flower shop is. His wife used to own it before she sold it and retired.'

'I don't like the creepy bookshop,' said Charlie, pointing at The Bookshop of Memories.

'But you liked the old antique store next door,' observed Scott.

Scott and Lexi exchanged a smile. They knew it wasn't the antique store she liked, but that she'd had the opportunity to visit Maisie.

Charlie got out two little paper bags. 'This is for you. I've got one too.'

'What is it?' Lexi looked from Charlie to Scott as she took the bag. He just smiled.

Lexi handed Scott the flowers so she could open her paper bag as they walked out of the cobbled yard. 'Hey, it's a bracelet.'

Charlie opened her bag and showed Lexi one very similar.

Lexi stopped to admire the smooth stone with an orangey yellow hue.

'It's an amber bracelet to match the necklaces you bought us.'

'You made this yourself?' Lexi said in surprise.

'Yes, Maisie showed me how.'

'It is very pretty, Charlie. Thank you.' Lexi put her arms around her and gave her a hug before they set off again.

Charlie glanced at her dad. 'It's Maisie's birthday next week.'

Scott looked at her. 'Is it?'

'Yes.'

Lexi looked at her too. 'Has Maisie invited you to her party?'

'Yes. It's going to be a sleepover at her dad's house. There's going to be lots of her friends there too, from her school.'

'Maybe you can go to her party and meet them? Make some more friends.' Lexi eyed Scott. 'Wouldn't that be nice?'

'I want to have a sleepover. I've never had one of those before.' Charlie looked up at her dad with imploring eyes. 'Oh, please can I go, Daddy? Can I?'

Scott came to a halt before they walked out of Cobblers Yard. He glanced over at the shop. 'Perhaps you'd like to pop over to the shop and tell Maisie you can go to her party.'

Charlie ran up to her dad and threw her arms around him before running across the yard to the antique store to tell Maisie the good news. Before she opened the door to the shop, she paused. She turned around and shouted at her dad, 'You're the best!'

Lexi thought so too as she smiled at the good-looking guy who had, in the space of a fortnight, stolen her heart.

26

'Hey! Someone stole them.'

'Stole what?' asked Scott and Charlie in unison.

Lexi crouched down beside the gravestone, looking for them, but they were definitely gone.

She stood up and told Scott and Charlie what she had left at her father's gravestone – a hand-painted stone along with a large, smooth conker. Only the bunch of freshly cut flowers that she'd brought with her on her last visit on Tuesday was left at the base of his headstone, along with a bouquet that was not from her.

Staring at that bouquet, she also told them what she'd discovered the last time she'd been there; that someone else was laying flowers at her father's grave.

'Are these the same flowers?' Charlie asked. 'Or has the person been again?'

Lexi got out her phone and looked at the photo she'd taken. Charlie was right: the flowers, although similar, were not the same. 'You're right. They've been back.'

Charlie grinned. 'Do you know what this means?'

'It means you would make a good detective,' commented Lexi. 'Did Ray tell you that he's a retired police officer?'

Charlie said, 'No.'

Lexi saw Scott's expression. He'd been happy, smiling and light-hearted all day, but the old Scott, the one she'd first seen, worried, anxious, and almost fearful, was back.

'We don't really want to get involved with the neighbours.'

Lexi frowned. But he was involved, and so was she.

'Present company excepted,' said Scott, cracking a smile.

'But she's not really a neighbour.'

Lexi turned to Charlie wide-eyed.

Charlie shut her mouth.

Lexi guessed that she'd remembered her promise not to tell anyone about Lexi's squatting.

Scott looked at his daughter. 'Whatever to do you mean? Lexi is right next door. If she's not a neighbour, I don't know who is.'

Lexi changed the subject. 'Now, about this stone. What were you saying, Charlie?'

'Oh, yes. Well, it's obvious – isn't it?'

Lexi didn't understand what Charlie was trying to say. 'What's obvious?'

'This person is a relative, I presume …'

Lexi exchanged a glance with Scott, who was also trying to keep a straight face. She guessed they were both thinking the same thing; Charlie sounded like a detective from a police procedural. Perhaps that wasn't surprising, as Charlie had told her she watched a lot of that sort of thing with her dad. They both loved CSI.

'The stone,' said Charlie, 'hasn't been stolen. It was taken.'

'Same difference.'

'Uh no, it isn't, Dad. If it's stolen, it's an opportune thing.'

Lexi looked at Scott who just shrugged as if to say, *don't ask me what my daughter is talking about.*

Lex said, 'An opportune thing ...?'

Charlie screwed up her face, concentrating. 'Ah, no, I meant an *opportunist* thing. Someone happened along, liked what they saw, or thought it was worth a bob or two.'

'Worth a bob or two?'

'Yeah – and took it.'

Lexi nodded. 'So, you're saying this wasn't an opportunist?'

'That's right. I mean apart from anything else, the stone isn't worth anything. You said yourself you're not really an artist, so I bet it wasn't that good either – no offence!'

Lexi smiled. 'None taken.'

'So that leads me to my conclusion.'

Lexi stared at Charlie. 'Which is ...?'

'The person who laid these flowers was just as surprised as you to find someone else had visited the grave.'

'But couldn't it have been a kid or a dog?' asked Scott.

Lexi looked at Charlie for her thoughts.

'Yes, you have a point, Dad, if one or the other were missing. But the fact that's it's both means—'

'Someone definitely took them,' said Scott.

'And the only person who would do that was the person who—'

'Laid these flowers,' Lexi concluded, staring at Charlie.

'Yes.'

'But that still doesn't explain why they did it – why take them?' said Scott.

Charlie stared at the grave. 'Either they thought they'd been put there by mistake, and tossed them away in the bin.'

Lexi hoped that wasn't the case. 'Or ...?'

'My theory is that they took them for sentimental reasons.'

Scott looked at his daughter. 'Sentimental reasons? Do you know what that means?'

'Of course I do. I am ten, you know.' She gave her dad a look, dismissing his silly remark, and turned to Lexi. 'That person who has laid those flowers knows who you are.'

They all turned to look at the grave. They were silent for some time. The only sounds were the rustling of leaves from the branches of the old chestnut tree, which was gently swaying in the sea breeze, and the odd cry of a seagull.

'Lexi, can I leave my stone on your dad's headstone? I never knew your dad, but I'm sure I would have liked him a lot because I like you, Lexi.'

'Oh, that is so sweet of you, Charlie.'

Scott smiled affectionately at his daughter. 'That's really thoughtful and kind, Charlie.'

Charlie knelt down and placed her stone down on the base of the headstone. She looked around her, got up and went over to the old chestnut tree.

'What are you looking for?' Scott asked.

'I found a nice one.' Charlie brought it over to Lexi. 'What do you think?'

Lexi smiled. It was a nice, large, smooth conker, very much like the one she had placed next to her stone. She watched Charlie place it on the base of the headstone. 'I decorated the stone for you, Dad, but I really wanted to give it to Lexi's dad because her one is missing.'

Lexi had read Charlie's simple message to her dad, which was not unlike the one she had written herself.

Charlie turned around and looked up at her dad when she didn't get a response. 'What's the matter?'

Lexi looked at him too. Were those tears in his eyes? He wiped his eyes and placed a hand on her shoulder. 'I don't deserve such a wonderful daughter. I drag you from pillar to post. And I don't listen to you and what *you* want.'

Charlie was quick off the mark when she heard that. 'Does that mean I can go to school, and we can stay here?'

Lexi wasn't surprised that Charlie didn't want to leave, now that she was making friends. Lexi didn't want them to leave either. She stole a glance at Scott, hoping the evenings on his boat continued – especially if they were like the previous one. Although they'd have to be careful if that happened again. One morning, Charlie might discover that Lexi had not slept on her own houseboat.

In all their conversations over dinner during the past week, and through all the late nights snuggled up together on the sofa, enjoying one another's company, Scott still hadn't confided in her what he did for a living, and what was going on. She knew something was up. They moved around a lot. Charlie didn't go to school. They didn't have any friends, relatives, or grandparents that either of them had mentioned. And he had flinched when she'd told them that Ray, their next-door neighbour, was an ex-cop.

'So, what are you going to do with those?' Scott asked, breaking the silence as he eyed the bouquet in her hand.

Charlie stamped her foot and walked off.

Lexi watched her. She didn't go far, just a few paces, but she had folded her arms, and turned her back on her dad when he didn't answer her question.

Lexi turned back to Scott, guessing that the topic of conversation was already closed before it began. She looked at the beautiful bouquet in her hands. She stepped to her left to pay a visit to

Billie. 'I thought I'd call on my dad's neighbour again.'

As she placed the flowers on Billie's grave, Lexi glanced at her own neighbour. She didn't want him to go anywhere. She was looking forward to many more evenings spent snuggling up with him on his sofa, falling asleep in his arms in front of the television.

27

'What's the matter now? It's not about that stone and conker, is it? Because I told you before, I don't want to hear another word.'

'No, it's about this!' Margot had walked into the hallway and opened the front door as soon as she'd heard Meredith's car on the driveway. Meredith had been shopping. She'd brought along a bag of groceries to cook Margot's dinner. They hadn't spoken since they'd had that falling out a week ago over the stone and the conker that were still sitting on Margot's desk.

Margot couldn't believe it was Saturday and an entire week had gone by since Meredith's last visit. That was unheard of. She had been starting to worry that her best friend wouldn't come back.

Margot held up the key to the houseboat. She could see that Meredith recognised it instantly as she shuffled into the hall with the bag, aiming for the kitchen. 'Yes, I can see that is the key to the houseboat. Does that mean you finally went to fetch the notebook?'

Margot followed her into kitchen and watched her unpack the shopping. 'I don't think you gave me the right keys, Meredith.'

'What are you talking about?'

'It didn't fit. You gave me the wrong key.'

Meredith stopped unpacking the shopping, and turned around. 'I did not give you the wrong key. That is the key that was in the plastic bag under the flowerpot, just where you'd left it.'

'Well, if that's the case, explain to me why it didn't fit the lock!'

Meredith eyed her friend. 'I know exactly why.'

'Can you enlighten me?' Margot folded her arms.

'When did you go?'

'Last night.'

'On Friday evening when it was pitch dark?'

'Yes.'

'Did you have a torch?'

'Well, no. I know that path and my houseboat like the back of my hand. Besides, the houseboat next door that's rented through Airbnb had a light on. Their curtains were opens, so it threw some light on my houseboat.'

Margot didn't add that she'd caught a glimpse inside the houseboat next door and had seen a young couple snuggled up on the sofa together, the young man's arms around the young lady. She'd thought they looked very much in love.

'But you didn't have a torch,' said Meredith.

'No. I told you I didn't need one.'

'Oh, Margot. I know what happened. I bet you had the key upside down. It happens to the best of us. I've done it myself. It's obvious. You were trying to put the key in the wrong way up.'

Margot looked at the key in her hand. 'Oh, god. I'm an idiot.'

'Look, do you want me to go and fetch it? I can go right now before I put the dinner on.'

Margot glanced at the time. 'You know what? I'll go in the morning. I don't care who's around. The neighbours can see me, for all I care.'

Meredith laughed. 'Good for you. Now, shall I get the dinner going?'

'Yes please.' Although Meredith had left plenty of home-cooked frozen meals in Margot's freezer, Margot preferred her meals freshly cooked. It wasn't because they tasted any better than the ones she'd cooked earlier and frozen, it was just because she wanted Meredith's company. They always had a chat while she prepared a meal.

She wouldn't normally stay for dinner. Meredith had a family to go home to, but Margot always asked her, 'Will you join me?' She hoped that on this day her friend would say yes. She'd missed her terribly.

'Yes, I will join you.'

They stood for a brief moment, smiling at one another, Margot realising all was forgiven.

Margot pulled out a kitchen chair and sat down. 'I've been a bit of a fool lately, haven't I? What with the stone and the conker. You know, you're right: I was reading far too much into it.'

'I'm glad you've seen sense, Margot. I mean, wouldn't it make more sense for someone who was visiting his grave to have left flowers rather than a stone and a conker?'

Margot pursed her lips and thought of the small bunch of freshly cut flowers she's seen at the base of the headstone that she hadn't mentioned to Meredith. She hadn't disturbed those. She did remember the easterly wind that day and thought perhaps they had blown over on to her son's grave by mistake.

'You haven't been back since the Friday before last?'

Margot shook her head. 'I'm sure when I return there won't be anything else there other than the flowers I left there on my last visit.'

Meredith nodded. 'How could there be? Alexandra's gone, just like Sophie.'

'I know.'

They stared at each other, both lost in thoughts of that wretched summer day, and the grief that never went away, no matter how much time passed. 'She's gone, Margot, and no amount of hoping or praying or sitting at your desk wishing you could turn back the clock is going to bring either of them back.'

'I know that.'

'It's time to start living again. I think it should start with you telling your lovely neighbours, and Alan, the truth.'

Margot frowned. 'Why Alan, in particular?'

'Oh, for goodness' sake, Margot. Are you blind?' She raised her eyebrows.

Margot stared at her. 'Oh, I'm too old for that.'

'No, you are not. I know you like him.' Meredith turned around to put the oven on. 'Let's eat. Tomorrow you're going to fetch that notebook and find out all about your father. It's going to be a good day – you'll see.'

Margot sat at the table, watching her best friend prepare dinner, and thought – *Is it? Is it going to be a good day?* She was already feeling trepidation about what was in the pages of that notebook – and what her mother was going to tell her about a man she'd never known – her father, Kit. Her mother had finally told her his name, but that was all – she would tell her nothing more until she retrieved the notebook.

28

'Oh, no!' Lexi looked at the time on her phone. She'd overslept. She'd stayed next door far too late again the previous night, but had been careful to make sure she returned to her own bed – or in actual fact, Margot's – because she was due in work.

As she got dressed, she smiled when she thought about what they had done after they'd visited the graveyard a week earlier. Lexi had insisted on buying Charlie a present. She knew it wasn't her birthday, but Charlie had made her a lovely present – the amber bracelet she was slipping on her wrist right now – so Lexi had wanted to do something for Charlie in return. She hadn't been able to make her anything, or buy her a puppy, but she had been able to take her to one of the little boutique shops in Aldeburgh and buy her a dress to wear to Maisie's birthday party the next month.

The lovely Joules dress she'd bought Charlie had probably sent her bank account into overdraft, but she didn't care. She smiled when she remembered the look on Scott's face. His daughter had walked into the changing rooms wearing baggy jeans that looked too big for her slender frame, a boyish checked shirt and dirty white trainers, all making her look younger than her years. She'd walked out of the dressing room wearing a beautiful, colourful knee-length dress and a pretty pair of sandals with a slight heel. Lexi had even quickly braided her hair, surprised that she still remembered how to do that; she had always done her sister's lovely long blonde hair when she was little.

Scott's face had been a picture. For a moment, she'd thought that seeing his daughter dressed like a proper little girl had brought a tear to his eye. Then he'd cleared his throat when Charlie had asked, 'What do you think, Daddy?' He had quite clearly been lost for words.

Lexi was still ignoring that little voice in her head that was reminding her that she had to stop living in the moment and work out what she was going to do when all this came to an end. After the last week had flown by, she had no doubt that the next week would fly by just as fast, and time would move inexorably closer to the end of the summer and Margot's return to the houseboat. *You've got to start making some plans*, Lexi told herself.

She still hadn't checked her new bank account. She knew why; she desperately wanted to find her allowance in her new English bank account. Andrea said she'd transfer it from her account in the States if it turned up. If Lexi received her allowance, it meant that she could stay, find a place to rent, and move out of the houseboat. Not that she wanted to leave it. Despite her aversion to water, the houseboat had grown on her. She liked it. No, that wasn't true – she loved it. But was it because of the boat, or her next-door neighbour?

Lexi didn't have time to think about all that. She hastily washed and dressed. Outside, she could see the rain lashing down. 'Oh, bother,' she muttered. It wasn't going to be fun walking into work, but she had no choice. She grabbed a slice of toast and a cup of tea as she did her hair and makeup, dressed in jeans and a cotton shirt, threw on her raincoat, and pulled up the hood. She grabbed her bag, slipped her phone inside and opened the door, shaking her head at the great British weather. How could it be perfectly sunny and warm one day, with a beautiful cloudless blue sky, and like this – the sky completely grey and overcast, and pelting down with rain – the next? And this was meant to be summer? No wonder the weather was a national obsession. She stepped outside and locked the door behind her.

For a moment she hesitated as she wondered if she should leave the key under the flowerpot, just in case she lost it. It was something that went through Lexi's mind every time she locked up. She shook her head and popped the key away in her bag.

Lexi pulled her hood tightly around her head, deciding there was no point trying to put up an umbrella in the driving wind and rain. She carefully made her way to the path. This wasn't the sort of weather that made her relish being on a boat. Once on the path, she turned in the direction of the bridge, hood pulled down almost over her eyes, and walked at a pace, staring at the ground.

'Sorry!' exclaimed Lexi, almost bumping into a lady walking fast in the other direction. Lexi hadn't seen her coming, and they'd almost collided.

'No harm done,' replied the lady as she strode past and continued on her way. The lady also wore a raincoat and, like Lexi, had her hood pulled down, obscuring her face.

Lexi glanced over her shoulder, wondering in passing where the lady was heading this early on a Sunday morning. She didn't have a shopping bag that Lexi had noticed, so she hadn't been to get the Sunday newspapers or a loaf of bread. The path did lead past the houseboats, and she could be planning to continue on a walk along the riverbank. But she didn't have a dog to take for a walk first thing in the morning, and it wasn't exactly the weather for a nice morning stroll.

Lexi shrugged and continued towards the bridge. Ten minutes later, just as the rain started to ease, she stepped into the library and removed her wet coat. She hung it on a coat rack by the door.

'Good morning, Lexi.'

'Morning Jill. Sorry I'm late.' Lexi couldn't stop smiling, even though her hair felt a bit wet where it had escaped her hat, and she imagined her makeup had run, and her jeans, below the knee, were soaked.

'Did you mind coming in today?' It was Sunday, and Lexi would rather have spent the whole weekend with Charlie and Scott, but it was raining so there wasn't much they could have done except hang around the houseboats. But if that meant sitting on the sofa, cuddling up with Scott while the three of them played board games, which they'd done the previous night, then she would rather do that. However, she'd committed to working Sunday. Jill had been so kind and bent over backwards to help her out in the beginning, so she wasn't about to let her down.

Jill caught sight of her wet jeans. 'Oh, dear.'

Lexi looked down at them too. 'It's really raining out.' Jill had arrived by car. Her grey hair, makeup, and pressed clothes looking perfect, there was not a strand of hair out of place or a single rain droplet on her person.

'The hand dryer in the ladies' toilets is quite hot and powerful. There's nobody around but you and me at the moment. Why don't you—'

'Good idea!' Lexi headed off to the toilets, stripped off her jeans, and placed the trouser legs, one at a time, under the hand dryer. While she was there, she brushed her hair and got a tissue to wipe the mascara that had run. She looked at her face in the mirror and felt much more presentable. She shook her jeans to keep the dryer going for a bit until they were damp rather than soaking wet. 'That will do,' commented Lexi, putting them back on.

When she walked back into the library, Jill was standing the other side of the door with her coat on, holding Lexi's raincoat. Lexi looked at her. 'Are we going somewhere?'

'Oh, yes. Today we take out the mobile library.'

'Mobile library – what's that?'

'It's a little van stocked with books that we take around the community to people who otherwise wouldn't have access to the public library because they can't travel here.'

'In this weather?'

'I'm afraid so. I can't let the residents down. They do look forward to our visits immensely.'

'Residents?'

'Of the local care home.'

'That's right. They're not the only ones we visit. There're the small villages that have lost their bus services and are quite a few miles away from town, so you'll meet some mums with their little ones who enjoy coming inside to choose a book.'

'Okay.'

'First stop is the care home in Southwold.'

Lexi remembered reading about the vacancy for care home assistants, but she was happy in her job at the library. She looked at her raincoat. She didn't fancy a trip out in this weather. She glanced at the other library assistant. 'I could stay here if you wanted someone else to go with you,' offered Lexi.

'I'm afraid I can't leave you manning the shop, so to speak.

But this will be a good experience for you. It's something we all take turns with.'

Lexi took her raincoat, realising she didn't have a choice. 'So, we're going to the care home first?'

'Yes. Perhaps by that time the shower might have passed.'

Shower? Lexi frowned. If that was just a shower, she'd hate to think what a full-on storm looked like.

In the van, Jill asked if she'd spoken with Ray about finding some English relatives.

'Yes, he advised joining AncestryDNA.'

Lexi had been back to Aldeburgh the previous week with Scott and Charlie. While Charlie had visited Maisie at her mum's shop again in Cobblers Yard, and Scott had browsed in the shop, Lexi had popped into The Potting Shed and used the old computer upstairs to join AncestryDNA. Lili had made them each a cup of tea and they'd had a little chat. Lili had embarrassed her by remarking on how gorgeous Scott was, and that they made a cute couple.

Lexi looked at Jill as they walked to the door. 'I hope you don't mind, but I used the library internet during my tea break earlier in the week to log in to the site.'

'Not at all. Have you turned up anything yet?'

Lexi shook her head. She would have liked to find out whether Andrea had checked her account too, to see if anybody English had flagged up as a relative. She'd kept checking her phone, but Andrea still hadn't replied to her texts. As time went on, her hopes that she'd received her allowance were receding; Andrea was avoiding getting in touch because it was bad news.

'Ready, Lexi?'

'Oh, yeah sure.' She wasn't, though – not really. She thought of Scott and Charlie in the houseboat and wished she was there with them, snuggled up on the sofa, playing board games.

She reluctantly slipped on her raincoat and stepped outside.

❖

The first thing Jill did was to introduce Lexi to the care home manager, Nicki. Lexi tentatively smiled at her. Lexi had helped Jill carry over some books in large plastic containers. Jill had told her that in the villages, the residents came out to the van. That wasn't the case at the care home, obviously. Most of the residents had difficulty getting up and sitting in chairs. They couldn't be expected to troop outside and climb in the back of a van.

Lexi helped Jill organise the books, distributing them between two trolleys, which were not unlike the ones that they used in the library to return books to the bookshelves.

'Now, I'll take this corridor, and you can take that one.' Jill pointed in the other direction. We'll take odd and even floors too. 'I'll take the even floors.'

Lexi thought she caught a look pass between Jill and the care home manager. She pursed her lips, wondering if she was going to come across some difficult customers. She imagined that Jill knew exactly who they were, and what floors they were on. She bet it wasn't the even-numbered floors either.

Lexi slowly wheeled the trolley down the corridor. Jill told her to politely knock and call out, *Library Service*. If no one responded from behind the door, then she should move on to the next one. It sounded easy enough, but Lexi imagined that the reality would be different. She expected that some of the residents would complain about the newbie, complain about the books, and just generally complain because someone had happened along who they could just have a good moan at.

Lexi rolled her eyes and set off. She hoped most of the residents weren't in their rooms but were sitting in the lounge; apparently the care assistants would go round the lounge and ask the residents if they wanted books before fetching them off the trolley. That would be much easier.

Lexi headed down the hall, knocking on doors. 'Library Service!' she called out. The trolley was heavy, and she was tired after her late night. All she wanted to do was curl up on the sofa with Scott in front of a warm fire. There was an imitation one in the Airbnb houseboat, but it was rather nice with the light and the plastic logs aglow in a soft orange electric light. She glanced at her watch. She couldn't wait until the end of her shift. It was curry night again, and she was looking forward to seeing which curry Scott was going to cook.

❖

Lexi could see the end of the corridor, the last room on the right, and then the lift which would take her down to the ground floor, and the lounge, where she was going to have a well-earned tea break while the care assistants helped the other residents choose a library book if they wanted one.

Lexi tapped on the door, and said, 'Library Service,' for the umpteenth time. She closed her eyes hoping she got no response.

'Who is that?'

Lexi opened her eyes. 'It's the library service.'

'I know that, but who are you? You're not Jill.'

Lexi stared at the door. 'No, I'm Lexi. I'm new.'

'Are you, now?'

'Yes. Do you want a book or not?' Lexi frowned. That sounded rude. She though she heard a chuckle come from behind the door. 'I haven't got all day,' Lexi added.

'Neither have I, so you'd better come in.'

Lexi breathed a heavy sigh as she glanced at the lift, thinking, *so near but yet so far.*

'Well, what are you waiting for?'

Lexi felt like just getting in the lift and pretending she hadn't heard the woman behind the door. What could the woman do about it – run out and catch her? The lift door opened. Lexi looked at the door, looked at the trolley, and thought *I've had enough of this.*

She'd started wheeling the trolley towards the lift when a care assistant walked out and looked at her, then at the last door along the corridor. 'She didn't want a book, then? That's unusual.' The care assistant lowered her voice, and added, 'I wouldn't blame you if you just ignored her and got in the lift either. I expect Jill told you she's a difficult customer.'

Lexi frowned. 'No, she did not.' Or the fact that the difficult customer was on an odd-numbered floor.

'Well, perhaps she's okay with Jill, but personally,' she continued in a hushed voice, 'I find Esme difficult.'

'I'm sorry – did you just say *Esme*?'

'Yes. She doesn't want to be here. Well, most of them don't, obviously, I mean – would you?'

Lexi looked at the young care assistant and vehemently shook her head, *no.*

'She keeps asking if she can go back to her houseboat.'

'Her – *what*?'

'Houseboat. I heard that she asks her daughter every single time she visits. Of course that's impossible at her age, isn't it? But she just doesn't get that, obviously. Then it's the temper tantrums because her daughter keeps saying no.'

The care assistant held open the lift door. 'You coming?'

Lexi turned her head and looked wide-eyed at the door to Esme's bedroom. 'I want to meet her.'

The care assistant looked at Lexi as though she was barmy. 'Well, er … good luck with that.'

'Where are you?' Lexi heard Esme shout from behind the door. 'I want a book!'

29

Lexi opened the door slowly and started to push the trolley laden with books through the doorway.

'Well, come on – don't dawdle.'

Lexi frowned at the old lady, who was dressed in a rather loud, flowery cotton dress, and was sitting in a comfortable chair by the window, barking orders at her.

Who does she think she is? Lexi glared at her. 'I am not dawdling. Do you know how awkward this thing is?' Lexi barked back. She caught Esme smiling at her. Was she finding this funny?

Lexi managed to get the trolley around the door and into the room. 'Right, can we make this quick? I've got to leave soon.'

'Who do you think you are, young lady? Nobody orders me around!' exclaimed Esme.

Lexi folded her arms. Was she after an apology? If that was the case, she'd be disappointed. Lexi wasn't going to apologise for being terse, not to the rude old lady sitting in front of her – she'd started it. 'Well, there's a first time for everything,' she replied.

The old lady appeared to gag, and Lexi rushed forward. *Oh, god, now she's choking!* Lexi spotted a glass of water on the side table in front of her chair. She picked it up. 'Here, have some water.'

Esme pushed the glass away. 'What are you doing, child?'

'You were choking – weren't you?'

'Don't be a fool! I'm laughing.'

'Oh, right. Sorry.' Lexi frowned into the glass. She'd told herself she wasn't going to apologise.

'Put that down.'

Lexi did as she was told and put the glass of water down on the coffee table.

'Bring the trolley over here.'

'A please wouldn't go unnoticed,' Lexi replied.

Esme looked at her, her lip curling in a smile. She raised an eyebrow. 'Please.'

Lexi wheeled it over and took a seat in the chair by the window opposite Esme.

Esme eyed her. 'Did I say you could sit down?'

Is she for real? Lexi thought. *She's treating me like some sort of servant.*

'No, you did not,' she said. 'I've been on my feet all morning, trundling that heavy trolley up and down corridors, and in and out of lifts, so I am sitting – and that's that!'

She stared at Esme, who held her gaze for what seemed like an age. Then the old lady got up and walked over to the trolley.

'Anything take your fancy?' Lexi asked, drumming her fingers on the arm rest, and looking out the window. At least the weather wasn't great this morning, otherwise she'd be missing out on another enjoyable weekend at the beach with Scott and Charlie.

'What's this?'

Lexi turned her head to find Esme standing over her, a book in her hand. Lexi recognised the book instantly. She looked at her handbag. The clasp had come undone. 'Hey, that's my book!'

Esme turned Margot's book over in her hands. She looked at

Lexi. 'Have you read it?'

'Have you?' Lexi asked, holding out her hand for her book.

Esme smiled as she handed it back. She glanced at the trolley. 'Well, what delights have you brought for me, then?'

Lexi looked at her. 'Do you want a book about boats?' she asked off-hand.

'Boats? Why do you ask that?'

Lexi shrugged nervously. She didn't want to make out that she knew Esme's story – or at least what was written in the notebook. Instead, she said, 'One of the care assistants said you want to go home to your houseboat.'

Esme resumed her seat, carefully lowering herself into her chair. 'It's true.' She exhaled. 'I don't want to be here – would you?'

Lexi glanced around the room, then turned to face the window. 'You've got a nice view.'

'I had a nice view where I was.'

Lexi pursed her lips. She knew exactly what Esme was talking about. She fixed her gaze on the older lady. She wanted so much for Esme to tell her all about her time as an IW on the canal boats during the war. What an exciting time it must have been. She wondered how to broach the subject, how to get her talking.

'You know, I first stepped on to a boat in the war.'

Lexi leaned forward, holding her breath. She remembered to breathe. 'You did? What were you doing on a boat in the war?' Of course, Lexi knew the answer, but she couldn't very well tell Esme that.

Esme turned to glance out of the window. 'I was an IW. I don't expect you'd know what that was.'

Lexi stared at Esme, trying to suppress a smile. 'Can you tell me?'

Esme turned to look at her. 'It's what they called us, you know, the women who worked on canal boats in the war. Someone nick-named us Idle Women because of the badges on our uniforms which said IW. It stood for the Inland Waterways.'

'What was it like, your job in the war?'

'Oh, child. I had the time of my life.'

Lexi frowned. After reading Esme's notebook with Charlie, she'd thought the work sounded hard, the conditions harsh. How could Esme possibly have had the time of her life?

'How come? I would have hated it, being on a boat, working twelve-hour days.'

Esme's shifted her gaze to Lexi. 'How do you know that?'

'Oh, er … I guess you were, like, carrying coal and supplies up and down on canal boats.' Lexi looked at her sheepishly. 'I'm just imagining it was hard work.'

'It *was* hard work all right. My family were appalled when I volunteered. I came from a very well-to-do background, you know. But I wanted to do my bit, and have an adventure.'

Lexi thought of Kit. 'And was it an adventure?'

Esme eyed her a long moment. 'It was the biggest adventure of my life.'

Lexi caught something in her expression as she said those words.

'What were the others like? I guess you worked in a crew.' Lexi remembered their names, Joan and Margaret. She'd read a bit about them in Esme's diary, but she wanted to know first-hand what they had been like.

'I made some exceptional friends, life-long friends that I would never have had the good fortune to meet otherwise. That's what happens, you see, when you are transplanted from your normal, everyday world, thrust into a place that is so foreign, so new. And yet so exciting, so full of possibilities.'

Lexi thought of her trip from Connecticut, finding herself in England on the Suffolk Coast. She'd made new friends. She was about to make more – Lexi was thinking of Lili, Abigail and Hannah. Would they become life-long friends? Lexi sincerely hoped so.

She'd made a very special friend too, someone she didn't think she'd find, another soulmate; someone other than Brandon that she felt she could spend the rest of her life with. But she was scared by the thought that, like Brandon, she might lose him.

Lexi tried to push that thought to the back of her mind. She focused on Esme. 'What were they like?' Lexi asked again, 'The others on the boat?'

Esme offered her a rare smile. 'Now, there was Joan, who told such funny stories and always made me laugh. I don't know how she kept her sense of humour when I think back on it now. Her husband had gone to war; he'd been sent to the Middle East – Egypt I think. She hadn't seen him for four years. They were newlyweds when he left. They had no children, so she volunteered to keep busy. He returned, you know, from the war, and they had the family she'd always wanted. Four children.'

Lexi smiled. It was lovely to hear that Joan's husband had returned from the war.

'Then there was Margaret. I think she was around twenty. She had a fiancé. They were planning to marry when he next had leave, but ...' Esme trailed off.

Lexi stared at her. She guessed that unlike Joan's, Margaret's story did not have a happy ending.

'She did meet and marry, some time after the war, but she never forgot her first sweetheart.' Esme smiled. 'Then there was me, the youngest. Oh, we had such fun – sometimes a little too much.'

Lexi leaned forward in her chair. 'How so?'

'We were so young, probably younger than you. There was a pub not far from where we moored one night, so Joan went and bought some alcohol. What a party we had that night, with the little wind-up radio, taking turns to dance the waltz with each other out on deck, imagining we were with a sweetheart as we danced.'

Esme closed her eyes and was moving her head as though she was listening to music, lost in the past.

Lexi sat watching her. She pursed her lips, and said softly, 'Did you have a sweetheart in the war?'

Esme's eyes shot open. 'There was a boy.' She turned to look out the window.

Lexi waited, wondering if that was it. Maybe she wasn't going to say any more. Lexi was just about to ask his name when Esme said, 'I discovered him hiding in my cabin. He was so young, like me, but so frightened. He'd been hiding out in disused barns, travelling around the countryside, finding shelter where he could. He was a deserter. I couldn't blame him for deserting.' She shook her head. 'When I look back on it now, to think that in the midst of war, when young men, boys, were dying on the battlefield, there I was, having the time of my life, free from the constraints of my family and being a young woman in those times.'

Esme turned from the window. 'You know, my parents were going to marry me off to the son of a local earl. My future was all mapped out. It was a future I didn't want.' She stared at Lexi. 'I don't suppose your generation would understand or have any inkling of someone else controlling your life, your destiny. It was different back then.'

Lexi stared at her. Esme had no idea how much what she'd just said resonated in Lexi's own life.

'Of course, I was having none of it, don't you know.'

Lexi smiled. 'So, you helped this guy?'

'Yes, I did. We all did.'

'The other two on the boat knew about him?'

'How could they not? Although my sleeping cabin was on the other boat that we towed, we all lived and worked together. I couldn't hide him in my cabin indefinitely without out one of them finding out. You know, he ended up like part of our crew. Although we had to share our rations between four instead of three, we couldn't complain. Our lives were so much easier with a young man on board, travelling up and down the canals, helping us load and unload.'

Lexi hadn't known, from reading Esme's diary, that Kit had spent quite some time aboard the canal boat, and that the other two young women had known that Kit was a stowaway.

'How did they find out?'

'We'd left the canal boats moored up, and the three of us had gone out into a local town one evening. He'd followed me.'

'You were young, and ... in love?'

Lexi noticed that Esme didn't correct her. So, they *had* been in love.

'There was a dance.'

Lexi desperately wanted to know what happened. Had one of her friends betrayed him? Esme hadn't written about it in her diary. There was obviously a lot she hadn't included. Lexi had an idea why. They had been harbouring a deserter, after all. And she imagined there would have been a penalty for that if it had been discovered that they'd all been in on it, so she had not written down that her friends knew about him.

'What happened to him?' Lexi asked.

'I don't want to talk about it.' She got out of her chair and stood by the window.

But you were talking about it just a moment ago, thought Lexi. *Why stop now?*

'Fine!' Lexi felt *so* disappointed. She glared at her back. 'Do you want a book – or not?' She knew that sounded rude, but she couldn't help feeling cheesed off with Esme.

'I don't know how we got on to the subject,' muttered Esme. She turned around to look at Lexi.

Lexi got out of her seat and stood by the trolley. 'I'm leaving now, so if you want a book, you'd better hurry up about it.' Lexi looked at the clock on the wall. Weren't they meant to be there just for the morning? The clock was ticking, and it was nearly twelve. She wanted to get out of there. She put her hands on her hips and looked at Esme impatiently, thinking, *Come on, make up your mind.*

'I want *your* book.'

She must be joking, Lexi thought.

'I haven't read Mar ... I mean the author's work for quite some time. I fancy re-reading her book.'

Lexi had the second book in the trilogy, which she'd found and bought in the second-hand bookshop when she was in Dunwich with Sarah and her art class. Lexi had already read the first book. She was looking forward to reading the next book. She knew there would be a copy in the library, but it wasn't on the trolley, and Esme was standing there with pleading eyes.

Lexi breathed a heavy sigh, and opened her handbag. 'Okay, fine. Whatever.' She handed her the book thinking she'd probably find a copy in the library to read.

Esme took it.

'Don't I even get a thank you?'

Esme offered her a whisp of a smile instead.

❖

'Ah, there you are,' said Jill. 'I was about to send out a search party.'

'Huh?'

'I wouldn't be surprised if you'd got lost in this place – there are lots of floors and corridors.'

Lexi thought she'd got lost alright, in Esme and her story. She couldn't wait to tell Charlie who she had found today. She knew she could text Charlie, but she wanted to see her reaction when she told her she'd found Esme, the woman who had written the notebook.

Lexi had been shocked that it was really her, the lady who'd worked on the Inland Waterways in the war. She was dying to ask her all about it, and what had happened to Kit. But how could she without giving away the fact that she'd found her notebook? It was frustrating. But still, she'd found her. And now she just had to find a way to return the notebook. She hadn't said anything to Esme – how could she? She was, after all, squatting on the houseboat. She hoped Charlie could help her out with her little quandary; how could she give the notebook back to Esme without letting on where she'd found it?

As Lexi piled the books into boxes, helping Jill put them back in the van, she paused when she had a thought. On their next visit with the mobile library, she could bring the notebook with her and leave it in her room.

Jill shut the van doors and got in the car next to Lexi. 'Oh, by the way, before I forget, I heard from one of the care home staff that you'd made quite an impression on one of the residents.'

'Oh, really? Who was that?' Lexi said. *And how is that possible*, she thought. She hadn't stopped to talk to them, apart from Esme, whom she'd been quite rude to, which she felt a bit guilty about now. She looked at Jill and couldn't imagine which one had put in a good word. Although there had been a guy on the ground floor who had been a bit too forward. He had kept saying how pretty she was, and asking if she had a boyfriend.

Lexi looked at Jill and realised that she might not have meant what she'd said in a good way. 'Oh, am I in trouble?'

'No, not at all. In fact, she said that next time, she wanted you to visit her with the books. As I said, you've made quite the impression on Esme.'

'Esme?'

'Yes, that was a bit of a surprise. You probably didn't realise, but she doesn't like anyone. She's quite the difficult customer.'

Yeah – that's why you were avoiding her, and left me to that floor. Lexi gave Jill a sideways glance and kept that thought to herself.

'I don't understand why she asked for me. I didn't say anything. Well, I did. Look, I'm sorry, but I was actually quite rude.'

'Really?'

'Yes.'

Jill surprised her by laughing out loud. 'Well, who would have thought? All these years, everyone has been pussy-footing around her, and it takes a slip of a girl to put her in her place. Oh, Lexi, you are amazing.'

30

'Right, that's it for today,' said Jill. 'My goodness – didn't the day fly by!'

Lexi didn't think so. She'd been watching the clock on the wall, counting down the minutes until they could leave. After they'd returned from their morning out with the mobile library, the afternoon had seemed interminable. She couldn't wait to see Scott. He was never far from her mind. *That's what happens when you're in love*, a little voice in her head said, surprising her.

They both walked to the door. Lexi glanced outside as she put on her raincoat. 'I can't believe it's still raining.'

Jill put her coat on too. 'It's really lashing down, isn't it? There's quite a wind too.' She turned to Lexi. 'I'm going to take you home in my car. You can't possibly walk in this. You'll get soaked, and with that wind, you wouldn't want to walk near any trees. Who knows what might come down in that storm.'

'Oh! Er, no – I'll be fine.'

Sheet lightning suddenly lit up the dark grey sky. A crack of thunder followed.

'Lexi, I won't take no for an answer. Come on.'

They stood together outside while Jill locked up. Lexi followed her to her car, a blue mini. 'Now, where do you live? It was a houseboat, wasn't it?'

Lexi nodded. 'It's in Walberswick, but if you just drive through Southwold and drop me outside The Harbour Inn on the quay, all I have to do is cross the footbridge to the Walberswick side of the river.'

Jill said, 'There's a car park in Walberswick, by the quay.'

'Yes, but it's a bit of a drive, out of Southwold inland to the main road, to get to Walberswick.'

Although Walberswick was virtually next door to Southwold, the fact that there was no road bridge meant that it was quite a detour to get there from Southwold by car. Lexi stared out of the front window. The rain was lashing down on the windscreen. 'I don't think in this weather you should be doing an unnecessary journey – do you?'

More sheet lightning followed by another crack of thunder made them both jump. Jill started the engine. 'Yes, you're right.'

'The houseboat isn't that far along the path. I'll be fine.'

They set off, driving through the town along the deserted high street. With the bad weather, hardly anyone was out and about, apart from a couple of dog walkers. Jill asked, 'Have you got any plans for this evening?'

'I'm visiting my neighbour next door for dinner.'

'It's quite a storm,' commented Jill, flicking her windscreen wipers up a notch.

The library closed at two in the afternoon, but the terrible weather and the massive grey storm clouds made it appear quite dark and much later in the day than it was.

'How are things going with your genealogy search on AncestryDNA? I noticed you on the internet on your lunch break and thought you might have checked the site again.'

'Yes, I did log on.'

Have you found any long-lost relatives yet? Sorry, I don't mean to pry – it's just that I thought I heard you talking on your mobile phone to Ray?'

Lexi pursed her lips. Andrea had finally texted to say she'd logged on and checked the site and had still turned up nothing. In her text, there was no mention of the bank details Lexi had forwarded to Andrea or transferring money into her bank account. She knew why; there was no allowance this month – not for as long as she stayed in England.

Lexi had texted her sister back a thank you for checking AncestryDNA. She did not mention money or an incongruity she'd discovered when she logged on to the site; nothing had flagged up on Andrea's account, but something – or rather someone – had on Lexi's. That did not make any sense. Lexi had phoned Ray during her break when she'd discovered this. She was still mulling over the conversation she'd had with him.

He'd asked her how things were going with tracing her English relations. The first thing Lexi had said was that she didn't think the site was very reliable. He'd asked her, 'What makes you say that?'

Lexi had told him that Andrea still had nothing, whereas for Lexi when she logged on today, there was a match, a relative she had no idea she had. She hadn't pulled up the details. How could she get her hopes up when she thought it must be a mistake? Unless it was because Andrea was logging on in America, and she was in England.

'Nope, it's an international site – there would be absolutely no difference in the results whether you joined here or across the pond.'

'Then, there's been a mistake,' Lexi had told him, 'because my sister and I should have the same result.'

That's when Ray had made a suggestion that had thrown Lexi completely. 'Is Andrea a full sibling?'

Lexi stared at the road ahead. *Is Andrea a full sibling?* She'd asked him what he'd meant by that. But of course she knew what he was saying. If Andrea was a half sibling, then there could be relations out there, someone on the site who was related to her and not her sister. But that wasn't what was bothering her so much. It was the possibility that they *were* half-siblings. *That just can't be true*, thought Lexi. It meant her mum would have had an affair.

She couldn't believe it. 'How would I know that for sure?' she'd asked Ray. 'It's not like either of my parents are alive to ask.' That was when Ray had told her that they didn't need their parents. 'You can take a DNA test with your sibling.'

Before she'd ended the call, Ray had said to her, 'Think long and hard, Lexi, about the consequences of exposing family secrets.'

'Are you advising me to let sleeping dogs lie and not to contact this person or tell my sister?'

He'd said, 'No, Lexi. That is not my place. I can't make that decision for you. I'm just saying that—'

'I might not like what I find?'

'Yes, and neither might Andrea.'

Lexi stared out of the car window, lost in thought.

… *reports of a tidal surge, so batten down the hatches, folks* …

Jill turned the car radio off. 'Here we are.' She pulled the car to a stop outside The Harbour Inn. 'Well, it's not letting up, is it?'

The rain was still lashing down, and the wind howled around Jill's little car. She turned to Lexi. 'I'm worried about you being in a houseboat in this weather.'

Lexi was worried too.

'Look, why don't you come home with me and stay the night? I've got a spare bedroom. One of my children is back from university for the summer, but the other one is off travelling. You are more than welcome to use her room. I've got fresh sheets and towels.'

Lexi was tempted, but she wanted to see Charlie and tell her about Esme, and retrieve that box from under the floorboard.

'That's so kind of you, Jill, but I'll be fine. Besides, I've got a date with my neighbour next door.'

'A date?' Jill raised her eyebrows and grinned. 'How lovely.'

Lexi had it on the tip of her tongue to say, *It's not what you think*, but actually, it was.

'That's right – you did say it was curry night.'

Lexi didn't mention that it had been curry night every night, for the past fortnight. She knew now that it was a euphemism. She might as well call them what they were – date nights.

Lexi pulled her hood up. 'Thank you so much, Jill, for the lift.'

'See you tomorrow, Lexi.'

'Yes, see you tomorrow. Safe journey home.'

'Thank you.'

Lexi got out of the car and had to stand her ground against the tremendous wind and rain lashing against her face. The weather was ridiculous. What had the weatherman said on the radio? Lexi hadn't been paying attention. Something about a tidal surge? What did that mean? She really hoped it wasn't going to be too choppy that night on the houseboats.

31

'Where have you been? I've been waiting for you for ages! Quick – come in here.' Margot beckoned Meredith inside the house. 'Come quick!' Margot headed down the hallway.

Meredith sighed. 'Hold your horses. I've got to take my coat off. It's blooming raining cats and dogs out there.' She slipped off her shoes. 'Oh, bother, my socks are wet.'

'Never mind that, come in here!'

'What is this about, that you dragged me out in this weather and couldn't tell me over the phone?' Meredith looked at her. 'You've got the notebook, haven't you?'

Margot's bright, cheery face dissolved into a frown. 'No, I haven't.'

'What? I thought you were going to get it?'

'I did. First thing this morning.'

Meredith shook her head, 'And ...?'

'The key didn't fit the lock.'

Meredith threw her arms up the air as she walked down the hallway. Talk about déjà vu. She couldn't believe they were having this conversation all over again.

'No, really, Meredith. The key does not fit the lock.'

'Well, I know I gave you the right key.' Meredith stopped. 'Are you saying the locks have been changed?'

'Yes. Look, I took a photo on my phone to prove it.'

Meredith walked up to the study doorway where Margot was standing and looked at the photo on her phone.

'See? You know how old my lock and door furniture was.'

Meredith popped on her glasses to take a good look. 'That looks brand new. Your locks have been changed.'

'That's what I just told you.'

'Oh, my goodness, Margot. You've got an intruder!'

'I know. I can't believe they've had the cheek – the audacity – to change my locks.'

'Neither can I. This sort of thing just doesn't happen in Walberswick.'

Margot put her hands on her hips. 'Well, it does now!'

'Did you call the police?'

'Yes.'

'When will they be here, Margot?'

'I don't know. They said they'd be here as soon as they can, but who knows?' Margot frowned. 'To be honest, I got the impression from the person I spoke to that they weren't exactly treating it like an emergency. I told them a crime has been committed – someone has broken into my property.'

'So, I take it that whoever it is was not on the houseboat when you were trying to get the old key in the new lock?'

Margot shook her head.

'When was this?'

'Like I said, first thing this morning.'

Meredith stormed back up the hall and started putting her coat on.

'Where are you going?'

'To the houseboat, of course. It's teatime. I bet someone is there now.'

'But—'

'No buts, I'm going to knock on the door and find out what they think they're doing squatting in your houseboat – and changing the locks. What a cheek! Are you coming?'

Margot hesitated. 'Yes.'

'Good.'

'But before we go, I've got something to show you.'

'Really, Margot, can't it wait? I'm sure it can't be more important than this.'

'Oh, but it is.'

Intrigued, Meredith followed Margot into her study. 'Look.' Margot pointed at her desk.

Meredith put her glasses back on and walked up to Margot's desk. There, in front of her, were two hand-painted stones with messages of love for a father, and two conkers.

Meredith slowly took of her glasses. She needed to sit down.

Margot sat down in her chair opposite Meredith. 'You know what this means, don't you?' said Margot, eyeing the second stone and conker. 'She's been back and discovered someone had taken her stone and conker, so she returned to the grave and replaced them. It's the only explanation.'

Meredith looked across at her friend. 'How is this possible?'

'I don't know, Meredith. But my granddaughter is here, and it's a bloody miracle!'

❖

'Margot, an umbrella won't stay up in this weather.'

They both stood by the front door in their raincoats. Margot put the umbrella back in the base of the coat stand. She turned to Meredith. 'It's awful out there. Do you really think we should brave it?'

'We must if you want to find out who's living on your house-boat.'

'I do.' Margot nodded. 'Let's go.' She opened the door and the wind caught it. 'Good god, it's ferocious!'

'I know!'

They both stepped out, pulling their hoods up, finding it quite trying, walking against the wind. They made it to the gates, and Margot opened them.

'Hey!' A neighbour Margot recognised, a firefighter with a young family, who must have been off-duty today, called out, 'I wouldn't go out in this. The weather is really bad, and there's meant to be a tidal surge.'

'A what?' Margot couldn't quite hear him above the wind.

'The RNLI called me.'

Margot heard that bit. He was also a volunteer for the Royal National Lifeboat Institution. She wondered if he'd been called out to a sea rescue – probably a fishing boat in trouble in the rough seas.

Meredith and Margot joined him in the street. He shouted above the wind, 'I'm going down to the quay.'

'Why?'

'The people living in the houseboats need to be evacuated. The people down by the quay might not be aware of the tidal surge. They've got to vacate their boats. We've got to warn them. It's heading their way – fast!'

'I'm coming too.'

'Why?'

Margot and Meredith exchanged a glance. Margot said, 'We want to help.'

The young man glanced through the gates at her large cottage. 'Is there any chance you might be able to provide shelter? I imagine it's going to be a rough night, and these people probably have nowhere to go.'

'Of course I can. Let's go.'

Meredith took Margot's arm and leaned in close, whispering to her as they hurried towards the quay, 'But they're all going to find out that you're not in London, and that you're right here in Walberswick, living in that!' Meredith pointed behind her at Margot's cottage as they hurried down the road towards the quay.

'What would you have me do, Meredith? Abandon them in their hour of need?'

'Of course not.'

'They're my neighbours, my friends.'

'I know, Margot, but that's my point. They might not be your friends for long when they find out the truth.'

'Don't you think I don't know that!' Margot snapped. She sighed, aware she was sounding just like her mother. 'I'll just have to cross that bridge when I come to it.'

Talking of bridges, they'd reached the car park on the quay and could see the footbridge up ahead. Margot stopped. In all the years that her mother had kept the houseboat on the quay, she had never, ever seen anything like it.

'Climate change,' mumbled Meredith.

Margot heard her. The river had swelled enormously such that the water was coming up to the footbridge. Some of the houseboats were already listing precariously.

'Can you see your houseboat?' Meredith asked.

'No.' But she didn't expect to see it from there because of the larger boat next door, rented out through Airbnb – not to mention Ray's even larger houseboat next door to that.

The young firefighter shouted at them. 'Stay there!'

They didn't object.

Meredith turned to Margot. 'What about the notebook?'

'Meredith, there are lives at stake. We can't worry about a decades-old notebook.'

'You're right. But what about the person squatting in your houseboat?'

'Yes, I see your point.' They both turned to look down the path. People were already abandoning their homes, taking whatever they could reasonably carry with them.

Margot watched them heading her way along the path beside the river. 'Well, if they're all coming round to mine, they will soon get found out, won't they? There will be nowhere to hide.'

Meredith smiled. 'How very true. And when the police arrive at your house ...'

'The culprit will be right where I want them, ready to get their comeuppance.'

32

'Lexi?' Scott grabbed her hand. 'Where are you going?'

'Back to the boat.' He'd spotted Lexi hurrying down the path towards the houseboat after Jill had dropped her off outside The Harbour Inn across the bridge. He thought she must have heard someone shouting out for people to leave their houseboats and evacuate the quay, so what was she doing there?

Scott and Charlie were racing up the gangplank as she passed them by. Scott had sent Charlie ahead, running up the path. He stopped Lexi's forward momentum. She'd just opened the gate.

'Scott, let me go!'

'What are you doing? Didn't you hear? There's a tidal surge. We've got to leave everything and just go!'

'Oh, like you have!'

Scott realised that Lexi must have caught sight of his backpack.

'It's just a go bag.'

'A what?' He saw Lexi cup a hand to her ear and realised that she couldn't hear properly through the driving wind and rain.

Scott had been sitting in the houseboat when he'd heard someone shouting out, and had looked out of the cabin window to see neighbours abandoning their boats.

He'd already read about the tidal surge in this area on the internet and decided to abandon ship, just to be on the safe side. He'd grabbed his phone, laptop and the go bag he always had at the ready. He'd never expected to use it for anything of this nature. *Climate change*, he'd thought.

The go bag was always on standby for an emergency flight of an altogether different nature. It was where he always kept their passports, a first-aid kit, a burner phone, a wad of cash, and a bank card, all wrapped in cellophane in little plastic bags. When they came for him – and he anticipated that they would catch up with him one day – he could grab the go bag, and Charlie, and run.

Although they hadn't caught up with him yet, he felt as though he'd been running since his wife left him. He looked at Lexi. Her presence was the first taste of normality that he and Charlie had had in a very long time. And he was not about to lose her now.

He would have been quicker to abandon the boat and would have caught Lexi further up the path if it hadn't been for Charlie's actions. She'd dived back into her bedroom, when he'd expressly told her not to, to grab her backpack. He'd run in after her. 'You don't need that!' he'd shouted.

He glanced at Charlie's retreating figure as he blocked Lexi's way.

'Please let go of me, Scott. I have to get inside the houseboat.'

Scott saw it bobbing up and down, getting precariously close to the Airbnb houseboat. 'No, you can't. It's too dangerous!'

'But the notebook!'

'What are you talking about?'

'I need to fetch the notebook.'

'Seriously, Lexi, nothing is worth drowning for. For god's sake, just leave it! There's no time – look!' He pointed at the river. It had risen, precipitating something devastating coming their way.

They both heard Charlie shouting out from further up the path, 'Daddy, hurry up!'

'Come on!' He pulled Lexi towards him, and holding hands, together they made a run for it along the path, and quickly caught up with Charlie, who had slowed behind other people making their way along the path towards the quay.

A young man squeezed past them. 'Is everyone off the boats?' he shouted out.

Murmurs of *yes* arose.

'Good. Quickly, follow me! A neighbour of mine is going to take you all in.'

Margot heard her neighbour. She turned to Meredith. 'Let's go back to the house and fetch blankets, towels and, more importantly, I'll put the kettle and start making some sweet tea for our guests.'

'You're not going to stay and see who it might be whose been squatting on your houseboat?'

'Nope, they'll be at my house in a moment. I'll know soon enough.'

'How will you know?'

'Because one of my neighbours must have seen something.'

33

Lexi held Scott's hand tightly as they made their way past the quay and up the familiar street where Lexi had followed Meredith two weeks earlier. As they left the quay, the tidal surge started to batter the boats. If she'd been inside, she might have been knocked unconscious and no one would have known she was there. She might have drowned if the houseboat then sank.

Lexi shuddered at the thought. Drowning had always been her biggest fear.

She avoided a backward glance as they left the quay. She didn't want to see the little houseboat sink and know that Esme's little notebook was lost forever.

Lexi slowed to a complete halt when she saw which house the small group were walking towards. The last time she'd seen the place, the wrought iron double gates had been closed. This time, they were wide open.

'Something the matter?' Scott asked.

Lexi looked at him. She wasn't the only one who'd come to a complete standstill. She thought, *I could ask you the same thing.*

'Hold on – I just want to find out whose house this is.'

Lexi gave him a sideways glance, aware that he didn't need to ask anyone else – she could tell him herself. But she kept her mouth shut.

Scott walked up to the young man standing at the gates, who was waving them all through. It gave Lexi an opportunity to have a quiet word with Charlie. 'You've got to promise me that you won't tell anyone I was living on that houseboat.'

Up ahead, Lexi could see Ray and Alan walking into the house. She guessed it didn't matter if Charlie promised not to spill the beans, because she wasn't the only one who knew. Lexi glanced at Scott. If she walked in holding his hand, then it would appear they were a couple renting the Airbnb for the summer. She thought of Ray and Alan. Unfortunately, she knew that a ruse like that wouldn't last long. Worse still, Scott had no idea that she had been squatting next door to him. What would he think of her when he found out?

'I promise, Lexi. I don't want to get you into trouble.'

Lexi smoothed down her hair. 'I know, sweetheart.'

'You won't go to prison – will you?'

'No one is going to prison.' Lexi didn't believe that for a second. *The truth will out*, she thought. Before long, Margot was going to find out all about her squatter, who was now under her roof. Lexi didn't know whether to laugh or cry at the absurdity of her situation.

'My dad said that if we don't keep moving around, they'll find him and take him to prison.'

'Pardon?' Lexi looked at Charlie. 'What do you mean?'

'Ah, that's all right then,' said Scott re-joining them. 'Turns out the lady who owns this place, Margot, is a writer, or was. I don't know. Anyway she's just a little old lady, so that's ok.'

Lexi stared at Scott.

He caught her staring. 'What?' Scott looked at his daughter. Charlie was standing there nervously chewing a fingernail.

Lexi noticed that too. She guessed Charlie knew she had said too much.

'Oh, nothing,' said Lexi. She had enough problems on her plate just then, as they stepped up to the front door, without finding out the guy she'd fallen for was a criminal; a fugitive from the law. Just when she'd thought she was making a life for herself in England, it was all going to end – and so suddenly. But she'd known that none of it was real; that it couldn't last. It had all been built on a lie, which was about to be exposed. She shook her head. And as for Scott – was that even his real name?

After what she'd just heard from Charlie, Lexi didn't feel inclined to take his hand, but he took hers as they stepped inside the house. Margot and her friend, Meredith, were waiting to greet them in the hall.

Lexi had the impulse to run. But where would she go? She was there now. She did notice that Ray and Alan had walked into another room and hadn't noticed her.

The three of them walked in behind other members of the houseboat community by the quay. It was a bit chaotic, with lots of people milling around the hall, being greeted by the two older ladies, who were handing out mugs of tea and blankets.

Lexi hung back. She said to Scott, 'Can you ask them where the bathroom is, please?'

Scott nodded. Thankfully he didn't question why she couldn't ask them herself. He walked up to one of them to ask, and returned with two cups of tea. 'They seem nice.'

Lexi looked at the tea, and thought, *They might appear nice now, but wait until they find out what I did*. 'Where's the bathroom?'

He pointed down the hall. 'Under the stairs. She had it converted to a downstairs cloakroom, apparently.'

Lexi looked at him. *God, now he's chatting to them*, she thought. She wanted to keep a low profile. 'I'm going to spend a penny.'

'I need to go too!' said Charlie.

Lexi took Charlie's hand. 'Come on, then.'

They walked around the people in the hallway. Lexi kept her head down. Charlie ran ahead. 'Hey, what do you think is in here?'

Lexi caught up with her as Charlie was about to open the door at the end of the hall. She grabbed the handle and pulled the door closed. 'The toilet is under the stairs, remember?'

'But I wanted to have a look.'

'It's the study,' said Lexi.

'How do you know that?'

Lexi frowned. 'I don't know.' Before she could stop her, Charlie had opened the door. They both caught sight of bookshelves before Lexi quickly closed the door.

Charlie turned around and stared at her. 'You were right.'

'Lucky guess. Now, what did you say about not wanting to get me in trouble?'

'Sorry.'

'If you want to explore, you'll have to ask Margot, the lady who owns this house. Perhaps she'll give you a tour.' Lexi imagined what a fascinating place this must be to a child; an old cottage-style house with all its little nooks and crannies, and a back garden with a fabulous old willow tree.

Lexi frowned again. She didn't know where that had come from. She'd spotted a willow tree in the front garden. Why did she think there was one in the back garden too?

Lexi found the door in the stair panelling. She stepped inside the modern downstairs cloakroom and turned around to look at Charlie in the doorway. 'I'll go first.' Lexi didn't need the toilet. She needed to make a private phone call. She was about to close the door when Charlie surprised her by barging in and slamming the door behind them. She locked it and turned to face Lexi.

Lexi looked at her in surprise. 'If you're that desperate …' Lexi stepped away from the loo.

'I don't need to go. I wanted somewhere private to talk to you.'

'Okay. But before you say anything, there's something I've been dying to tell you.' Lexi guessed now was as good a time as any. 'I found Esme!'

Charlie's eyebrows shot up. 'Esme? The IW?'

'That's right.'

'Where is she?'

'Just across the bridge in a care home in Southwold. She's old now, Charlie.'

'We have to give her back the notebook.'

'I know, but I don't think we can. By the look of that storm surge, we'll be lucky if there's anything left of the houseboat tomorrow.'

'I've got something to show you.'

Lexi watched her take the backpack off her back and unzip it. She held it open for Lexi to look inside.

'You have got to be kidding me!' exclaimed Lexi, her eyes wide.

'Am I in trouble?'

'In trouble? Oh, my god, how could you possibly be in trouble?'

'Because I stole it from the houseboat. I wanted to read it again, so I … I took it.'

'When was this?'

'It was when you were at work.'

Lexi frowned. 'But you haven't got a key to the houseboat.' Lexi stared at her. 'Wait, I remember.' She recalled a conversation with Charlie when they'd first discovered the notebook, and spent the afternoon reading it until her visit had been cut short by her dad calling her home for tea.

Charlie had wanted to continued reading the notebook. She'd asked if she could take it with her. Lexi had said no. It didn't belong to her, so it wasn't hers to give. Instead she'd stowed it safely back where she'd found it.

Lexi guessed what had happened. Charlie had sneaked back on to the boat before the lock was fixed, when Lexi was at work, and taken the notebook.

'I thought you'd find out it was gone.'

Lexi shook her head. She hadn't noticed it was missing. She'd assumed the tin was still safely stored under the floorboard where she'd left it. Lexi just hadn't had time to revisit Esme's notebook and her story. She'd barely thought about it until she'd met Esme earlier that day and had started trying to figure out a way to give her back her notebook.

Lexi flung her arms around Charlie. 'Oh, Charlie, you are amazing, do you know that?'

'So, you're not cross?'

'Oh, my goodness, not in the slightest. I could never be cross with you.' Lexi hugged her close once more, before she drew back. She looked at her for a long moment, wondering how she was going to tell her that this was it – she was leaving.

34

There was no easy way to tell her. 'Look, Charlie, I've got to go.'

'Go where?'

'Back to America.'

'No! You can't!'

'I have to, Charlie.' Lexi cupped a hand gently around Charlie's cheek. She didn't understand. Lexi had nowhere to live. The houseboat would be in no fit state to return to, even if it had survived the tidal wave, and although she still had the key to the little flat above Lili's shop, she couldn't go there now. She was in big trouble. She'd told Lili about squatting on a houseboat, but she realised belatedly that if she stayed in Lili's flat, it would only make things worse; the fact that Lili already knew what she'd been up to made her an accessory to her crime.

'How long will you be gone?'

'I don't know, Charlie.'

Charlie's bottom lip quivered. 'You're not coming back, are you?'

Lexi pursed her lips. She knew she could lie, but she'd been lying all this time to all these amazing people she'd met, who called her a friend. She didn't deserve them. Lexi took a deep breath and said, 'Honestly, Charlie, I don't think so.'

'But why? Is it because you've got nowhere to live? You could stay with me and my dad. He'll find somewhere else to live. Somewhere that's not a boat, because I know you don't like the water.'

'It's not about living on a houseboat.'

Charlie wasn't listening. 'But he's good at finding places to live.'

Lexi thought of Scott's go bag. From what Charlie had told her, they had to keep moving around, otherwise he'd end up in prison. God knows what he'd done, but the fact was, she'd gleaned they were on the run. How long did he think a relationship would last, if he was constantly moving?

How could he have done this to her – keep the truth from her and let her fall in love with him? *Damn him.* She'd fallen for Scott, but she needed a home, stability, a life. It was obvious that he couldn't offer those things. *He can't feel the same way about me,* thought Lexi. *I was just a holiday fling before he moved on.*

Lexi stared at Charlie. She was so sorry that things had to end this way. The fact was that she loved them both, and it was breaking her heart to leave them.

Charlie wasn't giving up. 'I overheard the lady say that she can put us all up for as long as we want. You can stay here.' Charlie wasn't going to accept that Lexi was really going.

'Oh, Charlie.' Lexi shook her head. 'The houseboat I was squatting on belongs to one of the ladies here. If she finds out—'

'She won't. I made a promise, didn't I? I won't tell, and neither will my dad.'

Lexi looked at her. She was wavering. There was just one problem – or two, in actual fact – Ray and Alan. At some point very soon – it could be happening right now, for all she knew – Alan or Ray, or both of them, would bring up the broken lock. It was inevitable. There was no way round the fact that if she didn't sneak out of this house, she'd be outed. There was no houseboat-sitting company. There was just a young woman taking advantage of Margot and squatting on her houseboat.

In hindsight, it would have been far better if she'd called on Margot the moment she discovered where she really was, given her the letter, and explained what had happened in London and how she'd come to be living temporarily on her houseboat, waiting for her to return. Perhaps she would have let her stay for the summer. *Who knew?* But it was too late now.

Isn't hindsight a wonderful thing, Lexi thought bitterly. 'I am so sorry, Charlie.'

Charlie wiped her tearful eyes and runny nose with the sleeve of her jumper. 'As soon as my dad has found somewhere else to live, I'm going to text you, so you can come back.'

Lexi breathed a sigh. She'd already told Charlie she wasn't coming back, but the poor child just didn't want to listen.

'Do you promise you'll come back?'

Lexi did not want to make a promise she couldn't keep. She'd done enough lying for one holiday.

'Please say yes, Lexi.'

Lexi guessed she would come back to visit England at some point, and she could call in on Charlie. Feeling a lot less guilty after that thought, Lexi said, 'Yes, I promise.'

Charlie threw her arms around her. 'I knew it. I knew you love my dad.'

Lexi pursed her lips. Perhaps visiting Charlie was not one of her better ideas. It wasn't that she didn't want to see her again; it was the thought of Scott moving on and finding someone else.

When Charlie stepped back, throwing her a big smile, Lexi

took her by the shoulders. 'Charlie, this is important. I need you to do two things for me.' She knew she was asking a lot.

'What is it?'

Lexi opened her handbag and got out the letter for Margot. There was no way she could give it to Margot herself now. She needed to leave right away. She couldn't put the letter in the post-box by the houseboat it had blown over in the wind. And if she posted it through Margot's door, it might get trodden on and lost with all the comings and goings in the house.

She had thought of leaving it on the sideboard in the hall, but once again, she thought something might happen to it. What if it fell on the floor and got trampled?

Lexi held up the envelope. Her mum wanted it to be handed to Margot personally. It would be. Just not by herself. 'I need you to give Margot this letter. It's not for her friend, Meredith, it's for Margot, the lady dressed in the bright red house coat.

'The colourful lady?'

Lexi looked at her. That's just what Ray had called her. 'Do you think you can do that for me?'

'Yes, I can.' Charlie took the letter.

'Good.' She watched Charlie put the letter in her rucksack for safe keeping. 'Now, you won't forget, will you?'

Charlie shook her head. 'I won't. Cross my heart and hope to die.'

Lexi smiled at her, remembering that it was what she and her sister had always said to one another when they were young.

'Now, the other thing. You're going to have to be quite grown up for this.'

'You can trust me, Lexi.'

Lexi stared at Charlie. She got the impression that her father had asked a lot of her over the years too. She still didn't know what was going on in their lives, but she expected that Scott had had similar conversations with his daughter.

'I want you to take that tin and give it to Esme.'

'Okay.'

'She lives in a care home across the bridge in Southwold.' Lexi glanced at her rucksack. 'Have you got a pencil and paper in there?'

'What for?'

'So I can write the address down for you?' Lexi frowned. She couldn't remember the street it was in. 'Or directions – at least.'

Charlie got out her phone. 'What's the name of the care home?'

Lexi knew that. She gave her the name and watched Charlie doing something on her phone.

Charlie looked up. 'I've got the walking route. It will tell me directions as I walk there.' Charlie held up her phone.

Lexi could see the street they were in now, and the red flashing dot which was the care home, and Charlie's destination in Southwold. There were little dots marking the route on the street map, and a button to tap when she wanted to begin. 'Oh, you are so clever, Charlie.'

'Nah, it's just Google maps.'

Lexi gave her another hug. 'Did I tell you how amazing you are?' This time, Lexi noticed that Charlie wouldn't let her go. She had to prize her arms from around her waist. 'Now, are you happy with your missions?'

'Yes.' Charlie reluctantly went to open the cloakroom door.

'Wait! You can't give Margot the letter just yet.'

'Why not?'

'Can you wait a little bit?'

'You're leaving now, aren't you? And you don't want me to hand it to her until you've gone.'

'Yes.' As soon as she called for a taxi. Lexi found her phone in her handbag. She hoped one would come out, despite the weather. Thinking of which, she said to Charlie, 'The visit to Esme will have to wait until the storm has passed. Do you understand? You can't go out in this.'

'Yes, Lexi. I'm not stupid. I'd rather not get washed away in a tidal surge.'

Lexi smiled at her, relieved. 'I'm glad to hear it, Sophie.' She couldn't bear it if some happened to her all because she'd persuaded her to do something.

'Who's Sophie?'

Lexi frowned at her. 'What do you mean – who's Sophie?'

'You just said, *I'm glad to hear it, Sophie.*'

'Did I? Are you sure?'

Charlie nodded.

'How strange.' Lexi opened the door a crack and looked outside before she let Charlie go. 'Now, off you go. And remember what I said – you have to wait to give her the letter.'

Charlie stepped into the hallway. She paused outside the door and turned around. 'What shall I tell my dad?'

Lexi slowly closed the bathroom door.

'Lexi?'

She sat down on the toilet lid and burst into silent tears.

'I'm going to tell him the plan, that as soon as we've got a place, you're coming back,' Charlie whispered from behind the door.

35

Someone tried to open the cloakroom door. She heard a stranger comment, 'It's still occupied.' Lexi imagined it was someone from the houseboat community. She heard footsteps as they walked away.

She wiped her eyes dry with a tissue and flushed it down the toilet. She took a deep breath and willed herself to get it together. She had to leave.

She scrolled through her phone for the taxi company she'd used before. She phoned them. 'I'm at ...' Lexi had forgotten the name of the street. She gave the name of the pub up the road instead. She thought perhaps it was for the best that she didn't wait outside Willow Tree Cottage for the taxi.

'Can you arrange a taxi for me now. Where to? The airport. Yes, London Heathrow. Do you accept cards?' Lexi knew she'd have the taxi fare to London, even though it would probably be most of what was left in her checking account after payday.

She didn't care about that. What did worry her was what she was going to do when she got to the airport. She had nowhere to stay, and although she still had that flexi open ticket, she hadn't had time to check when the next flight was back to New York. She hoped there was one that day. It would mean she'd have to catch a night flight, as it was already teatime and she imagined it would be at least a three-hour drive to Heathrow Airport. But she didn't care about that. She didn't fancy trying to sleep on a hard plastic seat in the terminal overnight.

Lexi shook her head, thinking about how things had changed in one horrible afternoon. If it hadn't been for the weather, she'd be sitting with Charlie on the sofa in the houseboat while Scott cooked another delicious curry.

The receptionist on the phone interrupted her thoughts. 'A taxi will arrive in ten minutes.'

'Thank you.' Lexi put her phone back in her bag. She had another call to make, but she was going to do that in the back of the taxi. If there wasn't a flight that day, she imagined it would be costly to book into an airport hotel, and she just didn't have the money. Lexi had no choice but to contact her grandparents in case she couldn't reorganise her flight for that night. She wasn't too concerned. They'd sort out things out, especially when they found out she just needed a one-way ticket. Despite her promise to Charlie, Lexi knew she wasn't coming back.

As Lexi slipped out of the bathroom, she glanced down the hall and noticed that the study door was open. 'Charlie,' Lexi said under her breath. She knew it was her. Once she got something into her head, she just had to do it.

Charlie reminded her of someone, but it wasn't Lexi's sister. Lexi brushed that thought aside. She glanced through the open door. Charlie was nowhere to be seen. Lexi spotted a patio door out into the garden. Was it unlocked? Could she get out of the house that way, and circle the cottage through the gardens back around to the front gate?

She'd have to if she wanted to avoid Scott, Margot, Meredith, Ray and Alan. Lexi cast a quick glance over her shoulder and ran into the room, straight past the desk. There was an easy catch on the door that she just had to turn, and the patio door opened. Lexi whipped outside and closed it behind her. She pulled her raincoat tightly around her, put up the hood to hide her face, and ran out into the garden.

She wasn't watching where she was going and a branch hit her in the face. 'Ow!' She stopped and brushed the branch aside, only to be met by another one. Lexi frowned. She pulled her hood down and realised she was standing by a willow tree. Lexi froze when she saw the light switch on in the study, and Margot and Meredith walk in.

❖

'That's odd. The study door was open,' commented Margot. 'I'm sure I shut it.'

'Perhaps someone walked in here by mistake. There's nothing missing, is there?'

Margot looked at the desk. 'Nothing important.'

Meredith followed her gaze. She looked at the hand-painted stones and the two conkers.

'How are you going to find her?'

'I'm going to stake out the graveyard every single day until she returns. I'll take a book. There's a bench I can sit on under the chestnut tree.' Margot looked at her best friend. 'I wish—'

'I know what you wish, Margot, but nobody stole away my grandchild from me in the way that yours was stolen. I don't know how it has come about that she came back after all these years – neither of us expected that. I thought she was gone for good. But what happened to my grandchild was different. We both know that. Sophie isn't coming back. Sophie died that day and no amount of wishing can change that.'

❖

As Lexi ran from the willow tree, hoping she hadn't been spotted, she had the sensation that she'd been there before. The thought was soon relegated to the back of her mind when a police car passed her as she hurried up the street to the pub.

She could see that the taxi had arrived already. Lexi breathed the biggest sigh of relief as she opened the passenger door and got inside.

'I'll just have to drive down to the quay and turn around.'

'There's been a tidal surge, so I'm not sure if that's a good idea.'

'Don't worry. It's all over now.'

Lexi noticed the wind had died down considerably, and there were only spots of rain. As they passed the police car parked outside the gates to Margot's home, and two police officers stepped out, Lexi hunkered down in her seat. At the quayside car park, Lexi sat up. As the driver turned the car around, she saw the state of the boats. They were piled on one another, some listing, many broken beyond repair. 'How awful,' said Lexi, close to tears.

'Don't worry, love – I'm sure insurance will cover that. It's been quite a tidal surge all along the East Coast of England – worst for sixty years, apparently. Looks like you didn't choose the best time for a holiday. American, are you?'

Lexi nodded. 'Yeah.' She didn't want to get into the whole English thing right now.

As they passed Margot's house, she saw Scott running out of

the house, followed by Charlie, who was trailing behind. She'd told him. Unfortunately, he spotted her in the taxi.

Lexi turned in her seat to see him running, waving frantically at the taxi, before he slowed down to a stop. She turned around in her seat, tears rolling down her face.

'Heathrow airport – wasn't it?'

'Yes.' Lexi got her phone out to make that call.

36

Lexi looked up as Brandon handed her a cup of tea. 'Is that your grandpa again, asking when you're coming home?'

Lexi put her phone down and took the cup of tea. She turned back to the window. She was sitting on an upholstered chair, her legs tucked under her, staring out at the New York skyline. The text message she had been reading wasn't from her grandpa, it was from Charlie. Scott and Charlie had taken a room at The Harbour Inn while the houseboat was being repaired. Charlie wanted to know when she was coming back.

'I'm still surprised your grandfather organised a seat for you on a flight to New York rather than Connecticut.'

Lexi could have flown back on her flexi-ticket, but it was standard class, and there were no standard seats available for a couple of days. She hadn't had the money to stay in an airport hotel or afford the extortionate price of an upgrade to business or first class on the next flight out of Heathrow. But her grandparents had. She'd flown first class back to New York.

'I would have thought he'd want you to go straight home to Connecticut.'

'He did, Brandon, but I needed to collect my new bank cards.

I thought I told you that.' After she'd been pickpocketed in London at the start of her trip, and had cancelled her bank cards, the bank had reissued new cards and posted them to her registered home address – the apartment in New York. When she'd arrived at the apartment, Lexi hadn't expected Brandon to still be there.

The bank cards weren't the only reason she'd returned to New York. She'd told her grandfather that she wasn't ready to join the firm, and that she wanted to return to New York and find a job. Unsurprisingly, her grandparents hadn't been happy. She knew they'd have been even less happy if they'd known that Brandon was still there too.

'How's the job hunting going?'

Lexi gave him a look.

'That good, huh?'

Lexi sighed. Her heart just wasn't in it.

'Why are you bothering? You don't need one.'

Lexi turned from the window. It was raining. The rain had never bothered her in the past. Now it did. A great deal. It reminded her of England. 'Brandon, I can't sit in the apartment all day, every day. I need a job.'

'No, you don't. I can look after you now. It's about time. Now we've got what we always wanted, what you've always wanted – independence from your family. We're free. No more worry over getting your allowance. No more jobs working you into the ground. And your family can't call me a good-for-nothing so-and-so any-more.' Brandon smiled. He was relieved Lexi wasn't returning to Connecticut any time soon. She'd got England out of her system, even though he was surprised she hadn't really spoken much about her trip or shown him photos. Lexi had told him that she'd visited her father's grave, so it hadn't exactly been a vacation.

She hadn't found any English relations, so it didn't surprise him that she wasn't exactly raving about her time there. She was back on speaking terms with her grandparents. He thought it was a bit extreme, cutting her allowance off like that over a trip to England. He'd wondered what that was about. He'd asked Lexi, but she was still as much in the dark about it as he was. Apart from that, the only fly in the ointment was her sister, Andrea. Perhaps it had been her texting Lexi?

'Was that Andrea?'

Lexi glanced at her phone and shook her head. 'I thought she would have been in touch, now I'm back.'

Brandon had thought so too. 'Perhaps she expected you to return to Connecticut, and she's not happy that you've returned to New York?' *And me*, thought Brandon. But they couldn't complain about him now, could they? He imagined what her family had thought of him – sponging off his girlfriend and not getting a *proper* job. He wondered what they were thinking now everything had changed.

Brandon stared at Lexi. Unfortunately, some things hadn't. Since she'd returned a fortnight ago, they'd been sleeping in separate bedrooms. When was she going to forgive him?

'You know they're calling me the new Kurt Cobain – can you believe that?'

Lexi shifted her gaze from the raindrops running down the windowpane and looked at Brandon as he pulled up a chair and sat down opposite her.

Lexi shook her head. 'I think everyone was really surprised – shocked, even.'

Brandon knew that when she said *everyone*, she was talking about her family.

Lexi smiled. 'Not me, though. People just see a success story, don't they, but you and I know that it's taken you years of hard work and sacrifice to become an overnight success.' Lexi had cried when she had discovered that Brandon had secured a recording contract – and not only that; there were already predictions that the sales of his first album might well mean it going gold or even platinum. The sales of his first single were already going through the roof, suggesting that Brandon had a real hit on his hands.

'You were the only one who believed in my dream.'

'I believed in you, Brandon. You're my best friend – how could I not?'

'Yeah, and look how I repaid you.' He looked away, thinking of the women he'd slept with. That had stopped. It was all in the past. He'd told her that the moment she'd returned. He still couldn't believe she was back. But every time he'd broached the subject of his infidelity, hoping she'd forgive him and things would go back to the way they were, she'd changed the subject. He could tell she still didn't want to talk about it, so this time *he* changed the subject.

'When did you discover the money in your bank account?' That was another sore point, but Brandon was not going to back down on this one until she got the message. 'Do you remember?'

Lexi's smile faded. Of course she remembered. She'd been sitting in the departure lounge at Heathrow Airport, about to board her flight to New York, when it occurred to her that she'd want to buy a cup of tea and some snacks.

The taxi fare to the airport had cost a lot of money, as she'd expected it would, but she really didn't know how much money she had left in her account or whether she'd gone overdrawn already. Her grandparents had resumed her allowance – she had known they would – but the money would not be paid into her English bank account, obviously. So she'd known she would have to make do with whatever was left in the account she'd opened with the bank in Southwold. That's when she'd got the shock of her life. She'd logged into the banking app on her phone, and an account balance on her screen had flashed up that she'd thought could not be right.

Lexi had nearly gone without the tea and snacks until she'd found out she hadn't had to pay for them – they were complimentary in first class. She had sat and wondered about her account balance, thinking that there was obviously something wrong with the app. How could her account be over one hundred thousand dollars in credit?

'And that's just the tip of the iceberg,' Brandon had told her when she'd turned up at the apartment to discover he was still there, and she'd mentioned the stupid English banking app that didn't work. Except it did work, perfectly well. It matched the exact figure – give or take the wages from payday that were still in her account – that he'd deposited in there. He'd tried to persuade Andrea to hand over Lexi's English bank account details. Andrea had refused – and he knew why. She didn't trust him after the way Lexi had supported him financially over the years. Despite his reassurance that all he wanted to do was deposit money into Lexi's account, she hadn't believed him. So he'd sent off a cheque to Andrea instead.

At that point, Brandon hadn't known if she was coming back. He'd got the impression from Andrea that she was not, so he'd asked her to pay the cheque into Lexi's English bank account.

Lexi stared at him. The way his album sales were going, Brandon would probably turn out wealthier than her grandparents.

Brandon wasn't one to gloat, but Lexi could be. She imagined what her grandparents would say; they'd spent decades of hard work building up a sustainable business to pass on to their grandchildren, and all Brandon had done to make a pile of money was to write some songs. She knew they'd make it sound so easy, as though hard work hadn't gone into that too, and would intimate that what he was earning was out of all proportion.

Lexi knew that a lot of other people might think the same way too, but she didn't. Brandon had a rare gift for song-writing and music, and his music had obviously touched a lot of people. His record and download sales were testament to that.

Lexi thought that Brandon deserved every cent in recompense, but that she didn't deserve a cent of it. She knew what it was – guilt money from Brandon over his sleeping around. He said he'd put all that behind him. That was guilt talking too, now she was back.

'Brandon—'

'I know what you're going to say.' She'd told him many times, since she'd been back and discovered that he'd signed over fifty per cent of all his royalties to her, that she would not touch a cent of his money and that he had to tear up that contract. 'I didn't sign anything,' she'd said.

She hadn't had to. It was Brandon's choice what he did with his money.

'I can't take your money, Brandon. I really can't.'

'Yes, you can.' He knew she wasn't happy at all that he'd also signed over half the rights to his songs too.

'They're *your* songs. I haven't had any input into the creative—'

'That's just not true, Lexi. How would I have had the time to write all these songs if I hadn't lived in your apartment, rent-free, for all that time? And where do you think some of the lyrics came from for my songs?'

'How do you mean?'

'You, Lexi. You've been my inspiration, my muse.'

She stared at him, aware that although it was rock and roll, they were all love songs. Lexi frowned. That still didn't make her feel any better. 'Perhaps you should give the royalties to my grandparents. It was their money, after all, that really supported you. I would never have afforded this apartment without my allowance.

'Absolutely not. You supported my dream, Lexi. You never gave up on me. I wouldn't have made it if it were not for you. I mean, you even let me stay here when I—' The words caught in his throat. 'I couldn't believe you came back to me.'

Neither could Lexi. When she'd discovered Brandon was still there, and that he was intending to buy the apartment from her grandparents, she'd thought she'd just collect her new bank cards and leave. But she hadn't. She just wasn't ready to return to Connecticut and the life she knew was waiting for her.

When she'd told him the reason she'd stayed on in the apartment, he'd said, 'But don't you see? You don't need a job now. You don't need to return to Connecticut, step into their shoes and take up the reins of running their business. Let Andrea do it. You don't have to do anything that you don't want to do. You're going to be independently wealthy. That hundred grand is just a drop in the ocean, and nothing is going to change that.'

He was talking about the royalties. Lexi knew that he was still hoping she'd come back to him and resume their relationship. They'd been sharing the apartment since she'd returned from England, but sleeping in separate bedrooms. Brandon had said, 'Look, stay as long as you like, no strings.' Of course, there were – he wanted her back. But an awful lot had changed in the weeks she'd been gone. She'd just failed to tell Brandon that.

37

'I've got a lot of stuff to process right now,' she said to Brandon, avoiding the big question – would they get back together? It had been three weeks since her return to New York. She had not rekindled her relationship with Brandon, just their friendship.

Lexi sighed heavily. Scott was all she could think about. Was he okay? Why was he on the run? What would happen if whoever they were caught up with him? What would happen to Charlie?

Brandon interrupted her thoughts. 'I've been preparing to go on tour.'

'Have you?' Lexi said absently.

'I was hoping you might come along?' Brandon had been building up to asking her. The trouble was, he was leaving in a few days' time. Now, he wished he'd asked her sooner. 'We're going to be on the road, moving from city to city, but we're staying in fancy hotels. You'd enjoy it. It's an American tour, but the record label is already organising a world tour in a few months' time too.'

'I can't, Brandon.'

Somehow, he'd known she'd say that. He knew something else too – they weren't getting back together. Deep down, he'd known for some time. It wasn't that she couldn't forgive him for cheating on her; it was something else that perhaps he hadn't wanted to acknowledge. When she'd left him, their time apart had made him realise something. Perhaps she'd realised it too.

'You're going back, aren't you?'

Lexi glanced at the laptop sitting on her lap; she'd been Googling flight details to London, Heathrow.

'I've left things ... unresolved.' She could feel the colour rising in her cheeks as she avoided eye contact.

Brandon took her hand. 'How long have we known each other?'

She looked up. 'You know how long.'

He smiled. 'It was a rhetorical question. What I mean to say is, I know you. You're unhappy. You'll always be unhappy living here.'

'You don't have to move on my account.'

He smiled. 'That's not what I meant. Your heart is elsewhere.'

Lexi stared at him. How could he know? She had never mentioned Scott.

'Your heart is in England. I know that's where you belong, not here in New York, or a mansion in Bel Air.'

'You've bought a mansion in Bel Air?'

'Not yet, but it's on my wish list. It's much easier to work out there in LA. That's where the record label is based, and I'm thinking of collaborating with other artists.'

'What will you do with the apartment?'

'I'm going to keep it, Lexi. I love New York. This place ...' He glanced about him. 'It's got special memories for me.' His gaze settled on her.

'For me, too.'

'Assuming your grandfather will sell it to me. I'll offer him a very good price.'

Lexi smiled. 'I know you will. He'll sell it to you.'

'How can you be so sure?'

'He's a businessman, first and foremost. He'll sell at the right price.'

'Great, because I thought we might meet up here in New York from time to time. There's plenty of space to accommodate you and anyone you might bring with you.'

They sat staring at each other, realising that this was it. They were each other's comfort blankets; had been for years. He was, after all, her best friend, and she was his. It was something they'd realised while living together for the first time on a platonic basis. They were the best of friends. They always had been, and it should have stayed that way. But they had ended up in a relationship, when in fact they would have been far better off if they hadn't. The fact was that for the first time in her life, Lexi had fallen in love.

'He's an English guy, isn't he?'

'Who?'

Brandon cocked his head to one side. 'I know you don't want to hurt my feelings, but from the moment you returned, I knew there was something different about you. It wasn't just because you'd travelled to England. It was something more. You'd changed, you were different, and I couldn't put my finger on it, until it dawned on me what had happened. You've met someone and fallen in love.'

Lexi didn't deny it.

'Why didn't you tell me?' he said sternly. 'Best mates tell each other everything.'

'Best mates?'

'In hindsight, I think we made a lousy couple, but excellent best friends.'

Lexi leaned forward and flung her arms around Brandon. 'I couldn't tell you because I couldn't bear the thought of losing you. Since I returned, I have been wracking my brain over how I could possibly choose – you or Scott.'

'You don't have to choose. You won't lose me. And I won't lose you. I couldn't work out why this past week things have been so great between us. I bet it's been confusing the hell out of you.'

Lexi nodded her head vigorously.

'It's simple. We're best friends. We always have been. We've just complicated things by becoming a couple. We were just kids, teenagers, when we started dating, but I think we both realise now why we loved each other but were attracted to other people too. We need each other, as best friends do, but we need that other person too – y'know?'

Lexi stared at him. 'Have you been seeing Kimberley?'

'No, even though she left her husband. But I think about her all the time. All the time. At first I thought I was going crazy. I want you back in my life. I can't live without you, but …'

'You need her too.'

'Like you need the English guy, Scott.'

They sat there holding each other's hands, realising that their lives were going in very different directions, on different sides of the Atlantic. But it wasn't them breaking up, not like before; it was them cementing their friendship. 'Remember when we were little and we made a promise to each other that we would get married some day?'

'The pinkie swear?' She felt stupid about that now, embarrassed.

'Well, I know it was implied, but we didn't specify to each other.'

Lexi laughed. 'No, that's true.'

'Well, I propose another pinkie swear.'

She stared at him, feeling a little silly. All the same she held out her finger. He took it in his. 'No matter where we are, we will talk every day, on the phone, social media, whatever. I'm always here for you, Lexi – no matter what. Promise.'

Lexi smiled. 'I promise too.' Her smile faded. 'You won't do anything stupid, will you?'

'What do you mean?'

Lexi wasn't talking about the fact that he'd handed over half his royalties. 'You know, drugs and ... stuff.'

Brandon gave her reassuring smile. 'Of course not. I've got you to ground me.'

Lexi grinned. 'Yes, you have.'

'I'm going to be coming to England on tour in a few months' time. I want to meet Scott.'

Lexi frowned. 'I don't know if he'll still be there.' Although Charlie had texted that they were back on the houseboat, it didn't mean he'd still be there when she returned. She thought of that go bag and her heart sank.

'Well, he'd be stupid not to wait for you.' Brandon glanced at her laptop. 'When is your flight?'

Lexi looked down at her phone. 'I've booked it for a few days' time. I have to see my sister first ... and a guy in Detroit.'

'Detroit?'

'I'm flying there first.'

'Why?'

Lexi didn't have time to get into all that. She'd been sitting at the window, wondering how to tell Brandon that she was packed and that a taxi would be turning up soon to take her to the airport.

She'd finally plucked up the courage to check out the person who'd been a match on AncestryDNA. Lexi told him what she'd discovered when she'd visited the cemetery where her father was buried – that someone else was leaving flowers on her father's grave. 'I really thought I had an English relative, but when I joined AncestryDNA, it turns out the only hit I had was some old American guy living in a residential care home for the elderly in Detroit.'

'Oh, Lexi, I'm so sorry.'

'Yeah – I got my hopes up. But I guess it was just a good friend who left the flowers.'

'So, this old guy in Detroit, what's his name?'

'Christopher Gleason.'

'Ring any bells?'

'Not in the slightest.'

'What relation is he to you exactly?'

Lexi bit her bottom lip. 'According to the DNA, he's my great-grandfather.'

'Pardon me? What's he doing in a care home in Detroit?'

Lexi immediately guessed what he'd assumed. 'Oh, er no, he's not my maternal great-grandfather.'

Brandon frowned. 'So, you're saying he's your paternal great-grandfather?'

'Yes.'

'Oh, your father's side.' Brandon added, 'Sorry, that's stating the obvious. I'm just trying to wrap my head around this.'

Brandon wasn't the only one. 'So am I.'

'But your father was British.' Brandon paused. 'I don't get it.'

'Neither do I.'

Brandon stared at her. 'There's something you're not telling me.'

Lexi smiled at him. He knew her too well. 'Here's the thing. Andrea joined the site some time ago when she got it as a present from Chad one year. Nothing came of it. I don't know if she let her membership lapse. But anyway, she went on it again, and still nothing.'

'You mean she's not related to this guy in Detroit?'

'No. Ray, that's one of my neighbours where I was staying ...'

'Squatting.' Brandon grinned.

Lexi frowned at him. She wished she hadn't told him. He hadn't laughed when she told him about evading the police at Margot's house, but she could tell he'd been amused at the fix she'd got herself into. 'God, Lexi, if only you'd answered my texts and calls.'

If she had read his texts or answered his calls when she was away in England, she wouldn't have had all those worries over money and squatting on the houseboat. Brandon would have paid for a hotel room for her. *But then I wouldn't have found that tin with the notebook hidden inside.* She thought of Charlie and wondered how she was getting on, whether she'd made it to the care home, and what Esme's reaction would be when she saw the notebook.

'Earth to Lexi.'

She looked at Brandon. 'Sorry.'

'What were you saying about Ray?'

'Oh, yes. Well, he suggested ...' Lexi took a breath. She still couldn't believe it.

'He suggested *what*?'

'That Andrea might not be a full sibling.'

'What does *that* mean?'

'She might be my half-sister.'

Brandon stared at her, a look of incredulity on his face. 'Does

Andrea know about this?'

'No.'

Brandon leaned forward in his seat. 'Is there any chance the results could be wrong?'

'You mean about me being related to this guy, Christopher Gleason?' Lexi pursed her lips. 'I contacted Ray to check it out. He says not.' Lexi frowned. He also said something else, something he'd said before. *Think long and hard, Lexi, before you expose a family secret, and what the repercussions might be.*

'Now I'm afraid to open my letter.'

'What letter?'

'You know, the one my mother left me.'

Brandon looked surprised. 'You *still* haven't opened it?'

Lexi had planned to. She'd had far too much time on her hands since she'd arrived back in New York. Today, with the rain lashing down on the windows, and with Brandon busy working on his next album, she'd finally decided, in light of finding that guy in Detroit who was apparently her great-grandfather, that perhaps the letter would shed some light on it all. But she still couldn't bring herself to open the letter and read her mother's final words. She told Brandon how she felt. 'Crazy, isn't it?'

He leaned forward in his chair and took her hands in his. 'Not at all. She's your mum.' Brandon understood, just as Lexi did, that opening that letter and reading her final words meant coming to terms with the fact that she was really gone.

Brandon said softly, 'The letter might explain why she wanted you go to England and return the letter to that English lady – what was her name?'

'Margot.' Lexi frowned. That was the other thing. What if the letter did shed some light on that? Lexi didn't want to know, because she felt guilty for giving Charlie the responsibility that was hers.

'You didn't give Margot the letter, did you?'

Lexi hadn't told Brandon everything about her trip. 'No.'

'Was that part of the unfinished business you were talking about?'

Lexi looked at him. She guessed it was. Lexi had texted Charlie to check if she'd given Margot the letter. She hadn't had a reply to that text. *Had she forgotten? Had something happened and she'd lost the letter?*

'When is your flight to Detroit?'

Lexi checked her watch. 'In three hours. I phoned for a taxi. Sorry, I should have told you.'

'It's all right. You've got your life, and I've got mine. I understand.' He smiled. 'I could take you to the airport, Lexi. You must have seen my car on your way in.'

She thought how it would have been difficult for her to miss it. 'I don't think you should leave your red Porsche parked on the street like that. I'm sure a secure underground car parking space comes with this apartment building.'

'Yes, two actually, but they're already taken.'

'You bought three cars!'

Brandon looked at her sheepishly. 'I haven't bought them yet. They're on loan from a garage. It's free publicity for them. They took my photo with the cars. It will be hard to choose when the money rolls in. I really like all three.'

'Really, Brandon.' She chastised him. 'Perhaps I will keep hold of half your royalties, for safekeeping.'

'But there will be plenty more where that came from.'

Lexi wasn't really cross with him. She understood. Unlike her, he hadn't grown up with money. This was what she imagined people went through who won the lottery. He'd soon tire of spending money on a whim, and all the material things he could buy.

But he hadn't won the lottery. When he'd done spending money, he still had a purpose in life – his music. And it was that, not the Porsche or the fancy house in Bel Air, which would really make him happy.

His music was his happy place. It was what Lexi had been searching for all her life too; something money couldn't buy – a meaning, a purpose in her life, and friends, and a place to call home. She'd always thought she'd find that in England. She still believed that. But whether her happy place was with Scott, she had yet to find out.

Lili had texted her, asking her where she was, and reminding her that she was still holding her to that promise to go out with her, Abigail and Hannah on a girls' night out. She'd said it wouldn't be the same without her, which had brought a tear to Lexi's eye. Lili had also told her that Ray was worried about her.

He hasn't seen you since the night of the tidal surge. He spoke with Charlie at Margot's house. She told him you'd returned to the US. Please come back, Lexi. We all miss you.

Lexi had eventually let Jill know that she'd returned to America, feeling terribly guilty that she'd just dropped everything, including her job, and left Jill in the lurch. She'd told Jill she had some family issues to attend to, and that she didn't know if or when she'd be back.

Lexi hadn't expected a very nice response to her text – if any. After all, she hadn't even had the decency to phone Jill and tell her. She'd been very cowardly and had done it in a text.

To her surprise, Jill had responded immediately, telling her to take as much time as she needed, and that her position in the library was still there for her when she was ready to return.

Lexi had cried when she'd received the lovely reply from Jill, still feeling terribly guilty. She felt that she didn't deserve it. It did make her wonder why Jill assumed she would be back; she hadn't said for definite that her plan was to return.

'So, can I take you for a spin to the airport in the Porsche? Or the Mustang. Or would you prefer the Ducati?'

'The *what*?'

'Come down to the garage, and I'll show you.'

'No, thank you, Brandon.' She looked over at the door to his music room. 'I'll stick to the taxi. Besides, you've got work to do if you want to buy a Ducati – or whatever it is.'

'It's a sports car.'

Lexi had guessed that. She smiled to herself. He'd soon tire of expensive toys.

She looked at her laptop. She'd been catching up on the local news back on the East Coast of England. She glanced at the article she'd been reading before she closed down her laptop:

Anonymous Donor Saves Houseboat Community. An anonymous donor came forward to pay for the repairs of the houseboats on the quay in Walberswick that had been badly damaged in the tidal surge ...

Lexi hadn't been exactly truthful when she'd told Brandon that she wouldn't touch a cent of his money; she already had. But she hadn't expected it to make news headlines.

She slipped the laptop into the bag beside her chair. Her suitcase and coat were waiting by the door. Brandon followed her gaze. He hadn't noticed them until now. He turned to look at her. 'So, I guess this is it.'

Lexi stood up and slipped on her shoes.

'Phone me and let me know how you get on in Detroit.'

'I will.'

He hesitated.

Lexi looked at him. 'What is it?'

'If this guy really is your paternal great-grandfather, and not Andrea's, it means that your paternal grandfathers were not the same, and that means—'

'My sister and I haven't got the same father. We really are half-sisters.'

'Which means that ...' he trailed off.

'You don't have to say it.' Lexi said it, instead. 'My mum had an affair.'

'Sorry. I'm sure that scenario has played out in your head. But the question remains ...'

'Yes, what is it?'

'Is the guy buried in the cemetery your father or Andrea's?'

Lexi stared at him.

'Sorry, sorry. God. I'm an idiot.' Brandon just realised that was a scenario that had not even entered her head. 'That hasn't occurred to you – has it?'

Lexi's mouth dropped open.

'It's just that when you said the guy – Christopher Gleason – is in a care home in Detroit, it didn't make sense to me because your father was British. Unless …' He trailed off, staring at her. 'Say something, Lexi.'

'I've got to go. My taxi will be here any minute.'

'Please let me drive you.'

'No!' Lexi stalked off to the door.

'You forgot something, Lexi.' He'd caught sight of the letter from her mother on the arm of the chair.

Lexi turned around and saw what was in his hand. 'I don't want it.' Her face softened. 'Come over here.'

Lexi surprised Brandon by putting her arms around him. 'I don't want us to part on this note. Best friends always make up.'

Brandon hugged her tightly. 'Will you be okay? I can come with you.'

When they parted, Lexi shook her head. 'I need to do this on my own.'

Lexi turned for the door. She'd always thought she was a Brit – well, half-British. Now she wished she'd listened to Ray about exposing family secrets. If she had listened, then she could have continued through life in blissful ignorance. But that genie was out of the bottle, and now there was no going back.

Her one consolation was that at least no one else would get hurt by the revelation. She wouldn't have to tell Andrea about their mum; she need never know. The consequences, the repercussions of all this would stop with her and the man she was about to meet. She hoped.

As she made her way down to the waiting taxi, which would whisk her to the airport and an appointment with an old man in Detroit, she had an uneasy feeling in the pit of her stomach that when it came to family secrets, things were never, ever that simple.

38

The care assistant popped his head around the door. 'You've got a visitor.'

'Pardon? Did you just say I've got a visitor?'

'She's waiting outside.'

'She?' He got to his feet with difficulty. 'What's her name?'

'Lexi.'

He shook his head and sat back down. 'You've made a mistake. I don't know anyone by that name.'

Lexi was standing behind the door, listening. When she'd turned up at the care home, she'd discovered that they hadn't told Christopher Gleason they'd made an appointment for her to go along and meet him. It was the care assistant who had noticed a match pop up on the AncestryDNA site one day when their oldest resident had fallen asleep in his chair in front of the computer. He'd thought it would be amazing if it was all organised as a surprise.

Lexi had only found this out when she arrived.

'Is she English? I thought she was English.'

'What made you think that?'

'I don't know. Never mind. I don't want to see her.'

The care assistant, Joe, walked out and closed the door. 'I'm sorry, but he doesn't want to see you. I don't know why.'

'But I've come all this way.'

'I really don't know what's got into him. Do you know how long he's waited for this? It's been years. Decades. He was one of the first, if not *the* first person to sign up to one of those sites. I really thought he'd be incredibly happy about this. I don't know who he was looking for. I know his history. He didn't marry or have kids. Poor guy has nobody, so you can imagine my surprise, everybody's surprise, when you popped up.'

Lexi turned to go. After all that, she was beginning to wonder if there really had been a mistake on the DNA site. Lexi's spirits soared. That meant—

'Kit, she's going now. Are you sure you don't want to see her?'

Lexi came to a sudden halt. She whirled around halfway down the corridor and looked at Joe talking to Christopher through the closed door. 'Did you just say, *Kit*?'

'Yes.'

'But his name is Christopher.'

Joe said in a hushed voice, 'Yes, but he's always preferred to go by the name Kit.'

Lexi stared at him. She hurried back and stood there outside the door.

'Miss, are you all right?'

'I'm not sure.' She took a breath. 'Kit, it's Lexi.'

He didn't answer.

'I found your letter and the ring.'

She waited but there was still no response. She looked at the Joe who just shook his head and gave her an apologetic shrug.

Lexi turned to the door once more. 'I found Esme.' She

stepped back when the door opened.

'Kit, what are you doing out of your chair?' Joe rushed forward and grabbed his elbow to steady him.

'Get off me. I can walk, you know.'

'Yes, but you haven't got your sticks. You might take a tumble.' He fetched them. 'Here.'

Kit leaned on one. He peered at Lexi. He suddenly grinned. 'I knew it! Oh god, I knew it!'

Lexi stared at him. 'Knew what?'

❖

'But you promised you were coming home.'

Andrea made it sound as though Lexi had said she was returning to Connecticut for good. But Lexi hadn't made any promises to Andrea. She'd just texted to say that she was coming to see her. She hadn't mentioned the real reason she was doing a pitstop in Connecticut – she wanted to see her sister before she returned to England.

But now that pitstop in Connecticut would have to wait. 'Andrea, I can't come to Connecticut after all. There's something very important I need to do first.' She glanced at Kit, who was busy packing his suitcase. Joe had been going over the medication that he would need to take with him for the trip when Lexi's phone rang. Lexi had been surprised it was her sister; Andrea hadn't contacted her at all since she'd returned to America. She thought it might have something to do with the fact that Brandon was still in the apartment in New York.

'But I need to tell you something, Lexi.'

'It will have to wait.'

'But it can't. Where are you?'

Lexi hesitated. 'I'm in Detroit.'

'Detroit? What are you doing there? Are you with Brandon? Has he got a concert there?'

Lexi glanced at Kit, who was folding some shirts and placing them in his suitcase. 'Look, I'm flying back to England in a few days.'

'You're returning to England – already?' The way Andrea spoke made it sound as though she already knew that it was inevitable her sister would return.

'Yes.'

Andrea fell silent for a moment. What she said next stunned Lexi. 'I'm coming with you.'

'What?'

'I'll get an internal flight and ... and meet you in Detroit. We can catch the flight to England together.'

Lexi glanced at Kit. She didn't think that was a good idea.

'Please, Lexi. This is important. I want to come.'

Lexi stared into space, wondering why. Was there any way Andrea could have found out about the results that had been thrown up by the AncestryDNA site? About Kit and the fact that they were half-sisters? About their mum?

Lexi shook her head. Brandon wouldn't have told her. That couldn't be it, so it had to be something else. 'Is everything okay with Chad?'

'Yes, of course. Why do you ask?'

'No reason.'

'Please, Lexi. I really want to come.'

Lexi sighed heavily. She couldn't fly to Connecticut and collect her sister, not with Kit in tow. 'All right, but can you catch a flight in time?' *And will there be seats left on the flight to London?* Lexi thought it was a bit extreme to travel across the country and join her on an international flight to England just to tell her something.

'I'm online now. There's a redeye to Detroit. No, wait, that's next week. *Damn*!'

'What's going on, Andrea?'

'I can't tell you over the phone.'

Lexi glanced at Kit. Should she tell Andrea her news? But if she were to tell her the truth, she didn't want to do it over the phone either.

'When exactly are you flying to England?'

Lexi heaved a sigh. She had no choice but to tell her. 'Tomorrow.'

'Tomorrow?' Andrea went quiet for a moment. Lexi thought she heard her tapping on a laptop in the background. She heard her sister say, 'Right, I've found an international flight to London on Friday out of Bradley International Airport. What time does your flight land at Heathrow, Lexi?'

Lexi reluctantly gave her the flight details.

'Great. I'll be there three hours ahead of you. I'll wait for you. Can we meet in the arrivals lounge? Will you text me when you land? God, I'll need to book accommodation. Have you got accommodation?'

Lexi's head was spinning with all the questions. 'Don't worry about that, Andrea. I'm staying at The Harbour Inn – it's a pub on the East Coast of England. It's a twin room, so if there's no other vacancies, you can stay with me.' Lexi didn't mention that she'd booked two rooms, nor the reason she'd booked another room. Lexi couldn't believe she was on the phone arranging for her sister to come too. She glanced at Kit. Under the circumstances, Andrea was the last person she wanted on this trip.

'Right, I think we're all set,' said Joe, packing the medication in the case as Lexi put her phone back in her bag. 'Are you sure you're up for this trip, Kit?'

Lexi looked up. She caught the concern on Joe's face as he asked that question. Over the last few days in Detroit, while she was putting plans in place to return to England with Kit, she'd got to know Kit and what he had done with his life after the war.

She had also got to know a little about his care assistant too, and the reason that of all the residents in the care facility, Joe had formed an attachment to Kit in particular. It was because of people like Kit that Joe hadn't turned to drugs or become homeless. He had a job and was training to be a nurse. Joe had taken her to one side and said he owed his life to Kit and all the other veterans like him who had worked tirelessly all their working lives so that subsequent former veterans like himself had access to support when they left the military.

Lexi discovered that after the war, Kit had dedicated his life to the US army and its personnel. Lexi was surprised to hear that Kit was a veteran. She'd assumed from what she'd read in Esme's diary that, as a deserter, he'd been taken back to America and tried in military court, and that he had served time in prison. She didn't know anything about the ins and outs of what happened to deserters when they were caught.

It turned out that Kit had been convicted and was about to receive a dishonourable discharge and be imprisoned for a year. It was Joe who had told her all this. But the court-martial process allowed for his commander to have the final say regarding whether his conviction and sentence stood, or whether it was commuted; he had the authority to reduce the punishment or overturn the conviction completely.

Kit had asked for clemency, which he was allowed to do, in the form of a clemency petition. In view of his age – or rather his having been underage when he joined, and the subsequent situations he'd found himself in after deserting, where his age and naivety had been taken advantage of – Kit had expressed remorse, regret, and the strong desire to prove to himself and to the military that he was worthy of wearing the uniform and serving his country.

Lexi was so thankful that Joe had told her what Kit had confided in him. Seeing the proud and slightly obstinate man sitting before her, she couldn't imagine he would have opened up and told her all this – not straight away; not until they had got to know one another better.

Kit had returned to the military, where he'd served around the world for twenty years before leaving and taking advantage of the United States' GI Bill, whereby he could enrol for a college degree.

He'd eventually joined the US Department of Veteran Affairs, which provided educational benefits to US military veterans, along with many other benefits – from compensation, pensions, health care, and home loans, to practical help with rehabilitation, finding employment and even help with burial and funeral expenses.

Joe also told her that Kit had volunteered in his spare time for the Veterans Crisis Line and another organisation – a charity set up to support those serving in the military as well as their families, and which assisted them in all sorts of ways. It was through these organisations, and people like Kit, that Joe – who had loved his life in the military but had been pensioned out of the army after an injury – found the support to move on and start studying for a college degree, as well as finding work. Joe had started volunteering himself, as Kit had done, in order to help others in similar situations to find their feet in life 'on the outside,' as Joe called it.

'It can be a lonely place out there once you return to civilian life,' Joe had said. 'You can feel quite lost, very alone. People like Kit, and the organisations he's worked for and volunteered in, literally save lives.'

Lexi stared at Joe, thinking back to those conversations she'd had over the last couple of days. She was so, so proud of the great-grandfather that she was so lucky to have the privilege to meet, and to get to know, and the amazing way he'd turned his life around after the war.

39

'Stop fussing, Joe. The doctor said I'm as fit as a fiddle. I'm just suffering from one ailment that won't go away.'

'And what's that?' asked Joe.

Kit rolled his eyes. 'Old age – what do you think all those pills are for?'

Lexi smiled. He'd been checked over by a doctor before she'd booked their flight, who had made sure he was as fit as he could be, considering his age, to make the journey.

Lexi had suggested she could get in touch with the care home in Southwold and he could have a Skype call with Esme, but he insisted he wanted to see her in person and surprise her. Lexi understood. Despite the enormous passage of time, he was still in love with her. Even if he died trying, he insisted that he wanted to make the journey, just to see her, hold her hand, and tell her how much he loved her and had missed her.

Lexi had cried on hearing that – and the other thing he'd told her. Kit had said that he had been convinced that Esme had been pregnant when he'd left England. Esme hadn't told him. But it was the reason he had joined AncestryDNA as soon as it had launched a DNA test in the US in 2012, hoping that one day he might find out whether what he had suspected was true – there was a child out there somewhere, his child, and he wanted to find them.

Lexi wondered if that was the reason he had continued in one of his voluntary support roles, even now, in his nineties. It was something close to his heart. Joe told her how he often found Kit had fallen asleep in front of his laptop, still trying to find people.

He had helped scores of ex-servicemen over the years, most of whom had served in Vietnam, find the women they had fallen in love with. In a lot of cases they'd had children they would never have known otherwise – children who would have grown up without knowing their fathers if it hadn't been for Kit.

But Joe told her the sad part was that Kit had never found his. He was aware that Kit always hoped that he would find a match before he died. Sometimes, Joe said he'd wondered if it was wishful thinking on Kit's part, the idea that the woman he loved had had his child. Until that is, the most amazing thing had happened – Lexi had appeared.

Lexi smiled at Kit as she remembered what he'd said that first day they'd met. Although he couldn't explain it, he'd just known as soon as he looked at her that she was his descendant – his great-great-grandchild, as it happened.

Kit took her hand. 'I've been looking for you for a long time,' said Kit. 'You said that you found my letter and the ring that I'd left for Esme, so you know my story.'

Lexi thought back to when she and Charlie had discovered the tin, together with the unopened letter that they suspected Esme had not discovered beneath her notebook. The letter told of what would take place that terrible night, what Kit had planned. But he hadn't planned to betray Esme and her friends. Quite the opposite. Lexi stared at Kit and thought of his incredible story, and the price he had paid to protect Esme and her friends.

Lexi had read his story in the notebook, and his letter, but she still wanted to listen to her great-grandfather tell his story.

I'm ashamed to say that after I joined up and we landed in France, I ... I deserted. It was a cowardly thing to do.'

'You were only seventeen.'

'I thought going to war would be an adventure.'

Lexi imagined there were many young men who had relished the opportunity to join up and leave their mundane lives behind, with no idea of the hell that awaited them.

'I was so young and naïve. I fell in with these men, older than me, who were American deserters in Paris. They called us deserter gangsters. We pillaged to survive. But sometimes they did things ...' He shook his head. 'They were a bad bunch. I wanted to get as far away from them as I could, so I stowed away on a boat from France. I thought one of them was my friend, and I'd confided in him my plan to leave France for England. He came too, organised it all. I had no idea that I hadn't escaped them. Little did I know that it was all part of their plan.'

'Their plan?'

Kit nodded. 'I discovered that our destination once we came ashore in England, in the dead of night, was the Inland Waterways. I'd never heard of the English canals. I didn't end up on Esme's boat by accident. It was all part of their master plan to rob the Bank of England. I didn't know it at the time when I boarded the boat for England that I was being set up.'

Kit heaved a sigh. 'Once we got ashore and travelled to the canal, that's when I realised how naïve I'd been. They weren't going to let me go. They made me board that boat. I don't know where their intelligence came from, but they'd discovered gold from the

Bank of England would be transported along the canal, passing the very canal boat that I would be stowed away on. It was my job to hide in *The Butty*, the boat they were pulling along, and throw the cargo overboard so there would be room for the gold.'

'But there was a complication,' said Lexi.

'Yes. They'd had people staking out the canal, and there were always two crew – women. They hadn't factored in a third crew member who was sleeping in *The Butty*.

'Esme.'

'I was just as shocked as she was to discover someone else there that night.'

Lexi knew the rest of the story. They'd fallen in love, but all the plans they'd made to be together after the war were not to be.

'I didn't hear from the gang for weeks. I thought that was it; they'd abandoned their plans to rob the Bank of England as fool-hardy and would just leave me be. They'd told me the meeting point, but after weeks of not reaching it, I thought they'd put me on the wrong boat, going in a different direction, and that was that.'

Kit slowly shook his head. 'Then one day, I found out from Esme our next destination, and my blood ran cold. That was the meeting point along the canal. They'd be there. They knew when the boat with the gold would pass by. They wouldn't tell me the rest of the plan. They'd kept that to themselves. But I had a jolly good guess. Once I'd off-loaded the cargo when the girls were asleep, and the boat reached the rendezvous point along the canal, they'd take the boat. They needed the girls out of the way.'

'You mean they were going to—'

'Murder them, most likely. I had to do something.'

Lexi had read his letter. 'So, you contacted the police.'

'I did. There was a payphone in one of the villages. I called the police and told them the whole plan, and the rendezvous point. By the time we arrived, the police had rounded them all up. And then they took me.'

'Why didn't you tell Esme what was going on? Why didn't you escape when you had the chance?'

'I had to be sure the police would be there. I had to stay on the boat. I wanted to protect Esme and her friends in case something went wrong. I was afraid they might get hurt. If I'd told her ...'

'She would have made you leave, escape.'

'Yes. When we arrived, it all happened so fast. The police came onboard to arrest me. I didn't have a chance to tell her. I knew that would happen. So when she was fast asleep the night before, I found her notebook in the biscuit tin, and I wrote her a letter and gave her the ring I'd worn – my mother's engagement ring she'd given me for luck before I went to France. I tucked the letter under her notebook.'

He closed his eyes. 'I'll remember her scream to my dying day when she thought I didn't really love her, that I'd used her, betrayed her.'

Lexi sat there staring at Kit as he shook his head from side to side. 'I was taken by the American Military Police to jail. When I was eventually released, I returned to England – it was some time after the war – and made my way back to the Inland Waterways, searching for her.'

Lexi felt so sad that he hadn't been able to find her.

'I eventually found one of the girls – one of Esme's friends who had been part of the crew on that boat. I ran into her in a pub and begged her to tell me where Esme was. But she would not. She told me I'd broken Esme's heart.'

Lexi didn't know how to tell him that Esme had never read his letter or found the ring. If only she had, she wouldn't have gone through life not knowing the truth of what had really happened that night. So far, Kit hadn't asked the question – how had Lexi come by the letter?

Lexi thought of Charlie and wondered if she had delivered the tin with the notebook and that letter inside. Was Esme reading it right now?

40

'Good morning.' Margot greeted the care assistant at reception as she walked by. She was not looking forward to telling her mother that her boat had sunk, and with it she'd lost the notebook forever. She'd been putting off telling her on her last visits, stalling until she plucked up the courage to tell her what had happened on the night of the tidal surge.

Margot had woken up that morning feeling terrible that she'd fobbed off her mother yet again the previous Tuesday when she'd asked where her notebook was. Although it was Saturday, and it might surprise Esme when she turned up twice in the space of a few days, Margot knew she couldn't put it off any longer; the next day, it would be four weeks since it happened.

Esme obviously hadn't seen it on the news or read about it in the newspaper. Margot wasn't surprised. Esme spent most days either reading novels or staring out of the window. Margot knew she had to break the news that her boat was gone, and with it her notebook.

'Excuse me.'

Margot glanced over her shoulder and caught the young woman on reception beckoning her over. Margot backtracked to the reception desk. 'I'm here to see my mother.' She didn't think she needed to tell her that. She'd seen the care assistant before. They all knew she visited her mother more or less every Tuesday, although for once she'd deviated from her normal routine. She was the only visitor Esme had.

'Your mother is with someone at the moment.'

'Oh, god. Is it the doctor? Is she okay?'

'She's fine. She's just got a visitor.'

Margot looked astonished. 'Someone else came to see my mother?'

'Yes.'

'Who?'

'She said her name was Charlotte.'

'Charlotte?' Margot shook her head. 'Never heard of her. What does the woman look like?'

'Well, er … it's not a woman.'

Margot peered at her. 'What do you mean?'

'It's a child. I guess she's around ten.'

'Ten? Wasn't she with an adult?'

'No – just her.'

'What did she want?'

'She wanted to visit Esme.'

Margot looked at her.

The young woman shrugged. 'I didn't ask why.' She added, 'I just thought you should know.'

'Okay, thank you.' Margot hesitated. Should she wait? Perhaps it was a child from the Brownies, visiting people in the community to earn one of her badges. She glanced around reception. There were no other children there. And the girl clearly wasn't with an adult.

Margot set off for her mother's room.

'Mum?' Margot opened the door and saw her sitting in the chair by the window. A slim girl, around ten years old and wearing jeans and a t-shirt, stood by the window.

Margot stepped into the room, eyeing the child. 'Who are you?'

'I'm Charlotte – Charlie.'

'What are you doing here?' Margot asked. She saw her mother glance over her shoulder, tears rolling down her cheeks.

Margot rushed forward. 'What happened?'

'It's not my fault,' Charlie said quickly. 'I didn't make her cry. It's the letter.'

Margot looked at Charlie. 'What letter?'

'The one from Kit.'

❖

Margot carefully folded the letter and slipped it between the pages before slowly closing the notebook – the one she had thought was lost. Now she knew everything about her parents – how they'd met, and how they'd parted, never to see one another again. She sat looking at the ring in her hand that had belonged to her father. 'He never knew about me, did he?'

Esme slowly shook her head. She sat in silence, staring out of the window. She hadn't said a word.

Margot wasn't surprised. How devasting to discover that for so many years she'd been broken-hearted because she'd believed that Kit hadn't loved her, when nothing could have been further from the truth. How different their lives might have been if only she'd known; how different *she* would have been.

Margot shifted her gaze from her mother to Charlie, who was sitting by the bed. She had an old rusty biscuit tin on her lap and was busy doing something on her mobile phone. Margot studied her. She was sure she'd seen her somewhere before.

Margot held up the notebook. 'How did you come by this?' She was dying to know, but she'd wanted to read the notebook first.

Charlie looked up.

'And how did you know to bring it here, to my mother?'

Charlie stared at Margot. She suddenly stood up and slipped the phone in her pocket. 'I have to go.'

Margot watched her pick up her backpack and put her arms through the straps, slipping it on her back. That's when it came to her. 'I *do* recognise you. You were at my house with the other people who had been evacuated from the houseboats on the quay.'

Charlie started walking to the door.

'You found this on the houseboat – didn't you? On *my* houseboat.' Margot stared at her intently. Even if Charlie was about to deny it, Margot knew it was true; Charlie's expression had betrayed her.

'Is that where you've been living?'

Charlie shook her head vehemently. 'Me and my dad were living in the houseboat next door.'

'You and your dad? Is he the one who found this?'

Charlie shook her head again. This time she avoided eye contact.

Margot had a peculiar thought. 'You're protecting someone, aren't you?'

Charlie put her hand on the door handle. 'I have to go now.'

'Wait! Who was that woman who came with you to my house? Was that your mum?'

Charlie frowned. 'No.'

Margot thought not. She guessed it was the woman who had been squatting in Esme's houseboat – and Charlie knew. And that woman had found her mother's notebook and had sent Charlie there to give it back. But how had she discovered that Esme was living in this care home? She must have met Esme. Had she been there, in this room, with her mum? Was it someone who worked there? If so, why hadn't they given it back sooner?

She looked at Charlie. 'Did the lady who gave you this notebook work here?'

Charlie shook her head.

'How long have you had the notebook?'

Charlie looked at her sheepishly. 'That day all the boats were wrecked by that big wave, my friend told me to give the notebook to Esme.'

'You mean the tidal surge.' Margot couldn't believe she'd had the notebook all this time. 'That was four weeks ago. Why on earth didn't you give it to her sooner?'

'My dad doesn't know I'm here. He's getting things ready to move back onto the houseboat that's been repaired. I said I'd stay in the hotel room this morning while he went shopping for groceries.'

Margot nodded her head. She got the picture. That was why Charlie was here on her own without an adult. But it didn't answer Margot's question about how the lady who was squatting on the houseboat had found Esme.

Charlie said, 'Why did you take my stone?'

Margot turned around. Charlie was still standing in the doorway.

'I'm sorry – what?'

'I saw it on the desk in your study. You took my stone, and

hers too. You *stole* them from the graveyard where we left them.'

Margot turned from the window to look at Charlie.

'She asked me to give you a letter, but I don't like you. I don't like people who steal stuff.'

Margot stared at her. She took a tentative step forward. 'Please can you tell me your friend's name? I didn't mean to take it.'

'That's a lie. You should have left it there. I felt bad for Lexi so I gave her my stone that was meant for my dad – and you took that too!' Charlie's bottom lip quivered. 'Why did you do that?'

'Lexi – is that the name of your friend?'

Charlie nodded.

'Oh, Charlie. I took it because I thought my granddaughter had come back. I thought it was hers, and I ... I just needed to have something real, tangible, so I took it home because I needed to know that I wasn't imagining things. That's my son's grave, you see. And I thought my granddaughter had returned. I haven't seen her in so long, since she was a very little girl, younger than you.'

'How come?'

Margot walked over and sat down on the end of the bed. She was going to say, *it's complicated*, which it was. 'There was an accident on the quay ...'

'What sort of accident?'

'Someone drowned, Charlie. It was all my fault, you see. I made a terrible decision.'

41

Margot stared at Charlie. She wished she hadn't mentioned the accident. She would never forget that day. How could she have foreseen that such a wonderful day would end in tragedy? It had started like any other day, with the two girls running up to her attic, where she had a trunk full of old clothes. How they had loved to dress up.

She'd woken up to another beautiful summer day. She'd been able to hear the girls running around the attic upstairs, their childish giggles and laughter reverberating around the house. On the spur of the moment, Margot had decided to take a rare day off from writing and take the girls to Thorpeness instead. She'd planned to do something she'd never done before – take them out on the boating lake.

It was the girls who had given her the idea. They'd come running into her study, with Meredith hot on their heels, but not quick enough to catch them before they burst in, waving plastic cutlass swords they'd found amongst decades of bric-a-brac in the attic. Margot had remembered those old swords, and the eye patch one of the girls had been wearing. They'd found old costumes she and Meredith had once dressed up in, and toys they'd played with when they'd been young children living in the house.

'No, stop. Girls, Margot is working!' Margot remembered Meredith's look of horror at the girls bursting into the study and disturbing her work, running in circles around her desk, chasing each other.

Margot had looked at the two girls – dressed as pirates with their bandanas wrapped around their heads, wearing their eye-patches and waving their plastic cutlass swords – and had immediately got up from her desk and pretended to sword-fight with them.

'Come on, Meredith,' she'd said, dragging her into the study. 'We need to fight off these pirates before they capture our ship and take all our booty!'

Margot sighed as she recalled her decision to take the girls to Thorpeness to play pirates on the lake. Meredith had whipped up a delicious packed lunch for them so they could have a picnic lunch on the beach after their adventure on the high seas, visiting the islands to see if they could find treasure.

She'd tried to persuade Meredith to drop everything and join them, but she wouldn't; she'd said she still had chores to do and shopping to get in the town. In fact, she'd been rather pleased that the girls were being taken out and weren't under her feet all day.

If only she had come with us, thought Margot, *then perhaps it wouldn't never have happened.* But she would never blame Meredith. She had only herself to blame.

On their return, rather than going straight back to the house, Margot had parked the car on the quay. She couldn't even remember the reason she thought she needed to go to the houseboat there and then. She vaguely recalled there was something she wanted to pick up. *Why, oh why, didn't I just drop the girls home to Willow*

Tree Cottage and then go by myself? It was a question that had played over and over in her mind during all the years since.

Of course she knew the answer – it was simply that it had been more convenient just to park on the quay and pop there first. It would have saved all of ten minutes, if that, but the repercussions of that fateful decision would last a lifetime.

Margot stared at Charlie. There were a multitude of *what ifs* about that afternoon. What if she'd insisted they wait in the car? But of course, they had refused. They had wanted to go too. Margot never took them to the houseboat on the quay. There was never any need. They had all they wanted – a big garden to play in, toys, dressing up clothes – all back at Willow Tree Cottage.

But Margot had seen no harm in taking them with her, and no harm in letting the girls run ahead, waving their cutlasses, and continuing their game of pirates on the houseboat for a few minutes. How could Margot foresee the tragedy about to unfold as the girls continued their game of pirates on the houseboat?

Sophie, who had always been the more outgoing and fearless of the two of them, had climbed up on the lip of the boat, balancing precariously with her sword as she pretended to walk the plank.

Margot had listened to the children's laughter as she'd walked along the path towards the houseboat, smiling to herself, so happy that she had decided on a whim to take the day off and just spend it with her grandchild and Meredith's granddaughter, Sophie.

That was when she'd heard a splash, and a scream. Running towards the boat, she had seen her granddaughter leaning over the side, her hand reaching out, screaming, 'Sophie!'

As Margot had run along the path, she'd seen that her neighbour, Alan, had got to the houseboat first. He'd dived into the water and pulled Sophie out. But it had been too late. She had gone.

Margot's thoughts turned to that unfinished manuscript that had languished in her desk drawer for the past twenty years. Every summer, she'd returned to Willow Cottage, unable to bear the thought of staying on the houseboat in the summer months; at the time of year when the tragedy had happened. Meredith had done her best to encourage her to finish the story. Margot often tried, but she could not. She knew she could never write again.

What if it had rained and they hadn't gone to Thorpeness on that fateful day? Or whatever it was she thought she desperately needed on the houseboat – why hadn't she left it and fetched it another time? All sorts of scenarios that didn't end in losing two girls that day – one to the water, and the other ...

'Who drowned?' asked Charlie.

Margot turned to look at Charlie. 'My best friend's granddaughter.

'I wish I'd never taken the girls out that day – then it wouldn't have ended in tragedy. But I wanted to spend time with my granddaughter. She was not going through a good time.'

'How come?'

'I'm afraid she found out that her parents were getting a divorce.'

Charlie was still standing by the door. Her hand dropped from the doorknob. 'My mum and dad split up.'

'I'm sorry to hear that.'

'Yeah, well, these things happen.'

Margot looked at her. That sounded like something her dad had probably said. Margot sighed. Alexandra had found out about the plan to split up her and her sister.

Alexandra shouldn't have been at the top of the stairs listening that morning. Margot's son and daughter-in-law had brought the children to stay with her in Walberswick that summer, trying to patch up their marriage after her son had discovered his wife's infidelity, which had taken place three years earlier. Their marriage wasn't working, so they had decided to go their separate ways – her son would take his child, and bring her up in England, and her daughter-in-law would take Andrea and return to her parents to bring her up in America. Margot hadn't been happy about the plan either. All sorts of arrangements had been made to fly back and forth between England and American during the holidays so the sisters could see each other. But they had all known, Margot included, that it probably wasn't going to happen nearly as frequently as they imagined, if at all.

Then it had happened. Out of the blue, her son had had a heart attack. Margot had put it down to the stress of discovering that his wife had had a one-night stand, and that his youngest child wasn't his.

It could have been that or simply, as the doctor had said, an unfortunate hereditary heart condition. Margot thought of her husband. He'd also died young of a heart condition. But whatever the reason, it wasn't going to change the fact that her son was gone, and with him had gone all the plans they had made for Alexandra to remain in England, living with her dad and her grandmother, Margot, in the big sprawling Willow Tree Cottage in Walberswick.

Despite her heartbreak at losing her son, and the fact that deep down she'd blamed her daughter-in-law, Margot had invited her to stay and live with her, and bring up the girls in her house.
Unfortunately, her daughter-in-law had refused. She had wanted to return to America, and take the girls with her. Margot had known that the children's maternal grandparents were rich, and she

had suspected they'd given an ultimatum; she'd heard her daughter-in-law on the phone one night saying, 'You know that I can't afford to be cut off.'

When Alexandra had found out she was leaving for America, Margot had tried to reason with her that she had her mum and her sister, but she'd screamed, 'I want my dad – and I want you!'

'You can visit,' Margot had said. 'You can spend the entire summer here with me and Sophie.' Meredith had often taken Sophie with her when she was working at Willow Tree Cottage, especially during the school holidays while her daughter and son-in-law were working. Alexandra had been having such fun playing with Sophie that day. But those future visits were never to take place.

Although Sophie had been pulled from the water quickly, no amount of CPR had been able to empty her lungs of water. Margot knew she would never forget Alexandra sitting on the houseboat, hugging her knees, rocking back and forward, saying over and over, 'It was all my fault.'

Charlie frowned. 'Why was it her fault? Did she push her?'

'Oh, no, nothing like that – but she blamed herself for Sophie's death. She said it was her idea, the walk-the-plank game, and that she told Sophie to go first.'

Margot had tried to convince her that she mustn't think that. It had just been a game – a silly game that lots of children played. 'It wasn't her fault it went so very badly wrong; it was my fault for letting them run ahead, for allowing them on the houseboat unsupervised, for not dropping them home first.'

Margot took a breath, remembering something else she would never forget. The next morning, Alexandra had woken up and asked when Sophie was coming round to play.

At first they all thought it was a cruel joke, although Margot couldn't imagine her sweet-natured granddaughter would behave that way. But then it had dawned on Margot, Meredith and Alexandra's mother that it wasn't a joke – not at all.

To protect herself from what had happened, her granddaughter had built a subconscious wall around the memory and shut it away in the dark recesses of her mind. It was then that Margot realised that she'd lost not only her son, but her only grandchild. The plan to have her come over to spend the summers in England at Willow Tree Cottage, along with Andrea, who would always be welcome, could never be, lest she remembered what had happened that day.

Everyone had agreed that a young child shouldn't live with the guilt of believing it was her fault that her best friend had died. One life had been lost, but why ruin another? It had been decided that she needed a fresh start, otherwise one day she would wake up and remember. Knowing Alexandra, Margot knew she would never forgive herself, even though there was absolutely nothing to forgive. Children will be children, and as Meredith had said all along, it had just been a terrible accident.

Of course, it was always a possibility that wherever she was, one day the memory would resurface. But she had only been six. Why would it? Unless she went back there. But she never would.

Margot wondered why she'd ever agreed to cut off all contact. It seemed, in hindsight, extreme. She knew why she had done it – she would have done anything to protect her granddaughter. But over the years it had crossed her mind that perhaps Alexandra's mother wasn't protecting her eldest child, but was protecting herself from something neither of her children knew about – the affair.

Losing her grandchild broke Margot's heart, but it was what had been agreed: Margot must never look for her. But that didn't mean she'd ever stopped wishing that one day Alexandra would walk back into her life.

She had thought for a split second that the day she'd always dreamed of had come – but the young woman who'd left that stone wasn't Alexandra. Whoever she was, she had clearly made a mistake when she was at the graveyard.

Margot smiled at Charlie. 'I want you to tell your friend that all is forgiven.'

Charlie frowned at her.

'I think we both know that your friend was squatting on my houseboat.'

Charlie bit her bottom lip.

'What I'm saying is that I won't press charges. She's not in any trouble.'

'It wasn't her fault, you know. She lost all her money. Someone stole it, so she had nowhere to live.'

'I see.' Margot didn't believe that for a second. She looked at Charlie, feeling so sorry that a grown woman could lie like that to an innocent child. What was the world coming too? She decided not to mention the fact that her locks had been changed.

'What about your lock? She won't get into trouble about that – will she?'

Margot raised an eyebrow. So, Charlie did know about the lock.

'She didn't mean to break your lock. Ray did it.'

'Ray? My neighbour – Ray?'

'Yes. Lexi lost the key, so he tried to pick the lock and well, he wasn't very good at it. It broke.'

Margot raised her eyebrows. 'He picked my lock?'

'Yes, and broke it, like I said.'

'I see.'

'So Alan, that's our other neighbour, he came and fixed it.'

'Did he now?'

'Yes.'

Margot raised her eyebrows. *Just who is this Lexi character who has my neighbours running around after her, aiding and abetting her squatting in my houseboat?* thought Meredith. She knew it was unintentional, helping out the squatter. She imagined that, just as she'd done with Charlie, this Lexi must have spun them a yarn so that they believed she was living their legitimately. It made her wonder what they'd say when they found out.

'She only came here to give you the letter.'

'I'm sorry – what?' Margot remembered Charlie had mentioned a letter. She'd momentarily forgotten about that. 'What are you talking about?'

Charlie walked over, took a seat on the end of the bed, and slipped the bag off her back. She thumbed through the bag and brought out a white envelope with Margot's name on the front.

Margot looked at the envelope. 'What's this?'

'The letter Lexi asked me to give to you.'

'But I don't know your friend.'

'It's not from Lexi, it's from her mum. That's what she told me.'

'Okay,' said Margot slowly. She had no idea why a stranger's mum had written her a letter. Maybe she'd been a fan of her books way back when.

'So, Lexi won't go to prison when she comes back?'

'No.'

Charlie got out her phone.

'What are you doing?'

'I'm texting her to let her know. She promised she'd come back when me and my dad had somewhere to live. We're moving back into the houseboat today. I texted her and let her know.' Charlie frowned. 'She hasn't texted me back. I really want her to come back. My dad likes her a lot and so do I. She's got to come back.'

'Come back? Where is she?'

'She's in America.'

'America?'

'Yes.'

Margot looked at the letter in her hand, and swallowed. She said to herself, 'But I don't know anyone called Lexi.'

Charlie stood up and shrugged. 'She's like me, you know.'

Margot looked up at Charlie. 'How so?'

'Our names. My name is Charlotte, but I prefer Charlie.'

Margot shook her head. 'Sorry, but I still don't understand.'

'Oh, right. Well Lexi's real name is Alexandra, but she prefers—'

Margot shot out of her chair.

'—Lexi.'

42

When Lexi arrived at Heathrow with Kit after a night flight leaving on Friday, she really hoped Andrea had missed her flight. But it was not to be. As soon as the plane landed mid-morning on Saturday, Lexi got a text. Andrea was already waiting for her in the arrivals hall.

She introduced her sister to Kit. It was a bit awkward not to. But the introductions only extended as far as their names.

'Kit, this is my sister. Andrea, this is Kit.'

The look on her sister's face was priceless. In any other circumstances, Lexi would have found it funny. Andrea had not expected her sister to turn up in the arrivals hall so quickly, on a buggy driven by one of the airport staff; for someone Kit's age, priority boarding, priority *everything*, was the name of the game. That was why it had taken several days back in Detroit to make all the arrangements. It hadn't just been a matter of booking the next available flight – not with someone Kit's age. But it had given Lexi more time to spend with Kit and get to know him a little better.

However, it wasn't Lexi's mode of transport, getting her to the arrivals hall in double-quick time, that had Andrea standing there open-mouthed when she arrived, but the very old guy who was with her. Lexi had had no choice but to tell Kit she had a sister, and the ramifications if Andrea were to discover just who Kit was.

On the plane, Kit had been sworn to secrecy, although he had said, 'Oh dear – I'm the proverbial skeleton in the closet, aren't I?' He had smiled at that point, diffusing a very awkward conversation, although they both knew it was true. 'Don't you worry, Lexi – I will keep my mouth firmly buttoned up,' he'd said before drifting off to sleep for most of the flight.

The trouble with Andrea, though, was that she never let things go until she'd got to the bottom of whatever it was that was bugging her. She'd been like that since she was little – it was just the way she was. Lexi could have done without it just then.

Lexi sat in the back of the taxi with her sister. Kit was up front in the passenger seat, next to the driver.

'Who *is* he?' Andrea whispered as the car set off from the airport.

Lexi whispered back, 'I told you, I'll explain everything – I promise.' Lexi frowned. Would she explain everything? She already knew that she'd made a promise she couldn't keep. She was stalling.

'Why can't you just tell me? You obviously know each other.'

Lexi rolled her eyes at Andrea's insistent questions, her hot breath in her ear as she whispered in the back of the car, 'What's the big secret, Lexi?'

Lexi could have sworn that Kit heard that because he turned his head.

Lex whispered back, 'Look, Andrea, just give it a break, will you? I've hardly slept on the flight over, and I've got a lot on my mind right now.'

'Yeah, well, you're not the only one.'

Lexi gave her sister a sideways glance. She watched her fold her arms and turn her head to stare out of the window. *What is she doing here?* Lexi wondered. She hadn't bugged Andrea about that because as she'd just told her sister, she had enough on her plate.

Lexi glanced at her phone. Andrea wasn't the only one who'd sent her a text. Charlie had sent her one too. She got out her phone and re-read it. They were moving back into the houseboat that day – the one they had no clue that Lexi had paid for, along with the repairs of all the other houseboats on the quay. All bar one, the one that had been wrecked beyond repair – the very one she had squatted on.

She was surprised by how it had affected her, knowing that the little boat was gone. Her only consolation was that Charlie had the tin with the notebook, and Kit's letter and ring.

Charlie had texted to tell her that she'd delivered it to Esme. And Margot had been there.

Margot.

Charlie also told her that she'd given Margot the letter from her mother. And not only that, but Margot had found out that she'd squatted in her houseboat. But everything was okay, she could come back now, because she didn't have to go to prison.

Lexi had smiled at that. She thought, not for the first time, *Oh, to be ten again, when life was that simple.*

Lexi knew why Margot had forgiven her, why it was inevitable she would – because Margot was her English grandmother, her father's mother. And if Lexi had had any doubts that this was true, Charlie sent another text just to let her know that Margot had taken her stone, but had she said she was sorry.

Lexi took a sharp intake of breath when she read that text.

Andrea heard her. 'Are you all right?'

Lexi turned to look at her sister. All the pieces of the jigsaw were finally coming together, explaining why she had an American great-grandfather. Of course the tin was hidden in Margot's houseboat because that boat used to belong to her mother, and Lexi's great-grandmother, Esme.

She remembered taking the library books to the care home, and what the care assistant had said. *Esme keeps asking if she can go back to her houseboat. I heard that she asks her daughter every single time she visits.*

Lexi shook her head. It hadn't occurred to her that Margot was living on her mother's houseboat. Why something that obvious had not crossed her mind before, she had no clue. It wasn't until she had found Kit, and discovered he was her great-grandfather, that everything had fallen into place.

Lexi realised that far from throwing doubt over whether the English man she'd always called Dad was her father, the discovery that her great-grandfather was Kit only confirmed that the man whose grave she had visited was indeed her father. Nowhere in Esme's notebook had there been a mention of the fact that Kit was American, but now she knew that her dad's mother was Margot, and his grandparents were Kit and Esme.

Now she understood why her mother had entrusted her, and her alone, to deliver that letter, in person, into Margot's hands. It wasn't the letter she was delivering, but Margot's long-lost granddaughter. *Why have I been kept from seeing my paternal grandmother all these years?* Lexi wondered. Was the answer in the letter from her mother that she had yet to read?

'Have you opened your letter?'

Lexi's eyes went wide. Was her sister psychic? She'd just been thinking of the letter. Lexi turned to look at her and shook her head.

'Why not?'

Lexi sighed. They'd had this conversation countless times over the last few months, with Lexi saying she wasn't ready, and her sister looking at her sympathetically; her response had always been that she would know when the time was right.

'I think you should.'

Lexi raised an eyebrow. That was the first time Andrea had said that. 'Why?'

Andrea bit her lower lip, looked at her sheepishly, then avoided eye contact.

'Andrea?'

'I'm going to text Chad and let him know I've landed safely.'

Lexi watched her get out her phone and turn to the window to send her text. Lexi faced the front and wondered what was going on. It wasn't like her sister to be evasive and not answer a direct question.

Lexi leaned forward and asked the taxi driver, 'How long now?' It was taking longer by road than train – the way she had travelled from London to Suffolk before. But they had to go by car. She was conscious of the fact that Kit, although extremely spritely considering his advanced years, tired easily. Waiting on platforms for trains, and climbing in and out of carriages, would not have been practical. She glanced out the window at the queue ahead. They were stuck in a traffic jam on their way out of the airport.

'Once we get on the motorway, the rest of the journey will be plain sailing.'

Lexi hoped so. She glanced at her sister and thought once again, *What is she doing here?*

43

Esme sat alone in her room by the window with the notebook on her lap. She stared across the rooftops of the town at the sparkling sea in the distance, thinking about how her life might have been, how *she* might have been, if only she'd known the truth. Her heart had been broken, and her life had never been the same again.

She thought back to the conversation she'd had with Margot before she left.

'I've been a terrible mother,' she'd said.

Margot had shaken her head in disagreement, as Esme knew she would. 'Come home with me. Please.'

'No.' She didn't deserve to return to Willow Tree Cottage. Her daughter had been through her own heartbreaks, losing a son, being widowed at a young age, and then losing her grandchild. After everything, Esme thanked god that Meredith hadn't turned her back on Margot. But she wasn't family. The only family Margot had left was sitting in this room, and Esme had treated her daughter abysmally over the years, when it was no fault of Margot's that she looked the spitting image of Kit.

She'd told her all this, knowing her daughter would forgive her for her failings as a mother – she had done so a long time ago.

'Then come back with me. Let's return to Willow Tree Cottage together. We could be a family again.'

'You haven't got time to look after me.'

'Oh, Mum, I've got all the time in the world,' she'd said.

Esme had shaken her head, and then she'd had a thought. 'All right, I will. But first I want you to do something for me.'

'Oh, anything.'

'Find my great-grandchild – your grandchild. Find Alexandra.' To her lasting regret, Esme had had nothing to do with her. She remembered that summer when they'd come down from London to stay at the house with Margot. Esme hadn't left the houseboat, hadn't visited even once to see them. She regretted that. She regretted lots of things. She'd lost Kit, but she'd lost Margot too. She'd spent all her life wallowing in self-pity, as though the whole world owed her something; as though she wasn't like everybody else who went through life with their own share of heartbreak and just plain bad luck. Everyone else had to learn to live with it. Why couldn't she? *Because I loved him too much.*

Esme looked at the rusty tin that Charlie had left behind on the table by her chair. Why had she kept it all these years? Esme had made sure to keep it hidden from her daughter. That was the reason she hadn't left it in the house, but on the houseboat where Margot was never allowed to venture.

Just to be on the safe side, she'd still hidden it where she thought no one would find it. But what if she hadn't? What if she'd left it in Willow Tree Cottage instead, and a young Margot had come across it? Would she have been inquisitive like Charlie and found the letter and the ring? She imagined she would have.

It crossed her mind that if she hadn't refused to tell Margot all about her father, and shown her the notebook all about her life in the war instead, then she would have eventually found the letter and the ring herself. Esme hadn't intended to be cruel by not telling her. All these years, she'd been trying to protect Margot from the heartbreak she had suffered herself while thinking he'd cruelly betrayed her.

Charlie reminded Esme of Margot when she was a child. If only she'd let Margot join her on the houseboat. They could have had such fun together. But she never had. She'd spent the long summer holidays avoiding her only child, avoiding that face, those eyes that she didn't want to see, day in and day out, reminding her of him. She had been happy on the boat because it transported her back to the happy time when she had worked on the Inland Waterways, before she'd met Kit and her life had changed forever.

Her best friends, the two women whom she'd worked with on the canal had often visited in the summer. They'd spend time together, reminiscing. Unfortunately, they were both gone – and now, so was her houseboat.

But I don't need that now – I have this. Esme looked at her notebook with the letter inside. She took the letter out of the notebook and held it against her chest, her heart. She whispered, 'I know I'll never see you again. Some might say one must never give up hope, that it's never too late. But at our age ...' She trailed off, looking around the empty room. 'But I'll always have you in my heart.'

❖

'Esme.'

She hadn't heard the knock on the door. She turned in her chair to find Nicki standing in the doorway, looking very solemn. Esme stared at her. She was always so happy and cheerful. Esme frowned. 'What's the matter?'

Nicki suddenly burst into tears.

Esme stared at her and felt her heart pounding in her chest, afraid of what the care home manager was going to tell her. 'Is it Margot? Has something happened to my daughter?'

'Oh, no, that's not it.' She wiped her eyes. 'I am so sorry. I just didn't expect to get all emotional. I'm the biggest sap when it comes to—'

Esme looked at her. 'When it comes to – *what?*'

'Happy endings.'

Lexi stood behind the care home manager, listening. Kit was standing beside her, leaning on his walking sticks, grinning from ear-to-ear. Lexi turned to Kit. 'Let me walk in first. I think I should warn her.'

'Who's that?' Esme asked. She'd heard someone else talking behind the door.

Lexi stepped into the room. 'It's me.'

Esme put on her glasses. 'I know you. You're from the library. Have you come with more books?' She frowned. 'But it's not Sunday.'

'No, Esme, I'm not visiting from the library today.'

Nicki said, 'Lexi has brought someone to see you.'

Esme stared at her. 'Lexi? Are you ...?' She swallowed. 'Are you Alexandra?' Esme held out her hand. 'Oh, my dear, come closer. Sit with me.' She looked over at Nicki. 'Is Margot here?'

Lexi shook her head. 'She doesn't know I'm here yet.'

'Why not? We must tell her.'

Lexi said, 'We will. But first there's someone else here who wants to see you.'

Esme frowned. 'Who?'

Kit stepped into view in the doorway. 'Hello, Esme.'

44

Lexi slowly closed the door on her great-grandparents, who were sitting quietly, holding hands, staring into each other's eyes. They'd barely said a word to one another as Kit had walked into the room and taken the seat next to Esme in front of the window. Lexi guessed there would be plenty of time for that, but right now, in that moment, they were finally together, and no words could express what it meant to them.

'Lexi!'

She jumped at the sound of her sister's voice behind her. Lexi whispered, 'What are you doing here? I told you to wait in the car.'

'I got bored waiting.' She looked at the door. 'Who is she?'

Lexi clicked the door shut, realising that Andrea must have caught a glimpse of the couple. 'I'll explain later.'

'Oh, really? You've been saying that the whole way here.'

Lexi grabbed her sleeve. 'Come on.'

They walked out of the care home to the waiting taxi.

'Where to now, Miss?' the taxi driver asked as they got in the back seat.

'Can you hold on for a little longer?'

Andrea said, 'What are we waiting for?'

They both turned their heads when they heard someone shouting out. 'Esme! Where do you think you're going?'

Esme and Kit were walking towards the taxi. Esme halted, turned around and lifted one of her walking sticks in the air, waving it at the care assistant. 'Go away!'

'But you can't just walk out!'

'Watch me! I am not a prisoner. I am free to go where I like.'

'Where *are* you going?'

'I'm going home to my family.'

❖

'Where are we?' asked Andrea. She peered out of the window as the taxi stopped outside the double gates to Margot's home in Walberswick.

Lexi turned to her. 'Don't you recognise this place?'

'No – should I?'

Why would she? Lexi thought. Andrea had only been three when she was last there. Lexi wondered whether she was doing the right thing, taking Andrea with her. She could have left Andrea at The Harbour Inn in Southwold, where she'd booked a room. They'd stopped briefly to check in and offload their suitcases. She could have then gone on alone with Kit to see Esme.

The plan all along had been for Kit to break Esme out of the care home, as he'd put it. The trouble was, Lexi didn't know where they would go after that. Kit had told her that once he'd spoken with Esme, he'd figure it out. He'd said, 'I don't know if she met someone in the intervening years, and fell in love and married, but she has my ring, and although I might not be able to get down on bended knee, it would be my dream come true if she'd do me the honour of being my wife.'

Now they'd all returned to Willow Tree Cottage and were about to give Margot the surprise of her life.

Lexi glanced at her sister and thought once again how she too was in for a surprise – but not like Margot; not in a good way.

Up until they'd returned to the cottage, she was still debating whether she was doing the right thing, telling her sister that their mum had had an affair, and that they were half-sisters.

Lexi realised even as they arrived that there was still time to change her mind and just drop Esme and Kit off at the cottage. She could take Andrea to the hotel in Southwold, and then pop back later, without Andrea, and finally be reunited with her grandmother, Margot.

But something stopped her in her tracks; Andrea had a right to know who her father was. It was during a conversation on the flight from Detroit that Kit who had persuaded Lexi to tell her sister the truth. He'd said that one day, as time marched inexorably on, it would be too late; he'd be gone. And the conversations Andrea might have had with him, knowing who he was, would be lost forever. Kit had said that Lexi would never forgive herself.

And so here they all were.

Lexi and Andrea helped Kit and Esme out of the taxi, and they all walked through the double gates. As she looked up the short drive to the front door of the house, Lexi said, 'You two go ahead.'

'What about you?' asked Esme. 'Margot is going to be so surprised to see you.'

Lexi glanced at Kit. 'One surprise at a time.'

Esme grinned. 'Ah – I get your thinking.'

Lexi hugged them both. 'I will be along in a moment. There's something I need to do first.' She caught Kit nodding his head and offering her a reassuring smile – she was doing the right thing.

Lexi turned to Andrea and caught her looking at them all. 'Lexi, will you just tell me what is going on?'

Lexi took her arm. 'Come on. There's something I want to show you.' Lexi thought it might jog her memory.

Andrea sighed heavily as she was led away from the drive, through the front gardens and round to the back of the house. 'Lexi, will you please tell me who those people are and what we are doing here?'

'Just a minute. Ah, there it is.' Lexi had found the weeping willow, the one she'd walked into when she'd ran out of Margot's house, trying to evade her before she flew back to New York. If only she'd handed Margot the letter as she'd promised, then all would have been revealed. There was no reason to run. There was every reason to stay.

'Lexi?'

'Oh, sorry – yes. Do you recognise it?'

'What?'

'The willow tree, of course. We used to play hide and seek in this garden, around the willow tree. Don't you remember?'

'No.' Andrea stared at the house. 'Are you saying this is where we lived when we were in England?'

Lexi pursed her lips. 'For a little while, yes.'

Andrea looked up at the tree.

Lexi followed her gaze. A memory suddenly came to Lexi of a girl around her own age. Her name was Sophie.

Sophie.

'Lexi, are you all right?'

'I remembered something. I think I had a best friend called Sophie who used to come and play with me here.'

'What happened to her?'

Lexi looked towards the house. 'I think ... I think she drowned.'

'She drowned?'

Lexi thought back to that episode on the quay when Charlie had fallen into the water. 'I think I was there when it happened.'

'Do you remember anything else?'

Lexi shook her head.

Andrea sighed. 'Perhaps that's just as well. It's not the sort of thing you really want to dwell on. But it does explain one thing.'

'What's that?'

'Why you were always so afraid of the water, and hated those holidays on Grandpa's yacht.'

'Yes – I did, didn't I?'

'I'm surprised you were living on a houseboat.'

Lexi had told her sister that she'd been living on a houseboat, and about the guy next door, Scott, and his little girl, Charlie, whom she was very fond of. Andrea had quipped, 'I don't think it's just Charlie that you're fond of.'

She'd ignored that comment, but she had told her sister that despite her fear of the water, she had grown very fond of living there. Her heart had been broken when she'd discovered the little houseboat was beyond repair. She had offered, anonymously, to pay for it to be replaced, but Margot had refused the offer.

They fell silent for a moment, both listening to the rustle of the branches. And then Andrea and Lexi said in unison, 'I've got something to tell you.'

45

'This is going to come as a shock, Lexi. I've thought long and hard about this. I hate secrets, so I just have to tell you. I'm so sorry, but here it is.' Andrea took a deep breath.

Lexi noticed she appeared to be struggling with whatever it was she had to tell her. 'What is it, Andrea?'

'I thought Mum might have explained in her letter to me, but there was nothing.'

'Explained what?'

'I wouldn't expect there'd be anything in your letter. After all, what's it got to do with you? Sorry, that sounded rude. When are you going to read yours, anyway?'

Lexi looked at her sheepishly. She already had. Standing outside Kit and Esme's door, something had spurred her on to tear open that envelope. She'd found the letter in her coat pocket when she'd slipped her hand inside soon after arriving in Detroit. She recalled casting it aside in the apartment in New York. She smiled when she realised Brandon must have surreptitiously slipped it in her coat pocket when he hugged her goodbye. She'd kept it close in her coat pocket until she'd finally decided to read it. Perhaps it was seeing Kit get closure; maybe she felt she wanted that too –

and she would only have it by opening that letter and reading her mother's last words.

She had run though all sorts of scenarios around what might be in her letter, but what she hadn't expected was that her mother had written in her letter the truth about her affair and the identity of Andrea's father.

Lexi eyed her sister. *How am I going to tell her?* she wondered.

'Look, I don't know how to tell you this, Lexi, so I'm just going to say it. Mitch is my dad.'

Lexi stared at her. *How on earth did she find out?* she thought.

Andrea took another deep breath, and said, 'Sorry, I know this must come as a shock. The fact is, Mum had an affair when we lived in London. It was short-lived. Mitch and our mum knew each other from high school. They'd been high school sweethearts but then they'd gone their separate ways, until one day they bumped into each other in London, and well, I was obviously the result. They broke it off when he returned to the US. Then your father died, and we moved to Connecticut. Mitch found out and got in touch, and the rest is history. As I got older, he guessed the truth, but she said she'd leave him, deny it, if he ever spoke a word of the affair.'

'How did you find this out?'

'You know the DNA thing? I hadn't been on it for ages. So I did like I promised, and went on AncestryDNA again, and it turned up a paternal relative.'

Lexi stared at her. 'You didn't tell me.' Now Lexi realised why Andrea had gone quiet, and hadn't replied to her texts or voice messages.

'I expected to find an English relative, but it was an American – a cousin on my father's side. I suspected that something wasn't right. You know me, I never let things go. I wanted to get to the bottom of just how this person was related to me because I didn't see how that was possible, as my father was English. Unless ...'

'We had different fathers.'

'Exactly. That's why I couldn't contact you. After I found out, I thought perhaps it was better to leave you in blissful ignorance.'

Lexi glanced up at the house, thinking of Kit. She hadn't told her about the relative she'd found either because, like Andrea, she had been trying to protect her sister.

'I thought at first it was better not to tell you, but then again, you were in England – what would you uncover? I confronted Dad, I mean Mitch—'

'He's your dad, Andrea, you don't have to not call him that in front of me.' It seemed funny that now she'd found out he was her real dad, she was calling him Mitch – she never did that.

'Mitch told me everything. I was just so mad at them all, our grandparents included, that they had hidden this from us, from you.'

'They knew too?'

'Yes. They've written you a letter. I have it in my handbag. I told them all that I was going to England and I was going to tell you everything. I believe it's a letter of apology to you, Lexi.'

Lexi frowned. 'I think it's my grandmother they should be apologising to.'

'Yes, that's what I told them.'

Lexi smiled at her sister.

'They wrote a letter of apology to Margot too. I didn't force them to do it. They'd already written one. They told me that when you returned to Connecticut after breaking up with Brandon, and they found out from Mitch that you were thinking of going to

England, that was when they sat down and wrote the letters, hoping to see you before you left.'

'But I told Nana I was returning to New York.'

Andrea looked at her incredulously. 'And you thought Nana didn't see right through you? You thought she believed you?'

Lexi looked at her sister and sighed. *How stupid of me to think that I could pull the wool over Nana's eyes*, she thought.

Andrea's expression changed. She looked at Lexi, tears welling up in her eyes. 'You never saw your grandmother while you were growing up, all because of Mum's secret – because of *me*. I am *so* sorry.'

Lexi shook her head. 'It really isn't your fault, Andrea.'

Andrea paused and eyed her sister. 'I must admit, you're taking this surprisingly well for someone who's just found out our mum had an affair, and we're half-sisters.'

Lexi turned to look at the house.

So did Andrea. 'You knew, didn't you?'

'Not at first. Like you, I did the DNA test and it turned up an ... anomaly, shall we say. I discovered I had a relative on my father's side that we didn't share.'

'Who?'

'Kit.'

'Kit?'

'Yes, he's my paternal great-grandfather.' Lexi told Andrea all about the tin she'd found on the houseboat along with the letter and ring, telling of a love story that went all the way back to World War Two. She hadn't known it at the time, but she had been reading her great-grandparents' story.

'When Kit decided he was returning to England with me, I told him you were coming too, and swore him to secrecy. As Esme and Kit are my great-grandparents, not yours, and the woman who lives in this house, Margot, is *my* paternal grandmother, I didn't want you to come, Andrea, in case you found out. I didn't know how to tell you. But then again, I wanted you to have a chance to find your father.' That was what Lexi had been thinking before she'd read the letter from her mother and discovered that her sister had known him all along.

'I've always been his favourite – haven't I? And I've always called him Dad. I just thought it was because I was little and he was the only daddy I'd ever really known. But now ...' Andrea trailed off.

'Now, you know the truth.' Lexi smiled.

'You didn't seem at all surprised when I told you it was Mitch.'

Lexi reached in her handbag and got out the letter from her mum.

'Is that your letter?'

'Yes. I opened it when I was waiting outside the door for Esme and Kit just before you appeared. Here.'

'What does it say?'

'Read it, Andrea.'

She took the letter and started to read ...

❖

Lexi, my darling. You went to New York to forge a life for yourself, like I did in England when I was young, but I knew there would always be a part of you longing for something more. This is the reason I am sending you back to England with a letter – so you can meet your English grandmother. I'm so sorry that I didn't do this sooner, but I am a coward. I hope you can find it in your heart to forgive me, both of you.

I wanted you to know that I loved your father. Don't you ever think that your father or you were a mistake. He was my best friend, but I loved another.

Mitch was the love of my life. I realised that when I met him again in London. I tried to make a go of it with your father after that, lying to myself that Andrea was not Mitch's child. But it didn't work. Your father and I had decided to go our separate ways. We'd made plans. You were going to live with your father in England, and I was going to take Andrea back to America to live with my parents. But then your father died and with him went our plans.

Margot wanted us to stay and live with her, but I wasn't brave enough to go against my parents' wishes. They wanted us to return to America. So we left, never to return. Something happened that summer, and I will always regret using it as an excuse to cut all ties with your English grandmother. It was easier that way so the truth of my affair would never come out – the truth about Andrea. Because if it did, it would hurt both my children.

I didn't expect to meet Mitch again. But I suppose it was inevitable – that's love, isn't it? If fate or serendipity – call it what you will – has a way of getting you back together, it will.

Why, you may wonder, have I not written about all this in Andrea's letter? Andrea has found her place in the world – she belongs with Chad, and working for her grandparents, and she has Mitch, the only father she has ever really known. So, why not let sleeping dogs lie? Why even tell you?

I think reading this, you know why. If I send you back to England, which I just feel compelled to do – it is where you have belonged all along – the truth will out, as they say, and I need to make it clear to you that you were not a mistake; neither of you were. I loved two men in my life, Lexi – it's just that Mitch turned out to be the love of my life. I hope in time you come to understand.

When Lexi had first read the letter, she had paused at that point and thought of Brandon and Scott, before she resumed reading ...

What you choose to do with this, with regard to Andrea, I must leave in your hands, which is an awfully big responsibility, I know. But I trust you to make the right decision. I always have. And I think you trust yourself.

Well, I have to leave you now to live your life and trust your instincts – if you do that, then I know that you will be okay.

Find your happy place, Lexi – but I suspect I know where that has been all along. It is just up to you to find whom you will share that place with.

Goodbye, my love. Mum.

❖

Andrea stood there under the willow tree, reading the letter. She looked at Lexi in surprise. 'She told you about Mitch in your letter.'

Lexi said, 'I'm glad she did. I don't want there to be secrets anymore.' Lexi looked at the letter in Andrea's hands. 'She couldn't tell you herself. She couldn't bring herself to tell me either. But as the years went on, I think she realised that she didn't want to take the secret to her grave. She entrusted me with her secret. I think she knew I would find the right moment to tell you.'

Lexi knew that her mum had been aware of how much she hadn't enjoyed those summers they'd spent in Florida and Hawaii with Mitch and her maternal grandparents. Lexi imagined her mother probably realised that her oldest child would have loved to be on the Suffolk Coast, spending her summers with her grandmother.

Lexi thought of the letter her mum had written to Margot. She guessed that, just like the affair she'd kept hidden from them, her mum hadn't known how to tell Lexi about her paternal grandmother in England. So she had hatched a plan to encourage her to return to England, where she knew she belonged.

It was all there in her letter that she hadn't read. 'I've been so stupid, not opening the letter.'

'But don't you see, Lexi? If you had opened it, you wouldn't have joined AncestryDNA to look for English relatives. You would never have found Kit.'

Lexi smiled. She hadn't thought of that.

'And you would never have found that tin. It would have been lost, along with the ring when the houseboat went down. And Margot would not have been reunited with her father.'

Lexi felt tears running down her cheeks. 'Oh, Andrea, you are so right.' She stepped forward and embraced her sister.

When they drew back, Andrea said, 'Do you think they will have made it up the drive to the front door yet? It's not far, but it's still a bit of a walk at their age.'

'I should think so,' replied Lexi. Esme had taken her hand when she'd helped her out of the taxi, and told her that she wanted to walk with Kit, to take him home.

They both turned to look at the house, thinking about the reunion that was about to take place inside.

46

'Margot, there's someone at the door,' Meredith called out.

Margot was sitting in her study with the letter that Charlie had handed to her. The envelope was cast to one side, and the single piece of notepaper was lying on the desk in front of her. She stared at the letter. It began, *Forgive me, Margot.*

Just one short sentence followed. It contained all that needed to be said.

I brought her back to you.

Margot's thoughts were interrupted by the insistent ringing of the front doorbell.

'Shall I answer that?'

Margot looked up, 'Yes please, Meredith – I'm busy.' Margot was busy trying to work out what she was going to do. With this letter, her daughter-in-law had brought Alexandra back to her, in a manner of speaking. She still couldn't quite believe that her granddaughter had been right there, in the house, and that she'd lost her again. She was gone, back to America. How would she find her?

Margot had asked Charlie for her granddaughter's mobile number. Charlie had willingly given it to her. She wanted

Alexandra to come back just as much as Margot did. But now, stupidly, she'd been afraid to phone the number; afraid to find out that her granddaughter wasn't coming back.

Margot shook her head. Poor Charlie was under the impression that Alexandra would be back. But as Margot had discovered in her life, nothing was certain, and sometimes everything you took for granted, the life you had with the people you loved, could be lost in a blink of an eye.

Margot was thinking of her son, and her granddaughter, and her daughter-in-law. If only she had stayed there with her daughters after being widowed. How different things could have been.

Margot was just reaching for the phone on her desk, deciding it was now or never – she had to phone Alexandra – when she saw something out of the corner of her eye, a movement in the garden. She thought it was just the branches of the beautiful willow tree swaying in the wind. Even so, she got up from her desk and walked up to the French doors to look outside. It was a blustery day, the end of the summer, and the beginning of autumn was in the air. Margot frowned when she saw two women standing in her garden.

Margot put her hands on her hips. *Where did they come from? And what do they think they're doing, trespassing in my garden?* Her breath caught in her throat. *Alexandra? It can't be. She's in America.*

Margot opened the door and called out, 'Alexandra?'

From down the hallway, she could hear Meredith exclaim, 'Oh, my goodness, you've got to come quick, Margot.'

She glanced over her shoulder. 'Just give me a minute.' Whatever it was could wait. She stepped outside as the two young women turned in her direction.

'Grandma?'

Margot could feel her heart pounding in her chest as she ran across the lawn. 'Oh, Alexandra – it *is* you!' They embraced, tears running down their cheeks. Margot saw the other young woman backing away.

'I'll er ... go now, Lexi. Which direction is The Harbour Inn where we're staying?'

Margot looked at her. 'Andrea?'

Andrea stopped. 'You recognise me?'

'Of course I do. Aren't you going to give your grandma a hug too?'

'But I'm not your—'

So, she knows the truth, thought Margot. 'You are to me, Andrea. I loved you then, and I love you still. I've missed your cheeky smile and your determined little character.'

Andrea looked wide-eyed at Margot.

'Come here.' Margot held her arms wide.

Andrea walked over and got the biggest hug from Margot.

Now it wasn't just Margot and Lexi with tears streaming down their faces.

When they'd finished their embrace, Margot turned to Lexi. 'And you, Alexandra, my little adventurer. Oh, how you loved playing hide and seek among the willow tree branches. You've certainly given me the run around, haven't you?'

Lexi said, 'I'm sorry about squatting on your houseboat.'

'Don't be silly.' She realised that her granddaughter had told Charlie the truth about what had happened in London, losing her money.

'If only I'd known the lady I was supposed to hand the letter to was my grandmother, but I didn't. Mum left a letter for me explaining everything, but stupidly I only opened it today, otherwise I would have found out the truth a lot sooner, about you.'

Margot watched Lexi take her sister's hand and give it a reassuring squeeze.

Margot still couldn't quite believe they'd both returned to Willow Tree Cottage. 'Now, you must both come inside. What's all this nonsense about you staying at The Harbour Inn? You are staying here with me.'

'Why didn't you want your houseboat replaced?' blurted Lexi.

'How on earth did you know about that?'

Andrea said, 'Lexi's former boyfriend is now a big rock star, and he's giving Lexi lots of money. She used some of the money and had everyone's boats fixed up after the storm, except yours because it was beyond repair.'

Lexi exclaimed, 'Andrea! That was meant to be a secret.'

Andrea frowned at her sister. 'What happened to not keeping secrets anymore?'

Margot smiled. 'You know everyone in the houseboat community thinks it's me who paid for all their boats to be repaired because I felt guilty over lying all these years about the summers I spent away. I denied it of course, but they just think I'm far too modest to admit it.' Her smile faded. 'You liked the houseboat, didn't you Alexandra?'

'Call me Lexi.'

'Of course.'

Lexi said, 'Yes, I did. They grow on you, don't they?' She noticed that her grandmother hadn't answered her question. Lexi knew that the houseboat had originally belonged to Esme. She guessed it was her decision. Perhaps the reason was that, unlike the other houseboats, hers had been beyond repair, and it was irreplaceable. Or perhaps it was the case that Esme saw little point in someone going to the expense of replacing it, as she had accepted she could never return to live on it. That chapter in her life was over.

It certainly is now, thought Lexi, smiling. Esme had her letter and the ring, and now Kit. She didn't need her houseboat anymore. She'd returned to Willow Tree Cottage. Her happy place was right there, with Kit and Margot. The cottage was her home.

'It surprised me,' commented Andrea, 'when I found out that Lexi stayed on a houseboat. You've always hated boats, Lexi. But now I know why.'

Margot raised an eyebrow.

'Sophie,' said Lexi.

Margot looked at her, wide-eyed. 'You remember Sophie?'

'She was my friend and she drowned, didn't she? I remember that you let us go ahead to the houseboat on our own, and my mum, well she said in her letter that something happened that summer and she regretted using it as an excuse to cut all ties with you. I think it was what happened to Sophie.'

Lexi added, 'I think it wasn't just that. I bet our maternal grandparents made her sever all ties with England. I imagine they wanted us to themselves.' She gave her sister a sideways glance. Andrea didn't object to that possibility. In fact, she was standing there nodding her head, as though it was obvious that it was what had happened. She opened her bag and handed Margot a letter.

'What's this?' she asked, taking the envelope.

Lexi replied, 'It's a letter from our grandparents – a letter of apology. Can you ever forgive them?'

Margot sighed. 'They were protecting you, Lexi.' She would never forget her granddaughter waking up the morning after the accident and asking when Sophie would be coming round to play.

'No, Mum used it as an excuse to leave,' Andrea cut in. 'I think she was protecting herself from either of us finding out she'd had an affair with my dad, Mitch, the man she went on to marry.'

Margot stared at Andrea. Maybe there was some truth to it, that what had happened had given their mother an excuse to leave and cut all ties.

She put the letter in her pocket, and held their hands tightly in hers. 'That's all in the past now.' The wind was picking up. She had to raise her voice to be heard. 'I'm so glad you're back – both of you.'

Meredith breathlessly appeared at the French doors. 'Oh, Margot, there you are,' she called out. 'I've been looking for you everywhere! You'll never guess who is here.'

'Yes, I know – it's Alexandra and Andrea.'

Meredith looked from one to the other, her expression confused. 'Oh, my goodness, is that really them?'

'Oh, yes!' Margot called back as they walked towards the house.

'There's someone else here,' Meredith said as they approached.

Lexi and Andrea exchanged a glance and grinned. Lexi said, 'I brought someone back with me from America.'

Margot looked at her. 'Yes, you did – Andrea.'

'No, not just my sister. I found someone. Someone I think you will want to meet.'

Meredith exclaimed, 'Margot, it's your father!'

'My ... father?'

Lexi smiled. 'Come on, Grandma. Let's go and meet Kit.'

Margot stepped into the study, her legs feeling wobbly, but she had her two girls with her. Lexi held her hand as they walked down the hall.

Meredith said, 'They are in there, Margot.'

'They?'

'Esme's home.'

'Mum's home?' Margot looked confused as she stopped outside the door to the lounge.

Lexi and Andrea exchanged a smile. On the way there in the taxi, Esme had proudly shown them her ring and had told them of the proposal Kit had made.

Meredith wiped a tear from her eye as Margot opened the door.

Kit said, 'Hello, my darling girl.'

47

'Let me make you two girls a nice cup of tea.' Meredith looked at them. 'Oh, my goodness, I can't believe you're both here. I know you probably don't remember me. I'm your mum's best friend.' She hugged them both before leading the way down the hall into the kitchen. As they sat down at the kitchen table, Lexi's phone buzzed with a text. She happened to glance at Andrea before she read it. Andrea was chewing a fingernail, looking around the room. *Is she avoiding eye contact?* Lexi wondered. She knew that look. 'What are you up to?'

'Oh, me?' Andrea shrugged. 'Nothing.'

Lexi read the text. It was from Charlie, asking when she was going to arrive. Lexi stared at the text, bemused. 'How does Charlie know I'm back?' She glanced at Meredith, who had turned from the kitchen counter with two mugs in her hands. She shrugged and walked over, placing the mugs on the table in front of them. Lexi's eyes settled on Andrea.

Andrea was still avoiding eye contact.

'Andrea ...?'

Her sister looked at her sheepishly. 'When we dropped off our cases at The Harbour Inn ...'

Meredith interrupted. 'We'll have to sort out collecting your luggage. You girls are not staying at The Harbour Inn. Although it's a lovely place, you're staying here at Willow Tree Cottage.'

'Is there enough room?' asked Andrea. 'I get the impression that Kit and Esme are here to stay.'

Meredith smiled as she stirred her cup of tea. 'Margot will be so thrilled to hear that her parents are moving in. But of course there's still plenty of room for you both to stay here.' She looked at them eagerly.

Lexi smiled at Meredith before she fixed her gaze on Andrea across the table again. Lexi held up her phone. 'Andrea? Now, about that text from Charlie. What were you saying – about when we dropped our luggage off?'

Andrea was still avoiding her gaze. 'Meredith, I've got a question. Something I still don't understand.'

'Fire away,' said Meredith.

'Lexi's grandmother. Her name is Margot Dorey, but our surname is Dawson. Lexi's dad's surname was Dawson.'

Lexi looked at her sister. 'I guessed it was a pseudonym she'd used for her writing.' She looked at Meredith.

Meredith nodded and smiled. 'If she hadn't reverted to her maiden name after her husband died, you'd have realised you were related, Lexi, far sooner.'

'I wish I'd known who you were, Lexi, when I met you at the library. But then how were you to know that Margot was your grandmother?'

'Mum never told us about her,' admitted Lexi. She did leave me a letter. I should have read it earlier, but I didn't.'

Meredith nodded. 'It's okay.'

Andrea said, 'Why did she change her name back to her

maiden name after her husband died?'

'She didn't want to but because she was using her maiden name for her books, and they became extremely popular, it was just easier for income and tax purposes to do so. So Margot Dawson became Margot Dorey.'

Lexi was relieved that Meredith wasn't angry with her over the episode at the library. She wasn't surprised Meredith remembered.

Lexi turned to her sister. 'Now, about that text from Charlie,' she said again, wanting to get to the bottom of the mystery of how exactly Charlie knew she was back.

Andrea looked at her sheepishly. 'You know when we dropped off our cases in the room, and you nipped to the loo?'

'Yes.'

'I picked up your phone when you got a text.'

'You picked up my phone?'

'You left it on the bed. It was a text from Charlie, so I might have … er … replied.'

'What?'

'And told her that you were here.'

Lexi was already looking at her phone, scrolling through the messages. She found the reply that Andrea had sent from her phone. She looked up. 'Andrea! Why did you do that?'

'Because I think you were going to avoid them, and it would have been the biggest mistake of your life.'

No, the biggest mistake would be if I saw Scott again, Lexi thought, frowning at her sister. Andrea didn't understand. Scott had a go bag. How long would he and Charlie be on the houseboat before he had to leave again, disappear?

She didn't know what trouble he was in, but whatever it was, she knew she couldn't leave with him. Lexi had found her home on the Suffolk Coast. She desperately wished Scott and Charlie could stay, but in her heart she already knew that it was most likely never going to happen.

Lexi felt terrible, but she had decided not to reply to Charlie's text. The idea had been that Scott and Charlie would never know she'd come back. It would mean living with Margot for a time before she found a place. Perhaps she'd look for a home in Aldeburgh, on the seafront, although her heart was really in Walberswick.

But Andrea had scuppered that plan. Lexi shook her head. 'Andrea, you don't understand ...'

'I do,' said Meredith.

Lexi swivelled her head in Meredith's direction. 'What do you mean?'

'It's Scott isn't it? And the trouble he's in.'

'You know about that?'

Meredith nodded. She walked over with her mug of tea and a plate of homemade cakes, and put them down on the table before pulling up a chair. 'Margot met Charlie when she visited Esme at the care home. Charlie confided how she and her father moved around a lot. She wanted to stay in Walberswick and wait for you to return, Lexi. She wanted to stay and start school here in September.'

Lexi nodded sadly. She knew all this.

Meredith continued. 'She told Margot that she thought her dad was in some kind of trouble. So Margot accompanied her back to The Harbour Inn where they were staying. It was moving day, and Charlie thought that they were going back to the houseboat. But they weren't. They were packing up and leaving the Suffolk Coast for good.'

'They're leaving?' Although that would solve her problem of trying to avoid them, Lexi's heart sank. It didn't come as a surprise – she had already envisaged just this scenario – but she really didn't want them to leave. 'Where are they going?'

Andrea eyed her sister. 'I thought you didn't want to see them again?'

'Just hear me out, Lexi.' Meredith continued. 'When Scott arrived back at The Harbour Inn to collect Charlie, it turned out that he'd been to the agency in Southwold to tell them he wouldn't be returning to the houseboat, and to tell the owner he was leaving. That was when they'd told him that the houseboat had changed hands.'

'Changed hands?' said Andrea. 'What does that mean?'

'Whoever had paid for all the houseboat repairs had bought out the owner. There's talk among the other houseboat owners that they paid an excessive amount so they would agree to sell.'

Andrea turned her head and stared wide-eyed at her sister. 'Lexi?'

Lexi avoided her gaze, 'Go on, Meredith.'

'When Charlie found out they weren't going back to the houseboat, she grabbed her bag and ran.'

Andrea turned to Meredith. 'Oh, my god. Where did Charlie go? Did they find her?'

Lexi already knew the answer to that question. She opened her mouth to say, but Meredith continued her story.

'Obviously Scott didn't know who Margot was. He didn't want her to get involved in their private business. That was when Margot told him that she was already involved because Lexi is her granddaughter, and she guessed that you were in love with him.'

Lexi bit her lower lip, avoiding Meredith's gaze.

'Margot told him that whatever was going on, she could help. She's got a lawyer friend. But first they had to go to the houseboat. That was where they found Charlie.'

Lexi wasn't surprised. When Meredith had said that Charlie had run away, that was where she'd thought they must have found her. 'What happened next?'

'That's when the whole sorry business about the predicament Scott had got himself in came out.'

Lexi leaned forward in her seat. 'Is it something bad? Will he ... will he go to prison?'

Meredith breathed a sigh. 'Charlie's mother walked out when Scott was back in England on leave, so Scott deserted his post in the army. The official term is Absent Without Leave. He did it for family reasons. He loved his job, but he was stationed abroad. He was afraid that his daughter would end up in care.'

Meredith shook her head. 'There are no grandparents to look after her, no relatives who could take her in. So, he has lived in constant fear that the military police will find him and that he'll be court-martialled and sent to prison. He's read about others who've got around eight months. It doesn't sound long, but what would become of Charlie? Who would look after her?'

Lexi could feel the tears welling up. She'd had so many people who had taken care of her after she'd lost a parent. Even now that she was in her twenties, and an orphan, she had her sister, she had her grandparents, she had her stepdad. And she now had the lovely Meredith, and her wonderful paternal grandmother, Margot. She didn't know what it must be like not to have that extended support network.

'So, you can see why he constantly moves around, looking over his shoulder, wondering when the MOD will catch up with him.'

Lexi breathed a huge sigh. So many things had gone through her mind, primarily centred on one thing – what had Scott done, and was he a bad person? Now she knew the truth. 'So, what can be done?'

'In hindsight, he realised there may have been other options. Perhaps if he'd talked to his commanding officer, there would have been a mechanism by which he could have been discharged from the army on compassionate grounds. But he did not have that conversation, so he never knew there might have been a way out of all this that didn't mean taking his daughter and going on the run.'

Lexi stared at Meredith. 'What about now? Is it too late?'

'Margot's solicitor friend says there are specialist lawyers who could help him, but Scott said he wouldn't have the money to hire one. Apparently, he's already used up most of his savings.'

Lexi looked at Andrea. 'I've got the money. I can help him.'

'Margot has offered to help him financially too.'

'So, what happens next?' Andrea asked. 'He's still here, isn't he?'

Meredith nodded. 'Margot persuaded him to stay. And to give himself up.'

'No!' Lexi got out of her chair. 'He can't do that! What if they take him away?'

'They will, Lexi. But he may avoid prison. And even if he doesn't, Margot convinced him that it was better for him, and Charlie, to get through a few months in prison rather than spending years looking over his shoulder. That way, he can give Charlie the life, the stability she needs.'

'But what will happen to Charlie if he's court-martialled and goes to prison?'

'She's going to stay here, with Margot. At least, that's the plan. She's discussed it will her lawyer friend regarding a temporary custody agreement, and hopefully that can be arranged.'

Lexi looked around her. 'I imagine she'd love to stay here. But I think there's somewhere else she'd prefer.'

Meredith raised her eyebrows. 'Where's that?'

Lexi shot out of her seat. 'I've got to go!'

Meredith said, 'Where?'

But Lexi had already run out of the kitchen.

Meredith turned to Andrea.

Andrea stared after her sister and smiled. She thought of Lexi's great-grandmother, Esme, returning home to Willow Tree Cottage with Kit, and said, 'She's going home.'

48

Lexi was running down the path towards the houseboat when her phone rang. She didn't stop to answer it, even though it kept ringing insistently. As she neared the boat, she shouted out, 'Scott! Charlie!'

She heard Scott's voice. 'Lexi – you came back!' She came to a halt at the gangplank. Scott had stepped out of the houseboat and was wiping his hands on a tea towel.

'I hoped I'd find you here!' Lexi exclaimed breathlessly. She had recalled that although they'd been staying at The Harbour Inn, when Charlie had run away, Meredith and Scott had found her at the houseboat.

'I went back to the agency to enquire about renting the houseboat because I'd changed my mind about leaving. They'd had a message left from the new owner saying I'd find a key under the flowerpot on deck by the door. I thought that was a bit odd. Stranger still, when I got out my wallet, they said it had all been taken care of, but wouldn't elaborate.'

Scott was staring at her, the same bemused expression on his face, as though he couldn't quite believe she was there either.

'I must admit, I feel like a squatter, not paying any rent. It's all rather odd.' He looked at her, and grinned. 'I knew you'd be back, if for no other reason than to stop Charlie's incessant texting – that's pester power for you.'

Lexi rushed forward into his embrace. She stood back. 'Where's Charlie?'

'She's organising her room, getting settled in. I'll go and fetch her.' He stopped. 'Do you know who owns the houseboat?'

Lexi grinned at him.

He looked at her and laughed. 'I don't believe it.' His smile faded. 'This isn't going to last – us here – even though someone persuaded me to stay.'

'Yes, I heard – my grandmother, Margot persuaded you not to leave.' Lexi said, 'Meredith told me everything – she's Margot's best friend. I know all about what happened, Scott, when Charlie's mother walked out. We're going to figure it out. We're going to get through this.'

Scott's face broke into a grin again. 'I know we are. With you by my side, I can get through anything.'

Lexi grinned too. 'So can I.' She knew that this was the power of love. As long as they had each other, everything would be all right in the end. Lexi watched Scott go inside the houseboat. She was about to follow when she heard him call out to Charlie that there was a surprise out on deck. Lexi still hadn't answered her phone. She assumed the call was from Charlie, who had yet to find out she'd returned. Lexi was about to answer the phone when she heard a dog barking and Charlie's voice calling out, 'Hey! Where are you going, you naughty puppy!'

A yellow Labrador puppy shot out of the houseboat.

Lexi knelt down, and the puppy ran straight into her arms. 'Hey, there. Where did you come from?'

Charlie ran out of the houseboat too and stopped dead when she saw Lexi. She ran up to her, threw her arms around her and burst into tears.

Scott walked out behind her. 'Oh, dear. She had the same reaction at Maisie's birthday party when Maisie got a puppy for her birthday, and she got one too.'

'Oh, Charlie. I have missed you so much.' Lexi looked up at Scott. 'You bought her a puppy?'

'Yep, there was one left in the litter. The naughty one, as it happens.' Scott looked at Lexi. 'I hope the houseboat owner doesn't mind pets.'

Lexi cried tears of joy.

'Aren't you going to answer that?'

Lexi had momentarily forgotten about her phone's incessant ringing. She held it up wondering who on earth was so desperate to get hold of her.

'Hello?'

'Is that Lexi?'

'Yes.' Lexi stood up and put an arm around Charlie's shoulder, pulling her close. She glanced at Scott, who picked up the puppy and held her in his arms.

'Hello, Lexi. It's Hazel. From the publishers.'

'Oh, hello.'

'I don't know what you did, Lexi, but she's writing again.'

'Pardon?'

'Margot got in touch just a moment ago. She said something about an unfinished novel she was working on years ago that she's intending to complete, and she said she's going to write another book too.'

'No way!'

'Yes, it's called *The Stowaway*.'

Lexi grinned. 'Of course it is.'

'She told me the story line. It sounds fascinating. You know I've never heard of IWs. She mentioned three women in the story. Actually, I think it would make a marvellous trilogy, each book telling one woman's story. I might suggest it to Margot. What do you think?'

Lexi smiled thinking of Esme, Joan and Margaret. 'I think Margot might have another bestselling trilogy on her hands.'

Hazel said, 'Those were my thoughts exactly.'

Lexi had yet to tell Hazel that the bestselling writer was in fact her grandmother. She thought she'd save that story for another phone conversation.

Hazel added, 'Mind you, I do have one problem.'

'What's that?'

'The illustrator of her original trilogy was an amazing person.'

'Can't you try and get in touch with them?' Lexi was aware that it had been years since Margot had last published a book. The illustrator could be retired by now. Even so, she said, 'Perhaps they'd like to work with you and Margot again?'

'I'm afraid that is just not possible. It was such a shame. He was so talented, and they were a lovely family.'

'Who?' Lexi had no clue what she was talking about.

'You know, he met his future wife at my little publishing company when he was illustrating Margot's books. He'd pop in from time to time, and she was temping here, as I needed the extra help when Margot's books took off.'

'Temping?' Lexi thought of her mother, who had temped at a publishing agency in London years earlier.

'Yes, she was American.'

'American?'

'Oh, yes. They married and had two lovely little girls. I often wonder what happened to them. They used to come into the office with their daddy sometimes and sit at my desk and do colouring-in while he illustrated his mother's books.'

'Margot's son illustrated her stories?'

'Yes. One of his girls, the older one – now, what was her name? Oh, yes – Alexandra. Now, she was quite talented at drawing, you know, even then. I could see she could have been a talented illustrator. Her father said so too.'

Lexi stared at Scott. 'He did? He said that?'

'Oh yes. He died young, I'm afraid. It was so sad. Soon afterwards, Margot stopped writing. I had a rather lovely thought when she rang, that Margot's grandchild could illustrate her new trilogy. But I didn't like to ask her in case, well, something had happened to her. Perhaps you could ask, as she seems to be quite taken with you. It's amazing that she is writing again.'

Scott put a tender hand on Lexi's shoulder and mouthed, 'Are you okay?'

Lexi nodded her head and gave Scott a reassuring smile as she wiped a tear from her eye. Lexi hadn't had a chance to ask Margot about her father. She imagined that Margot had photo albums of her dad from when he was a baby; they were something she was looking forward to leafing through. She wanted to find out all about him and her late grandfather.

Hazel added, 'So, where do you want me to send the cheque?'

'The cheque?'

'You know – remember when you visited my office in Bloomsbury looking for Margot Dorey, and I promised you a finder's fee if you found her and persuaded her to write again?

Although for the life of me, I'm still not sure how you did it.'

Lexi smiled. 'Oh, yes – right.' She looked at Charlie and Scott. 'Send it to my home address.'

'Oh, wait, first things first. I'll need your full name. It was Lexi Dawson, wasn't it? I better write it down.'

Lexi paused. 'Actually, my full name is Alexandra Dawson.'

'Right, so that's Alexandra Daw—'

There was a sudden silence.

'Hazel, are you still there?'

'You're her – aren't you?'

Lexi smiled. 'I am, yes. I'm Alexandra. I am Margot Dorey's grandchild.' She glanced at Charlie, realising that if she had given Hazel her full name to start with, Hazel might have realised who she was at the start of her trip when she had visited Hazel's little publishing house in London.

'Oh, my goodness. I had no idea – not until you told me your full name.'

'I had no idea either until ...' Lexi thought of Esme and the notebook, and her lovely great-grandfather, Kit. 'Look, it's a long story, but would you mind if we got together one day and I'll tell you all about it?'

'Oh, yes. I'd like that very much. In the meantime, will you ask Margot?'

'Ask her what?'

'Why, if you can illustrate her books of course. You had quite a talent, you know. You got it from your father.'

Lexi thought of Esme and realised that her father had inherited his talent from her. Lexi started to shake her head. 'I've had no training. I have no qualifications in illustrating or art—'

'Oh, poppycock. No amount of schooling or creative courses

or degrees in art can teach you the one thing you need above all else.'

Lexi thought of Maisie and knew what Hazel was going to say.

'Raw talent. Even if you haven't practised your art since your father died, it's still there Lexi, waiting to be rediscovered. Take your grandmother. I bet she hasn't written a word in twenty years, but that doesn't mean she's lost the ability to write – does it?'

Lexi shook her head.

'Of course not. Now, how about it? Will you promise you'll ask her? Ah, wait, I think I'm getting ahead of myself. I'm sure she'd love you to, but I suppose the question I should be asking is if would you like to follow in your father's footsteps and illustrate her books?'

'Oh, I'd like nothing more.'

'Good, now we must meet up. I'd love to hear your story and meet with your grandmother again. I've missed her and her wonderful writing. I'll bring the cheque with me. So, where are you living?'

'I'm on the Suffolk Coast in Walberswick.'

'Ah, wonderful – my favourite part of the world.'

Lexi smiled. It was hers too. She followed Charlie and Scott into her new home. 'You'll find me on the houseboat by the quay.'

'How will I know which one?'

'You can't miss it,' said Lexi, smiling as she stepped inside. The name was emblazoned on the side of the boat, where everyone would see it, including the postman and her grandmother when she went looking for Charlie. Lexi smiled at the thought that Margot had seen the name of her houseboat and decided it would be the perfect title of her next book.

Lexi said, 'The name of my houseboat is *The Stowaway*.'

The Sunrise Coast Series continues in

The Bookshop of Memories

Paperback and Kindle eBook available soon from Amazon

If you enjoyed *Return to Willow Tree Cottage* I would be grateful if you would leave a review on Amazon.

For further details about the author and her novels please visit the author's website.

www.elisedarcy.com

Printed in Great Britain
by Amazon

18955107R00202